Poaching The River

A Novel

by

Rod Fleming

PlashMill Press

D1380825

Published in 2006 by PlashMill Press

First Edition

A CIP catalogue record for this book is available
from the British Library.

ISBN: 0-9554535-0-X

Printed and bound by CPI Antony Rowe, Eastbourne

PlashMill Press
The Plash Mill
Friockheim
Angus DD11 4SH
Scotland.

For my wife, Madeleine, and my daughter, Charis.

Thanks to all those who helped in the long process of writing this book and preparing it for publication and in particular to Sine Robertson and David Grant for their support, advice and encouragement throughout.

PROLOGUE

Once, a little girl stared deep into a tide-pool at her feet. She had her knees scrunched up tight to her chest and her arms wrapped around them and her bare legs still bore the traces of sea-water and sand and mud. She was a skinny girl, long boned and fine, with black, black hair and brown skin and deep brown eyes that were almost as black as her hair, and she was pretty, too, pretty in a way that foretold of great beauty, with her white-toothed smile and her big eyes and her fine-shaped bones. But this was no Mediterranean scene; this little girl was sitting upon a rock, green with seaweed and coarse with barnacles and limpets and chitons that lay—still lies, for all I know—where tide and tempest had tumbled it, on a pebbly beach below a towering cliff somewhere on the north-east coast of Scotland. Before her extended that grey and troublesome North Sea, one of the most unpredictable and treacherous stretches of water in the world, that has since time immemorial yielded up its riches only to those who were brave and skilful enough to take them; and yet it has taken its tithe and more in return.

But the little girl thought not of that; she was as aware of the sea as most people are of the air they breathe, and forbye, just then, she might have been all that was left of the world; for it was softly defined by the thick grey haar that obliterated everything more than ten feet away. The light within this earthbound cloud was so directionless that it seemed as if it was the objects around her that emitted their own light, and by a curious trick of refraction, the water in the pool that so fascinated her seemed to be the brightest light of all.

But she could hear. The distant blast of the foghorn on the harbour wall at Arbeg that warned of a reef that extended into the sea like a deadly finger. The mourning, chillful wail of the seagulls as they swung and swooped about their nests high up in the red-sandstone cliffs that massively and invisibly towered above and behind her, encircling the little bay. Footsteps clattering through the pebbles of the beach. The sounds of muffled voices, perhaps not far away, but then again perhaps very far; the mist distorts sound too. The sound of spade striking deep into the soft yielding sand as the men dug bait. A village dog barking, higher up even than the gulls, for the little girl's village was atop the cliff. But all of this was but the harmony, the counterpoint, to the endless rhythm of the fundamental melody; the slow rolling of the sea. Now she was in a quiet passage, the spring tide right out, and her wavelety tendrils but tapping time upon the muddy sand of the foreshore, but in her strident times she could come thundering up out of the night in her foaming legions, in the black, howling cacophony of a gale, a Force 10 or yet a Force 12, full

1

hurricane, hurtling out of the grey-black pit of her belly and smiting the shore with such violence that the very bones of the land shivered in awe, blasting spume sixty, eighty feet up in the air, gnawing at the bones of the land, gnawing, and knowing, too, that in time all of this land would be hers, for it cannot resist forever, and is doomed to be finally ground up into that same sand that squeezes so delightfully between toes.

The little girl upon the rock shook her long black hair and a shower of tiny droplets that had condensed upon it sparkled the surface of the pool. Within the pool there were whelks and winkles and hermit crabs and urchins and starfish and brittle-stars; anemones and shrimps and gobies and sand-eels and green partans. But she had seen something else, with her sharp child's eye, moving slowly in the seaweed; two long whip-like tendrils emerging from under a rocky shelf, and she knew full well to whom they must belong. At her side, lying on the rock, was a rusty length of iron bar, about three feet long and curved into a hook at the end, called a cleik, and she softly uncurled one arm and found it. But a streak of mischief was never far below the surface of her, and she determined to have a little sport before inserting her cleik into the hole and attacking the blue-jacketed lobster from behind with its hooked end, driving him out where she could get a quick and sure hand upon his weskit aft of those nippers of his. So she let her toes drop into the water, which was chill for it was early summer yet and the cold of it bit her.

How lang will ye let me tickle ye, Maister Lapster, afore ye come oot in yer rage at me and nip with yer great black claw? How lang can I dangle this wee pink toe in front of ye afore I have tae lowp back wi a yipe or mebbe be nippit?

CHAPTER ONE
The Auchpinkie Hotel.

B ig Sye was thirty-six years old, and by that process of slow accumulation that gradually silts life up, he had, over the years, acquired most of the things that he needed. He lived in the village he had been born in, Auchpinkie, a tiny community, but two lines of brightly painted cottages at the end of a road that went nowhere else, on the rounded coast of Angus. Though the village was small, it had all that you might think necessary; a little one class school, a kirk, the Auchpinkie Hotel, and his Auntie Mae's corner shop, where you could buy everything from a pint of milk to a twenty-five ton shackle, post your letters and get the local news. Both of these last were in the square at the end of the single street, and Big Sye lived there too, in a cottage he had built himself on a postage-stamp of ground his mother had given him; its position was such that every morning he was ashore, when he looked out his bedroom window, the first thing he saw was the white-painted facade of the Hotel. And that just suited Sye fine. It made him feel quite at home.

Mark you, he'd done his fair share of wandering; Auchpinkie is a fishing village still, even if the big boats all berth at Arbeg three miles down the coast, and once the sea is in the blood, it's a sair fecht to filter it out again. So Sye had worked the trawlers, and then joined the Merchant Marine. He had travelled the most part of the globe, and if he had the mariner's view of the lands that he had visited—that they all comprised of beaches and docks and seamen's bars—nevertheless he had still been there. He was a natural seaman, as you might expect, and no mug neither. He had worked hard and studied the great tomes on Seamanship, even though it was a penance to him; and it was all made worthwhile when he at last got his Master's ticket, and soon after, the command of a small freighter. He thought he was set up, and within a year the line went bust and he was on the beach.

It happened at that sad time when the once great British merchant fleet was being almost destroyed as companies rushed to abandon the old Red Duster and register with flags of convenience. There was a flood of men seeking berths. Sye signed on the register, stretched, and waited for a ship. He had a lifelong pal christened William Teviotdale, but whom everybody knew as Peem. Sye and Peem had been near as dammit inseparable since boyhood—why, Peem even married Sye's wee sister, Isabel—and they had aye shipped together when they could. Peem had been Engineer on the freighter, and the pair of them got washed up on the same wave. They set to drinking their redundancy together, but

3

when they saw the bottom of the bucket they decided that it was high time to Dae Somehin. So they scratched their chins and rubbed their temples and kicked the rail of the Public Bar of the Hotel, and then went and trained to be divers so they could work on the oilrigs in the North Sea. The living in it was good, right enough, and for a puckle years it filled their pockets and the bellies of Peem's steadily increasing brood. But Sye had got a taste for being in command, and anyway he had come to the view that the only employer a man could be sure of was himself. Then a seiner, steaming into Arbeg with her hatches carelessly open to save a few minutes at the market pier, got broached by a freak wave in a ripening force ten. Knocked flat on her beam she was, staggered, filled, started to right, got hit by another wall of water and down she went, slap in the middle of the fairway. Sye lost no time. He bought the wreck from the insurance company for one pound sterling on condition that he cleared the channel of her within thirty days.

Our men set to work, and despite the continuing foul weather, they managed it; not without adventure, it is true, but that is another tale. Once the wreck was raised they had a long job drying her out and refitting her, but after that they were in business, with their own dive-boat. That had been three years before, and now the pair of them had pretty well as much work as they could handle, and the future, Sye at last allowed himself to think, appeared secure.

Maybe just a bit too secure. There are some seafarers who can take a berth and be there until they slip their anchors, happy to have a job, sending the money back home, and taking their leaves when they come. And then there are others who always seem to have something itchy in their bunk. It makes them restless, like. They can't sleep at nights and they get into squabbles. They get all fankled up like a line that's been coiled the wrong way and then they have to give themselves a great big shaking and a shoogling to get all the kinks out. They can't help it; it's just the way they are, and there's not a seaman in the world doesn't know one of them when he sees him, nor can honestly say that he has never felt that way himself sometime. Our Sye was one of these, and it goes a long way to account for all the scrapes he'd got himself into over the years. Despite Peem's constant attempts to contain his friend's impetuous whim, the pair of them had seen the inside of every Sheriff Court from Peterhead to Leith.

And right at the moment, despite the house, the BMW, the money in the bank, being his own boss and the Rolex Submariner on his wrist, Big Sye felt like he was wearing shuin two sizes too small, and it pinched him something rotten.

One afternoon in late April when the first greening of the trees tells of the arrival of a long awaited spring, Big Sye was in the Public Bar of the Auchpinkie Hotel, jammed firmly into the angle between wall and woodwork in an attitude that could only have come with long practise. And, indeed, when he straightened up, he revealed—like some characteristic spoor—the ingrained mark left by his right hip rubbing against the plasterwork. He was as big as his name, tall, rangy, with bones far too big for him, and a pint tumbler vanished in the lover's clasp of his fingers. His elbows rested on the bartop, and one foot was crossed over the other.

Now, the Public Bar of the Auchpinkie Hotel was a proper sort of a bar where the art of drinking was taken as seriously as it should be. To be sure, you could argue that it lacked something in the finer points of human comfort; the wooden chairs could begin to gnaw at a body's backside after an hour or two at the chap, the tables were rickety, the flagged floor grim-hard and the draughts hard to bear. Still, good ale and whisky and the company of like-minded friends works wonders. Tourists and anyone else who preferred something softer than sawdust to tread on were directed to the lounge bar, the domain of Dave the barman's wife Agnes, where plush carpets and soft seats and a jukebox and chilled wine betrayed the lurking presence of the late twentieth century.

This afternoon the haze of smoke and dust revealed the shape of only one other in the room besides Dave the barman and Sye, and it'll be no great surprise to learn that this was Peem, who was parked on a rickety bentwood chair by the tiny fireplace with his feet extended to the hearth, where instead of dancing flames there was a sprig of heather, for Dave had decreed that summer had arrived, official. Upon the mantle within comfortable reach, was a nippy and a pint jar; his chair was pushed back on two legs, and a copy of the *Arbeg Guide* lay spread over his lap. If Sye was tall and rangy with bones one size too big, Peem was small and compact, you might even say dapper, had his attire been less comfortable. He had a wispy blond beard, doe-soft brown eyes and an unlikely shock of sun-bleached ringlets. But the striking thing about him was his lopsided grin, which gave him the allure of a crazed leprechaun.

Peem was the only son of Jess Teviotdale, a woman whose idiosyncrasy and furious temper were legendary. When he was little, he had been the most beautiful boy you could imagine, with his golden hair and his big eyes with the corners slightly turned down, his cheeky grin of white teeth and his upturned nose; as delightful to the eye as any Christmas Card choirboy. He was the image of his Da, whom Peem never knew. Then, one night when he had been out on the ran-dan, he came home to a row with Jess. Neither of them really knew, later, what their battle royal had been about, and it certainly wasn't the first they'd had, nor by a long chalk would it be the last. But that night Peem had been jilted by his girlfriend, and he had had a long conference with a bottle of Glenmorangie.

After Jess went wrathful to her bed, Peem pondered upon the metaphysics of life. It occurred to him—being brought up in the Presbyterian faith—that there was only one Being who could be responsible for his troubles, and he fancied a word with that Being *right now*. Give him a piece of his mind, like. So he stormed out of the house and up the lane towards the Ness, where the cliffs cut perilously close to the path, so close indeed that a dry-stane dyke had been erected to prevent the wayward accidentally making this their last journey; Peem, who planned to do so deliberately, clambered up on the wall and prepared to launch himself to oblivion.

It was perhaps fortunate that he was as completely and entirely drunk as he was; for at the crucial moment Peem slugged back the last of his Morangie, shook his fist at the heavens, tripped over his shoe-laces, twisted round in space, and measured his length on the narrow ledge above the cliff, coincidentally smashing out the front teeth of both his jaws and damn near achieving his desired end by braining himself on a half-interred boulder. There he lay unconscious until the painful dawn broke and he staggered back over the wall and along to his bed. By the time he woke up in the morning, half-remembering the events of the night before, and got himself to Casualty, it was not only too late to save the teeth that had broken his fall, but several others forbye, his broken nose had set itself squint, and the lacerations round his mouth had needed more stitches than a curtain hem. The doctors and dentists did what they could, but what they could was not much, and Peem wasn't really beautiful afterwards and for ever more his ill-fitting dentures and hastily-repaired mouth gave him a pronounced lisp and a crooked smile. These days he was quite blasé about the whole thing and would cheerfully pop out his dentures and relate the story to complete strangers if he thought they were feeling awkward, like.

In the end, and by-the-by, things had worked out though; for Peem, by the time of his little accident, had long been the subject of a romantic interest on the part of Isabel Swankie, Sye's wee sister, an interest that had never borne fruit, because Peem was that used to seeing her as the wee pest that spoiled the childhood ploys he and Sye had gotten up to he hadn't noticed the changes that time wrought upon her. But in the wake of the accident—as everyone tactfully called it—Izzie had seen her chance and risen to the challenge, appearing to Peem as an angel of mercy, and more than that, revealing herself to be a very shapely and attractive one. Iz wouldn't be Iz if she didn't know how to get what she wanted in life, and it had not been long before our Peem was hooked, body and soul, and not a thing could he do about it. Which was fine, because if Iz was no angel, she was a perfect match for Peem. But we'll meet Iz in the flesh later; meantime back to the bar.

Absent-mindedly, Sye fumbled a battered pack of ten Players Navy Cut—untipped, of course—from the pocket of his checked shirt, withdrew one, tapped the end on the back of his free hand, found a match in his trouser pocket and struck it casually on the front of the bar. The brief flare of the match in his cupped hands threw his features into sharp relief as he puffed, his eyes narrowed against the smoke. He flicked out the match and tossed it into an ashtray, and a gesture as subtle as any auction-room shark's sent Dave to work pulling a fresh pint of beer as Sye gazed thoughtfully through the smoke at his own tousle-headed reflection for a few moments.

"Peem, ma loon," he said at last, words of gravity that sunk but slow into the shimmering silence of the bar, "A'm beginnin ti feel pest hit. A'm aa seizin up in aa ma jyntes. Is it no aboot time we hud a bit action aboot the place? Yer a lang time deid, y'ken."

With an inscrutable expression upon his hang-dog face, Dave placed the fresh pint of beer on the bar before Sye and raised an eyebrow toward Peem, who, in turn, checked his reserves upon the mantle, glanced at his watch, stretched, and nodded. "Aye, A've aboot time fur anither een afore Izzie comes ower an lassoes me. An gie's a," he let his eye scan the shelf behind the bar, "Gie's a Wood's Navy an aa, willye Dave? Hank ye affa muckle." He got up, stretched again, slouched to the bar and installed himself next door to his pal. He watched as Dave set about pouring the drinks.

Dave had once been a big man, but the years had shrunk him, a million times reaching down for bottles and glasses bending him into his familiar stoop until he could not have straightened out even if he had wished to. His hands were those of a man who had laboured hard, but over the damp days of a publican's life they had become red and puffy until his fingers looked like link sausages on a butcher's plate. When things were busy he'd scuttle from end to end of his bar, never leaving the sanctuary, in a curious mincing shuffle incongruous on such a big man, his spaniel eyes with their sad wrinkles earnest and eager to please, his slight deafness giving a him a quizzical air, his ingratiating smile, half-hidden by his old-fashioned handlebar moustache, never far from his lips. It was easy, especially if you were carrying a dram or two to lubricate the cockles of your heart, to feel sorry for him and think that he'd jump at the chance to be gone from the shackles of his toil. But under the mask of his longsufferance Dave was as disgustingly content with his lot as any of us could ever wish to be; his manner was just a defence.

He and Agnes had bought the bar at a knock down price at a time when everybody was tight for cash, and the previous owner had done a moonlight flit with the bank's siller. Canny Dave had been saving his wages as grieve at Hawkhill farm, and had just enough to make the deposit. It was not long before he discovered that certain of his clients, when over-imbued with the drink, were likely to take a good swing at the biggest man in the bar just for the hell of it; and all too often, Dave would be that man. Now, anyone who has spent a good part of his life in the bothy is no stranger to roughhouses. Dave had never minded a bit sparring; quite enjoyed it in fact, but when Agnes pointed out that it was bad business to be forever knocking nine bells out of his best customers, Dave Paterson the grieve, a muckle bear with a glinting eye, a roaring voice, and a tattie-dreel swagger, the holy terror of St. Cyrus on merkat-day, had become Dave Paterson the barman, as meek and kindly and innocuous a soul as you'd ever meet.

Mark you, there were times, at the end of the day, when he let the old Dave out for a wee bit saunter and a swagger and a lean on the yett that was his bar, and then he would roar and laugh and swap the news with any who'd take him on. But by and large by the time he got to that stage the rest of the party were too pie-eyed to take any heed of the drink talking on him anyway. Aye, Dave had the barman's curse, all right, and not being the type to live in paradise without tasting the fruit, he took righteous pleasure in his indulgence. Not that his admittedly prodigious habit ever came close to damaging the business. A man would need a camel's thirst to drink the profits of the Auchpinkie trade.

This thirst had gifted Dave with a nose as red as a cherry and a tremor in his hands that was mesmerising. It would begin when he took the order. His muckle hands would dive into the shelf of glasses and lift out two, three, four, a puffy finger in each. At once there was the sound of spoons being played, or maybe castanets, and you would glance around in surprise until your eye fell on the cluster of glasses, the source of this weird syncopation, as it made its way to the fonts. As each glass in turn was raised under the spigot and the handle pulled, the increased muscular effort meant that the St. Vitus' Dance of Dave's fingers stilled for a moment, and the onlookers—for by this time every eye that could see it was fixed on this process, all conversation had stilled, and the air was thick with the projected consciousness of the watchers, every one willing those fingers to remain still—would think all was going to be all right, and relax a bit but then gasp! For as soon as the pressure on the handle was released, bang would go the shakes once more, and over the side would go the top half-inch. And then everyone would shrug their shoulders and get back to business.

Since it was entirely impossible for Dave to pour a full pint, with or without the psychic assistance of his patrons, the only way to get your own back for the inevitably short measure was to ask for a spirit with it, and make sure it was one that was not on optic. Everyone knew that there was no way that Dave could pour a dram into his tiny pewter quarter-gill hand measure without skelling a good mouthful over the side and into the waiting glass. Ah, what an affliction for an honest publican, what a sore trial indeed; how fitting that the years of imbibery should be thus revisited upon the sinner. For the more Dave screwed up his face and furrowed his brow and clenched his teeth and held his breath, the more violent would his shaking become and the more his customer would benefit.

Think on't; here was a man that had been known to thole his bar so cold that ice would form on the inside of the windows for his reluctance to throw another lump or two of coal onto the measly flicker of flame on the hearth, now condemned to practically giving away his liquor. The terrors of purgatory hold no more sublimely conceived an ordeal. Once, and only once, Dave had worked out a scheme to beat it, and that many years before. Sly dog, he'd put the price of a nippy up from fivepence ha'penny to fivepence three farthing (this being in the days of real money), kenning full well that as the evening progressed, few folk would notice if they didn't get their farthing back from the tanner. For a while Dave had been triumphant, a knowing smile had lurked under his doleful bassett-hound features, and a new air of conviviality had shone across the bar.

Then, in an unerring stroke of officially-inspired malice directed straight at the heart of the proprietor of the Auchpinkie Hotel, the Government of the day had abolished the farthing altogether, and the price of a nippy had had to go up to sixpence, anyway. Agnes had borne the brunt of Dave's spleen, without really understanding.

"But surely, dear, all it means is that you're a farthing better off on every nippy?" she pointed out innocently. "In fact, the way I see it, you're really a ha'penny better off."

"Ach, ye dinnae see it at all at all," roared her husband, beside himself in frustrated ire. "*That's* no the point. Look. Fit wey can A get whit's mine back when A'm aaready chergin for it? D'ye see? If it costs fivepence three farthin an A skell a farthin's worth intae the gless, an keep the farthin, then aa's square. But if it costs saxpence an A skell a farthin, nou fit wey dae A get it back? A cannae exactly ask for seevenpence jist so's ti gie them three-farthin back and anyway the rotten buggers hiv done awa wi the farthin in the first place! D'ye see? D'ye see nou?"

Agnes would have had to admit that she did not, but nodded for the sake of peace. Dave huffed mightily for months, cursed the Government and its officials black, and all orders for spirits were served under a thunderous cloud. Everyone else thought it was a hoot.

So it was that Peem took his harmless delight at the familiar spurned-dog look in Dave's eyes as he passed over his drinks, and made a great show of his pleasure as he sipped the rum. Peem could smell mischief in the air.

"Weel," he said, "Fittirye gingin ti dae aboot it?" he said to Sye at last.

Sye swung round to get a look at him. "Daa ken. Fit aboot we organise a tiddlywinks league?"

Peem laughed.

"Mind," Sye continued, returning to the observance of himself in the mirror, "It's near time for the Spring Run."

Peem shook his head. "Ach but thir no muckle sport in at ava. Syne the auld laird de'ed, e'en Geordie's no hud his hert in it. Mark you, A suppose the Spring Run's still the Spring Run for aa that."

Dave's hands had stilled and he was regarding the two men with a querulous expression on his face. He hated it when he didn't know what people were talking about in his bar and he hated even more the fact that all of his customers knew it.

"Did ye ken thiv sellt the pliss?" demanded Sye. "The new fellae's makin muckle cheenges. They say it's gingin ti be a Country Club." He puffed thoughtfully on his cigarette. "Some Englishman's bochten it, so A believe."

"Fit's at?" demanded Dave, at last overcome by curiosity. Sye looked at him with an amused expression on his face.

"Balgoonie Grange, min. D'ye no read the pippers? Official openin in twa weeks."

"Aye but fittsat ti dae wi this fellae Geordie's hert?"

Peem crossed his arms and leaned forward on his elbows, speaking gently. "Dayvit. Ye ken fit wey the Pinkie is supposed ti hae this great run o Fish the first spring tide efter Mayday? Weel, me an him aye ging an trawl een or twa foul-hookers across the estuar just sae's wi cin hae a puckle Fish fur wir freezers, like. Ken afore the toffs gets tore in aboot them. Ye ken fine we div cos ye aye buy a puckle yersel."

"Here, izzit at time o year again?" Dave's expression cleared. "Jings time flees."

"Aye, it is an aa. An the spring tides comes the same week thir openin the Grange........Here, did A no read somehin in the *Guidie* aboot at?" Peem returned to the table and picked up the paper. "Oh aye. Here wi gae. Thir awa ti hae aa sorts o extra patrols an aa that jist ti discourage the poachers, di daa, di daa muckle mair shite.........Here, bi the cringe, d'ye ken thiv e'en managed ti talk the Fishery Protection inti staundin affshore.......My, my. A wunner fit wey thi managed at."

"The Protection?" Dave's expression darkened again. "Fit hiv they ti dae wi hit? Neen o thir ingans, shairly? Thir affshore ur they no?"

"Aye weel, aye an no," answered Sye. "Fur a stert-wi the estuar's tidal an at gies them jurisdiction. An thiv made the Pinkie a Protected River forbye. At's jist anither wey o sayin the likes o me an him cannae fish it, like, but cos it's a Ect o Perliament, rether'n hit bein jist up ti the landlord ti stap wis, thi cin cry on the Protection an aa. Agents o the Croon, fittiver at means, see. Loadae guff, really," he mused. "But it mecht jist mak it guid fur a lauch. Fittdye hink, William?"

Peem grinned. "A hink if Iz finnds oot fit wir intil A'll be fur the high jump. But A jalouse thir mecht be eneuch sport in't fur me ti sling a bit hookie ower a bank ae derk necht. It's no worth it fur the siller, like. They fish-fermers his near as dammit made the poachin no worth the effort."

"Yer recht thir," mused Sye. "Still they mak no bed eatin for aa that. Fell rich, like, but no bed." He grinned. "Yer on the bell, ye ken."

CHAPTER TWO
Mae's General Store, Chandlery and Post Office

Across the square in a north-easterly direction from the
Auchpinkie Hotel is Mae Swankie's shop. This is a combined
grocer and gen-eral store, chandlery and Post Office, supplier
and stockist of everything from tea bags, Scottish Plain and toilet roll to
ship's paint, tar, corlene line, shackles and nails, where you can cash the
Giro on Thursdays forbye. Before Mae had it, her father did, and before
that, his. Mae herself rarely went anywhere else, being as how she lived
in the flat above. No, excepting funerals weddings and necessary excusions
to Arbeg, Mae would be behind the counter, from 8.30 to 5.30 six days a
week, fifty weeks a year.

Mind, Mae was not alone. Mae liked cats. And cats liked her;
with the inevitable result that her shop was permanently thick with them.
There were all sorts; tabbies and blacks and ginger toms and even a couple of seven toed Bristol cats. Any time you liked to have a look, there
would be cats sleeping in the coils of rope, on the shelves, in the piles of
mailbags, upon the newspapers and under the pot-belly stove. Even Mae
didn't know how many there were, and only the most favoured half
dozen had names. One of these, who was the undisputed ruler of the
bunch, was an enormous silver tabby named Davey Jones, whose locker
was the sunny middle shelf in the window, from which he had a clear
view down The Street with its cottages all different colours. Young or
old, whether they had names or not, each and every cat got fed when
Mae boiled up a huge pot of porridge and any left-overs that were going
upon the kitchen range in the back shop. There would be a calamitous
yowling and a scratching at the door, and Mae would coo soothingly
over her shoulder and cluck her tongue before braving the furry storm
and pouring the grey sticky mess into the ancient enamelled ashets that
were kept under the counter for this very purpose. Then there would be a
sound of greatly contented cattery.

And if the question of hygiene were ever raised, Mae would
proudly insist that she had never seen a mouse or a rat in the place.

Just as Davey Jones kept his watch, from his crow's nest amongst
the corlene and marlin-spikes in Mae's window, so it was from the same
shop that Mae and her cronies kept theirs. The Street, the square with the
hotel, the manse and the school at the far end of the village, and the
concrete obscenity of the Public Convenience, none could hide from their
scrutiny. For if the Public Bar of the Auchpinkie Hotel was where the
menfolk plotted and did their deals and passed their hours, Mae's was

where the women of the village gathered to pass their opinions. At the core was a group, unelected and self appointed, who, despite this, served as the village's Committee of Social Etiquette. And the power of this committee was not diminished by its ad-hoc nature.

Besides Mae herself, this select group comprised Agnes Paterson, wife to Dave the barman and joint owner of the Auchpinkie Hotel; Nan Swankie, the longsuffering wife and mother of two Alexander Swankies, the younger of whom was currently propping up the bar in the hotel, which was not so very unusual a circumstance; and Jess Teviotdale, whose son was beside him. Last but not least was Morag Paterson (no relation.) At one time this committee had been much larger, but the grim reaper had thinned the ranks sorely in the last wee while and the drift of younger folk to Arbeg and further in search of work meant that no-one had joined the ranks for over twenty years.

Their meetings were not always held in Mae's shop; the members frequently held sub-committee meetings in such places as the checkout queue at the Willie Low's or the Palace Bingo Hall in Arbeg. But Mae's shop had the distinction of being a sub-Post Office and so had an official legitimacy. Sort of. In any case since Mae refused to leave her shop during trading hours, Agnes's patch across the square was ruled out. This saddened Agnes, who had a weather eye on the till receipts, and because she found the atmosphere at Mae's a wee bit pungent. But Mae aye had a pot of tea on to stew on the range and she would even fortify the already electrifying brew with a drop of the craitur when required. Which was some consolation.

While the ladies of Mae's shop (the Hag's Huddle as some of their less reverent victims called them) saw no limits on the range or variety of their remit, the crack most often concerned the lives of their own families and friends. Oft-times did the subject of Big Sye come up, and not just because he was Nan's son. Nor was it only because of his notoriously ambivalent attitude to questions of legality, for regarding the law as an inconvenience that should be circumvented whenever necessary was normal in Auchpinkie. No, it was because Thon Bugger His Gotten Ti Be Hirty-Sax Year Auld And Nae Bluidy Sign O Him Gettin Wad Yet.

"Och, ye've nae idear ava," Nan was moaning. She was a round, plump, soft skinned, grey haired woman. She was standing by the metal-grilled counter that was the "Post Office" part of the establishment with her back to the door. "At laddie. Ye ken, he's still got twa motorbikes in bits in ma coalshed and ye wanty *see* the attic. Atween him an at faither o his ma life's jist no worth the trachle. A jist wish tae hell he'd finnd some bit lassie—some pair lass at cid thole him—an settle doon. At wey we mecht git some peace aboot the pliss."

Jess, who was short and square with an air of determination about her and a voice like two sheets of sandpaper being rubbed together, assented. "Aye. Hivvint A no been sayin fur mair years'n A cin remember at it wis high time he wis naillit doon? Crivvens, thir maun be some quine oot thir wi the smeddum tae tak him on."

"It's no takin him on at's the boather," observed Mae from behind her counter drily. "It's the keepin a hud o the bugger efter the fect, gin ye git ma meanin, at'll try her mettle. Yon laddie's niver hud ony trouble ava gittin lassies ti tak him *oan*. Him an at loon o yours, Jess. The een's as bed's the tither."

"A'll vouch fur at," agreed Nan, darkly.

"Here, youse," growled Jess threateningly, her eyes flashing. "Did ma Wullie no git himsel tethered? An he's brochten up a bonnie pack o his ain. Youse jist watch whaur yer castin yer axpersions."

"Och, it's always the same story," intoned Agnes. She, uniquely amongst this group, was not from the village and had a habit of trying to "talk proper" in front of the others, a habit they universally detested. "This problem with Sye has been going on fur years. Ever since—well, you know what I mean."

"A daa mind ye flingin yer ain dochter at him," rasped Jess. "Ye wis fleet eneuch ti get her awa ti varsity an ootin the reach o ony the loons fae roon here, the wey A mind o't." She reached into her bag and pulled out a packet of cheap cheroots. "A jalouse ye didna hink thi wis guid eneuch roon here fur yer ain quine. Ony o youse want a cheroot? Nu'? Aarecht, A'll jist hae een masel."

Agnes watched Jess happily lighting up with an expression of distaste. "Now, Jessie, ye know fine well it wasn't that. Celia's a talented girl and she had to be helped to develop herself."

"Aye it bluidy wis," growled Jess, squinting through the foul-smelling reek. "An daa ye cry me Jessie. Ye ken fine A canna abide at an ye jist dae hit tae fash me. Celia! B'Christ! Fit gart ye trachle the puir bit lassie wi a haunle like thon onywey? Nae wunner she'd idears abune hersel."

"I don't think you should say Celia has ideas above herself," retorted Agnes, her nostrils flaring. "Just because..........."

"Here, wid the pair o youse twa buggers hud yer wheesht an lay affa the constantly nigglin at een anither," snapped Mae. "Yer worse'n twa bairns ye ur wi yer bluidy yappin. An forbye it disnae alter the simple fect that gin he disnae look oot at laddie's gingin till wind up like yon auld gowk Boab Smuth. An fa the hell wants that? Pair Nan'll niver be shot o him."

Nan nodded. Agnes, who was not about to be quieted so quickly, said, "Aye, I know, I know; but there's not many unmarried lassies left hereabouts, is there?"

"Aye, an at's a fect," gravelled Jess reflectively. "Here, thir aye Mary Smuth. Ye ken." She pointed her cheroot out through the window along the street. "Hur doon by. She wis engaged ti yon loon Sturrock the butcher's son fae Arbeg but at's feenished lang syne. She wis a bonny quine fan she wis younger."

"Izzat aa ye kin come up wi?" moaned Nan. "The game's a bogey then. Ye ken fit *she's* like. Thon lassie hisnae gliskit at a man syne Sturrock's loon dumped her."

"Aye, but mebbe she's hud a cheenge o hert syne yon auld bat o a mither o hurs de'ed," put in Jess, with a grin.

"Jess, really!" cried Agnes, who was well known to have a thing about miscrying dead people—a thing that was regarded with utter contempt by the rest, who figured that at least with a dead person, there was no chance of being slandered back. "Let bygones be bygones!"

"Ach get real, eh?" muttered Nan. "Crivvens it's ten year gin it's a day at Sturrock's loon threw *her* ower. An A doot ony man wi bluid in his veins wid look at her twice nou. She's gotten that skinny she gars me feel hungery jist hinkin aboot her. Bluidy fell peety, for she *wis* a bonny-like quine in her day, an she wis jonick eneuch. Christ she's aa skin an bane nou tho, an she's a puss on her like she's been at the Soor Plooms ower lang." She shook her head sadly. "Na, ye'll need ti come up wi a muckle mair toothsome chickie'n at tae tempt ma Sye, trow me."

"An anyway, you're not really suggesting that a mousy wee lassie like that could keep a hold o *him*, are ye?" continued Agnes, who hated being ignored.

"Naehin wrang wi ma Sye. He's a braa laddie," Nan snapped back. She hated being ignored just as much.

"Och i the name o the bluidy wee man gie's a *brek*," snapped Mae, who was fed up to the back teeth with the bickering. At least she was as long as she didn't have the upper hand. "The fect o the metter is that Agnes is recht—fur eence," she went on, ignoring her victim's bilious glance. "It'll be a gey gallus besom at's got eneuch smeddum tae settle Sye's hash."

Morag Paterson was listening in silence to the voices behind her while she looked out of the window. She was not a woman of imagination or quickness of thought; and this, combined with the fact that she spoke so slowly she drove Jess to distraction, gave to her rare utterances a certain, false, air of sagacity. Looking out windows was an occupation which she indulged in whenever she could. She liked to see what was going on, did Morag, and forbye that she could see no point at all to the conversation about Nan's wayward son; Morag was a strict Presbyterian, and as far as she was concerned Sye was guaranteed a one-way ticket to a very hot place indeed.

"By," she said, her peculiar cracked little-girl voice stilling the chatter that went on behind her. "Izzint that no some bodie flittin intil Etta's auld hoose at the gushet o Foontin Square?"

Jess looked up, and, because she knew better than ask Morag for an explanation—it took ower lang—shouldered in beside her to get a look. You had to shoulder Morag; she was of considerable mass and not fleet to move it. "Far?" she demanded, and squinted through the hanging festoons of sun-bleached plastic buckets and spades. Then she let out a low whistle. "Jings, help ma boab," she breathed. "D'ye ken fa thon is? By! Thon's Etta's quine, Rae, isn't it no? By that'll pit the baudrons in amangst the doos willint it no jist?"

"Fa? Fit dae ye mean?" Mae charged out from her buckie and

peered hard through the panes, after clearing the grime with the corner of her peenie. "At cannae be *hur.* Cannae be. Etta aye sayed she'd gie the hoose tae the Cat Refuge afore she'd let thon quine o hers intil it." She breathed on the glass, gave it another dicht and then gasped.. "Here by the cringe yer recht eneuch, ye ken." She began to cackle. "By aye, efter aa the bluidy times Etta miscried thon lassie, thir she is, the same quine, flittin in sonsie as ye like."

"Fittdye jalouse happened?" Nan had joined the others.

"Daa ken," mused Jess. "Aiblins the thrawn auld carlin wis ower grippit tae pey a lahyer tae mak a Will ti lave young Rae ootin. Aiblins she wis jist fu o wind an pish as yaseyell."

"Yer recht thir, b'Christ. At wis aye somehin Etta had a feck o. Jist like the bothy cat," said Nan. "Fittiver, at's her dochter flittin in, an Etta's plantit sax fut unner, sae A jalouse we'll ne'er ken fit she wis hinkin." With this there was general accord.

CHAPTER THREE
Rae moves in

Rae Swankie, the woman that had caused such cackling amongst the teuch old hens that scarted about Mae's Shop, threw her self down on the sofa temporarily parked in the middle of the living-room at Number One Fountain Square and sipped at a welcome mug of tea. Around her all was chaos; boxes, cartons, black plastic bin-liners stuffed plumply full, suitcases bulging fit to burst; a life, in fact, all packaged up. Thankfully, Rae thought to herself, she was going to have a few days grace before starting her new job.

She looked around the room and its bare walls with the dingy paint and cobwebs. It was a sad sight, but Rae did not see these material things; she saw the room as it would be, and she nodded. It would be right nice, she thought. It would suit just fine. She luxuriated for a while, drinking in the calm that the departed bustle of removal men had left behind them; it was better now, it was quiet and tranquil and most of all it was *hers*. Hers and hers alone and no bugger could take it away from her. The thought made her feel warm and she snugged down and sipped the tea, kicking off her shoes and extending her feet onto a box as she did so. This was *her* place. At last. She had never thought it would be, but now it was.

Rae had grown up in this house, but she had not set foot in it for thirteen years near to the day. She had always believed that her mother would carry out her promise to leave it to the local Cat's Refuge rather than leave it to her errant daughter; so it had come as something of a surprise—not to say a shock—to discover that in fact her mother had not made a Will at all, and that Rae, as the sole progeny, had inherited the lot; a tidy enough sum of money to be going along with, the house, and the furniture. Rae could only think that her stars had changed, and occasionally she had nightmares that some day the lawyer would phone up and say they'd found the Will and the Cat's Refuge had inherited after all. However, for the meantime her unexpected good fortune, even if it couldn't wash away the sadness that she had felt in her life, still seemed to have given it a bit lick paint so that she could live with it the better.

Rae smiled, and shook herself. It was silly to let yourself be fashed by fancies and nightmares. What was coming to you wouldn't pass you by, so why worry? That had always been her motto, and it had gotten her through times that teuch they'd have been the end of a weaker lassie. She glanced at her watch, and then out of the window. Willie should have been back by now; she had only sent him along to the corner shop to get some milk. A certain uneasiness mounted in her, and she almost got up to look along The Street after him, but then she shook her head and sighed again. It was going to take a wee while to get rid of these city habits, these fears and insecurities. And wasn't that why she had come back after all these years? To bring her son to a place where he could grow up without her having to worry the way a city mother worries?

Sure enough, soon she heard the reassuring clatter of the latch on the back door being lifted. "Mind an wipe your feet an not trail gutters into the house," she called, and there was an answering grunt from the lobby. "An then come through an give me a cuddle."

Rae felt warm as her son hugged her; she hoped he would never not want to do that, never become self-conscious, even though she knew he would. "Ye were awa a long time," she said.

"Aye. The woman in the shop gie'd me a bar chocolate."

"Did she now. An I suppose she was askin ye about us?"

"Aye," quipped Willie. "But A didnae let on onythin. Honest. A jist tellt her her cats wis great. Mum, how has she got aa they cats? A've niver seen anythin like it."

"Mae? Don't know. Maybe she's a witch."

"Naa. Witches are *really* ugly. She's no ugly. She's jist auld, that's aa." Willie frowned. "An how come *you* ken her name?"

"Oh, everybody kens Mae. And anyway, she's related."

"Oh." said Willie. "So A'm related as weel?"

"Aye. But don't worry about it, you'll not have to remember her birthday or anything. As a matter o fact, most folk round here are related some way or anither." Rae stretched. "Right," she said, "That's enough questions for now. We've got work to do. We need to mak up the beds and put all these boxes away. And ye ken what? I canna be bothered cookin the night. What about we go into Arbeg and get fish suppers?"

Willie's eyes lit up like torch-bulbs. "Great, mum! Real Arbeg fish suppers!"

Thank God for junk food, thought Rae, and went to fetch her jacket.

Fountain Square is in the middle of Auchpinkie; its name comes from the days before piped water when the folk made use of a spring in its centre to do their laundry. An iron cistern had been placed on an ashlar stone plinth to conserve the water from the spring, and all around it were stone basins with stone slabs beside them to scrub on, and great bronze taps. The rest of the village was just called The Street. There are three cottages on three of the sides of the little square, the fourth being open to The Street, and Number One, the cottage that Rae had moved into, was on the south-east corner.

Next door was empty; or rather, no one lived there. Big Sye's father, Eck, used it as a store. There was stuff in there hadn't seen the light of day in thirty year or more. Next to that was Peem's house. Immediately next to that, the two forming an angle, lived Peem's mother, Jess. You might think that two people whose relationship was so spectacularly fiery might choose to keep a little more distance between them; but that would have been very out of character for either. Mind, it would have suited Peem's wife, Izzie, who for the most part was referee to their squabbling.

Physically, Iz and Peem could have been designed to match; they were both of the same compact but comfortable build, due in his case to an over-fondness for 80/- ale, and in hers to an irresistible weakness for milk chocolate, and to be fair, the production of a small tribe of Teviotdales.

As Rae pulled on her jacket, she heard a tap at the door. The first, she thought. That didn't take them long. She opened the door to see Izzie on the doorstep. The two women looked at each other for a long while in silence. At length, Iz spoke.

"Hi, Rae," she said, as if they'd seen each other only that morning. Then she smiled her dimpled smile. "It's nice tae see yiz again." She looked at Willie and then at the house. "Hiv ye taen oan Etta's hoose, then?"

"Aye. I have that."

"A saw the removers van. And yer gingin tae bide here?

Rae nodded.

"Och, at's braa, hon. Hiv ye seen Peem yet?" Rae thought she saw the slightest trace of a shadow pass over her old friend's face, but it was so fleeting she dismissed it.

"No yet," she replied.

"Ach he'll be fair delighted tae see yiz. Ye'll need tae drap by for a wee dram."

Iz moved forward suddenly and hugged Rae. Rae wasn't expecting it, and she froze stiff at first, but Isabel Teviotdale was not the type of woman to be easily put off a bit physical affection, and Rae felt herself relaxing, enveloped in something very warm and pleasant. "A hope ye daa mind me cryin roon tae see yiz."

"No. Course not. It's good to see ye, Izzie."

Iz pulled back. "Efter aa, we're neebours noo."

Rae glanced away. "Ach we're more than that, Iz. We'll aye be more than that." Her voice was suddenly thick.

Izzie's eyes shone. "It *is* really nice to see yiz again, Rae," she replied, and Rae knew she meant it. "Ye've been awa ower lang. Listen, A canna bide noo, but gin thir onyhin ye need, ye ken far A am, recht? Recht? Mi casa su casa, ye ken, hon."

"Okay."

"Wha wis that, Mum," asked Willie as they got into Rae's car.

"An old friend. I'll tell ye about her later."

CHAPTER FOUR
Geordie Baird and the Balgownie Estate.

Geordie Baird knew fine well he was the subject of a certain deri-sion on the part of Big Sye and Peem; sentiments which he, for his part, thoroughly reciprocated. And this was quite in the normal way of things, for Sye and Peem were well kent to be the most scurrilous pair of poachers between the Tay and the Dee, and our Geordie was the Head Bailiff of the Balgownie Estate. And since Auchpinkie was within the boundaries of that estate, and indeed the Laird of Balgownie was Feu Superior to the village, their several paths crossed quite regularly. Mind, and this to Geordie's infinite annoyance, though their paths had crossed spatially, they had not as yet crossed temporally—that is to say, Geordie had hitherto been just that wee bit over slow off his mark to get his hands on the slippery customers while they were still in possession of incriminating evidence.

Some four miles north of Auchpinkie Ness, and still well within the bounds of the estate, the River Pinkie flows into the sea. Now this River Pinkie, though not one of the great Scottish rivers like the Tay or the Spey or the Tweed, is nevertheless a good river, its fine steady flow of clear water tinted with peat brown. It has full, deep, slow turning pools which you can't see the bottom of in even the driest summer, and in spate it is as exhilarating a torrent as any. It is worth the fishing throughout the season, but its fame amongst the angling fraternity rests upon the habits of the King of Fish, *salmo salar*, the legendary salmon himself, who has, since time immemorial, upon the first spring tide after Mayday, surged in his hundreds up from the estuary into the river. It is a run that glazes eyes wherever fishermen gather, and while those who can afford to cast their fly legitimately over the water, another kind of sportsman takes what he can by stealth.

Geordie had been a Bailiff on the river since he had left the school, following in his father's footsteps, and taking charge of the fishery in his turn. His efforts to improve the fishing had until two years before been hindered by the attitude of the old Laird, who was a cantankerous lunatic as long-lived as he was mad who spent most of his days wandering around his lands dressed as he thought an eighteenth-century Highland chief should dress, notwithstanding the fact that his was a Lowland estate, that he'd been born in Croydon, and the term "'45" meant nothing to him at all. He always left the day-to-day management of Balgownie, its lands and waters, to his factor, a moon-faced clot who had, to put it politely, moved from several other estates before winding up here. The factor and Geordie had never quite seen eye to eye.

In the end they found the old man, dying as daft as he had lived, lying flat on his back and sonsie as you like, in the middle of the overgrown front lawn of the Grange, frozen stiff as a board and wearing only his nightshirt and a beatific smile. The usual local sources of gossip whispered that the true cause of the Laird's death was the long-desired success of his advances towards widow Macrae of Crowhill Farm, the formidable fortress of whose virtue he had been assailing since the day after she buried her husband; and with his wish granted he was content to lay him amongst the gods. True or no, only Mistress Macrae might know, and there was no chance of her letting on. For his part Geordie was—for all that he was a regular kirker—quite delighted.

Needless to say, the Laird's widow, a woman many years younger than the departed, lost no time; before the Laird was fairly planted in the ground she called the lawyers and told them to sell the place lock, stock and barrel for whatever they could get for it, since she could not (she sniffed into her handkerchief) bear to remain there with her poor, dear husband gone, and meantime she could be contacted at an address in Largs. No one was the least surprised when the factor decamped to join her, in order, he said, to help his mistress organise the sale. For all that he was a nincumpoop, he was a braw looking laddie, and he had just about enough brains to see when his train was pulling out.

The Balgownie Estate remained on the market for some time, so Geordie assumed the role of Factor on a temporary basis. The Estate was finally sold to a property developer who had made a fortune in the South (of England) and who had had the foresight to get out before the bubble burst, and the idea of a Scottish Estate had tickled his fancy. Well, the thought of living like a lord for the price of a suburban semi affects some folk that way. Anyway, this man, whose name was Anshaw, liked to see change, and to be fair—for now—he was prepared to dip his hand, with care, into his pocket. He believed in Progress, something he never hesitated to advertise. Soon Geordie found himself hiring staff, and for the first time ever had a real budget to spend; and he was not too sad to give up his interim duties as Factor to a certain Mr Stoker, the new owner's Man Friday, as I believe that class of functionaries are called. We will have more to say about Geordie; this serves but as an introduction, in the way of being polite.

Big Sye's house was called The Chateau. He had named it thus in measure of his delight at having a house of his very own, which was enormous, rather than of the house itself, which was not. The Chateau was in fact a miracle of miniaturisation. It was built on the site where once, long before, had stood a rickety wooden shed that had belonged to Sye's greatuncle Peter. He had given it to Sye's mother when she married Eck and moved into the cottage directly opposite. Eck had torn down the shed and built a garage that was only slightly more substantial. It became Sye's when Nan realised that her son was a grown man of twenty-five, with little apparent intention of getting married. He was cluttering up the house so she gave him the plot, with the garage, much to Eck's disgust, and told her son to build his own.

Sye lost no time and called in the aid of one of his second cousins, who was an architect and, conveniently, in the same darts team as the local Planning Officer. The second cousin arranged for Sye to deliver a present to this last (by a most circuitous and totally innocent route) of a quantity of fresh lobster and several bottles of Bell's, and permission was duly granted to erect a two-storey, two-bedroomed house. I hesitate to use the term 'villa' for fear of implying a grandeur of scale that would be entirely out of place.

Sye built the house himself, with the help of a team of friends and vast quantities of beer, and when it was finished it did not deviate sufficiently from the plans for the Building Control Officer to refuse a certificate of completion. Which amazed everyone, except for Sye and his second cousin, who had been most foresightful with the Bell's.

Upstairs were the two bedrooms, the toilet and the bathroom. Sye had actually succeeded in squeezing a double bed into the 'double' bedroom. However, having done so he found that the door would have to be either permanently open or permanently shut, so he compromised and took the door off its hinges altogether. The minuscule toilet was provided with a washbasin, but the disposition of easement and basin was such that to wash your hands you had to sit on the seat, any adjustment of clothes had to be done before entering, and gentlemen had to pee sitting down. Sye never bothered putting a door on that in the first place and habitually relieved himself while standing in the hallway. The other bedroom, the 'single' served as a store, and we shall not discuss this fragment of chaos until we are feeling a little stronger.

Downstairs was the front room and the kitchenette. Once, soon after the house was finished (a relative use of the term if ever there was one) Sye had been in Aberdeen, having that morning come ashore. That was in the good old days when you could take your wages in cash at Dyce heliport. The pubs and professional ladies of Aberdeen have never quite recovered since the combined pressure of wives and civic authority put an end to the practise. Anyway, there was Sye with a hipper absolutely bulging with cash and already carrying a fairish cargo of the craiter, ambling down Union Street wondering whether to have a massage or a curry, or both, and if so in which order, and just coming round to the idea of having a pint to lubricate the cogitive process, when all of a sudden he stops in front of MacKay's Furniture and his eye is caught by a suite of two armchairs and a three-seater sofa, all in black leather and all In The Sale. Jings, thinks he, jist recht for the hoose. And in he goes and slaps his money on the counter and buys it on the spot.

Well, when the van arrived, it was *bigger* than the house, a fact that was duly noted by the two dozen or so onlookers, lamp-post-leaners and kick-the-baa-agin-the-dykers that congregated to watch the fun. The men from MacKay's—rising stoically to the occasion—unloaded the suite with troubled faces, scratched their heads and puzzled and muttered and pulled out measuring tapes and then adjourned for a livener before returning, removing the front window, frame and all, and sliding the sofa in through the hole. It slotted in as if it was made to fit, and then there was no room for anything else.

Sye left the armchairs on the pavement outside until he was due to go offshore again, and then he gave them to Nan as a Christmas present. (It was June). He said he preferred the sofa, like, so he could stretch out. The armchairs were, well, too restricting. His mother sighed and squeezed them into *her* front room, which she never used except at Hogmanay and funerals. They were unloved, and became lonely, those chairs. Eck's dog, a small black-and-tan mongrel by the name of Queenie, gave birth to a litter of nine pups in one of them, which afterwards so resembled a prop from *Texas Chainsaw Massacre* that it had to be consigned to the garden shed. Nan said it gave visitors the willies, like. Sye himself first-footed his Ma and Da some years later whilst in a predictably miraculous condition, tripped over the cat, measured his length, broke his fall on the remaining armchair and so distorted its frame that forever after, whenever anyone tried to sit on it, it would try to tip them out. It knew it was an unwanted and an unlucky chair, and the bitter kenning of it made it spiteful.

Life in The Chateau was shared between Big Sye and his dog, Pluto. Now I say 'his' dog, but I should explain that the precise nature of the relationship was far more complex, and perhaps better described by saying that Pluto was a dog who consented to sleep in the same house as a human he had adopted. Sometimes. It was frequently opined in Auchpinkie that Pluto was the only sentient being that could ever, ever thole living with Sye, which, if you ever got a right deek at Plute, would give you more than a clue about what was generally thought of Sye's domestic habits.

Pluto was an enormous and shaggy flea-bitten-grey lurcher of truly Baskervillian aspect, with pale brown eyes, feet like dinner-plates and fangs like can-openers, and an essential aroma of hound that had been known to make polite ladies' eyes water. Even the most dedicated annoyer of other people's mutts would be disinclined to irritate this one. The overall impression of a less than entirely charitable nature hinted at by the way he growled like a barrel rolling down a hill if you just looked at him for too long was emphasised by his habit of leering up at you with one baleful eye and the somewhat frayed edges to his ears; he was getting on, was Pluto, and the scars of his battles were many. Mind, the numerous replicas of himself that strutted around the village testified that he was still a long way from being over the hill.

"Pit it awa, ya daft mutt, an g'aff the settee," growled Sye as he squeezed past into the kitchenette. Pluto, who was stretched out on his back with his legs in the air, opened his good eye and stayed put. The back door of the house was open—it was never locked, so that Pluto could come and go as he pleased; burglary was not a big thing in Auchpinkie, at least not within the village, and in any case both Pluto and his master were well enough kent that the Arbeg low-life gave them a very wide berth—and Sye pushed it shut with his foot.

"A wish tae hell ye'd learn tae shut the door efter ye," he said to Pluto. Outside the window he could see Dave the barman's terrier digging a hole in Ma White's drying green. He yawned. Pluto, who had been following the human with his eyes so that he was now bent round like a letter 'c', straightened, stretched, farted, rolled off the sofa, shook himself, stretched again, a big one this time from the tips of his fore-toes right down to each quivering hind leg in turn, finishing the performance off with a flick of his excessively-long tail, yawned, licked his chops and slouched into the kitchen. He raised his tattered ears and his tail—which was his primary means of communication—waved from side to side as if to say "Any chance o a dod nosh?"

Sye glanced at his watch and nodded. "No a bed idear. Feelin a wee bit peckish masel," he mused, and had a look in the fridge.

"An far hiv youse been these past puckle days?" he demanded as he put half a can of dog food, a stale ham sandwich and a steak pie into Pluto's dish.

"Naewey special," wagged Pluto innocently.

"Aye, A thocht at's fit ye'd say," replied Sye as he set the dish in front of the dog. He screwed up his face in distaste. "Christ thon pie hums, min. Fit wey cin ye sup on at?"

He opened the eye-level cupboards above the kitchen worktop one by one and sighed. Better tell Ma tae pick up some stuff next time she was at Willie Low's, then. Then he rummaged in the bread-bin and found a heel, which he inspected carefully. "A jalouse it's toast fur me," he grumbled.

"Aye weel ye kin jist keep yer paas affa mine, youse," growled Pluto. He finished off his repast and wandered back to the sofa.

Meanwhile the human was scratching thoughtfully at a penicillin-mould growing on the heel of bread. "It's aa recht fur *youse*," he complained. "*Youse* wid eat onyhin. Jings thon pie musta been thir for weeks." He threw the bread at the dog, who caught it deftly and swallowed it whole. "C'mon," said Sye after a moment's reflection. "We'll awa ower tae the Hotel an hae a recht bite an a wee bit wet-the-thrapple."

CHAPTER FIVE
Sye meets Geordie and Alan

S ye noted, as he entered the Public Bar with Pluto in tow, the presence of Geordie Baird and one whom he did not recognise, but whose attire, of green waxed cotton jacket, knee breeches and deerstalker, advertised the fact that he was in the same line of business as his companion. Forbye, he had by his side a stalker's staff, upon the intricately carved bone head of which he rested one hand. "Fit like, cousin?" intoned Sye with a smile at Geordie. The appellation was accurate, strictly speaking, even though the relation was removed several times; but then, Sye only said it because he knew it annoyed the hell out of Geordie. Pluto sniffed once, disdainfully, and then threw himself down on the flags in the middle of the floor and yawned, his one good eye fixed menacingly upon the Bailiff.

"Whit brings ye doon tae hobnob wi the likes o wis?" grinned Sye. "A hinny seen yiz fer, ach, hell, A canna mind noo." *Lang time efter the last time you saw me, onywey*, he thought. "Will ye hae a wee somehin?"

Geordie swithered. To say no would be impolite, far more impolite than he had any reason to be, but to say yes was accepting drink from a known—well, at the very least thoroughly suspected—poacher. In the end he nodded. "Large Chivas, A'll hae," he said. Might as well gar the bugger pay, he thought. "D'ye ken ma new man here? Alan Gilchrist. He wis on the Tweed afore, ye ken. Managed tae catch a hale wheen poachers."

Gilchrist nodded coolly at Sye. "Aye. Landit them in the jile, an aa. A'll hae a Low Flyer. A large een."

"Poachers, eh?" mused Sye as he settled himself into his habitual position at the angle of the wall. He shook his head. "Ach, thir nae affa muckle o that gings on aboot here nou. Nae eneuch siller in't. Divvy, fit's Agnes got on the necht? In the wey o grub, like?"

Dave passed him a dog-eared menu. "Naa," Sye continued, "It's the fermin that's killed it. It's no worth the trachle ony mair. So A hear, onywey."

Gilchrist was still gazing at him steadily. "So ye hear, hey? That's a guid ane. A hear things tae, ye ken. A've been hearing gey mony things aboot the poachers roond here. An whit A've been hearin tells me there's poachers aboot aa recht."

"Hiv ye heard at, hiv ye, tho? Crivvens. Ach weel, see A widnae ken. A've nae got time fur they cantrips." Sye looked over to Dave. "Could ye mebbe cry through for a steak pie an chips ti me, Divvy?"

"Ur ye gingin ben the houss furtae eat it?"

"Ach, nou, Divvy, kin ye no see A've got ma workin claes on. A hink A'll jist sup here the necht an at wey A kin hae a wee bit news wi ma cousin an his chum tae."

Dave's eyebrows knitted. The Lounge Bar was for eating, but he knew that there was no way he'd persuade Sye. And since this little ritual was carried out several times a week, Sye knew Dave had to put on the show of trying. Agnes's orders. Dave glowered and muttered something that might have been interpreted as "Ah weel mebbe jist this eence," and shuffled through the connecting door.

"Ye widnae ken, eh? That's no whit A heard," sneered Gilchrist, picking up where he'd left off..

"Cousin Geordie, wid ye like tae pit yer wee bit dug back on his lead until A get ma supper, hankin ye kindly like? An while yer at it, tell him we daa consider it polite ti mak insinuations like at aroon here. Leastwise, no till ye've got some kinda proof," said Sye, a certain air of warning in his voice.

Gilchrist, who was a big man with fair hair and a florid expression, suffused red under his deerstalker, but a movement of Geordie's hand silenced him.

"Aye, c'mon nou, lads," put in Dave, as he stepped back into his domain, closing the door on the strains of *Stand By Your Man* from the juke-box. "Save that kinna hing fer ootside."

Gilchrist held his tongue, but his gaze became a glower.

"Hings aboot ready for the big day, then, Geordie?" asked Sye in conciliatory tones, and Geordie was glad of the opportunity to defuse the tension. He was only too aware that the quiet hubbub of chatter from the other patrons of the bar had stilled to near silence during the brief interchange.

"Aye," he assented. "The Grange is lookin recht dandy. It's aa been reddit up an pentit oot an aa. New carpets, new curtains, the works. Thiv even pit in a swimmin pool far yon auld conservytery wis. We've naehin tae dae wi thon side, like, but still, it's grand tae see it efter the wey it wis, aa run doon and fu o doo skyte. A heard jist the day we're bookit for the first week by een o they big life insurance companies. Seems they've got begs o siller tae spend." He drained his glass. "Hae anither?"

"A hink sae. Gie's a large Macallan."

"Heh, heh." Geordie winced, but had to thole it: The eighteen year old Macallan was the most expensive short in the bar. "Oh, aye. Seems thir gingin tae bring a wheen thir top dogs on the sales front or fittiver an gie them a chance tae try thir haun on the new gowf course, a wee bit scamper ower the moor ettlin tae see the erses o a puckle deer disappearin i the distance, an a shot at the fishin on the river. The hale caboodle wrapped up wi the finest grub ye can imagine, served by the bonniest lassies ye'd care tae run yer een ower. Thiv e'en got new tartan outfits, ye ken. Aye." Geordie sucked his tooth and managed to look pompous. "Big cheenges, aa recht, big cheenges. It's the coming hing, ye ken, an A'm no girnin ony. Nou A've got three men under me, besides Alan here, an that's got tae be guid."

"Weel A seen in the pipper ye've got aa sorts o new patrols an aa tae stop they blastit poachers," put in Sye, with no trace of irony in his voice. "A suppose that's how yer man thir's aa fired up wi himsel."

"Dinnae ye worry, Sye. If onybody tries it, we'll nab him. You mark ma words."

Sye lifted one eyebrow. "D'ye hink it?"

"Oh aye, A div that." chuckled Geordie. The whisky was warming him up. "But tae tell ye the truth, whit wi the three gillies besides o us twa an the Polis an the Protection bein i the airts forbye, A daa hink thir onybody'd daur. Heh, heh. They'd hae tae be fell gallus, like." There was an uncomfortable silence and Geordie was aware that there had once again been a lowering of the level of noise in the bar; he had the feeling that every ear was half-listening to their conversation, and he felt considerably relieved when the atmosphere recovered.

"Weel, ye ken, *Cousin*," said Sye as he drained his glass. "Thir some recht gallus billies aboot. A widnae be sae confydunt if A wis youse." He set the empty glass on the bar thoughtfully. "Be the wey, jist atween wis, like, jist fit wey *did* ye manage tae persuade the Meenistry tae staund a vessel affshore sae handily like?"

"Ach, weel, at wis the boss's daein. He managed tae pull some strings somewey. Some chiel he gingit tae the schuil wi's a heid een i the Meenistry. A jalouse at's fit wey the English dae hings. Onywey, officially thir on the lookoot fur the Bleck Fish, but seein as how thir aboot, like, thill gie wis a leg up gin we need een."

Dave the barman glowered across the bar at him. "Fittdye mean, the bleck fish? Fit the blazes kinda fish is at nou?"

Sye delicately picked a piece of tobacco off the tip of his tongue with his finger and smiled. "It's they quotas, Divvy. Aa the boats has got limits on thir tonnage o fish these days an fan they've landit aa thiv lave tae, thiv tae tie up. Thiv ti lave eneuch fish fur the Frogs an the Spaniards, see. Europe, ken."

"A ken *at*. But fit wey does it mak thum bleck? A aye thocht they wis aa whechtfish aboot here."

"No 'bleck', 'Bleck', he sayed," explained Sye.

Dave's expression darkened thunderously, and Sye grinned. "Ach it's jist a mainner o spikkin, Divvy. Jist means that whiles a canny skipper mecht come alangside at a wee wee bitty herbour that's no muckle yased far he kin land a couple dozen boxes wi'oot lettin on tae the Meenistry. Thon wey he kin mak oot he's catchit less'nn he has an no hivti tie up. An ye ken, a boat tied up—ach, at's like you sittin here aa day wi the door locket."

Dave, whose comprehension of business principles was awesome, nodded.

"Aye," added Gilchrist, in a quiet voice loaded with provocation. His gaze had not wavered from Sye. "Mebbe jist like yon wee herbour doon the bottom o the clift." He pointed downwards.

"Ach, they'd hivtae be skelly," replied Sye. "Aabody kens ye cannae get onyhin bigger'n a pot boat alangside doon thir noo. An be the wey, wi aa the exercise yer gie'in yer jaa, are ye no mindin yer on the bell? Wir cryin oot wi drouth ower here." Sye did not, and with good reason, mention that there was nothing stopping you taking a pot boat out and loading a dozen boxes or so from a passing trawler. He sipped his whisky and carried on, hoping to steer the crack onto safer ground. "Onywey ye canna really blame the skippers, ye ken. Efter aa, fit wey sid thi hiv ti tie up fur ti watch aa they furrin boats cleanin oot wir ain watter? Maks nae sense ava. A say guid luck ti them."

"Yer a guy cool customer, A'll gie ye that. This'll be the first time Alan Gilchrist's pit his haun in his pooch for a poacher."

Sye regarded himself for several minutes in the mirror before he said anything and then sighed. So Gilchrist really did want bother. "A'll hae the same again, freen, an be the wey, dae A no mind tellin ye aboot bein sae handy wi yer insinuations no ten meenits syne?"

"A'm no insinuatin nothin. A'm statin a weel-kent fa-"

"Far's yer mucker the necht?" interrupted Dave as Agnes passed through the steak pie and chips.

"The twins's got a tempyrature an he's bade in tae help Iz keep an ee on thum," answered Sye. "Yer aye fashed wi bairns, it seems."

Alan Gilchrist, who had had more to drink that he should have, but not enough yet to know it, seemed to dislike the way his last taunt had been parried. His blood was up. "Nae bairns yersel?" he demanded.

There was something about his tone that Sye didn't like. In fact there was plenty about *all* of him that Sye didn't like. And an top of that he was clearly in the mood for a fight, and Sye really couldn't be bothered. "Ne'er wad," he said, quietly. He had been in situations like this too often; he had offered the olive branch of a change of conversation, and it had been thrust back in his face, and Gilchrist was getting more and more het by the minute. Whatever was going to happen would happen, Sye knew that now.

"How no?" sneered Gilchrist, all veneer of politeness dispensed with at last. "Ower lang in the jile? Or is it jist that that's no yer fancy, if ye tak ma meanin?"

Sye sawed up his pie without saying anything. He swallowed a mouthful and then turned to Gilchrist. "Weel now, howsaboot we jist cry at neen o yer ingans, eh? Gin ye daa mind me sayin sae." He looked hard at Geordie and felt a bad anger mount in him. What was he doing, bringing this, this *animal* in to irritate him and stir up trouble? This was supposed to be neutral territory. What was Geordie playing at, bringing in some thug that didn't know the rules? Well, if they wanted to play dirty, then that was just fine. Sye Swankie had never been feared of a gamey all his days, and he wasn't for starting now.

But Gilchrist had not finished. "A dinna doot ye'll be the kind o lad that likes tae hang aboot ither fowks wives, then, eh? Mebbe hae a wee bit diddle at a sea-widow while her man's awa makin an *honest* livin? Aye, that's a rare kind o a poacher for ye!" Before Sye, who, to be fair, was not entirely averse to sea-widows, could reply, Gilchrist drove home the point of his knife. "Poach fish, poach weemen, it's aa the same, eh? Jist as lang's it's done ahent fowks backs, eh? A ken you lads. A've spent aa ma days efter ye. Ye think yer the bees knees, but yer jist a bunch o dirty, thievin, cheatin—"

Sye pushed away from the bar and his arms swung loose. Unnoticed by anyone, Pluto got to his feet. His hackles were erect and his fangs bared. Gilchrist pushed past Geordie, ignoring his protestations and made straight for Sye. But then there was a Bang! that crashed through the bar and silenced everyone. Dave the barman had slammed the bar top with the rounders bat he kept under it, a sure sign that he had reached the end of *his* tether.

"*OOT*side, wi thon, A tellt ye!" he roared. "A'll hae neen o yer fisticuffs in ma bar!"

"That's aa recht," said Sye, never moving his glare from Gilchrist. "A wis jist lavin. Tell Agnes thir's naehin wrang wi her grub, it's jist thir a queer-like guff in here the necht. A hink A'll tak me a wee daunder alang the strand tae get a breath o fresh air." Gilchrist barred his way to the door. "Scaise me," said Sye.

Gilchrist moved aside but slowly. "Dinnae ye worry, ma canty mannie," he muttered as he did so. "We'll hae ither opportunities fur wir wee hert-tae-hert."

As Sye disappeared into the gathering night, Gilchrist returned to the bar. He was laughing. "Weel, that's roond wan tae us. See's anither couple whiskies, barman. A hink A'll award masel a wee deoch an doris."

Dave didn't move. "Whisky's aff," he growled. He was still holding the rounders bat. "Fur that metter, the beer's aff an aa. An the rum. An onyhin else ye kin hink o forbye."

"Oh is that the wey o it?" Gilchrist turned to Dave.

"It is at. An daa ye even hink aboot stertin ony nonsense wi me. A'd gie ye sicca dunt on the nut ye'd be seein starns fur a week soon as look at ye."

"That's *eneuch,* Alan," interjected Geordie, his voice sharp with authority now. "A'm sorry, Dave. We'll be on wir roads noo."

"Good. Saves me the bother o flingin ye oot. Yer barred, the pair o yiz. Sup up yer drink an get gingin."

Sye did not, as he had said he would, head straight for the beach upon leaving the bar. Instead he walked along The Street to Fountain Square, turned right, and chapped on Peem's door. When Peem answered the door, he was dressed in a pair of jeans, the flies of which he was still doing up.

"Oh, here, sorry, like, Peem," said Sye. "A didnae ken ye wis busy."

"Ach it's yersel," said Peem, and winked. "Ye didnae interrup onyhin." He squinted at Sye quizzically. "Here, are youse aa recht?"

"Naa. But daa fash yersel. A'll see ye the morn." Sye turned to go, and Pluto cheered up.

"No ye'll no," exclaimed Peem, stepping out into the square. "Ye'll c'way in an hae a dram an tell us fit i the hell's gotten intil ye. Ye look like ye've seen Auld Nick. Izzie an me wis aboot ti hae wirsels a dram onywey."

Sye swithered. "Ye shair?"

Peem looked down at his jeans and laughed. "It's bath necht, Sye. Nuthin ti worry aboot. The pair o wis aye get drookit bathin the bairns."

Sye turned to the dog. "Awa hame, Plute," he said firmly, and followed Peem into the lounge. He sat down in an armchair by the fireplace. Peem picked up a sweatshirt from the back of another armchair and pulled it on, and then went to the cocktail cabinet, which, by the way, was superbly stocked and equipped. As if you needed to ask. Without asking he poured Sye a serious OVD and one for himself. Izzie came in as he was doing so, dressed in a pink towelling robe and mules. She walked over to Sye and turned up her face for him to kiss, as she always did, kissing full on the lips. As their lips met Sye was for a moment enveloped by the heavy scent of her. Then she pulled away and curled up on the sofa like a cat. "A'll hae a Bacardi an coke, hon," she said to Peem, pulling his sleeve. "Plenty ice."

"C'mon, then, Sye, spill the beans," she said, as Peem passed her the clinking glass. "Tell me *aahin*."

Sye sipped long on his drink, and then explained what had happened in the bar. Peem shook his head and clucked his tongue, but Iz just gazed intently at Sye with her grave blue eyes. It was a habit that took some people by surprise. When Sye finished she nodded slowly.

"Ye shid niver hae risen ti thon bugger's bait, Sye," she said quietly, reaching for her cigarettes. Her habit of hitting the nail on the head first time could be uncomfortable, thought Sye. "A've a feelin that thir somehin gingin on thir. But ye'll no heed me onywey." She sighed.

"Yer recht, Iz," agreed Sye. "An A'm sorry A done it, noo. But thon bastart hud me that roused. A mean Geordie's a jonick eneuch loon, jist he's on the ither side, like. Fit the hell wis he hinkin aboot bringin yon intil a civilised pub ti deev the likes o me?"

"Did ye niver hink that maybe puir Geordie had nae idear the mannie wid ging on like at? No hink mebbe he wis jist as embarrassed as ye wid hiv been in his place? Onywey, fit's done's done." Suddenly she stopped and twisted round in her seat. "Ian! Izzat you! Awa up ti yer baid *rechtnoo!*" Ian was Peem and Izzie's eldest son, and twelve years old. "That laddie? A cannae get him ti bide in his baid at necht fur love nor money, an see gettin him up in time ti catch the skale bus the morns? A trial." Izzie unfolded her legs from under her and crossed the room. She ran her hand through Sye's hair and then shook her head. "A should tell ye tae let the hale hing drap an forget aa aboot it. But seein as ye'll no listen, you just be careful an daa be gettin ma man in trouble." She looked at Peem.

"Daa you be bidin up jaain wi *him* aa necht either. That's an order. It's no as if ye didnae work thegither aa the day lang nor nothin."

"A'm gingin ti get that bastart, so A am," said Sye, after Iz had left. His anger was slow to catch light, but it burned long and steady once it was aflame. "A daa ken fit wey yet, but A ken A will."

"Ye no hink mebbe Izzie's recht? Best drap the hale hing?"

"Aye, a coorse she's recht. Ma sister's near as dammit aye recht, which is een o her mair annoyin sides. As ye'll hae noticed yersel be nou A jalouse. But A'm no like at. Ye sid ken better. Efter aa we've gotten intil thegither."

Peem laughed and got up to refill their glasses. "Daa you start on aboot fit we yased ti get intil," he said cheerfully. "We'll be up aa necht if ye dae. An that'll be me in the doghoose fur—ach, A daa ken. Lang eneuch."

CHAPTER SIX
The village and its harbour. Big Sye's Cave. Sye conceives a plan

The village snuggles contentedly like a colony of barnacles into the shoulder of Auchpinkie Ness, a vast, gnarled, wind-skelpit dug's heid of red sandstone that shoves rudely into the grey North Sea. Right on top of this rock is the kirk, a monument that has stood lonely against the sky for many long hundreds of years, and before they turned Christians the Picts that once ruled this land worshipped their gods there, and maybe those that came before them too. Who knows? Anyway, it's a landmark (and more importantly a sea-mark) visible two dozen miles away and more on a clear day. On misty days it shoves its spire up through the carpet of the haar into the clear sky above, so that from the air all that can be seen of the village is its solitary finger of slate, rising from the sea of grey like the masthead of a sunken ship.

Though the highest point is the Ness, the whole of the village is built along the top of a two-hundred foot red sandstone cliff; stone cottages brightly painted with the same good ship's paint the villagers use on their boats, so that you can tell whose boat is making for home as it flashes green or yellow or red through the rolling grey hump-backs, plunging like a gull over the billowy sea. Once, in the time before the fleet moved to the new harbour at Arbeg, and, to be sure, the living was harder than it is today, the women would watch from up thonder on the kirk road to see their men's boats coming home, and when they caught a glisk of that welcome flash of colour, they would rush down to the port—and before that the beach—to help offload the silvery harvest. But whiles it happened that a wife—aiblins a young quine fresh on the door-flag of married life, aiblins an old grey-haired grandminnie—would wait and wait and wait and wait until long after the night fell, before she walked slowly back to her cottage in her dool, with the other women-folk of her family comforting her with their quiet voices. For the sea has aye taken a heavy toll of those who dare plunder her.

The little pebble beach at the foot of the cliff and the harbour can only be reached by a steep and tortuous footpath (for the very brave) or an only slightly less steep track that descends along the bank of the little burn that you can at least get a motor down, so long as you feel sure that it will make it back *up*. At the bottom of this track is a little bay sheltered by the encircling cliffs. Before they built the harbour at Arbeg in 1860, the Auchpinkie fleet had been much bigger. In those days the harbour wall had been longer too, but it had been rudely truncated when a stray German mine broke its rusty mooring off the Tay and got thrown against it in a storm not long after the Armistice was signed. Some folk swore that bits of rubble from the blast stove in the windows of the old kirk at Auchengask, three miles inland. Nowadays all that remains of the fleet are three or four open pot-boats that habitually nod their heads on the easy swell within the harbour, and the half a dozen or so even smaller boats ranging from the smart and well maintained to outright hulks whose clinker planks have long syne sprung from being allowed to dry out, hauled up in a row on the strand.

Once these boats were hauled up out of the sea by hand, then by horse and now the job is done with an ancient, rusty Massey-Ferguson tractor that seems to belong to everyone and no-one. This item is by necessity kept at the top of the brae, the battery having disappeared in the dead of night years before, presumably to keep a local farmer's tractor going. There was never muckle love lost between the farmers and the Auchpinkie folk, nor is there yet. Since the tractor's steering is perhaps a little vague, and the brakes gave long ago under the attack of constant immersion in salt water, bump-starting the beast is not for the faint-hearted. It is wise, by the way, to make sure that no one *is* trying to start it before you climb the lane, because that tractor takes absolute right of way over all other road users.

The marram grass verges of the strand are piled high with the detritus of the fishing trade; lobster pots, the newly made, and the ancient and decrepit. Great skeins of net and festoons of plastic floats. Long lengths of ship's cable, rusty and long-seized winches, and two huge bronze screws from a steamer that foundered on the reef in 1897. The villagers thought to sell them for scrap in the First War when the price was high, and with great ingenuity managed to get them ashore, but then they couldn't get them up the cliff, so there they are still. There are a few postage-stamp gardens down here too, where some hardy souls grow their tatties; you would think they must arrive at the table ready salted, such is the proximity of the plots to the sea. There are a couple of pits full of old cinders where haddock is sometimes still smoked, a couple of sheds, and a few drying lines for those poor souls that don't have greens up in the village and are obliged to traipse all the way down here with their laundry.

Big Sye stalked slowly along the foreshore, his boots sliding as the rounded chuckies of the beach gave and held unpredictably under his feet. His hands were thrust deep into his pockets and he wore a glum expression beneath the tousle of sandy hair. From time to time he stopped, and his grey eyes swept the table of the sea. The slow swell sucked and chuckled at the shore, and above, as always, wheeled the circling maws and terns. It was early; hardly six o'clock in the morning and the sun was still low, though the warmth of its rays was already soaking through the carapace of Sye's blue serge pilot coat. It felt good. He surveyed the grey ocean once more. More than twelve mile offshore but seeming, through the crystal air, near enough to touch, the sugar white stalagmite of the Easter Rock lighthouse glowed pink on the horizon. Nearer to shore, a coaster made her way north, moving silent and stately and seeming far more beautiful than the noisy, rusting, paint-peeling workplace that she was. Nearer still two oil-rig supply boats steamed south in tandem, heading for the base at Dundee, busy little vessels that champed at the swell, their red-painted hulls high out of the water. Sye sighed and continued his trudge over the sliding stones.

It was mixing the drink that had done it. Sye shook his big head so that the shaggy curls flopped and then he stopped with a wince. He should've known damned fine to get out when he and Peem had finished that bottle of Wood's Navy. But Peem's eyes had had that wicked light in them, and when he'd rummaged in the back of the sideboard and emerged with a bottle of George Smith's, Sye had not had the heart to refuse. He knew its effect of old, and he knew better than to drink the damned stuff—until three or four had already slid down or he felt in the mood for a party. But after it was all over and he'd cast himself down in his bed at The Chateau in happy oblivion, that was when the trouble started. Three hours later he was awake, his head swimming, a drouth that could drink a loch and cramps in the backs of his legs that had him sitting bolt upright in bed before he knew what was happening. The only cure was water and walking, and Sye had worn out the soles of many a pair of boots in moonlight perambulation over the years.

He swore and shied a potato sized stone at a shag sitting on a rock. The shag, had he had a tongue, would have stuck it out as the stone splashed into the water a yard wide of the mark. Sye sighed. Oh that bloody clown Geordie Baird. He could cheerfully strangle him. But Sye knew fine it was all as much his own fault. *Yon galoot Gilchrist wis jist lookin for trouble. A should niver hiv teen the bugger on. A shouldae let him hae his wee bit rant and let him awa hame an niver let on.* Sye picked up another stone and let fly again. It fell even further from the mark and the shag, evidently bored with the game, took off and flapped languidly to another rock.

Sye flopped down on a convenient rock and let the memory of the previous evening wash over him for the fiftieth time.

He rubbed his eyes wearily. The damnedable bit of it was that he knew fine that however much he might say, no, he wasn't going to let on, they days was over, shake his head and walk away, without a shadow of a doubt he was going to end up doing something daft that at the end of the day would probably cost him much more than it was worth.

He remembered how once he'd slid a souped up Ford Escort—on its roof, mark you—the entire length of the Rossie brig in Montrose, a clear two hundred feet if it's an inch. His passenger, a junior reporter on the local paper whom Sye was trying to impress at least long enough to get her pants off, had dared him that he couldn't drive up on two wheels like they did in the pictures, so's they could get round the road works that was cutting off their escape from a jam sandwich in hot pursuit. Well he couldn't—drive on two wheels that is—but the attempt was genuinely impressive. The policeman whose smiling head appeared to Sye, upside-down, through the driver's window, said he'd never seen anything quite like it in all his time on the force, and he'd been on the force a long time, and if Sye was feeling quite well enough to get out and stand up, like, how'd he feel about blowing into this wee bag?

That little number had cost four hundred note and twelve months shanks' pony, never mind the Escort that afterwards looked more like a soup *can* than souped up. And to cap it all the young lady in question had thrown him over in high dudgeon and taken up with a photographer. Big Sye sighed again and kicked a lump of driftwood. After years of practise he could smell trouble and right now he was reeling from the stink of it.

After walking up and down the beach for several hours to clear the whisky fumes from his head, Sye continued his trail around the rocky buttress of the Ness itself. There was a path there that was only passable at low tide, and you had to take care not to get caught on the other side, or you faced a long cold wait on a ledge before the tide fell again, and a drouking or maybe even worse if the weather was bad. For once round the headland there was nothing; only a small bay encircled by cliffs where the hungry North Sea nibbled at the land. There was no way out for a man on foot to the north, for on that side of the bay the cliffs rose verti-cally from the sea and the rocks had a good covering of water even at the lowest of tides.

The rock-flats in the little bay itself were, however, rich in life, and it was this which had first led Sye, when he was a boy, to explore them, armed with a cleik, that most useful instrument for catching partans and lobsters.

Once, Sye had been caught by the tide, after staying over-long in pursuit of a particularly big and thrawn lobster. He didn't fancy having a go at swimming round the headland, as there was a fair sea and he knew well the risk of being smashed against the rocks, so he spent the time moving out of the way of the incoming tide and exploring the cliffs. It was then that he found the little cave right at the northmost neuk of the bay that was to become his own.

The entrance to this cave was actually in the water and when he first found it Sye had been reluctant to wade in, for fear of the rising tide behind him shutting off his escape. But on close inspection he realised that a narrow ledge high up on the side of the cave was always above the high water mark, and so, confident of his escape route, he explored it thoroughly. It led about forty feet into the cliff, where, through the gloom, Sye saw that further progress was impossible due to a mound of pebbles, a sort of subterranean beach which was, again, always above the waves. He had realised at once that a boat could be hidden here, safe from pry-ing eyes. You could enter or leave the cave in such a boat at any state of the tide, except at low-water springs, but thanks to the ledge, you could come and go yourself dry-shod whenever you liked, and the boat could be kept safely drawn up on the little beach.

Sye had kept an ancient clinker-built dinghy, that he had sal-vaged, there for years, until it had fallen apart, its place being taken by a

Zodiac inflatable with a powerful outboard engine which rested there still.

Over the years Sye had made several improvements to the natural qualities of the cave, and had further concealed the ledge that was its only dry entrance with driftwood and boulders. If anyone else had ever discovered it, they had left no trace. It was in itself no great surprise that he should be the only one who knew about the cave; these cliffs are as full of holes as a gruyere and there are many that are not fully explored, though the presence of some curious symbols carved into the sandstone of the walls high up at the nether end of the cave bore witness to the fact that long before someone else had been here.

Sye liked to come to his cave to think. He kept a store of things useful to this pursuit in one of several plastic drums with hermetically sealing lids; cans of beer, matches, packets of crisps, tobacco, shortie, a bottle or two of moonshine. The little still for the production of this last was buried under the shingle. The other drums contained items more appropriate to the practise of poaching than its abstract consideration, such as nets, lines, weights, and hooks.

Towards ten o'clock he arrived, removed a fourpack of Tennent's Lager from the drum, made a mental note to buy some more, settled himself on a rock by the entrance which had a suspiciously worn appearance, ripped the ring-pull from one of the cans and began to think.

By the time the fourpack was consumed, when the tide had advanced nearly to his feet and retreated again and the westering sun placed the cliffs in blue shadow and transformed the wheeling gulls and plunging gannets into sparks of fire, Sye had figured himself A Plan.

He got up from his perch and stretched. He flattened the empty cans with his boot and made his way to the back of the cave where he added them to the pile, checked, as he always did, the lids on all the plastic drums and tugged on the ropes that secured them and the Zodiac, and then set off back towards the port.

Peem was down on the shore attacking the barnacles that caked the bottom of a venerable clinker sailing dinghy with a scraper. He'd promised the year before to put the boat into order to take Ian sailing and his son was getting impatient. The air was filled with a rich bouquet of *fruits de mer* and Peem whistled cheerily as he worked. It wasn't much of a whistle, but given the state of his mouth, the surprise was that he could whistle at all. "Aye, aye," said Sye. Peem saw the broad grin on his friend's face and smiled in reply.

"Aye, aye, ti youse an aa. An fit hiv ye got ti be sae joco aboot? Gin A couldnae guess, like. Ye'll hae some hallirackit ploy fur landin the pair o wis in the nick, A jalouse." He put down the scraper and sat on the upturned boat, pushed his blue cap back on his head, crossed his ankles and folded his arms.

"Spit it oot, then, afore it chokes ye."

Sye pulled a packet of Old Holborn and some Rizla from his pocket and began to roll up a cigarette. Then he waved the makings at

Peem, who nodded, said "Ta," and did the same.

"See it's like this..........." Sye began, when they'd both lit up. One and a half roll-ups later—Sye always took his time about these things—he finished.

"By the cringe, Sye, at's no a ploy fur gettin the pair o wis in the jile, at's a ploy fur gettin wis baith killed." Peem shook his head from side to side with a smile of disbelief but for all that Sye knew his friend was hooked.

"So fan ur we gingin ti dae it?" he continued.

Big Sye laughed. "If A mind recht the moon an the tide'll be jist hunky-dory Monda next. But we can check it up at the pub. Davey'll hae a *Guidie* an A could fair dae wi a jar. A thon yapping doesnae half gie ye a dry thrapple."

"Aye, okay," said Peem, straightening up. "You're on the bell, mind."

CHAPTER SEVEN
Smuggler's Cave

Sye's was by no means the only cave in the area. The red sand stone cliffs which rise like stern ramparts out of the grey North Sea along this coast may look solid, but in fact the soft rock of which they are made is riddled with holes. Centuries of gnawing by the waves have gouged out hundreds of caves and tunnels as the corrosive mix of sand and salt water has worked its way along the weaknesses in the strata. And because the land here is still rising—still relieved that the burden of the Ice-Age glaciers has been lifted off its back—these caves and tunnels sometimes form interlocking systems on different levels, incongruously high up the cliff face.

It was in one such cave that Ian Teviotdale, Peem's son, had his den. It was the perfect hideout for a young outlaw, and he had made it his own. The entrance, being some twenty feet above the level of the highest spring tide, was always dry, and to make things even better, it was hidden by a brush of gorse that clung determinedly to its tiny crevice in the rock. And even if an intruder should stumble upon the little aperture that rose no more than three feet above the ledge and was about as wide, he would see little. You had to go in backwards, and then, just inside, the cave dropped down into a roomy chamber with a domed ceiling and a level shingle floor, entirely protected from the wind, lit with a soft light from the entrance. The disposition of these two spaces—the lobby and the front room, so to speak—was such that a laddie could stand on a fish box on the floor with his head in the lobby and keep watch on the curving strand of the bay.

Needless to say, Ian was not the first to have made use of the cave, though he was undisputedly the sole tenant now. He called it Smuggler's Cave, though if it had ever really been one—which was quite possible, the history of this coast being what it is—the smugglers had not left much in the way of contraband. Ian had excavated as much as he could of the shingly floor in the search for treasure, without any success. But previous users had left treasure of sorts; a rusty tin oil lamp that could light the cave at night; some fishboxes that made an ideal table; and a straw palliasse for a couch. To this Ian had added a trove of jetsam, the prize of which was the skeleton of an armchair which he had wriggled and forced with much sweating and swearing into the cave, whose bare springs were now upholstered with tattie-sacks and bits of net. Ship's rope was everywhere, and there was a collection of net floats. It was an entirely snug and pleasant little house where that privacy essential to the schemes of laddies was assured.

This Saturday morning, while the air outside was loud with the screams of mating seabirds on the cliffs, and Big Sye's head was loud with the ringing in his ears, Ian was putting right the last remaining inadequacy of the cave. Ian, you see, suffered from a grave social injustice: All the other bairns of about his age in the village were *lassies*. It was just not conceivable, at least to a twelve-year-old, that a lassie should be admitted to this haven of burgeoning masculinity, so till now Ian had played there alone. Though he was comfortable in his own company, whiles he wearied for someone to share his adventures and secrets with. But now a saviour had arrived, in the somewhat unlikely form of Willie Swankie, Rae's son. It was true that Willie was only recently come to the village, but given the extremity of the situation, Ian was prepared to overlook this minor obstacle. And in any case, Willie came from Embro; why there was no *limit* to his sophistication.

Ian lost no time. He had checked out Willie's suitability by the subtle probing at which boys are without peer, and had discovered that Willie was not a swot, not a tell-tale, nor had any other damning faults; and so this morning, bright and early, he had breezed along to Number One Fountain Square, a journey of some forty feet, and asked Rae if Willie could come out to play. To which Rae was delighted to answer 'yes', since she had been concerned about uprooting Willie from his friends in the city—and at the same time keen enough to extract him from the company of some of them.

After swearing his new ally to eternal secrecy on pain of warts, styes and boils—a standard enough hex—Ian had shown Willie Smuggler's Cave. Now, the two boys were in residence and passing idle conversation. Willie was good-looking, with the delicately shaped bones and the fine dark skin and thick black hair of his mother's clan, and blessed with her smile of dazzling whiteness. To Ian's delight, he had inherited her taste for adventure as well. Now he was lying on the straw palliasse with his hands behind his head, chewing on a stalk of grass and gazing at the ceiling. Ian, who was fair as his father, was reclining in the skeletal armchair. In his hand was a jamjar within which was a very large spider named Hamish whom he was exercising by slow rotation.

Ian was but rarely—outside of school hours anyway—without the company of his dog, Badger, one of Pluto's many offspring. It was as well for him that lurchers are valued for their ability rather than their looks, for Badger appeared to have been put together from the leftover bag of a doggy jumble sale. Presently he had his oversized chops resting on his young master's knee and was gazing up at the unfortunate spider's contortions with clear fascination, his toothbrush eyebrows seeming to crawl all over his head, and the tip of his whiplike tail twitching from side to side.

Willie got up from his couch and went to stand on the fishbox below the entrance. He stuffed his hands in his pockets and gazed out at the sweeping curve of shingle strand below. He sighed. "Ian," he intoned at last, "This is great, an aa.....But d'ye niver get bored up here?" Ian's hand froze and the luckless spider slid down the glass wall of his prison. Badger swivelled his great head and rolled his eyes. Ian twisted round in the armchair and gently placed the jar on a ledge behind him. He smiled as one does who knows he is about to impress.

"Uncle Sye wis roon lest necht," he said after a pause. "A cam doon efter Mum went ti baid an listened ti fit him an ma Da wis crackin. Tell ye, they wis some pished. They wis roaring an lauchin aboot the scrapes they yased ti get intil fan they wis loons. They wis gingin on aboot a hale wheen o hings, but maistly A mind how they said they'd eence made bombs."

"Bombs? Whit dae ye mean *bombs*?" Willie's voice was mocking. "Whit kinna *bombs*?"

"Foo mony kinna o bombs is thir? Bombs at *blaw up*, A jalouse."

"Aye aye. That'll be recht. A dinnae s'ppose ye owerheard fit wey they *made* these bombs, didye?"

Ian smiled. "Aye an A did tae! Syuger. Aye, thi yased syuger. Here, dinnae ye lauch at me like at. A'll gie ye somehin ti lauch aboot if ye daa cry canny. Syuger. An some kinna weedkiller. Sojum Klor-e-ate, wis fit Da sayed."

"Sojum Klor-e-ate? Niver heard o't. An sugar? Yer hivvin me on."

"Naa its *true*! A tell ye, they wis lauchin thir heids aff aboot fan they set the gress at Arbeg Links alecht wi the stuff and the Firies hid ti come an they couldnae pit it oot an thi aa thocht the Trades gowf club wid be brunt doon. Honest."

"Oh aye." Willie's voice dripped with contemptuous disbelief. "An whit else did they dae wi this sojum klor-e-ate an sugar?"

"They pit it in tinnies an set lecht til it so's it wid splode acoorse! Fit dae ye hink they did? Christ min, onybody'd ken at."

"They wis windin ye up." Willie warmed to his game, still with his back turned and a grin spreading over his face. "They kent ye wis thir an they wis hivvin ye oan."

"They wis *nutt* hivvin me *oan!*. They wis bleezin fou the pair o thum. Fit wey wid they wind me up? Fegs min, they couldna herdly staun up, nivver mind *wind* up." Ian clucked his tongue and shook his head and his right leg, which was slung over the stick that was one the arm of the chair, began to wave up and down and his eyes to flash, a foretaste of the quick temper he'd inherited from Jess.

Willie half turned, noted the other's rising ire and pretended not to. "Ach youse must be een o they lads that wid belave ony auld shite!"

Willie had timed the final insult to perfection, for Ian had just come to the boil, and he sprang from his seat and launched himself at Willie, who only just ducked a haymaker that was fain to knock his napper right off. The two boys grappled and fell to the floor, kicking and tearing at each other's clothes while Badger, who aye liked a piley-on, rushed round and round the rising cloud of stoor, barking furiously and wagging his tail at the same time. Hamish the spider observed the scene from the safety of his prison.

"Aa recht aa recht *aa recht*!" yelped Willie at last, who was handicapped in wrestling ability by being practically helpless with laughter.

Ian, who had been sitting on his chest, holding his wrists, and thus had had the upper hand, relaxed a little and rolled back on his heels, warily not letting go his grasp, and cocked an eye. "Submit?"

"A submit. Git *aff.*"

The boys helped each other to their feet and began dusting themselves down. Badger was still tearing round the inside of the cave, his tongue hanging out and his eyes rolling, barking furiously.

"So whaur," asked Willie, his eyes shining with mirth and enthusiasm, "F'Chrissake shut *up*, will ye ye stupit dug ye—whaur do we git this Sojum Klor-e-ate stuffy?"

Some time later, the two lads arrived outside Ferguson's Ironmongery Emporium in Arbeg High Street. A little thought had convinced them that even if Sojum Klor-e-ate was available at Mae's, any attempt to buy it there would be giving too much away to the enemy, and they had instead opted for the four-mile cycle ride into town. Mr. Ferguson of that ilk took them in from top to toe in a glance, and then surveyed them again, slowly, his suspicion patent. He clucked his tongue and leaned forward on the polished mahogany counter. His quick, monkey-brown eyes swivelled from one to the other in his tanned peanut head and he sucked a tooth.

"Fittizzit yer efter, leds," he said, at length.

"Twa pun sojum klor-e-ate, mister, please," asked Ian, a slight breathlessness entering his voice, a breathlessness that was not missed by his interrogator.

"S-o-j-um k-l-o-r-e-a-te." Mr Ferguson sounded out the words very slowly and screwed up the wrinkled brown skin of his face into a vision of theatrical puzzlement. Which was not surprising as he and his brother, who now stood habitually silent at the other end of the counter, were mainstays of the Arbeg Amateur Dramatic Society. Mr. Ferguson the elder had even been on the TV, though the boys did not know that. "Uh-huh," he continued, "And fit's at, fan it's hame? Hmm?"

"It's weedkiller," pleaded Ian. "Y'ken."

"Aye. Oh aye. Oh it is, is it noo." Ruminatively, Mister Ferguson scratched his earlobe with a long nail, and squinted at the ceiling of the shop, which was a hanging garden, a forest indeed, of tools, bicycle parts, and great coils of cord hanging from the pitch-pine rafters. "That's *sodium* klor-e-ate ye mean. A see noo. Mmmm-Hmmm. And fit did ye say it wis fur, sonny?" He snapped his gaze back to the boy before him.

"It's furtae kill weeds, mister." Ian shifted from foot to foot nervously and looked at Willie. "An A didnae say."

Willie kicked him.

"Funny, A kinda thocht it mecht be." Mr Alan Ferguson, character actor of some repute, allowed a certain irony to enter his brogue.

"The question that exercises me is *fa's* weeds?"

"*Oor* weeds acoorse." Irony was entirely wasted upon Ian.

"*Your* weeds?" Mr. Ferguson's eyebrows made a grab for his receding hairline and his eyes swivelled from one boy to the other, his facial muscles, which could clearly be seen moving beneath his thin and shiny skin, twisting his features into an expression of amazement. "Do *you* hiv weeds? My my. Really? By yer some young ti hiv weeds, youse."

"He means his ma's weeds, honest mister," put in Willie, who knew, having been brought up in the metropolis, when he was being strung along.

"Aye well. This "sojum klor-e-ate" at ye cry hit, is on the list." Mr Ferguson straightened a little and his tone was more serious. "The list o' dangerous chemicals, lads. That means A cannae sell it til a minor." He gazed at the boys intently and saw there disappointment and confusion. He sighed. "A minor is somebody at's under-age, see?" he explained, patiently. "No somebody at gings doon a mine."

There was still total blankness on the faces before him and he sighed again, took off his glasses and polished them carefully before putting them back on and looking over the top of them at the two boys. "Sodium Chlorate," he said, with emphasis, "Is a poison an highly," he paused for effect and swept his eyes from one to the other, "*Highly* inflammable. Wee laddies like you hiv been kent ti dae stupit hings wi hit an A am no allowed ti sell it ti ye till ye git tae be echteen. It's the laa. Zat recht Tam?"

His brother Tam, identically dressed in a grey coat, neatly laundered and pressed and the frayings on the cuffs trimmed back to a precise line, looked up from his copy of the *Arbeg Guide* and nodded sagely. "Yup."

"Och but mister, Ma needs it. She sent me aa the wey ti get it."

"Aye an me tae."

"The hale baith o yiz? By, your ma's feared ye'll loss yersels." Mr. Ferguson—he was the older of the two brothers and always took the formal title—still leaning on his elbows on the wooden counter, one wrist crossed over the other, nodded and sucked a tooth slowly. He did not trust this pair, and he was not about to sell them a chemical he well knew to be potentially explosive, not to mention the devastation it could cause when applied to an enemy's front lawn.

Willie leaned close to the other side of the counter. "Whit if we get a notey fae his Ma?" He nodded vigorously as if to encourage an affirmative response.

But Mr. Ferguson had experience of juvenile forgers, having been one himself once. "Nu'. Nutt on yer nelly."
"Please?"

Mr Ferguson's armour was unassailable. "Nu'. Ye hivty be echteen or ower ti buy thon stuff. An at's final."

"Aye okay," replied Ian suddenly, and he and Willie and Badger—who had come along for the run—turned and left the shop together.

Mr Ferguson remained leaning over the counter, watching the

three of them over his glasses as they crossed the street. He shook his head.

"At wis ower easy by half. A hink A've jist been had. A daa ken how, A jist ken it. Fit dae ye hink, Tam."

"Daa ken," said Tam, without looking up.

Sharon Paterson *was* eighteen, and on the dole. She was one of Ian's innumerable cousins, and she was also quite happy to buy cans of lager and bottles of cider on behalf of her younger relatives and friends, for which service she charged in fags. Ian had figured that this was not so very different and Sharon lived only five minutes walk away at the foot of Arbeg High Street. Ian talked her into it in less than no time, mortgaged against the price of ten Dunhill; for our Sharon liked to present a refined image to the world.

Ian and Willie watched from inside the Woolworth's front door on the other side of the street as Sharon carried out her commission. From their vantage point they could see the antics of Mr. Ferguson's eyebrows, and the entrancement of his brother Tam, whose gaze did not leave Sharon's fulsome buttocks as they strained against the black fabric of her mini from the moment she entered till the moment she left the shop. Ten minutes later they were on their way home with the contraband.

CHAPTER EIGHT
Ian and Willie's first Squib.

Rae could not help noticing a certain agitation on the part of her son as he wolfed his dinner. It was clear, at least, that he got on with Ian Teviotdale; a fact which pleased Rae greatly. But it has to be said that she was also a little concerned; being no stranger to mischief herself she knew it well enough when it walked in the door. However, she just smiled and narrowed her eyes as Willie bolted the last of his ice cream and fled the house.

By three o'clock, Ian and Willie were huddled together on hands and knees in the middle of the sandy floor of Smuggler's Cave. The sun-bleached furniture had been pushed to the side to make room for their experimentation, and on the floor lay an ancient and battered copy of 'A Children's Cyclopedia', much torn and fingermarked, which was opened at the entry for 'Nobel'. Other pages were marked with sundry bits of sweetie-wrapper, and had we but been gifted with the ability to read those closed pages, we would have found ourselves learning about Chinese rocketry, gunpowder in the Middle Ages and the theory of action and reaction. This book was Ian's—he had had it from Jess one Christmas—and from its worn pages had come the inspiration for many an adventure.

Their researches had convinced the boys that their squib would work better were it contained; to which end had they pressed an ancient and rusty cough-lossengers tin which had been part of Ian's store of Usefu Hings. His left hand now wore a large bloodstained clootie, witness to an injury sustained in trying to prise open the rust-fastened lid with a bent screwdriver. With breath held in furious concentration so that the silence of the cave was punctuated by explosive exhalations, the two of them pored over the task. Due to Ian's injury it was now up to Willie to complete the preparations. Badger, as ever close by the side of his young master, lay stretched out on the floor with his chops nestled into his forelegs, so still that the only clue that he was alive was the twitching of his caterpillar eyebrows as he observed every movement.

Ian had already, as carefully as any French *patissier* preparing his dough, mixed equal quantities of the two powders together in the Cortina hub-cap. With great care Willie spooned the mixture into the tin. Ian, inspired by an episode of *Bonanza*, had decided that the way to set the squib off was to punch a hole in the lid, and from there lead a trail of the mixture as a fuse, and so, while Willie filled the tin with the tip of his tongue stuck out in concentration, Ian punched a hole in the lid with a six-inch nail for a drill and a stone from the floor for a hammer.

At last the boys grinned their readiness at each other. Breaths held, and constantly alert for the unwanted presence of adults, they made their way out onto the ledge. Their bodies were electrified with excitement. Ian, his hand bandaged up, assumed the role of overseer.

"Aye. Pit it there, Willie. No, there, it's better. The gorse'll hide the flash fae the strand."

"Thir naebody doon thir ti see."

"Ach aye but thir mecht be. Ye canny be ower shair. Jist dae fit A tell ye, will ye?"

Under normal circumstances Willie would have immediately challenged his friend's right to give orders in this way—the society of boys is anarchic in the extreme—but right at the moment he was so preoccupied he hardly noticed. With great care and no little difficulty, he gouged a hole in the hard packed sand upon the ledge with his penknife, placed the tin in it with the hole uppermost, and then covered it over, leaving only a space for the fuse. The two boys then retreated backwards toward the cave mouth, Willie, his face a stony mask of concentration, gingerly sprinkling a trail of white powder from the hub-cap.

So great was their concentration, indeed, that they had forgotten about Badger. Now the dog is an animal whose association with man goes so far back into history that even the scientists cannot now be sure when it began; and most dogs, at least, are creatures of fairly predictable natures. You might almost begin to think that we would be so used to them and their ways, we, that is, the race of dog-owning humans, that we could never be surprised, never be caught off guard, would always be prepared for anything that our canine companions might possibly do. You might; but show me the dog owner who has never left a pound of sausages on the kitchen table while he ran out to the car to fetch in the rest of the groceries, and has never returned to see the guilty look and the string of links, the soft savoury evidence, hanging so pinkly from the corner of their beloved pet's mouth, and I will show you someone who is not quite human.

And so it was. It went, I suppose, something like this:

What is that thing that my young master has buried? And why has he done so? Does he wish that it should be hidden? If so he has done a very poor job of it. And why does it smell so peculiarly? Is it safe? Perhaps I should investigate. Oh yes I think that I really must, and if needs be just uncover it with my muzzle sooo gently—Hah! I have ye ye divil!

"Badger! C'wa ooti thir this meenit!" Ian roared at the dog and Willie swung his boot.

"Ye stupit dug! A'll hae ti dae it again. Noo, sit *doon*!"

The dog, obedient to the last, curls one last lip at the shiny thing and slinks back to the mouth of the cave, settling down on the sand and waving his tail in his desire of forgiveness. And it soon comes. For Ian returns to his side and hunkers down beside him.

"A'll lecht it."

"Ye will nutt," retorted Willie ferociously. "A done aa the work."

"A will sutt! The hale hing wis *ma* idear, so gie's the metches." Our heroes had to compromise in the end as the makeshift bandage on Ian's hand made it impossible for him to open the box, so Willie took out the match and gave it to him, and then he held the box up so that Ian could strike it.

"Here gings naehin," he said, and lowered the flame onto the white trail of crystals.

The three pairs of eyes, the two human and the one canine, widened as a little lilac flame began to dance and sputter along the path set out for it. Badger rumbled a low growl that seemed to originate from the end of his tail and cause the whole of his body to vibrate as it passed through him to escape between his bared fangs. Ian and Willie held their breaths as the dancing fairy of fire moved rapidly away from them, and all three of them unconsciously retreated further and further into the shelter of the cave entrance. Ian slipped his hand up and wrapped his fingers round Badger's collar, as much for his own reassurance as to restrain the animal.

And then the little flame reached the hollow, some ten feet away along the ledge, where they knew that their little squib was buried, and there it disappeared.

A moment's agony dragged its heels. What if the mixture was wrong? What if the stuff they'd got was not right? What if Big Sye had just been blethering with the drink? The two boys turned their heads to look at each other, and each saw written in the other's face the selfsame doubts.

The device went off with a bang that jumped them nearly out of their very skins. There was a vivid flash of light and an instant later they were peppered with pebbles and shards of rock. The crack of the explosion rattled a lazy echo off the cliffs on the other side of the harbour, and the chamber of the cave boomed in satisfied resonance.

Badger, unable to contain himself a moment longer, exploded into a roar of fury at the little pink dancing thing that had shouted so impudently.

"A'll show ye A'll show ye A'll show ye!" he bellowed at the top of his loyal doggie lungs, jerking free from Ian's grasp and leaping forward to do battle. But the boys hardly heeded him. A cloud of smoke hung over the ledge and as it cleared the result of their little experiment lay before their astonished eyes. Where before there had been a flat surface of sandy soil packed so hard a well-built boy could only with difficulty loosen it, was a saucer-shaped hole about eighteen inches in diameter and six deep. Of the tin there was no trace left at all.

Ian looked at Willie and Willie looked at Ian and Badger whimpered in bafflement and cocked his head from side to side and pawed at the empty space where the squib had been.

"Crivvins," said Willie at last.

CHAPTER NINE
The Village Cludge

Now, as I said before, Auchpinkie had a Public Convenience. It was the twentieth century, after all. In the days before flush sanitation the habit was to relieve oneself over the cliff-edge or in the tatty patch, but with the gradual slide of these northern communities into Southron politeness, change was inevitable. And since a Public Convenience was a Good and Necessary Thing, then of course it should be in a prominent position in the village— and where better than right in the middle of The Street, opposite Fountain Square with its old cistern, once the only source of fresh water, and its pretty stone basins and bronze taps. In fact, it could be said that this monstrosity, this bunker of grey concrete and slime-green paint, was the single most prominent building in The Street, set as it was apart from the rest, on a slight rise, with a commanding view on every side.

By the time of which we speak, all of the houses, save for one, had been introduced to individual Water Closets, with the outflow being piped to the shore far below and then, via a concrete-sheathed sewer gnarled with barnacles, out to sea. Not very far out to sea, I'll grant you, and gey queer things were sometimes found on the beach under the right—or wrong—combination of flooding tide and onshore breeze, but by and large it worked.

The sole house that was not so equipped belonged to a nonagenarian of uncommon stature named Robert Smith. He—Lanky Boab as he was known—had always insisted on fertilising the little tattie-patch at the back of his house the natural way. Until, that is, one arctic morning in a freezing February, his ancient knees had seized up solid in the act of squatting, and he had near died of hypothermia before he was rescued by his neighbours. Still he refused to have anything so unhealthy as a lavatory in the house, and had begun, more than ten years after the rest of the village had stopped, to use the Public Convenience, more commonly known in the village as "the cludgie". These days he had come to regard the little gent's cubicle as his own, keeping it swept out and fresh. But despite this there still remained one quirk in his habit. A lifetime of easing himself alfresco had given Boab a liking for the fresh air, and though he may have at last consented to use the village cludge, under no circumstances would he agree to close its door. It stopped the air circulating, he said, and that could not be healthy for a body. And his knees rapped on the back of it, on account of the length of his legs. Anyway, you had a grand view of the sea from the throne; right therapeutic so it was.

So, any morning you cared to look, at ten o'clock on the dot Boab opened his front door, walked from his cottage to Mae's shop, bought his copy of the Daily Record, ten Capstan Full Strength and a pint of milk, creaked back along the street to the cludge, opened the door of the cubicle, hung his cap on the hook, since he was technically going indoors, took his cigarettes and matches from the pocket of his ancient jacket, for Boab always, always, wore one of his three suits, unhitched his galluses, let his trousers fall to his knees, and settled down on the seat to smoke his fag, read his paper, and relieve himself. And though if challenged he would only begrudgingly admit that at least in the cubicle you could read the paper when it was raining but he didna ken if he didna prefer the tattie-patch for all that, the truth was that he had come to regard this morning ritual as something of a highlight of the day, and the featureless concrete cubicle as the ultimate expression of the luxury and the convenience of modern living.

The ground fell sharply away from the street on the far side of Boab's throne, and levelled off some ten feet lower into a broad plateau. Here stood a pleasant villa, larger than the cottages which faced onto the street above, though it did not at first appear so, for it was only when you came to the edge of the slope that you realised that it had two storeys at all. Its garden, with the proud square of drying green in the centre, was neat and well kept with borders of individual plants standing to attention in little seas of brown earth above which no weed dared show its head. This house was the home of Morag Paterson, whose acquaintance we have already made, and had been, more or less, for near enough the half-century now.

Morag was the youngest daughter of four and she had never married. Her mother had been a Presbyterian of the fanatical school who would have put skirts on the chairs themselves to hide the legs, had she not been over grippit to buy the cloth. No hint, no mention of sex had she ever allowed to enter the house. She even called the things the coal was delivered in 'begs' in order to avoid any possible confusion. Her born-again Calvinism had denied and warped her daughters, and had dried the very life itself out of her husband. Morag had suffered the most of all the girls at the hands of her mother's obsessions, for it had fallen to her to stay at home and care for the old carlin as she sank from life through senility to death. Her sisters had all taken good care to get themselves far from Auchpinkie as soon as they were able. Her mother had been long in the going, and it had been a sore trial for Morag; but a greater trial by far for the now middle-aged daughter left rattling around the house on her own was the bitter, bitter fact of her virginity, and her increasing conviction that she would pass her whole life without ever finding out what the blazes it was that all the fuss was about.

During her mother's life, not only had there been no place in the house for sex, but no place either for passion of any kind. Joy, love, fear, hate, even grief—it was all muted and as bland as processed cheese slices. Life for Morag had been like hearing Mozart with your ears stuffed full

47

of cotton wool; you knew it was there, but the detail was a mystery. She had been forced to listen, till she was near forty-five years old, to her mother threiping on about the evils of the flesh and how she hoped she wasn't going to turn out like those other three—wicked, the lot of them, over much of their faither in them—after whose early death, by the way, matters only got worse. As a result of the constant bombardment, reinforced by weekly doses from the pulpit, Morag had wrapped herself in a mantle of Presbyterian propriety that was demanding of her and judgmental of others. She had constructed, as best she could, a world in which sex, and bodily functions in general, simply did not exist.

At least while she was awake.

But as soon as she fell asleep, the whole lot came tumbling out again. Her mind was a kitchen press overstuffed to bursting with junk; upon opening the door the tiniest crack, it all came crashing down about her ears. Morag's world of dream was a Pandora's box and in the mornings she would be shocked that she was capable of dreaming such things. Especially as the only time she had ever even seen an erect penis was when she had watched, her nine-year-old mouth open and her eyes wide with shocked amazement, a heifer being served by a bull in the yard of MacPherson's farm. Anyone who has witnessed the act of coition in bovines will appreciate that this had given her impression of sex a somewhat larger than life quality, that was only amplified, if that is possible, in her dreams.

She had never been able to talk to anyone about her dreams, least of all her mother, and had only hoped that in time it would all go away. Which of course it hadn't, and as the years of her sexual frustration lengthened, her night-time adventures became more and more torrid, and more and more terrifying. Some mornings she would lie awake shaking with horror, and some nights she would pray softly into her pillow for hours rather than let herself fall asleep and face her torments. Morag, for all that she seemed unco douce and quiet, was an unexploded bomb waiting to go off.

Right now, she was at her kitchen window, which looked out over the drying green with its regimented borders. She spent a lot of time at her kitchen window, for she liked to see who was passing. As Boab hunkered himself down for his morning ablutions, she was finishing the washing-up. Her face was expressionless as she looked up at the ensemble of black boots, knobbly white knees, and newspaper, with a bit blue smoke rising in a curl from the top. It was her cross to be reminded daily of the existence of the lower half of the male anatomy by the most withered and desiccated specimen in the village, which was now resplendent before her, and whose owner, should he happen to notice her, would have the insufferable cheek to grin a toothless grin (Boab only wore his teeth for church on Sundays) and wave a friendly wave. A more imaginative character would have gone stark raving mad, but Morag only whitened her knuckles on the plates she was rinsing, and stacked them with muted violence.

CHAPTER TEN
Rae Starts work and meets Big Sye

Aweek after her arrival in Auchpinkie, Rae started her new job, as Personnel Manager at Cargill's Fish Processors, a canning plant a few miles along the coast. It is not a pretty sight, is Cargill's; and it has a certain aroma about it that can be a little off-putting. But for all that the firm, being an old family affair still run in the paternalistic tradition, was easy to get along with. Rae's new job, compared to the one she had given up in Edinburgh, was a good deal less high-powered and well-paid; but then it was also a good deal less stressful and time-consuming. But she was not concerned about that. As a matter of fact, she would be better off. Rae had used part of her inheritance to pay off the burdensome mortgage on her flat in Edinburgh, the source of so much worry over the years. She had thought of selling it, but on reflection, had decided to keep it as a bolt-hole; moving back to Auchpinkie was not a guaranteed success. But let out to students, the rent would more than cover the drop in her salary. And since she owned the cottage in Auchpinkie outright, and had money left in the bank forbye, she found herself a woman of some wealth and property. And this was something that Rae had never dared hope for. It was a pleasant feeling indeed.

Rae was amused by the reaction that her arrival had stirred within the village. After only a week she found that her friendship with Izzie, neglected for so long, was becoming as firm and as intimate as ever it had been. But then Izzie was like that. For her part, Rae felt guilty about the years of neglect, and had resolved to take better care of this friendship in the future. But others had reacted differently. She had expected that Mae and her circle of friends would take their time in warming to her, and in this she was not disappointed. As for the men, her effect upon them was miraculous; they were like putty in her hands. It could go to a girl's head, that, she told herself, to have every male in sight rushing to open doors for her, endlessly offering help and advice, and generally molly-coddling her as she had never been before. More than once she wondered if she had really changed so much from the teenager who had packed her bags and fled to the city more than a dozen years before.

The thought of that time still gave her nightmares, woke her sweating in the night, having found herself once again walking along a friendless city street with a suitcase in her hand, twenty-five pound in her pocket, pregnant and without the slightest idea of what she would do or even where she would sleep that night. All she had was the address of a friend of her cousin who was a student at the Art School. And a damned good thing she had that, too, and a damned good thing that the cousin's friend had enough room in her bedsit to put Rae up—sneaking her in and out so's the landlord wouldn't catch on—until she got herself sorted out.

There had followed years hard enough to give anyone nightmares; the baby; her mother, who had shunned her; the years of living in a flat in Niddrie trying her best to bring Willie up with the little help the state gave her; and then working; an office cleaner; a waitress; countless bar jobs. The decision to go to night school, and the hardness of the discipline; but she had thrived on the challenge, and Rae had always been bright. And then, miracle of miracles, a college place with a qualification at the end of it. Even that had been hard, for Rae found the college oriented entirely toward kids fresh out of school. Its peculiar discipline rubbed hard with her, a woman of twenty-three mature beyond her years. But she had stuck it out though there were times she had thought it would choke her. Rae got her diploma in Personnel Management; and so began that shaky ladder of career.

It was funny, she reflected, as she drove through the Angus countryside to work, drinking in the freshness and greenness and the hilarious yellow of the gorse; even six months before, mortgaged to the hilt and hardly a moment to herself, she would have counted herself content; funny the alacrity with which she'd let it go, for a part time job in a one horse village. She only hoped that this life that she had returned to would give her all that she was seeking. And to answer her own question, yes she had changed, out of all measure, from the unformed thing that she had been when she left. Now, when Rae walked into a room, she walked in a person of poise and confidence. But then she saw herself as herself, and that was that. It is said that you can never go back, for that which you left will have changed, and you will have changed too, and it will be a new thing that you embark upon. We don't see the changes in ourselves, neither we who leave nor we who stay. We just live our lives and are what we are, and it is rare that we have the opportunity to look at ourselves hard enough to see the changes. Change is such a slow thing; it is like the growth of a plant or the movement of the sand-dunes; too slow to see but inexorable all the same.

So Rae, when she bumped—literally, as neither of them were looking where they were going—into Big Sye as she staggered from her car, her arms laden with rolls of wallpaper, fumbling with her keys, was first surprised, and then glad, to see him. The suddenness of the meeting prevented her from getting all tense beforehand, which she surely would have done had she seen him walking along the street towards her and had had time to think about what she'd say. Hadn't this meeting been one of the things that had nearly persuaded her not to be daft, to sell the cottage and stay in the city?

Well, what she did say, smothering a laugh as he lunged to catch a roll of Sanderson that had fallen off the top of the pile, was "Oh, hi! It's yersel!"

Sye, on the other hand, found himself completely at a loss for words. His mouth suddenly felt as dry as if he'd stuffed it full of Weetabix with no milk, and all he could think of doing, once he'd saved the roll of paper, was to pick up Rae's keys, which had also been knocked flying. There was a moment's silence during which Rae realised that Sye had not a damned clue what to do next, and that the way was open for her to take control of the situation. "Would ye mind openin the door for me, since yer there, please," she said, and it gratified her the way he did as he was told. And when he had done so, and she had teetered into the house and deposited the rolls of wallpaper on her settee, she was delighted to note that he was still at the door, a roll of Sanderson in one hand and her keys in the other.

"Thank you," she said, flashing him a smile that would slay, and took the keys and the paper. For a moment they just stood there looking at each other, and then Rae said. "Look, I'm a bit pushed just now. But howsabout a drink some time?"

Sye spoke for the first time. "Aye," he croaked. The sound of his voice surprised him and he coughed. "Scaise me. Aye, okay. Aye."

When Rae closed the door she had to cover her mouth with her hand to stop herself shrieking with laughter.

Big Sye walked back to The Chateau in a state verging on shock. To tell the truth, for all his habitual bravado he was—as he had always been—completely overwhelmed by Rae, and Sye was not a man to readily admit to being overwhelmed by anyone, least of all—especially least of all—by a female member of his own family. Rae's father, you see, had been Sye's mother's big brother, which made them first cousins. Nothing unusual about that; the web of familial relationship in Auchpinkie being so complicated, like. Sye thought hard. It was difficult for him to equate the woman he had just met with the girl he had known—wild, yes, she'd been wild, had Rae, gallus as they come and often more than the boys. Gallus she had been, but gauche and awkward, too. Sye remembered how she had liked to ride pillion on his Norton; and Sye remembered a few other things too, and if he'd been a blushing sort of a man, he'd have blushed then. When was that? That was before he'd got his very first Mate's berth, on a Blue Flag fridge ship coming out of Rio carrying frozen beef.

At the door of The Chateau, he paused, thought hard for a moment, and then walked across to the bar. It was a full two pints before he felt quite himself again.

CHAPTER ELEVEN
Geordie Baird on Guard

Anshaw scowled. "But the salmon, George. Will they be on time?"Geordie coughed. He was used to being addressed as "Baird" by employers, and he found this employer's familiarity disconcerting. He could not help entertaining the horrific thought that soon he would be addressed as "Geordie", or even "Doad", and all the dignity of his position would be lost. He shrugged his shoulders and removed the stalk from his mouth.

"A hink sae, Mr Anshaw. Heh, heh. We've aaready got een or twa bonny fish lyin in the pools by the brig, an at's aye a good sign. Heh, heh." He could not himself remember when he had first adopted the affectation of his little chuckle when addressing toffs; it had become so ingrained a habit that he would have been surprised had anyone brought it to his attention. But despite his outward confidence, he was concerned, as he always was at this time of year. The reputation of the river before them depended on a couple of good runs of salmon in each year, the most important of which was due to begin any day now. But it was not a precise thing, and depended on circumstances beyond his or any human control; the feeding conditions under the distant Arctic icecap, where the salmon borne in these rivers gorged themselves upon prawns and made themselves into the powerful silver torpedoes that could make the journey back to the river of their birth, there to spawn a new generation. The tides, the pollution in the North Sea and the pollution that spewed out into the rivers themselves, masking the subtle scent that was the only beacon for the returning fish. Not to mention the depredations of the fishermen who took The Fish in their nets, legally and illegally, on his way back home.

It was Geordie Baird's misgivings about this last point—the taking of the salmon illegally—that had caused him to do that which under no other circumstance would he have dared to do, to beard the archdemon himself in his den. He wished to blazes now he hadn't, either. Alan Gilchrist had been far too aggressive. Geordie knew his cousin was bound to react badly. He had a hunch that even now Big Sye would be cooking a scheme up, and that thought worried him. Everybody the length of the coast knew that Big Sye from Auchpinkie thought it the most natural thing in the world to help himself to a few of the fish in the estuary. He'd been doing it since he was a boy, and his father before him, and like enough *his* father before him too. Sye, who never took that many of The Fish, and did it more for a bit sport than profit, subscribed to the view that a fish is a wild creature and so belongs to no one. This is not a view that is shared, however, by the landowners, who have used their political influence to accordingly arrange the law. But though he knew that his adversary was not a real threat to the stock of fish in his river, his blatant cheek annoyed Geordie enough for him to be determined to put a stop to his activities. It was a matter of professional pride, like.

Although, every year, Geordie Baird patrolled the estuary regularly through these nights in early summer when the water was still cold and The Fish had the urge on him to move, he had never come within a hail of catching his adversary in the act, and had only heard tell of Sye's success later, when somebody would sidle up to him in the pub on an evening and say something like "A heard Big Sye fae Auchpinkie's been in aboot yer salmons again, Geordie, izzat recht, like?" and Geordie would have to swallow his pride and smile like he enjoyed the joke too.

But things had changed now. Geordie could no longer allow himself the luxury of pretending that the relationship between himself and his cousin was just a sporting one. The new Laird, Anshaw, took a very dim view of anyone helping himself to his property without paying for it, and he was quite incapable of seeing poaching as anything other than common theft; which it is, I suppose, if you happen to be a riparian landowner. Salmon, to Anshaw, who had never cast a line in his life, were an abstract. They were swimming money with fins. Although Anshaw had bought Balgownie Estate for a sum that was downright laughable, he had long syne learned to love all of his pennies.

Even though he had just signed the papers that sold Crowhill and Backwater farms, one to the sitting tenant and the other to Ferguson of Meikle Howff, which sales had eased his cash flow position greatly, he was still anxious to see the Grange Country Club, as it was now known, 'washing its face', as he put it. And the fishery was the most important attraction. Oh, yes, the golf course was very pretty, and he'd even imported a minor tour pro to help design it; but then this part of Scotland is not exactly short of golf courses. Indeed a cynic might suggest that it was hard enough to find a bit sandy links between Dunbar and Montrose that was *not* a golf course already. And good restaurants and designer wine bars and heated swimming pools were ten a penny these days. Therefore it followed that the salmon must be protected; and that was Geordie's job. Geordie had better do his job, or else.

Now our Geordie may have been a little slow on the uptake whiles and not gifted in the diplomacy department forbye, but that doesn't mean to say that he was entirely daft. And to sharpen what reserves of native wit he did have was the goad of his considerable fear of this new boss of his. No. George Baird Esquire had no intention of letting himself be flung out of a pretty centrally heated cottage, a good salary with a pension and a Land-Rover Discovery to boot, for want of attention to detail. He knew the Pinkie Estuary better than anyone, better even than Big Sye and if there was one man who might have a chance of protecting it and its treasure against the poachers, this was that man.

The Tuesday before the official opening of Balgownie Grange, Geordie had walked the bank as usual and was gratified to see, lying lazily in the deep pools, their broad tails moving gently against the current, a fair number of the Fish. He made a note of the places where they lay and number and his heart was joyful. The amount of salmon in the river was not huge, but it was increasing, as it had been every day for a week. This was, if not a sure sign that the awaited spring run would not fail, then at least a reassuring and welcome hint.

And as the moon waxed toward the full, so did the pressure mount upon Geordie. For with the full moon would come the spring tide and it was then, as was well known by bailiff and poacher alike, that the great flood of the Fish would come up into the river proper on their way to the spawning grounds on the higher reaches in the Angus glens. At least, that was the way it was meant to happen. Some years the run failed, and only a few fish came in to spawn and then the river-people were sad, for the fish of these years were not only few in numbers but generally light and not well formed, though the occasional sulking giant was found. Usually these years were poor throughout the season and no-one did well. Then sometimes the Fish did come, but not in runs, rather in a steady stream throughout the spring and summer, and while there was good enough sport to be had in these years, everyone—and that included, most importantly, the paying rods—preferred the joyous bonanza of a true Spring Run, when the Fish surged into the river on the first spring tide after Mayday, mad in his mating passion, and jumped and cavorted and threw himself upon the hooks of anglers as he rushed to the mating grounds to consummate his lust and then float back down to the sea a spent and exhausted ghost of his majestic sea-fresh self, no longer even worth the catching.

All of Geordie's bailiff's instincts told him that Mr Anshaw was going to have a bumper crop for his opening week at the Grange. This looked to be a good Run, a glorious, gutsy run, when the King of Fish would reveal himself at his wildest and most passionate. This looked as if it would be a Run where the good rods would have stories enough to last a lifetime of winter evenings tucked in by the snug with less favoured souls, and where even the most inept beginner could be almost guaranteed to at least hook something, even if the landing of it was a different matter.

No one who has ever fished the Salmon can ever forget that first strike Bang! as a good spring run fish hits the fly, not timid and teasing and mouthing it fussily like a cautious high summer fish but uncaring and wild and full of contempt for man and all his devices; how every nerve in the fisherman's body jangles into life; the instant dryness in the mouth; the hiss of the line as it cuts at impossible speed through the tea-coloured water after a ghostly shape that seems as big as a shark; the bucking of the two handed rod already bowed into its perfect arc. Geordie had seen tyros left speechless and entranced for hours after a first strike like that.

Since his job depended on it, Geordie was glad to see those advance scouts, those darker shadows on the dark bottom with their sinuously waving tails, and he lost no time in assuring his boss that his guests were going to have a whale of a time at the fishing.

It was for that reason too that every night now, as nervous as a mother hen brooding her chicks, Geordie had his men out, Big Alan and the three gillies and a few casual hands besides, all night, walking up and down the banks of the river. They had dogs, retrievers mostly, police whistles, and they had their shotguns and their cudgels for self-defence. Some poachers these days play a hard game, and many was the tale of a bailiff or a gamekeeper who'd stumbled on a couple of poachers and had gotten his head well and truly kicked in for his trouble. It had never happened like that on this water, but Geordie was taking no chances.

For himself, Geordie took up nightly position on the south bank of the estuary just opposite the great shoal where he knew as well as Sye that the Fish would congregate, to get their first taste of the brackish water before moving into the river. He had his night glasses, and through the long chilly hours he swept them across the sea and the estuary itself. He felt confident that no one could get through the guard that he had posted, but he did not allow this confidence to dull his senses. These were the nights of the hunter and the hunted in more ways than one; the poacher hunting his salmon, the bailiff hunting him.

Each morning there would be a meeting such as this, with Geordie red-eyed from lack of sleep, and Anshaw his usual bumptious self, demanding to know how many fish were in the river, how big they were, where they were, and what they were doing. Time and again Geordie tried to explain to him that salmon were not like sheep and a river was not like a field; the fact that there were Fish in the river today did not mean that they would still be there tomorrow. But the appreciation of this point required a subtlety of understanding that Geordie despaired of ever seeing in Anshaw. You see, the great advantage of the Balgownie fishery was its proximity to the sea. It takes The Fish time to adjust to the decreasing salinity of the water as he moves upstream and it is this that makes him like to linger a little in the lower reaches, long enough for the physiological changes that were necessary to take place before he makes his way upriver.

All of this meant that as each run of fish passed through, the river here would, for two or three or four days, be packed full with fish that were mad and aggressive and reckless and just bruising for a fight; an angler's sort of a heaven. To which Anshaw sold the tickets. But—and it was a big but—as soon as the salmon had adjusted himself to the change in water, he would be off, following the irresistible scent of the upland burns and nursery streams where he had grown up, and there was nothing that Geordie or anyone else could do to stop him, save of course to catch him. What was important was that the salmon kept coming *in* to the river. Which brings us back to where we started and the reason why Geordie was a worried man.

CHAPTER TWELVE
The Bus Crash

Monday the seventh of May dawned a fated day. A puckle mile north of Auchpinkie, on the other side of the estuary, lived Jock Stott, in a white painted cottage on a hill inland of the main line to Aberdeen, yet still in hail of the sea. Below his kitchen window the land dropped away to the railway cutty, and on the far side was a promontory, a cliffy headland—though the cliffs were lower here than at Auchpinkie—a promontory that had a queer air to it, as if it was out of place, a misfit in the landscape. Upon this rounded lump that stuck out into the sea was a structure that, at first sight and silhouetted against the rosy dawn, looked for all the world like a fortress, a castle of some ancient and doughty Scottish legend, so square, squat, low, and massive was it. But in reality its provenance was more mundane, though of interest still.

It was no wonder that this headland seemed queer; for here in the midst of a coastline made entirely of red sandstone, issued a seam of limestone from the very bones of the earth. You would see, as you lingered in the early light, that the structure you had thought to be a castle had huge holes in its walls, and a few moments' close inspection would reveal it to be nothing other than a vast oven—or rather, several ovens. These were lime kilns, used for centuries to burn the limestone of the headland into lime for mortar and for the fields.

Latterly though, now that the building trade has lost the skill to use the old ways and lime was no longer dug and burned here, the kilns had become a favourite haunt in summer for young couples who thought that they might find privacy enough in the grassy hollows that were the long since blocked up chimneys of the ovens to engage their passions without fear of discovery; in fact the place was that popular the kilns were overbooked and you could hardly take a ten-minute daunder on a sunny day within a mile of the place without coming across some pair at it. But the local lovers had reckoned without Jock in the white cottage up the hill and his ex-MOD Barr and Stroud binoculars. Jocky looked forward to fine summer days as much as they, even if his pleasure was vicarious.

But now, as he slyly parted the curtains in his kitchen window with the back of one hand and peered gleefully out into the morn, it was not to watch the alfresco connubials of the local youth. For just on his side of the lime kilns was another cottage, set right on top of the limestone headland, which had once been the home of the kilnmaster, but was now lived in by a certain Mr and Mrs Tadger. Dick and Alice came from the south—Kelso, if you must know; he was an engineer and he had a good job at a food processing factory in Montrose. For six months of the year, when the factory worked flat out canning the potatoes, peas, beans, and soft fruit that were the produce of the fertile hinterland, Dick worked nights. He liked it; the night-shift bonus was substantial, he and Alice put the money away, and they had a nice little rainy-day hoard. Forbye that, Dick liked the gowff, and this regime gave him plenty time to indulge himself.

Alice was the daughter of a minister, and she had grown up into an uncommonly attractive and trim blonde.She also had the libido and morals of a well-brought-up alley cat, a fact that everybody but Dick was fully aware of. No-one was ever going to tell *him*, on account of his being built like a brick shitehouse and famously short-fused. Be that as it may, the year before, and not long after the Tadgers had moved into their cottage, Alice had somehow engineered a liaison with one Deek White, a driver for the North Star bus company. Deek was what you might cry a romantic young man, eager for instruction, like, and Alice was just delighted to oblige. She liked to keep busy, did our Alice. Got bored easily. And golf was not really her thing. Too vertical. Anyway, things could hardly have worked out better, for Deek—at Alice's suggestion—had volunteered for the early morning country school round, a job for which he had not much competition as it involved such an early start. But Deek was smart and reliable, so to sweeten the pill his manager let him take the bus home with him to save time in the mornings. So with little effort, Deek was ideally placed to profit from Alice's excess of urge.

This Monday was the first night shift of the new season at the factory, and Jock was up sharp with his binoculars at the ready; and he was not disappointed. At five-thirty on the dot the red-and-grey AEG Dreamliner bumped and rumbled down the rough track past his house to the lime kilns, did a three point turn with a rapidity that could only have been born of familiarity, parked outside the cottage, and out hopped Deek. His knuckles had not even fallen upon the panels before the door was flung open, a shapely—and naked, for Alice was not one to waste time—arm extended, and he was dragged inside.

Jock settled down with a mug of tea so strong the spoon would have stood up and a packet of digestives. He could hear his wife's snoring reverberating down the lobby and he switched.on the radio to hear the farming report. But mostly he had his binoculars glued to his eyes, for Alice had a thing about sleeping with the curtains open and the view was absolutely excellent.

Deek had a habit of leaving things until the last moment, and this morning, being the first of the new season in more ways than one, as it were, he could perhaps have been forgiven for being a little tardy. At seven forty-five, by which time he should already have had the first brats aboard, the cottage door flew open and out flew Deek, his jacket and tie over his arm, his shoes untied, his shirt unbuttoned, struggling with the zip on his trousers. He jumped into the bus and started it up and revved it with a smoke-belching roar of worn injectors (the bus's, not Deek's) that shook the earth, and then jammed it into gear and set off down the track in a shower of mud, whilst Alice leaned contentedly on the doorpost with a smile on her face, wearing only an Aran sweater to ward off the chill of the morning.

Fate handed out a cruel reward for the lover who had overstayed his time; for only a few moments before Deek had managed to disentangle himself from Alice's embrace, Paterson's cowman had gathered his herd from the field between the Tadgers' cottage and Jock's, and by the time that the ageing bus came bucketing down the narrow lane, the seventy-five Ayrshires were waddling and lowing their slow way to the milking parlour, their over-full udders spurting milk as they went waurstling up the brae. Poor Deek—his mind was elsewhere, you realise—rounded the corner and was almost upon them before he saw them. Cows being cows, they had thoroughly lubricated the already slippery road. Deek gasped, hit the brakes hard and the bus slid into a graceful sideways skid that was abruptly ended when it plunged off the road and into the ditch.

Jock, who had seen everything from his eyrie, threw back his head and opened his mouth. From the deepest recesses of his body came a shrieking, side-splitting, painful, quivering laugh that mounted rapidly in pitch and volume. He bent double and smacked his thigh and his dentures shot out and skittered across the kitchen floor. Della, rudely awakened from her noisy slumbers, shouldered her broad way in to see what her fool of a husband was making such a fuss about now, put her big toe in the false teeth, which promptly locked shut upon her pet corn, and fell to the floor with a wail. Jock sank to his knees and grasped the back of one of the chairs, now completely overwhelmed by the agony of his hysteria.

Meanwhile, Deek climbed, shaken and bruised and with blood trickling from a small cut on his forehead, from the cab and looked at his grey and red bus for a very long time. Then he kicked it. Really hard. Alice, who had watched the whole episode, horror-stricken, slammed the door and stamped her foot and swore, her mind jangling at the thought of the explanations that were going to be required when her husband arrived home in half an hour and found the lane that only led to his house blocked by a bus that had no business being there.

Paterson's cowman, who was named Tony and wore his hair in a pony-tail, was listening to Pink Floyd on his Walkman when it all happened. He never even noticed.

CHAPTER THIRTEEN
A Day Off School

By half past eight that morning the little group of children clustered around the gates of the primary school already knew that there was something amiss. For these were the older children who had already left Auchpinkie's little single-class school to take their places at Arbeg Academy. Each morning, rain or shine, they collected at the gate at eight-twenty to wait for the big red-and-grey bus that arrived at eight-twenty five to ferry them to their day's lessons.

Now, they could see there was no snow on the ground, so the fact that the bus was even five minutes late was a cause for some hope. The children chatted in hushed voices and cast regular anxious glances down the Arbeg Road, expecting any moment for the bus to come rumbling and wheezing and belching its smoke round the corner at Blair's farm. Each minute that passed without its arrival boosted their hopes a little further. By eight-forty-five they knew they were sure to miss the morning assembly and the start of their first classes, and when the younger children arrived to wait for Miss Middleton to open up the little school, their mood, which had grown increasingly lively and confident, was one of pure holiday.

Clandestine nautical activities had long been a part of Auchpinkie life, so that at one time the Crown had felt it necessary to station a whole squad of Coastguard officers here. Originally they were billetted in the village, but when their superiors discovered they were becoming a bit too friendly with the natives, they built new cottages for them on top of the cliff half a mile further down the coast, at the south end of the bay, overlooking the harbour. Out of harm's way, they thought. But then they didn't know the Auchpinkie folk, and there was aye an awful number of the single men that ended up getting married to local girls......And a man could hardly arrest his brother-in-law for smuggling. These were just Coastguards, after all—why, not even a Customs Officer would do that. Surely?

These days, though, the Coastguard patrol in blue-and-yellow vans from their base at Montrose and the houses were sold off long ago. Miss Middleton was a lady (she was always referred to as a 'lady', and as 'Miss Middleton', never as 'Muriel') who had never married and was devoted entirely and in equal measure to her school and to her garden. She lived in the southmost cottage, which she had bought not long after arriving. Some of the children (and not a few of the younger adults, for that matter) believed that Miss Middleton had *always* been there, but in fact she originally came from Paisley. But only a very few people remembered that.

Miss Middleton was of an age somewhere between forty and sixty; it was impossible to guess more accurately than this, though great was the speculation, due to her habit of applying her make-up with what the painters call impasto. You got the impression that she could take the whole thing off, quite intact, at night, and put it on again in the morning. Her hair was raven black and unruly, a trait which she effectively curbed by the use of super-hold hair spray, and when her scarlet lips parted she revealed a smile of teeth so uneven and haphazardly spaced as to resemble two rows of ancient and neglected tombstones. And her pupils had plenty of time to become familiar with the unique topography of her dentition, since her smile, bless her, but rarely left her face.

Miss Middleton loved children. In fact she adored and doted upon them in a way that is perhaps reserved for those who have none of their own. She had a miraculous power over them—doubtless inspired, in some animal way, by the sheer force of her love—which persisted throughout their lives, so that grown men and women with families of their own would shake themselves to attention upon her approach, take their hands out of their pockets, and refrain from using bad words. Miss Middleton—famously—detested 'muddle'. Muddle was a term she used to describe anything that was not quite just *so*, and it distressed her greatly. Miss Middleton liked everything in her life to be *so*. When she hung out her very laundry it was a work of art that drew comment from the passers-by.

That morning, when she arrived at the school on the dot of five to nine, as always and wheeled her bike into the little playground, she was confronted by a scene that was by any definition 'muddled'. Her pale blue eyes swiftly appraised the swirling meely of shouting and running children inside the playground. She locked her bike up, slipped the keys into the patent hand-bag that she always carried, and tugged straight the hem of her dog-tooth tweed jacket. She addressed the group with her normal radiant smile, and the effect was pure magic.

"Good *mo*rning, boys and girls," she intoned in a voice that would have carried with ease the Usher Hall and was still mellifluous.

"Good *mo*rning, Miss *Mi*ddleton," they all sang out together in response, and shuffled into something more resembling of order.

"Well, well then, what *has* happened? Why are you all still here?"

"Please Miss, the school bus didnae come, Miss." blurted Becky Spink, who had been teacher's pet before she went to the big school.

"Did not come, Becky dear. And do stand up straight. Well, we'll have to see about that."

Miss Middleton, after flashing a huge and crooked smile at Becky Spink, just to make sure her feelings weren't hurt, turned and walked smartly up to the school building and unlocked the door.

"Now, then, little ones to their places, please. Smocks on; we're going to do some painting," she sing-songed. Her voice was a miracle of gentle and loving authority. "Big children wait outside. I have to make a telephone call."

The older children, who had formed themselves without thinking into a loose crocodile, disintegrated into a fluid group around the schoolhouse steps as Miss Middleton disappeared inside. They could hear the muted tones of her voice from the little office that led off the classroom, and presently she returned.

"Now then, children," she began, smiling radiantly, "I'm sorry to have to tell you that the bus that should have taken you to the Academy this morning has been in an accident. Fortunately the driver was not badly hurt, but it seems that there is no transport available to get you to school for the morning session. However, those of you who wish to spend the morning revising, quietly, may sit at the back of my class. The rest of you," and here her eyes settled coolly, though her mouth was still smiling, upon Ian and the new friend whom she did not recognise but whom she suspected as being cast of the same mould, "The rest of you may take the morning off."

Miss Middleton's eyes narrowed perceptibly as she regarded the two boys. "There will be," she continued in a voice that now contained an overlay of command, "There *shall* be a bus to take you to school this afternoon. It will arrive at twenty-five past one. Your headmaster has informed me that absences shall be noted." She smiled beatifically and stood back from the entrance so that those who wished could enter. And it was no mean tribute to Miss Middleton's qualities as a teacher, given the sunny promise of the morning, that everyone except Willie and Ian trooped meekly inside.

Needless to say, by the time that the last of the other children had passed through the schoolhouse door, this same pair, with a canty step and a carefree air, were on their way down the track toward the strand. Miss Middleton sighed.

Willie and Ian were only too ready to take the morning off school, and there was no thought in either of their heads of turning up for the replacement bus that afternoon. The both of them knew perfectly well that there was little their teachers could do, for a half-day absence wasn't worth the trouble of a letter home, and the worst they'd get was a few lines. And they had a ploy in mind that would make *that* worthwhile. In any case you may rest assured that they were both well used to poking the school on much flimsier excuse.

Somehow a legitimate day off, when it comes as an unexpected bonus, has a better flavour to the more reluctant inmates of a school. Unlike weekends and holidays, parents have not normally formalised plans to deal with the presence of their brood. There will be no tedious chores to do or messages to run and no plans to visit *relations*—who were well known to be even more dull and enervating than the run of adult humans. And unlike those illicit days of adventure poked from the school on a morning's whim to go seagull-egging or ferreting or guddling trout from the burn, a boy on a day like this could actually let himself be seen, at liberty, in public, without fear of retribution.

And Willie, at least, had something in mind.

Some weeks before, Lanky Boab had caught Ian taking a short cut across his tattie-patch on his way to the beach. Now this was a short cut that Ian had used for so long that he had come to regard it as not merely a convenience, but a right. Boab, for his part, had long known about the practice; he could hardly, after all, have missed Ian's footprints, which had amalgamated into a path of hard packed earth in the middle of the patch. However, given his age and his rheumaticky joints, he had never actually been able to get a hold of the interloper in order to discuss with him his political philosophy on the ownership of private property and the thorny and troubled question of *trespass,* which does not exist under Scots Law. But that day, Ian had wandered across the patch with his mind not fully on the task—being more involved with how he could sneak his father's ancient .22 rifle out of the house to go pheasanting— and he simply walked straight into the old man's arms as he emerged as silently as a wrathful black cloud from his garden shed.

I suppose Boab can't have known that it was not Politically Correct to deliver a sharp cuff on the lug. So he did, more than once, while holding Ian in a horny grip as tight as a vice by the other. Lug that is. He had then, to the boy's utter horror, led him up the street by that same lug, knocked on the door of his own house, and delivered him into the hands of Izzie, who was sufficiently persuaded of the rightness of Boab's case as to ground her son for a whole week.

Ian was a douce sort of a lad at heart, and left to himself he would have taken the dunts and put it down to experience and that would have been that. But Willie was made of different stuff; there was more of his mother's smeddum in him than you might think. So when Ian related the tale to him, he was not long in coming up with a scheme for revenge. With their discovery of the sodium-chlorate-and-sugar banger, it appeared to Willie that the perfect means of delivering retribution was now to hand. So, very soon after being released from the drudgery of a day at school, they hied themselves to Smuggler's Cave, along with Badger, whom Ian had released from the miserable restraint of a long chain in his parent's back yard on the way, to put the finishing touches to the new device. Their skills had progressed considerably since their first primitive essays and this particular squib was prepared in an Andrew's Liver Salts tin. It promised to be even more explosive than the original contents.

The boys looked at each other conspiratorially as they prepared to leave Smuggler's Cave on their Mission.

"Let's synchronise wir watches," breathed Willie. "Right. Fan A coont three it's eleeven meenits pest ten. Een, twa, three. Got it?"

"Aye," replied Ian, clicking the winder on his Timex. This ritual was a sign that their expedition was of the weightiest nature; everything had to be done by the book, or else run the risk of Bad Luck spoiling it.

"Awright, then, let's dae hit!"

CHAPTER FOURTEEN
Lanky Boab's Dream

L anky Boab settled himself down, hunkering into the familiar con-tours of the toilet seat, and spread his Daily Record over his knees. What a beautiful morning it was. He pulled out the pack of Capstan Full Strength he'd bought at the same time as the paper—which latter would, after being read, be put to a more pragmatic, and some might say appropriate, use, the cooncil having omitted to apportion a budget for the supply of toilet paper—and lit up with a Scottish Bluebell match. He inhaled deeply and smiled. Capstan Full Strength are famous; the nicotine effect of the first one in the morning is like being in the back seat of a very fast car when the driver decks the throttle. You can't be a reformed person and smoke these things; you don't smoke them to have something to do with your hands.

Boab remembered Dr. Campbell's face when he found out.

"You smoke *what?* Good God, man, how long have you been smoking those?"

The patient had explained that he had been smoking them ever since Passing Clouds had become hard to get twenty years before. He still thought that Capstan Full Strength were a bit on the peely-wally side, and they certainly didn't have the same cachet as Passing Clouds, which were six inches long and oval, but they'd do until something better came on the market.

Dr. Campbell, a no-nonsense type of the old school, who had brought more into the world and seen more out of it than he cared to be reminded, almost let himself fall into the trap of giving Boab his standard lecture on the evils of smoking; but he stopped himself just in time. He had, after all, just examined the old craiter, and had found him to be in fine shape, except for his rheumaticky joints, which creaked like ancient doors whenever he moved. It was a question of balance; yes, the cigarettes might not help the rheumatism, but what other complex relationships within that venerable body that now sat in front of him, might be disturbed, and with what result, were he to withdraw the input of a clearly substantial daily dose of nicotine?

"Boab, you know you should take it easy on the fags," he said at last, in his best avuncular bedside manner, more because he knew he had to than with any hope of agreement from the old man.

"Ach, Doctor, A'm a charmed man, did ye no ken?" Boab chuckled and peered into the doctor's eyes. "Did ye ken A wis in the War? An A daa mean yon wee bit shindig in thirty-nine. A mean the trenches, min.

63

But A wis een o the chancy eens. A got awa wi hit. There was a wheen billies A kent deed an niver cam back. Heh-heh." He leaned forward, his great bony hands with the translucent skin of the very old gripping the top of his walking-stick, and he grinned a grin of ill-fitting National Health dentures. His frame began to shake and a curious gurgling, wheezing noise, reminiscent of a bagpipe warming up, emanated from his throat. At first Dr. Campbell, for all his thirty odd years experience in general practice was worried, until he realised that Boab was laughing.

Boab stabbed one horny finger at the desk top that separated him from the doctor, and his air became conspiratorial. "Aiblins A shidna be lettin on ti ye, but A daa jalouse thir muckle thi cid dae noo, and forbye ye've aye been a jonick eneuch loon. Ye ken, A leed ti get intil thon hell. Ye had ti be sivinteen, see, and ma twa brithers an me wis in Arbeg for the Coonty Show an thir was the Bleck Watch recruitin tent set up afore the yett, wi a piper blawin jist fit ti bust. Ma brithers wis courtin the lassies Keillor fae Friock, an no sooner dis they lassies catch a glisk o the recruitin-sarjint in his fancy duds an his bonny kilt than they starts up aboot foo brawlie a laddie mecht look aa pitten-on like at, an fit wey thir wis naehin a lassie mecht no dae fur a bonny sojer-boy like, if ye get ma meanin. Aye. Weel, Jock an Doadie baith hud a drink on thum an they wis at roused be fit the lassies sayed did they no jist ging an tak the shillin there an then like." He shook his head slowly, and audibly, and a long silence ensued; he was not laughing now.

"Fan they cam oot they wis canty as twa cocks, an they begood ti tease me fir bein ower youthie; but syne they wis back i the meely, A joukit back ti the Bleck Watch; A tellt the sarjint A wis sivinteen, but A wisnae; A wis herdly fowerteen, but A wis muckle, ye see, A wis aye muckle." He looked far out the window, and the surgery clock ticked many times in the silence that followed before he spoke again.

"Onywey, Doc, A daa ken foo mony year at maks it, but A mind o haein ma saxteent birthday on the Somme, and baith ma brithers wis deid— blawed inti smithereens be a mortar bomb—e'en then. Christ, for aa that Doddy wis nae farrer awa fae me nor ye are noo, we couldnae find eneuch bits o him ti mak it worthwhile caain a graft. We jist pit fit wi hud in wi Jock. An d'ye ken this, A niver had a scratch on me. Naa, Doc, gin the coffin nails ur gingin' ti git me A'll still hae hud aa that A've hud syne A got oot o thon hell for a bonus, the wey A see hit."

To the accompaniment of a series of plainly audible creaks from his joints, Boab extracted a crumpled handkerchief from the pocket of his jacket and shook it out, all the while leaning on the stick with the other hand. The doctor noticed for the first time how old the suit was, and how it had neat leather patches sewn on at the elbows, and tried to ignore what might be being released into the antiseptic atmosphere of the surgery by Boab's attempts to smooth out his hanky. At last the old man succeeded, deliberately dabbed each eye in turn, and then blew an enormous bugle-call into it. As he watched him return the once-white cloot to his pocket, the doctor could see that the old man's nostrils were still twitching.

"I thought you might see it that way," replied Doctor Campbell, smiling wryly. "And I suppose you're right enough. Though I wouldn't recommend it as a life's habit. And I must say, apart from the rheumatics, ye're in fine shape for a man of your age. I don't suppose you might try a....milder brand? No? Ah well. Here I'll give you a prescription that'll help make you more comfortable with the rheumatism......."

So it was that Boab lit up his Full Strength that morning, just as he always did, in the clear conscience that it was not *against* doctor's orders, anyway, and he flicked out the match and began to read the paper, holding the cigarette firmly between his lips, and screwing up one eye against the smoke. The sun warmed him to the core through the open door of the cubicle and he looked up. Over the top of Morag's house he could see a patch of sea that was struck by the sun into a great pool of shimmering crystal fire that hurt his watery eyes to look into.

But this morning Boab's eyes did not seem to hurt as badly as they should; for some reason, rather, they seemed drawn to the centre of the incredible luminosity that was as intense as that of the sun itself. Boab found, strangely, that the brilliant light seemed to form itself into shapes, shapes that moved with a purpose that was more than that of the dancing sun glinting off the waves so far away.

For a very long time, it seemed, he watched the milling patch of sunlight upon the distant blue sea, and then, at last, his lips began to move. For the far-off light had become very close now, and he began to know that which he saw, and he was glad, and a slow smile of recognition broke upon his lined face. And then he spoke, quietly, and as if to himself, though it was clear that he addressed another.

Once, in that War of so long ago, Boab had been lightly gassed, and had spent a week in Lille; there, whilst touring the soldier's bars and whorehouses, he met a pretty young whore who spoke no English and to whom he had given his virginity along with his sous. And now, despite the fact that her flesh-and-bone self had died a fat and grey-headed madame with whiskers growing out of her face thirty years before, it seemed to him that she appeared out of the shimmering light in all her youthful loveliness. "Angelique?" he whispered.

And on the instant that he did so, the eyes of Boab's earthly dust glazed over and bade farewell to the person who had inhabited it for such a very long time.

As Boab's hand sagged earthward, it took the lighted Capstan Full Strength with it; the fingers relaxed a tiny fraction, and the cigarette fell to the floor. That cigarette must have been hated, for while most cigarettes would have burned out on the concrete slab, this one did not, and instead managed to find a crack behind the toilet which no-one had noticed and roll in.

Perhaps I should explain that when the Cooncil built the Convenience, the contract was oiled by the usual pay-offs and sweeteners, and more care was given to cost than to precision. The Cooncil did not think to ask the villagers why there was no cottage on the site. If they had they would have been told that there was a crack in the cliff structure there, and nobody in Auchpinkie was daft enough to build a hen-coop over it, never mind a cottage. But they didn't ask, and just laid all the drainage, dumped down a concrete slab, and built their cludge, while the villagers grinned and tapped their foreheads. Not many years later the cliff shifted an almost imperceptible amount, and cracked the pipes, which began leaking into the strata. The inevitable colonies of bacteria which thus found themselves a home under the Convenience began to hollow out the rock and produce methane gas long ago

Now as any schoolboy will tell you, methane is explosive, but only under the right conditions. If you have too much gas and no air, the gas will not even burn; and if you have a little gas and a lot of air, you get a controllable flame. But if you have just enough air, and just the right amount of gas............

As Lanky Boab's spiritual vestige passed out of his weather-beaten remains, Willie and Ian, as we have seen, were placing their most recent squib against the back wall of the Public Convenience at a time at which they knew that Boab would be inside, taking his quasi-alfresco ease with a cigarette and the Daily Record. Then they retreated to a van-tage point to watch the show.

"This'll gie the auld bugger some fleg!" said Willie.

"Aye, at'll learn him ti tak hud o ma lug!" replied Ian, rubbing the offended part tenderly.

This latest squib was the first trial of a more sophisticated fusing device: a piece of sisal baler twine soaked in a solution of their mixture and dried carefully in the sun. Ian had been most attentive in chemistry class recently, and the teacher had noticed, not without some dark pre-monition, the depth and precision of his questioning.

So far the plan had gone exactly to schedule. Their first recon-noitre, carried out with the stealth of cats, had revealed the tell-tale trace of the enemy; the white bony profile of two ancient knees sticking out from the cubicle door, and the unmistakable aroma of Capstan Full Strength.

"There he's!"

They had rushed from the cover of one house to the next, stick-ing close to the walls and crouching down by each successive corner. At last their target was before them, the grey concrete edifice separated from the shed by which they sheltered by an open space of twenty feet or so. For a long time they remained there, before, with an exchange of mean-ingful glances, Ian—whose privilege it was on account of it being his ears that had been so abused—lit the dangling fuse of the squib with the Zippo lighter adorned with genuine U.S.A.A.F. insignia that he'd swapped for a complete set of American Civil War bubble gum cards.

At once the two broke cover together, sprinted to the Conven-ience, set down the Andrew's Liver Salts tin with its fizzing fuse and withdrew, in a clatter of footfalls and little explosions of smothered giggles, to the other side of the old cistern in Fountain Square.

Their tension was so great that their very bodies shivered, and from time to time one or other of them burst into suppressed fits of mirth, to be cloured promptly by the other. As the little sputtling flame crawled along the sisal baler twine, they became more and more excited, until at last the flame disappeared from view. The boys leld their breaths.

In her kitchen Morag dried a plate and glared at the motionless (and by the way now completely sensationless) figure of Boab above her, gazing out to sea, with his paper spread over his knees. In the Public Bar of the Auchpinkie Hotel, Dave the barman was sweeping the dust around the floor with a besom that had long lost its bristle. Mae and her cronies were deep in conference in the corner shop. Deek White was allowed to leave the Casualty Department of Arbeg Hospital, and looked forward with dread to his forthcoming interview with the depot manager. In the cottage by the limekilns, Dick and Alice Tadger, having had a row of historic proportions, were making frantic love on the kitchen table, while Alice's three cats lapped up the milk from the bottle that had smashed to the floor. Inside the little schoolroom, Miss Middleton chirpily encouraged and cajoled the infants while the big children pretended to study and instead fell asleep in the golden sunlit warmth. And inside the Convenience, Boab's Capstan Full Strength, as if on a mission of its own, rolled and dropped into the crack and tumbled down a fissure in the rock and at last fell upon an invisible tongue of methane gas.

The chronology of the next few moments is hard to recount; no-one who was there can remember very clearly. It is often like that with sudden and shocking events; time seems to slow and each sensation—surprise, fear, pain, takes its turn to appear and to be appreciated. We remember with incredibly detailed recall the clothes that people were wearing, the way the wind was blowing, the minutiae of that which came to pass; but, as any newspaper reporter or policeman will freely confirm, our sense of what happened when, and then, becomes hopelessly confused.

And so it was. The lighted cigarette end met the tongue of gas and they decided to have a party, and the tongue of gas invited all its friends, and then, with a Whoop! that stopped the entire village dead in its tracks and shivered the rocky bones of Auchpinkie Ness itself, all hell broke loose.

A rollicking, searing, cavorting, devastating blast of flame leapt lustily skyward through the fissured rock and escaped into the world. The precast concrete walls of the Public Convenience fell outwards like so many playing cards. The easement itself flew up into the air and then, on descending, exploded into a shower of shards upon the tarmac of The Street. The cast-iron cistern flew less high and when it came down stove in the roof of Bert Paterson's Ford Granada, which he had customised with the fiddlings of his dole money. Bert looked out of his window and burst into tears. The windows of six houses were blown out. The pine chainstore table in the Tadger's kitchen splintered and collapsed under the violence of the combined assault of the thrashing bodies upon it, and as she crashed to the floor, Alice at last achieved her long and most assiduously sought orgasm. She felt the vibration of the distant explosion and thought *Jesus Christ All-bluidy-mechty! So the earth really does move!* and passed out in amazement. No one ever saw the roof of the Convenience again.

The worldly remains of Lanky Boab Smith were blasted clear of the throne and launched majestically into the air. Morag dropped the plate and it smashed on the floor, as the figure, lifeless jaw hanging open and arms spread wide like a risen Christ dressed in a greasy black suit with the pants about its ankles, soared in a graceful arc towards her. She screamed. Boab's short flight came to an end and he descended upon the washing line on Morag's green, which miraculously held, and there he came to rest, suspended by the armpits, his bare knees on the grass, and his ancient family jewels dangling not ten feet in front of Morag's face.

Something big and tight that had been twisting Morag into an ever more uncomfortable shape for longer than even she could remember finally snapped, almost audibly. She rushed out of the kitchen door, and attacked the bared buttocks of the insensate Boab with the first thing she could lay her hands on: her yard-broom.

"Ye dirty old bugger.. Ye dirty old Bugger....Ye DIRTY ..... OLD....BUGGER.... *YE!*", this last ejaculated in time with a wallop that would have dirled every bone in the old man's body, had he been able to feel it.

In their hiding place behind the cistern, Willie and Ian rose to their feet and stood in silence, mouths agape in sheer and unadulterated horror, oblivious to the fragments of stone and concrete and shards of ceramic that pattered to the earth about them. Somewhere, with a corner of one ear that was not really listening, Ian heard a curious noise that tugged at his attention. Tonk-tonk-tonk, it went. Willie shook him by the his shoulders.

"Ian! F-F-F-F'Chrissake min lessgethehellootiherequick!"

Tonk-tonk, went the noise. Tonk-tonk-tonk-tonk, in diminuendo, and all the time coming nearer. At last it stopped. Ian looked down, at once unable to resist his curiosity any longer and quivering with trepidation at what he might see. At his feet lay an Andrew's Liver Salts tin with a hole punched in the lid. In a long instant that seemed a lifetime Ian came to know the meaning of terror. Slowly he stooped and picked the tin up. His very worst fears—fears he could never have imagined before— were only confirmed. The tin was still full and the fuse had gone out half an inch from the charge. Ian began to shake and he looked up into the eyes of his friend with a face ashen white and stricken with awe. Suddenly his mouth was as dry as a sun bleached bone.

"Run," he croaked.

CHAPTER FIFTEEN
Big Sye's Doings

What with all that commotion in the village, explosions and ructions and ambulances and police and firemen and loss adjusters from the insurance company (to adjust it so's it's your loss an no oors) and sanitation engineers from the Cooncil and the boys from the Watter Board and folk that nobody kent what the hell they were there for at all but they still had a right good deek and a stand around and a blether with their hands in their pockets before they slipped into the Auchpinkie Hotel for a bridie and a quick one or four along with the reporters and photographers and a lassie from Radio Tay and even a TV crew from Grampian who said they were on their way to a balloon launch when they got paged and I don't know how many other comings and goings and dogs barking and bairns greeting and car horns blaring and this that and the other and God only knows what else so's a bodie'd cry out for a minute's peace just so's he could get a hold of his thoughts, I've clean gone and forgotten to fill you in on what Big Sye'd been up to in the meantime.

So we'll leave that meely to get on with itself for a while and use the storyteller's right of free movement in time and space to turn the clock back a wee bitty to before all of this carry on broke out in the first place.

Big Sye, you will recall, had found himself on the receiving end of a dare, with provocation, and as anyone who knows him will attest, the one thing he cannot ever resist is a dare. It was only natural that after his confrontation with Geordie Baird and Alan Gilchrist, Sye would be pricked into doing something out of the ordinary. Geordie should have asked Nan, Sye's mother, for her advice; she would have told him that the surest way to get her son to do anything at all was to tell him that he couldn't and if he really wanted Sye *not* to do it, then he should tell him that he *had* to. She would have warned Geordie in the weightiest of tones that above all else he must not seem to be issuing a challenge; for if he did, her son would be certain—duty bound—to take up the gauntlet.

For Sye, as has been mentioned elsewhere, the poaching of the river was a sporting event; his depredations were not great and it was the fact of outwitting the authorities that gave him his pleasure. Not that he ever condescended to use a rod and line or anything so artificial as that, but a wee bit gaffing or tailing with a hankie wrapped round his hand so the fish wouldn't slip or trawling a heavy weight to which were attached several large treble hooks—of the type legitimately used to catch sharks—

across a few likely pools in the hope of foul-hooking a decent fish, was not in the way of being major-league poaching. Not like dynamite at least. Sye rarely even took money for the fish he took; he preferred to load up his own freezer and if there was a bit left over he'd give it to his Ma or any of his innumerable relatives who looked like they needed a bit feeding up and could be trusted not to let on.

But this was different. A Direct Challenge had been issued. Worse, he had been insulted and provoked in the Bar of the Auchpinkie Hotel, which was as good as saying in his own front room; and no dilettante approach would suffice now, for A Direct Challenge With Insult and Abuse called for A Very Serious Bit Poaching and No Nonsense Neither. And Sye had cooked up a total beezer, believe me.

You'll mind that Big Sye had explained his plan to the incredulous Peem down on the foreshore, the day after he and Geordie had had their row. Then, as you'll maybe also recall, the pair of them had gone for a drink—Peem said he bluidy needed one after hearing *that*—and consulted the tide table in Dave's *Arbeg Guide*. Sye had been right about the tide and the moon. Of course the thing about spring tides is that they are caused by the changing phases of the moon, and the biggest range, that is to say, the highest and lowest tides, comes with the full moon, and the no moon, and the smallest range at the half-moons. You still with me? Anyway the rising tide would flood the estuary of the River Pinkie after midnight on Monday the seventh, under a full moon. And that would add just that teeny bit of extra spice to the affair, for a full moon on a clear night is to a poacher the same as broad daylight.

The operation was organised with a precision and skill that belied our more familiar vision of Big Sye and Peem as professional bar-props. In fact they were only amateur bar-props. Diving, don't forget, was their profession. That they had both been working in the North Sea for as long as they had without accident testifies that they were very good at it. So, on the Sunday evening, they made their way to the little cave, arriving just after eight, in the dim light of the gloaming, wearing their dry-suits under overalls and donkey-jackets so they would look innocent enough. In the cave they checked over their gear; they spent the last few minutes putting on black balaclava helmets and applying camouflage make-up to each other's faces. They slipped out to sea in the Zodiac as night unrolled its velvety carpet, and moved north around the headland towards the Pinkie estuary. Big Sye rigged the little sail, for they could not risk using the motor, and propelled by that and the rising tide they made good time to the southern edge of the estuary, where they dropped the sail and began to row, muffling the oars with bits of rag wrapped around them. There was a little swell and not much breeze—a perfect spring evening.

Inside the estuary proper the channel hugs the north shore and the banks here are steep and undercut, with overhanging vegetation. They pulled the Zodiac in under this cover and dropped the little cleek-anchor. Peem swung himself over the side and dropped as silently as he could into the water. He rinsed out his mask and snorkel—they would not use scuba gear tonight, in case they got fankled up in the net—and pulled on his flippers. Sye passed him one of the blue plastic drums that contained the poaching tackle and took the other himself. The darkness was still complete, though the risen moon had turned the great bank of cloud that shaded its light into a vast silver zeppelin to the east. The two men, using the last of the rising tide to help them, swam silently upstream.

At last they reached the spot where that great finger of sand forms a bank in the estuary. This is the favourite place of the salmon, where he rests a wee, pumping the water through his gills and getting used to the change in salinity before moving up into the river proper. Our men moved upstream of this and as they did so the moon cleared the cloud and lit up the world. Instinctively Sye glanced toward where the Zodiac was moored, but could see nothing. Then he smelled, quite distinctly, wafting on the breeze, the unmistakable scent of tobacco-smoke, and smiled grimly. This was the dangerous part, where stealth and watercraft and their wits would be their only allies.

A little cloud masked the moon again and they began to put their plan into operation. Peem opened the drum and Sye pulled from it the end of a net made of monofilament nylon. I should tell you that being caught with such a thing *near* a salmon river in Scotland, never mind in it, will probably get you a custodial sentence. The plan—though daring—was simple. Starting upstream, they would encircle the bank with the net, which in design was similar to a purse seine, though small enough for two men to manage, and any fish that were there would be caught inside it. They quickly put their plan into effect, swimming slowly on their backs and allowing the net to stream out behind them, away from each other and along the sides of the bank. This part of the operation had to be done quickly and precisely, for though the current here was slack, the peak of the spring tide was past, and soon the water would begin to rush out to sea and they would not be able to control the net.

The bottom of the net was weighted and the top floated so that it hung vertically in the water like an invisible fence. Strung along the bottom of the net was a cord, which, when pulled tight, would ruck up the bottom of the net, eventually forming it into a bowl-shape with the bottom closed. A similar line threaded along the top of the net would then be pulled tight, forming a closed bag of netting, and any fish that had been within the encirclement of the net would be caught. The two men worked slowly and methodically, only occasionally letting their heads bob above the water to check their bearings. The slow minutes dragged by as they moved slowly around the bank, all the while their hearts pounding with the adrenaline that coursed their veins.

When at last they met up again on the seaward side of the bank, the tide was already beginning to do its work and they had no time to lose. A flash of teeth and white of eye was all they could see of each other in the gloom, and they began to pull the bottom line tight, scooping their prey into the bowl of the net. For Sye and Peem this was the most dangerous part of a dangerous enterprise. They could not remain submerged and work the lines at the same time. And it was hard work pulling at the lines and they could not avoid, however hard they tried, splashing a little. The sweat poured off them inside their dry-suits as they worked, but little by little they pulled in the line that was threaded along the bottom edge of the net until it was tight. No fish could escape now; the net was scooped tight beneath them and on every side was an invisible wall of monofilament nylon. Quickly Sye and Peem began to haul the top line and close the trap.

Suddenly they heard voices and froze dead in the water. They could feel the increasing weight of the tide-rush scrape the net along the bottom and they held their breaths. Suddenly a finger of light from a powerful torch snapped out across the estuary and Sye and Peem felt the cold hand of fear touch their hearts.

"Faazzat? Show yersel, the game's up!" A voice on the north bank, seeming dreadfully close.

"Ower there. Git the lecht ower there, Chrissake! Hey! You! A want a word wi you!" Sye immediately recognised Geordie Baird's voice and smiled grimly. Was this it? He looked over and saw the whites of Peem's eyes, but in the darkness he could not make out his expression.

We take the cards we are dealt in this life, and Geordie was as unfortunate as Sye was lucky at the chance of the slight cloud-cover and the advantage it allowed his adversary. For every moment of that darkness, as Geordie stood atop his dune with his walkie-talkie in his hand and Sooty, his retriever, at his side, the night seemed to prickle with alarms and flashes of light and to rustle with the sounds of myriad hordes raiding his fish. But it was only his imagination, and he heaved a sigh of relief when the moon was once again uncovered and he could search the area with his night-glasses. He could see nothing. Not a thing. No silhouetted boat, no outline of a man crouching where he shouldn't on the bank, nothing.

Nothing save the occasional bobbing of a black shape that could have been the head of a seal or an otter—both of which were plentiful in the estuary—circling the sandbank. Geordie peered hard through his glasses at the shapes, but they were too indistinct amongst the wavelets. Was there something odd about the way they moved? Geordie bit his lip. He was a traditional bailiff, as traditional as any upland gamekeeper, and in former years he would likely have drilled a bullet through the head of any otter that he had caught marauding his precious salmon. Although they did not know it, it was very lucky for Sye and Peem that a bailiff on the Tay had only the year before been fined and had lost his job for doing just that, the animals being protected by a for once wise law. Now all Geordie dared to do was to watch the furry pirates eat his fish. He swore and looked away and rubbed his eyes.

He put the radio to his mouth. "Alan? Come in Alan." Geordie habitually shouted into his radio at a volume that would have carried the estuary on a quiet night like this, and he found it tough going to keep his voice down to a stage whisper.

"Aye, aye. Geordie," came the crackled reply after a few moments. "Ye dinna need ti shout."

"D'ye see onyhin, min?"

"Na, nuthin. You?"

"Only they twa seals at the fish."

"Whit seals?" Alan Gilchrist was stationed among the trees on the opposite bank, not a hundred yards from where Sye's Zodiac bobbed patiently.

"They twa on the sandbank. D'ye no see them?"

"Oh, aye. A see the buggers noo. Oh, aye. Christ they're some size for seals ur they no?" Alan lowered his glasses and picked up the portable searchlight on the ground beside him, "Here A'm awa ti hae a shufti, Geordie, thir somethin funny...."

Just then, and before he could snap on the light, Alan was distracted by a grunt and a crashing and splintering of branches nearby: unmistakable sounds of a struggle.

"Here!" he yelled. "Fa's at?" He swung his light round and it lit up the trees. From further up the river bank on his side there came the sudden shriek of a police whistle. Geordie, across the river, flashed on his lamp and swept it across the pines that clung to the shore opposite. Sye and Peem, who were still floating with baited breath unsure of what was happening on the shore, submerged.

They could hear the splashing of one—now two–pairs of feet through the shallows, and then a heavier splash—somebody had fallen into the river. Then a finger of light stabbed onto the water over their heads, lingered for an interminable moment, and then swung away.

Above them, in the night, Gilchrist was closing in fast. He too could hear the sounds of running feet, and gussed—rightly—that one or more of the gillies had surprised someone on the bank. "Siccim!" he hissed, "Siccim, Dougie!", and slipped his dog's leash. A blacker shape in the black night bounded off into the darkness. A thought crossed Gilchrist's mind and he swung his light over the estuary. The seals had disappeared, if that was what they were. But there was no time to wait; he plunged into the undergrowth after the dog.

In the inky blackness of the estuarine water Sye and Peem were as still as dead men, only the breathing tubes of their snorkels showing above the waves. After the commotion and splashing on the north bank they could hear nothing. The minutes ticked by, each dragging its heels more slowly than the last, and they could feel the tide gathering speed. This was at once a blessing and a hazard; it meant that they were being silently moved away from the watchers on the shore, but the estuary runs a four-knot tide at springs and there was a danger of being swept out to sea. They could hear—or more like feel—the distant booming through the water of feet running along the river's edge. They felt the net tug as the fish took fright and swam into the monofilament. If they all panicked it was possible that the two men would no longer be able to control the net. Sye had no choice but to risk a look. The moon had come out from the clouds and shone brightly with its all-revealing light.

The cold made Sye's face burn, and he grimaced. The moon would soon, he could see, be obscured by a large bank of cloud, and he nodded his thanks. Away to the north, there came the sounds of pursuit carrying clear over the water. The action was much further away than it had seemed, for sound travels queerly through water. Sye heard crashing and splintering and shouting and dogs barking and police whistles blowing. Someone was being chased through the woods towards the road, but his pursuers were gaining. Suddenly Sye heard a car starting up. Its motor revved and it took off in a clatter of poorly adjusted tappets and howling rubber on tarmac. Sye smiled grimly. So there were two at least, and one had legged it to save himself. But the fugitive would still have to cross the brig to get away. Geordie was not fool enough to leave that door open, and then, sure enough, he heard the answering burst of noise from a big diesel engine as Geordie gunned his Land-Rover to close it.

Sye heard the chase on the ground change direction again—the one left behind had realised his mate had taken the car and knew there was no hope of escape along the road, so he had jouked back through the woods towards towards the estuary. But there was no escape that way either, as Sye well knew. It was only a matter of time now. The end came quickly and he heard the sound of pursuit transform into the sound of a struggle as several bodies landed on one body and the whole lot crashed to the earth. From the dancing arcs of the torches Sye realised that the men on the shore were no more than ten or fifteen yards from his Zodiac, and he remembered that if he and Peem were to get out of this caper unscathed, then they would need that Zodiac. He reflected an instant and then made a decision. With the tide now really beginning to rip out to sea, they were going to pass the boat in a matter of minutes.

"Peem! D'ye hink ye can hud oan by yersel?" he hissed urgently.

"Naa. A hink A'll awa ma bluidy holidays instead." Sye caught a glimpse of a flash of white teeth as Peem grinned despite the cold that numbed his face.

"A'm gingin fur the Zodiac. A'll need ti chance it while the moon's ahent yon cloud."

"Aboot time tae. But fit wey ur ye gingin ti finnd me? Cannae show a lecht noo, ye ken. Yon bank's gingin ti be hoachin wi baileys an polis aa necht."

"Thir a puckle piles a bit farrer oot— ye ken the eens? Ye kin see thum agin the lecht. Kin ye get thir an mak fest lang eneuch?"

"Nae boather. Mecht sneg the net, but A'll hae ti chance it."

"Aye. Listen.......If A'm no beck in hauf an oor, loss the net and tak aff. Recht?"

"Awa'n bile yer heid, eh, Sye? Jist git gingin. An mak it quick, A'm burstin fur a pish."

"Dae it in yer suit like aabody else." Sye disappeared into the night and Peem was left alone with his thoughts. And the fish, of course.

Sye had left not a moment too soon. The net, with Peem, was moving in the slacker water toward the southern shore where the water was still shoal, and Sye was unprepared for the violence of the sudden press of current as he moved into the deep water of the channel. There was little real danger, once away from the monofilament net and the possibility of entanglement. His dry-suit and the thick thermal under-suit not only prevented any water from getting to his body and chilling him, but were themselves a source of buoyancy. Indeed both men were wearing weight-belts to counteract this. Yet still the weird sensation of swimming against a mass of inky black water that was sweeping him rapidly out to an inkier black beyond was more than a little scary. When at last Sye sensed his sideways movement slacken, by some refinement of the inner ear unique to seafarers, he trod water and checked his position. The Zodiac was moored at the foot of a dead pine on the shore whose trunk and branches shone whitely in a passing glisk of moonlight, and Sye was surprised at how far he'd come past it, for all that he had been swimming upstream as he crossed the channel.

It took him another fifteen minutes to work his way as silently as he could back up the shore until he bumped into the black rubber boat. She still had water under her bottom and Sye breathed a sigh of relief. He pulled up the cleik and pushed her out from the bank. But he did not clamber aboard yet. Under the cover of the overhanging bank he had been insulated from sound and hidden from eyes, but as he moved out into open water he could clearly hear angry voices. They seemed so close that he felt he could reach out and tap one of the speakers on the shoulder, but he knew it was only a trick of the water, the darkness, and his insistently vibrating nerves. From the sounds they were making he knew that Gilchrist and his men were interrogating their captive with a certain vigour, and Sye knew he could expect the same or worse were they to catch up with him. Having once 'fallen down the steps' of a police station, he had little desire for the same treatment at the hands of the bailiffs.

It was a long time before he judged it safe to boost himself into the boat and silently ship the oars. He looked at the luminous dial of his Rolex. He was late; it was already three-quarters of an hour since he'd left Peem. He allowed himself a brief chuckle. His partner in crime was sure to have pished himself by now. He put his back into rowing across the mouth of the estuary. Out here the surf would mask the sounds of the oars, and the critical thing now was the race against the dawn.

It was quarter to four before he heard the muted cry of a curlew; which was no curlew at all but Peem hailing him as he approached the rotten pilings that had once supported a pier. Until the Second World War, ships had loaded there with logs of pine and oak floated down from the Balgownie estate's forestry, but now all that was left was a half a dozen sea-gnawed and blackened stumps.

Peem was good all right; he had not let the invisible bag of the net with its precious load of thoroughly bamfeezled salmon snag on the pilings. Sye helped him aboard and then they rowed far out to sea before at last they pulled the net. Behind them the fore-dawn was a rosy luminosity in the still black sky and both men knew that soon the sun would rise over the eastern horizon and they would be silhouetted against it from the shore. They knew that if that happened they could expect the quick attentions of a coastguard helicopter. They worked quickly and in silence but it was not easy work. The net was heavy with fish and each that came aboard had to be stunned with a sharp blow from a 'priest'—in this case a fourteen-inch pipe-wrench. Soon the boat was awash with the silvery creatures, and both men were shaking their heads in sheer amazement at their haul.

"No bed, eh?" chirped Peem in delight. Sye laughed.

Then he looked up at the sky and the laugh stilled on his face.

"Hell, Peem, luik at the time! B'Christ the sun'll be up in a puckle meenits an wis sat here like a bairn's deuk in a bath!" He looked hard at the outboard motor and then shook his head. "Cannae risk it. They buggers ashore hear at an the game's a bogie. C'mon, Peem, we'll hae ti row like the bars noo!"

Peem, who had been hauling the tail of the net, let it fall inboard and grabbed an oar at the same time as Sye. They were fit, and good oarsmen, but a Zodiac is not easy to row. It lacks the mass of a proper dinghy; it is ever the victim of a capricious breeze and a slight chop in the water plays hell with its rhythm, as it lifts and slaps rather than cutting through. Sye and Peem pulled as if all the devils of Hell were after them—which was not so far from the truth—the muscles standing out on their necks and their kists heaving. The sweat poured from them as they sweltered in the rubber dry-suits that had all night protected them against the deadly cold of the water but which now sapped their strength with the heat of them. Yet for all their backbreaking effort and the slight aid they had from the current, once in open sea their progress was slow. Sye looked over his shoulder. The great looming mass of the headland, black against an aquamarine sky, was still a good half an hour's rowing away. He pulled again, hard, and in silence.

Suddenly Peem swore.

"Fit?" gasped Sye.

Peem said nothing but nodded towards the north. Lights had appeared—the lights of a ship, close inshore.

"Bastart! D'ye hink it's......."

"Fa else wid it be but the Protection at close in at necht?" replied Peem, shortly. "A hink we've hud wur chips, Sye, ma loon."

Sye narrowed his eyes. HMS *Ellen*, without shadow of a doubt. Specialist fishery protection vessel, plastic hull, 140 feet, shallow draft, and fast—over forty knots he'd heard. He could see the finger of her searchlight sweep the shore in the distance. She was moving quickly southward, much faster than patrol speed. Even at that range Sye could see the whiteness of the bone in her teeth. He nodded. Geordie was not daft at all at all. He'd likely called the Coastguard at Montrose to let them know they'd caught a poacher in tidal water, with a shrewd idea that the Coastguard would radio the news to the ship, whose skipper would not be able to resist the temptation to call to quarters, wind up the motors and see if there was any trade for him.

It was just a pity that Geordie's desire to cover all possibilities had been so close to the truth.

Sye thought quickly as he pulled. Over the side? The shore was over a mile off and the tide was still ebbing. And if the fishery protection found a boat full of salmon, they'd search until they found the owners. He looked up. The dark shape of the ship was approaching the northern limit of the estuary, and she had slowed, her searchlight raking the shore. Luck, then, was still with the poachers; they had not been spotted from the shore and they would still, from the north, be a dark speck against the darkness of the coast. But not for much longer.

They rowed and rowed and the sweat hailed off them and their throats rasped. Twenty minutes, maybe twenty-five at the most till they reached safety; not a long time, but under full power that ship could catch them in under five; now she was nosing in about the estuary and her lights seemed close enough to touch. She began to move south again. Even at the speed she was going, she'd run them down in a quarter of an hour. They were going to have no choice; it was the outboard or be caught. Sye feathered his oar and leapt aft. The Johnson 50 that hung there was old, and tricky to start. Peem grabbed both oars, and doubled his efforts, his breath hoarse. Sye tickled the fuel and pulled on the choke and spun the motor with the starter cord. Ages passed as he tugged and tugged and twisted and twisted at the throttle, his face growing darker and darker, and the sweat beading on his brow. The sun was breaching the horizon now and any moment they expected to see lights and hear angry hails carrying from the shore.

Sye glanced north again and his heart froze and the hackles stood up on the back of his neck. The *Ellen* had changed course, and worse, she had hunkered down, her bow lifting and her stern digging in under the thrust of her powerful diesels, as she made full speed. Her searchlight swept towards them. They had been spotted, or picked up on radar. It didn't matter which. Sye swore and tugged viciously at the cord, but still the motor refused to start. Suddenly Peem, who had been watching with increasing agitation—or at least, as much as he could muster while breaking his back at the oars—cursed and pushed him aside. "Youse row," he snapped. He tinkered with the choke and tugged and the motor spat and coughed and sputtered a cloud of smoke. Peem backed off the choke entirely. "Ye've floodit it, ye daft bastart!" he hissed over his shoulder. He twisted the throttle wide open and gave the motor three fast spins. It screamed into life in a cloud of two-stroke, and the Zodiac surged forward. Peem settled down in the sheets, one hand on the tiller, and held the throttle wide open. The bow rose and Sye grinned and unshipped his oars and moved forward to trim the boat with his weight. Spray flew everywhere.

The chase was on. Even with the outboard howling at full power, the ship had the edge in speed, but maybe not enough to make up the ground. The Zodiac swept toward the headland beyond which was the safety of the little cave. But unless they could get there well before the ship, the entrance would be spotted, and a boat would be launched to arrest them. It was pretty well hopeless whatever, and both of them knew it.

Sye looked aft. He could see men moving on the fore-deck of the fishery protection vessel, and noted grimly that they were taking the covers off what looked like a gun but which he had a canny notion was a powerful water cannon. Once caught by that their motor would die and they themselves might well be swept into the sea under the ferocity of its blast. The ship's klaxon whooped and they heard even above the insane shriek of the outboard the commands bellowing over its loud-hailer.

"Heave to at once! You are under arrest! Heave to and stop your engine at once! That is an order! Heave to in the name of the Crown!"

Only seconds now to the cove beyond the headland, but with their wake a spoor thirty feet wide the two men dared no longer hope.

"Ower the side the meenit we roond the pynte!" roared Sye and Peem nodded grimly. What a waste of a night's work, not to mention the loss of the boat.

But then life has its surprises, and some of them are even pleasant, you know. For as the fugitives rounded the headland and looked to where Auchpinkie Ness should have been glowing fiery orange in the first finger of sunlight, they saw nothing. Nothing at all, save a wall of white. The cove, the bay, the port, and the whole coast to the south as far as their eyes could see, was entirely shrouded in dense haar.

"Waahoo!" yelled Sye and stood up, despite the peril of falling over the side. Peem's jaw dropped open in sheer disbelief. "Waa hoooo!" repeated Sye at the top of his lungs. "Ya bastart!" He turned and gave two fingers to the fishery protection vessel that was closing fast, as Peem steered straight into the haven of the mist. All in an instant the Zodiac, its hysterical occupants, and the salmon that should have been on their way up the river, completely and utterly disappeared inside its obliterating blanket.

Peem steered towards where he knew the cave to be and killed the outboard. They could hear the roar of the ship's motors and the boiling hiss of her screws cutting the water and the swish of her bow-wave. But they knew they would not be caught now. Close inshore, where the rocks showed high above the falling tide, their little echo would simply vanish amongst the clutter on the ship's radar screen, if it had ever been distinguishable in the first place. They took up the oars and began to row again, as silently as they could. They both knew the bay so well that they could pick their way through the rocks on a pitch-dark night, and even a peasouper like this was easy for them. Before long they found themselves nosing into the cave.

Out to sea the roar of powerful diesel engines had quieted to a rumble that made the air in the cave boom; the skipper had hove to when his ship rounded the headland and he had seen the fog. Only a fool makes speed close inshore in a pea-souper haar like that. Now he was sniffing and nosing like a dog that has lost the scent. But Sye and Peem knew they were safe. The ship had lost them, and they soon heard her discontented grumbling move slowly away to the south.

Our two elated poachers jumped into the shallows and dragged the Zodiac up onto the little stony beach. While Peem made fast, Sye rummaged in one of his plastic drums and pulled forth a bottle of clear fluid with a cork in it. He swigged deep and let the fire warm him. He passed the bottle to Peem.

"By Christ, we done it," laughed Sye, his joy and relief intermingled and fizzing over. "Can ye imagine Bairdie's face? But, by, thon wis some close. Christ, we actually done it!"

"See youse? Youse," replied Peem after a long suck at the bottle of moonshine, "Ur the jammiest bugger A've iver kent. B'rights the pair o wis should be in the brig noo, an no in here haein a dram. At's no bad stuff bi the wey—see's anither belt."

Sye grinned and wrapped his arms around Peem and hugged him. "Well, no jist luck," he laughed. "A'll hae til admit the Engineer saved ma bacon the day."

"G'aff ye great bloody nancy!" Peem shoved him away but his crooked grin gave away his delight. He raised the bottle. "Cheers, skipper."

CHAPTER SIXTEEN
How Willie and Ian were Converted, and Morag too

Sye and Peem got back to the village about six in the morning, still warm from the swift deoch an doris they had taken in the cave, and buzzing with elation. But they did not waste time on celebration. They knew they had to get back to their houses as quickly as they could. They did what they could to protect their haul from the attentions of passing seals or otters, stashed their kit, and hurried home, taking with them only the puckle fish they could safely hide in the village. They took their farewells in the square, and each went his way. Sye showered quickly, and then dried his hair with a hair dryer. Then he went to bed and pulled the quilt over his head to shut out the morning light. He had never gotten around to curtains.

And none too soon either. Not twenty minutes after his head hit the pillow he heard the scrunch of tyres on the gravel outside, and then someone hammered on the door. Pluto went into barking overdrive. Sye let them hammer for a while and then leaned out of bed and opened the bedroom window. He blinked. Below him he saw Geordie Baird and Alan Gilchrist and a policeman. Gilchrist had a dangerous smile on his face. Parked in the square was Geordie's Land-Rover and a police car with a glum-looking youth with cuts and bruises on his face in the back. Sye nodded. So they'd gone to the Estate Office to pick up the poacher that had been caught before coming here. He wondered what had happened to the other one—likely he'd abandoned the car and made off through the woods. Must have, for Geordie would never have let him cross the brig. He made a mental note to buy the poor lad in the car a pint if ever he ran into him. Had the Polis come here first, things might have been more difficult to explain.

"Mr. Swankie? D'ye hink we could hiv a wee word?" asked the policeman.

Sye made a show of looking at his watch and rubbing his eyes. "At this time i the morn? Can ye no come back later?"

"Naa, A daa hink sae. A'd like a word jist noo. It'll no tak lang."

"Aye, okay, okay. Hing on till A get ma breeks on."

As they waited, Gilchrist turned to the policeman. "Here, can ye no be a bit mair—*firm* as that?"

"Listen, we hiv aaready been doon the port. Thir wis nae sign o ony inflatable. Thir wis nae sign onybody'd haaled een oot. Even if thir wis een, A hiv on'y your word for hit that this led's involved. A ken yer suspicions, but us lot need proof, ken. Noo, we'll dae hit ma wey, an no hiv ony mair nonsense, eh?"

Gilchrist glared at him but held his tongue. Just then, Sye opened the door but left the security chain in place. "D'ye hink A could come in?" asked the policeman.

"How?"

"A hiv reason tae believe ye may be concealin stolen property."

Sye nodded pleasantly. "Okay. Youse an Cousin Geordie. No him."

"Whit?" Gilchrist flushed red with rage. "Ye cannae dae that!"

"Aye A can," said the Sye, smiling at him. "Een o ye is aa that's required tae identify fittiver't is yer luikin fur. A'm no obliged ti let onybody else in, an seein as how ye've nae warrant an nae hope o gittin een, ye'll jist hae ti thole it. Is at no recht, Constable?"

Gilchrist pushed forward but the policeman caught him by the arm. He had had quite enough of Gilchrist. In fact, he was half way to thinking there might be an assault charge against him if the laddie in the car's story was to be believed. "That's far enough. Mr Swankie kens his rechts. Een o ye *is* aa that's required. So *you* bide here."

Sye undid the chain, his other hand firmly holding Pluto by the collar, and pointed the way to the front room. "A'll pit the dug oot the back," he said, pleasantly, and then stopped. "Ye'd better get yer mucker ti c'wa fae the beck door first. Jist in case he gets a fleg, like."

The policeman looked hard at Pluto and nodded, pulling his radio from its lapel clip. "No a bed idear ava. Be the wey, A tak it ye've a licence fur at."

"A div," said Sye, who didn't. "Want tae see it?"

"Naa," replied the policeman, who knew it wasn't worth the hassle anyway. "Luik aboot?"

"Feel free."

"Ye been oot durin the necht, Mr. Swankie?", he asked, when Sye returned.

"Naa."

"Fit wis ye daein lest necht?" The policeman opened the fridge, winced, and closed it quickly. "Yer milk's aff."

"A wis oot fur a drink wi a auld freen," lied Sye, "Till aboot ten."

"Uhuh. Fa wis this freen?" The eye-level cupboards, one by one. "Jist a freen."

"Back ye up?"

"Gin she his til. But so wid Agnes at the Hotel ower by an a dozen or mair ither fowk an aa." Sye knew fine no one would let on different.

The policeman—who was not from Auchpinkie but had heard enough about the place to be forewarned—sighed and then nodded. "We'll no need tae bother yer lady freen, then. Seein how yer that sensitive." He looked over the back of the settee and then under it. "Upstair?"

"Efter ten o'clock?" he continued, as they entered Sye's bedroom. He looked under the bed quickly. "Yer missin a puckle socks an a pair o wye's A see." He straightened and looked Sye in the eye. "Weel?"

"A took Pluto doon the shore an cam back here. A had a dram syne gaed til ma baid."

"Onybody see ye?"

"Daa ken."

"Uhuh." The policeman opened the door of the spare room and let out a whistle.

"Hiv ye fund somehin?" Geordie was breathless and pushed forward enthusiastically. But the policeman just laughed, shortly.

"Div ye really live like this?" he asked of Sye. "No get a wifey in tae redd up a bit?"

"Fit's wrang?"

"Place is a midden, that's aa. But then, that's no illegal. Attic?"

"Stepledder's ahent ye. Wait an A'll set it up."

"Fit izzit ye div for a livin, Mr. Swankie?"

"A've a divin business."

"Ye've a boat, then? Far?"

"Tied up alongside at Arbeg. The *Rachel*. She's ower big ti bring intae the port here."

"Oh, aye, A ken the boat. That wis the een that sank? Yased tae be *The Mornin Star*? A thocht it wis bed luck tae cheenge a boat's name."

"Sae't is. But d'ye no hink she'd aaready hud aboot eneuch bed luck she could wi the auld name?"

The policeman laughed. "Yer mebbe recht. Got a freezer?" he asked, as he swept his torch-beam fruitlessly around the empty loftspace. "On'y tidy pliss in the hoose," he muttered.

"Aye, oot the back i ma shaid."

"A daa suppose ye've a inflatable wi a outboard," asked the policeman as they went down the stairs, with Geordie bringing up the rear.

"A've twa. Baith lashit ti the deck o the *Rachel*." Sye led the way through the kitchen out to the drying green and his shed. He unlocked the padlock and showed the way in.

"At's a sunker o a freezer," exclaimed the policeman. "Ye'd get a corse intil it."

"It belangit ti the Hotel. A daa really yase it, but Ma keeps her gear in it." The policeman lifted the lid and fished about amongst the freezer bags. "D'ye keep a boat here ava?" he asked.

"Aye. A've a twinty fit pot boat tied up doon ablow. The reid fibre-gless een wi the cuddy. But A daa hae time ti dae the pots these days an it's ma Da at yases it mair'n A div."

"A hud a look at it. Got a car?"

For reply Sye gave him the keys and pointed to the BMW parked next to the shed.

"Divin must be the business tae be in," noted the policeman as he opened the boot. "Aye. Weel." he sighed and handed back the keys. "A'm sorry tae hae disturbed ye, Mr. Swankie, and thank ye fur yer co-operation." he touched his hat.

"Hae a cuppae tay? " asked Sye pleasantly. "A hink A'll pit the kettle on noo A'm up."

"Naw hanks, no the noo. We'll ging roon the ootside an save trailin gutters in by."

The policeman and Geordie returned to the square, where the other policeman and Gilchrist were waiting. "Well, fit ur we gingin tae dae noo?" sighed Geordie.

"Weel, thon laddie in the back needs stitches, so A'm gingin tae Casualty wi him, an then A'll tak him tae the station an cherge him. Youse leds'll need tae drap ower tae gie wis a statement an aa."

"Whit? Ye cannae jist ging awa hame noo! We'll need tae ging along an chap up the ither een."

"No we'll no."

"Look," said Gilchrist, shouldering his way forward. "This pair is a pair o poachers, recht? Noo, either youse gae along an see the ither ane or we will. Recht noo."

The policeman nodded and smiled. "How'd ye like tae be arrestit?"

"Fit?"

"Ye've nae proof o nothin ava. A've nae reason tae ging chappin up half the village, an neither hiv youse. Somebody on a Protection boat hinks they mecht hae seen a inflatable oot at sea. But thir no jist recht shair. Fit disappeared onywey. An even if they did see somehin, thir nae laa agin bein oot on the open sea on a boat at fehve o'clock in the mornin. Or hud ye no realised that? Noo, A've aaready obliged ye the eence, an if A get ony mair o yer heckle, A'll hiv ye fer Breach. Youse get in yer motor an ging hame yersel, or else. An gin A hear ye've been back here steerin up, ye'll catch it."

"A'll spick tae yer Sarjint."

"You jist dae that. *Sir.*"

"Okay, okay. That'll dae, Alan. We'll be on wir wey." Geordie's voice was tired, for he knew that further protestation was futile.

"That's recht, Mr. Baird," replied the policeman soothingly. "You ging awa hame and get a bit kip the noo, an then ye can come by an gie wis yer statement later."

Sye, who was listening to every word through his bedroom window, smiled as he heard the cars start up, and crawled under his duvet.

He was rudely awakened a scarce three hours later by a rumbling concussion that near blew out his window. Sye sat straight up in bed as if he'd been electrocuted.

"Fit i the name o Christ izzit noo.....?" he said aloud, stuck his head out the window and looked along The Street. The plume of smoke and dust still hung lazily over the ruins, and a jet of water squirted high into the morning air above where the Convenience had once been. That air was filled with the screams of maddened sea-birds and the cacophonous barking of the village dogs, who resented being outdone. A prospect of utter chaos. Sye rubbed his eyes hard and then looked again. Nope, nothing had changed. From the other houses and cottages came the sound of voices and then people issued forth, running towards the scene of the disaster.

"Bluidy hell," said Sye to no-one at all. "Luiks like it's time ti get up then."

Willie and Ian did not stop running until they collapsed, their lungs heaving and gasping for air, upon the sandy floor of the inner sanctum of Smuggler's Cave. Badger, who had been tied to the skeletal armchair to prevent him from following the team on their mission, set up a chorus of mighty howls that would have broken the heart of the strictest dog-hater as soon as he heard the unmistakable sound of his master's footfalls. He dragged the armchair across the floor and when Ian entered he flung himself upon him and did his damnedest to lick the skin off him, as if they hadn't seen each other for a month.

Normally, at least in the presence of another, even his best friend, Ian would have spurned Badger and muttered something like "G'aff ye stupit dug," but not today. He flung his arms round the animal and hugged him tight. Then a thought seemed to strike him and his face, from being the mirror of perfect despair, began to reflect a ray of hope. He pulled away from the dog and threw himself onto his knees in the middle of the floor.

"Whit—whit in the name o' the wee man ur ye daein?" demanded Willie, dropping lightly into the cave and casting a suspicious eye at his friend. Badger cocked his head on one side and allowed the tip of his tail to twitch. He had not seen this game before and he wondered if it might be fun.

"Hud yer wheesht!" hissed Ian.

Willie turned and looked out of the cave entrance, his face resting on his cupped hands and his elbows on the floor of the antechamber. He sighed happily. "By the cringe we're gonnae hae some bother explicatin that een. Did ye see it? Did ye see it? Boom! Christ fa wid hae thocht a wee tinnie o yer stuff wid dae that!"

"Wid ye *hud* yer bluidy *wheesht* fer Chrissake—oh, eh, sorry, like—fur twa meenits, ye galoot? It wisnae yer wee *squib* done it."

"Fit dae ye mean?" demanded Willie aggressively. The squib had been his design and he was proud of its efficacy, even if he could see a good hiding and six months grounded looming before him.

"A mean it wisnae yer stupit squib at blew up ava, that's whit A mean, ye, ye *nincumpoop* ye."

"Fa ur youse cryin a nincumpoop? Yer fine an ladida noo, eh? A'll knock yer bluidy heid aff in twa meenits so A will. An onywey, *onywey*, fit wey de ye ken it wisnae ma squib done it? An tell me another hing, *smartypants*, fit wis it *did* dae it if it wisnae ma squib done it?" Willie swung round to face the other boy. "*Jeeeesus*, whit ur ye daein doon thir noo? Get up afore ye gie me the willies."

Ian, who had had his eyes shut and his hands clasped in an attitude he hoped was one of supplication, opened one eye tentatively. He quickly slipped a hand into his pocket, pulled out the battered Andrew's Liver Salts tin and threw it to the feet of the other.

"If ye ken fit's guid fur ye ye'll get doon here an aa!" he hissed, his face black with warning, before resuming his prayers, for that is what they were. Badger licked his face and was pushed away.

Willie stooped and picked up the tin. For a long time he turned it over and over and round and round. He examined the fuse, and the sellotape round the lid. He shook it and found it to be full. At last he let out a long, low whistle, and raised one eyebrow.

"Is this...........?."

"Uhuh."

"Sae fit wey.........?"

For answer, and without opening his eyes, Ian unclasped his hands and stabbed a finger towards the roof of the cave. Willie squinted upward. As far as he could make out, the Auchpinkie Hotel was directly in line with the indication. He returned his gaze dubiously to Ian and shook his head.

"Dave Paterson? Fit the hell hud he ti dae.......?"

"No Dave Paterson ye bluidy— sorry— idjit! Him! A mean *Him*! Ye ken? A mean *Goad* min, f'Chrissake—sorry—dae ye no see? D'ye no unnerstaun, ye unedgycatit galoot? It wis Him that done it! Fa the hell— sorry— else could it hae been? Christ—sorry— youse wid scunner a saint, so ye wid."

For the first time a chink appeared in the armour of Willies cockiness. He looked up at the roof of the cave and then he looked back at Ian. Badger whined and wagged his tail and rolled his brown eyes and made his caterpillar eyebrows rotate. Willie looked back at the roof and licked his lips.

"Ye daa ackchelly believe aa thon guff, shairly, dae ye? Dae ye?"

Ian opened his eyes and glared at him. "Here, if yer gingin ti talk at wey, talk ootside. A daa want tae be explotit like Boab!"

"Yer no real, youse. Fit wid.....fit wid *He* want ti dae thon ti Boab fur?"

"Fur tae gie him a tellin, mebbe." Ian shrugged. "Ye ken, like Sodomy an Gonnorya. Peelers o saat min. Ye ken."

"Peelers o saat?" Willie frowned. "Oh aye, A mind o somehin like at noo." Bible studies had never been his strong point. "But whit hud Boab done tae fash..........*Him?*"

"A daa ken. Aiblins it wis somehin he done a long time ago. Aiblins it wis the wey he aye hud a keech wi the door open. Aiblins Morag got oan the hot line. *A* daa *ken*."

Willie mulled this over a long time. Then, in a quieter voice, he dropped a bombshell. "Aiblins He done it cos o wis, an naehin ti dae wi Boab ava."

"Wis? Fit dae ye mean wis?" cried Ian, and a little shiver ran down his back. It was true that he had never been what you might call good. Certainly if called before the Elders of the Session, he'd have had a long job to explain himself; but since that went, and more, for most of the inhabitants of this village, including the Elders of the Session themselves, he'd never thought a great deal about it. He cast his mind back on the explosion and groaned. "Aw naw. Aw naw."

Willie looked hard at him. "Ye daa really hink it's at, dae ye?" He swallowed. "A wis kiddin, like."

"Naa but yer recht! D'ye no see? It wis—it wis a tellin ti wis, no ti Boab. Tae mend wir weys an—an *better fowk*, like."

Willie's face fell. "Fit dae ye mean? Like ging ti the kirk on Sundas an aa thon crap?"

"Aye! But no jist at! We hivty—we'll hivty dae *guid works*!"

"Jings, A didna ken it wid be that herd," muttered Willie, "Askin a bit muckle, izzint it no?" He let his eyes stray longingly to the entrance. Out there it was warm and sunny and not a care to be seen, and no end to the amount of divilment a boy could get into without fear of discovery. But then a vision of the blasting ball of fire that had devastated the cludge came into his head and he shivered. Ian was right. There was no escape.

"Kinda teuch on Boab, though," he muttered, as he moved to Ian's side nervously, casting a glance over his shoulder as he did so. "A mean, jist ti gie *wis* a tellin."

Ian reached up a hand and pulled Willie to his knees beside him.

"Widje kindly jist shut yer puss an git *oan* wi hit?"

As, the last of his scepticism swamped by this display of piety on the part of the wickedest—asides of himself—boy in the village, Willie sank to his knees and offered up his prayers for forgiveness to a God he had only the haziest notion of, a finger of dancing sunlight reflected off the blue sea, bounced into the entrance of the cave, shone onto the red sandstone roof and lit up the two kneeling figures in a cameo of such touching innocence it would have brought tears even to their mothers' eyes.

Badger whined and wagged his tail.

Deek White was undergoing a conversion too—in his case of a more mundane kind, from trusted and most favoured employee to something that crawled. He knew he was in for it when Ramsay Cameron, the depot manager, greeted him as "Derek", on account of his usual salute being "Fit like the day, Deek ma loon?" But Ramsay had let him stew till near dinner time before he called him into his smoky little office with the yellowing paint and the piles of dust-covered files.

"Tak a seat, Derek," said Ramsay, instead of "Park yer arse, Snaabaa." Ramsay always tried to speak in English when delivering a bollocking. He thought it sounded more appropriate. Superior, like. "You know, A'm really very sorry about all this. A really am. Up until now you've been ma most reliable driver. A right credit to the firm. No complaints whatsoever. And then all of a sudden you go and shove a bus in a ditch up a farm track where you had no business bein, miss yer school round, and forbye get me a rocket from ma boss. An Intercontinental Ballistic bloody Missile wi multiple festerin warheids, as a matter o fact. My lugs are still ringing wi hit. An how?" He regarded Deek with an aggressive intensity that somehow said that no answer would be required, and gathered himself.

"A'll tell ye how. Because yer brains has drapped intae yer skids. Oh, A ken all about it! Don't you sit there and shak yer heid! There wis a wee fellae up there at wis—who was—recht keen to let me ken fit wey you and a certain Mrs Alice Tadger—ye've got good taste, mind—hiv been, how shall we pit it?" Ramsay paused and circled the thumb and finger of his left hand and slid the index of his right in and out in the universally known gesture. He leaned forward for dramatic effect before speaking again, and as he settled into the stride of his bollocking, the effort of attempting to speak English became too much, and he abandoned it entirely.

"Oh aye. Playin hod the mealy puddin on the side," he snarled. "Luik. A'm tellin ye here and noo—ye'll be gittin it wrote doon fan Sheena thir feenishes daein' her nails an lays affa listenin to fit's neen o her ingans, daa ye fash yersel—that A hink this kinna cerry-oan is pure shite. No that A've onyhin agin ye dippin yer wick; naa, ye can awa an diddle half the females in Angus if ye like, but if ye iver daur play houghmagandie on ma time, or wi een o ma vee-hickles, again, A'll hiv yer guts for gairters, an A'll kick yer erse till its bleck and blue forbye. Recht?" He twisted in his seat and reached behind him to pull a packet of cigars from the pocket of his jacket, which was slung over the back of his chair. He was not the most supple of men, was Ramsay Cameron, and judging from the mild apoplexy the exercise produced, it would have been easier for him to stand up to get them; but that was not his gate at all at all. When at least he achieved his goal, he made his usual great production out of lighting up, and squinted through the smoke at Deek. In the background, Sheena, well known to be the most inefficient secretary on the East Coast, but then, you get what you pay for, began a painfully erratic tattoo on the ancient manual typewriter.

"Be rechts A shid gie ye yer jotters the day. I cid, ye ken. Gross misconduct, it's cried, an' gin fit you done isnae gross *an* misconduct at the same time A'm a Dutcher's uncle. But I'm no gingin tae sack ye, seein as fit wey yer my wife's wee sister's best freen's cousin's brither-in-laa. Hiv A gotten thon recht noo? They hings aye feckle me. At's fit wey ye got the joab i the first place, gin A mind recht—an A daa fancy explainin fit ye've been intil wi aa they females. A've eneuch aggravation wi'oot thon. An onywey." His lip curled and a triumphant glare came into his eyes.

"An onywey, *Snaabaa*, A've thochten o somehin fer, fer better fur youse." Ramsay breathed a cloud of acrid smoke across the piles of dust-covered paper at his victim, and smiled. "Oh aye. Somehin fer better." Leaning forward on his elbows he tapped the minute clear area of desk top in front of him with his forefinger and lowered his voice.

"D'ye ken, be ony chance, Cargill's fish processing plant at Invergarvie? Heh heh heh."

Deek felt a shiver of presentiment creep up his spine. "Aye, boss," he said, quietly.

"Oh goody gumdraps. Cos guess fa's got the contrack ti hurl the nechtshifts in an ootill Montrose?" Ramsay tapped his chest proudly. "Me. An d'ye ken fa's gingin ti drehve the bus?" His thick finger stabbed the air at Deek. "Youse." He pushed his chair back on two legs, kicked a space in the bundles of paper on the desk for his feet, clamped the cigar in his teeth, and put his hands behind his head. He smiled contemplatively at the yellowed ceiling for a long time. Then he removed the cigar from his mouth, and tipped the ash into the wastepaper basket that was already overflowing onto the floor, scratched his right ear with his left hand across the top of his balding head and chuckled. He took his time over a long stretch and a yawn and then grinned a yellow-toothed grin at Deek. But there was no succour in his smile. It was one of pure malice.

"Ken A've been scartin ma heid fur a week ettlin ti feegur oot fit een o youse buggers's pestered me eneuch to land him wi thon. Fa wid be the lucky led like. A *wis* gingin ti git Jock Duthie ti dae hit. Seems fell teuch but he's that dozent ye couldnae herdly dae him ony mair herm. But noo here an ye've solved the problem jist in the nick o time. By ur youse gingin tae hiv some fun. You hinny lived, Derek. You want weemin, A'll gie ye weemin. Aye, A'll gie ye weemin, a recht. Daa ye fash yersel, loon. Hiv ye iver, be the wey, bumped intil these parteecaler weemin—y'ken, the eens that div the nechtshift at Cargill's? The eens that youse ur gingin ti be takkin care o fae," he glanced at the clock for no reason at all, "Hauf echt the necht? A hink ye ken fit A mean."

Deek's heart sank to his boots. He was a sensitive soul under his devil-may-care disguise. An image came into his mind of the casual fish-gutters who worked at the plant; hardened women in blue overalls covered in fish blood stains, with hands like butchers and minds like sewers, Number 6's hanging from the bottom lip, loud lipstick smeared across their faces and smothered in Woollies' toilet water to mask the smell of fish-guts.

"Oh, aye, an d'ye ken fit?" continued Ramsay, still grinning an evil grin of triumph at Deek . "A rang Liz McGurk, the chergehaund, jist afore ye cam in. She's a hert o gowd, her. Aye delichtit tae help a bodie oot. Gings till the bingo wi Mrs Cameron whiles. Tellt her aa aboot ye an fit wey ye wis that keen on the lassies an aa aboot yer romantic inclinayshuns like. Aye. She was fair awa wi hit, ye ken. Said she'd tell aa her quines fit wey thir gettin a reglar, genyoowine Casynovy tae hurl them ti thir work." He pulled another sook on the cigar and beamed at Deek. "She sez thill mebbe even pit oan a wee surprise for ye, thill be that chuffed. Noo is that no jist ceevil?"

He squinted across the desk at Deek through a cloud of smoke and growled, "D'ye ken fit A hink? A hink yer jist aboot gingin till hiv eneuch ti thole wi wi thon shower. A hink ye'll need tae pit on twa pair o breeks wi padlocks on the spaivers and shove a Beano Annual doon the beck forbye, cos your erse, ma loon, your erse is gingin ti be sneckit till its bleck an blue an ye'll be a bluidy chancie billie if that's aa they div till ye. Hee hee hee. By the cringe, A'll warran yer gingin ti wish ye'd never kent fit a lassie wis afore the month's oot."

There was a long silence. Then Ramsay started up again, after polishing his nails on the greasy lapel of his jacket a while. "A daa jalouse ye'd like ti jist lift yer lines recht noo, eh? Save wis aa a loadae boather? Naa? Ach weel, we'll see fit yer sayin till't in a puckle weeks. Heh, heh. An anent the damage ti the bus an the cry oot o the brakdoon truck an the smaa metter o the fence ye sconed, howsaboot we jist cry it a tenner a week dockit aff yer wadges? At wey we mecht jist be evens by the end o the century." Ramsay tipped the ash from his cigar into the wastepaper basket and began to fish in the pile of papers on the desk. Small clouds of dust rose into the foetid air as he did so. At last he grunted and disinterred a copy of *The Montrose Gazette* and opened it. After some time he looked up at Deek, in apparent surprise.

"Ye still here? Cerry on, min, cerry on. Ye'd better ging hame fur some beauty sleep afore yer wee rondyvoo the necht." He waved his cigar at Deek, "Oh, an here, youse mind an keep ootin the wey o Dick Tadger. He can be a right unforgie'in bugger fan he's a mind, him. Heh-heh-heh. Christ, hiv ye ever teen a recht gange at the shudders on him? Ha-ha! He yased ti play for Hawick afore he flitted here, ye ken. Aff ye ging noo, sweet dreams, *lover-boy*." Deek closed the door on Ramsay's hoots of laughter and left the office a sad and apprehensive man.

CHAPTER SEVENTEEN
On the Price of Fish

Sye got up and showered and shaved. He had two cups of venomously strong coffee, and then he sat on the sofa with Pluto and fondled the latter's ear until he was delirious. The dog that is. He had some thinking to do. Sye that is. It was all very well having rubbed Geordie and that clown Gilchrist's faces properly in it; but it was another thing altogether knowing what to do with all the fish that was presently stashed under a weighted hap in the cave. There was more there than he'd ever had to cope with before, and it did want to be got rid of, because it constituted, if not conclusive evidence, then damned close to it. It would have to be brought up to the village, cleaned, and what wouldn't go in the various freezers, sold. Either that or given to the cats.

Sye had a small circle of regular outlets for such times as this, and he spent most of the morning phoning round. It was a depressing task. It seemed that the market for poached salmon was a little flat. It was the farming that did it; the hotels and restaurants could get their fish at two pound the pound, so the price would have to be less; the tourist season was not yet started, and as everyone knows, a frozen salmon is no use to a restaurateur. So Sye was selling a puckle of fish here and a puckle of fish there; it was hardly worth the effort, and it was not going to dent the pile of fish he had to get rid of. By one o'clock he could stand it no longer, and phoned along to Peem. Yes he was up, yes he was in, and yes he *would* like to go for a drink.

The pair of them met up outside The Chateau and without a word, turned their steps towards the Hotel. Pluto lifted his leg against the corner of the house and set off on a mission of his own. Our topers marched into the Hotel, turned sharp right into the Public Bar, and stopped dead in amazement. The place was absolutely stowed out, and worse, with people neither of them had ever clappit een on in their entire puffs. They shook their heads in wonder. Through the fug of tobacco smoke and between the heads of chatting drinkers, they could from time to time catch a glisk of Dave, his face purple with exertion and sweat pouring from his brow, scuttling crabwise up and down the length of the bar.

"Bugger *that*," said Sye, when he'd recovered himself. "The place is hoachin."

"Lounge?" asked Peem dubiously.

"Naa. Last Chance."

The Last Chance Inn at Inverbikie, on the main road north to Aberdeen, was a fine alternative; not that Sye and Peem were short of those. In fact, if either of them were to wake up, transported by some mysterious circumstance, at practically any location on the East Coast north of the Tay and within, say, ten miles of the sea, not only would they have known of a thoroughly decent hostelry in the immediate vicinity, but the chances were that they'd be on first name terms with the owner. But the Last Chance was special. It was run by an enormous Glaswegian by the name of Drew Gibson, who was a useful man to know if you needed to get rid of things to which you could not show proper title.

Sye and Peem enjoyed a pleasant lunch with Drew, and left with the promise to drop off a box of salmon as soon as they could; then they made their way back to the village. Time to clean and distribute the salmon they had already brought up from the cave.

CHAPTER EIGHTEEN
The Man Of The Cloth

Whilst Sye and Peem were up to their elbows in the gory business of cleaning salmon, Dr. MacCluskie, the pathologist at Arbeg Infirmary, was engaged in a similar sort of a task concerning the remains of Lanky Boab. Whether as a result of the explosion or not, he was sure that this old man had suffered a massive brain haemorrhage that would have felled a fit man of twenty, never mind a nonagenarian. This was the fact; and Dr. MacCluskie was a man of science and he loved facts. He cared not for the unexplained, the mysterious, the enigmatic. Dr. MacCluskie liked things that could be named and pigeonholed and researched and explained in safe, solid, scientific terms. That was why the horizontal contusions upon the old man's buttocks, where the skin was, despite its age, still baby soft and supple, troubled him so. Dr. MacCluskie had looked at a lot of dead bodies in his time and he had seen something like this before, but never on a very old man from a very quiet village; and what troubled him more than the simple existence of these worrying marks was that all the indications were that they were inflicted at roughly the same time as the death itself. Funny things happened in explosions, he knew that. And the bodies often had incongruous damage, often resulting from their treatment by the first on the scene; he knew that too.

But the more he looked at them, the more the myriad parallel, horizontal lines suggested to him that Robert Paterson's bare arse had been *flogged*, with something like a yard-broom, immediately after his death. But because he could not be sure, he mentioned the marks in passing, and left out his suspicions. "They must get up to some gey queer things down there, that's all I can say," he muttered, and signed the report.

Morag, whom, you recall, was the cause of the pathologist's concerns, had spent the most of the day recovering. She could thank her fellow villagers that her part in the day's events were not the subject of national news. The tabloid rags would fair have gotten their teeth into that. But long before the dust had settled on the ruins of the cludge, Jess and Nan had arrived on the scene with faces aghast with horror. They had thrown themselves upon the enraged Morag, who was still thrashing Boab's insensate buttocks and bundled her off to her bed; and had let it be known to anyone who asked—that is, any *official* who asked, that Morag had been out shopping all morning.

The poor woman was in a state of shock; a state which Nan had effectively treated with her own double-strength Valium and a stiff belt of whisky. Then she tucked Morag up in her bed and settled down in a chair to read the latest *Mills and Boon* and sit with the invalid. Pretty soon, Morag fell asleep, and the usual party started up in her head. Thing was, Morag spoke in her sleep—not that anyone knew this, because no-one had slept with her since she was a bit bairn and still too young to think such thoughts. But today she had an audience; Nan was listening. It was a good deal more colourful than what she was reading, too. She closed the book and leaned closer. At first she was shocked, and then intrigued, as she caught snippets of the mutterings. She rushed to the phone. "Jess? Jess? Izzat you? You git yersel ower here *toot-de-bluidy-sweet* an get a lugfu o this." A little later Agnes arrived too, and then even Mae was persuaded to leave the shop, which shows just how juicy Morag's ramblings were. Morag would have been surprised had she been able to see herself, propped up on the pillows in her bed, her every word caught in fascination by the four others, whose combined age was well over two hundred years.

Rae Swankie had been at work when the cludge at Auchpinkie had so spectacularly assumed the past tense; as far as she was concerned, Willie was at school and would not return till after four, and then would do his homework till she got home. In the stramash that followed the events at Auchpinkie, no-one had thought to phone her to tell her the news, which was fair enough, her being so recently returned to the village, and everybody being that busy, like. So Rae, all blithe and unknowing, had gone shopping in Montrose at dinner-time, where she had been so taken by a yellow shantung dress with an absurd price tag that she had bought it on the spot, and made herself feel even more deliciously bad by buying a pair of Italian shoes to go with it. She had grown used, after so many years of minding her pennies, to keeping a very tight rein on her fancy, and when she got back to the office she was feeling very satisfied indeed. Kinda like illicit sex without the mess.

Cargill's office secretary was called Gayle. Cargill's was an old fashioned firm; there was one secretary and what she couldn't do, you did yourself. Fortunately Gayle was one of those people capable of being in three places doing five things all at once, a five-foot-three whirlwind of energy and enthusiasm. Anyway, Gayle, who could never resist a juicy morsel, fizzed in to Rae's six-foot by six-foot kennel, before she'd got her backside right parked on her seat after lunch, with her eyes and mouth formed into three perfect 'O's, and blurted out, "There's been a splosion! At Auchpinkie! Of all places!" and rushed off to tell the Marketing Manager in the shoebox next door, leaving dust and bits of paper swirling in her wake and Rae high and dry and gasping for more. Rae almost wished Gayle hadn't told her. She told herself not to be silly; the house was insured and as far as she knew, Willie was safely at school, five miles out of range of any possible danger. But she phoned Izzie anyway.

It was not the most reassuring call she'd ever made. No, Willie had not been to school that morning, and he had returned to Izzie's with Ian for lunch—at which point Izzie had suddenly remembered her friend and had tried to call her, but Rae had been out shopping—and the pair of them had caught the bus to school for the afternoon session. All of which sounded fine. But there was something in her friend's voice that tugged at Rae. She listened to Iz making small talk, and then asked, bluntly, "Listen, is there something up?"

There was a protracted silence before the reply came. "We-e-ell, it's likely naehin......."

"Spit it oot!"

"It's jist—it's jist—they wis ower quiet, Rae. Niver breathed ae word aboot thon dreadful splosion that killed pair auld Boab. No a single een. An if ye ask me.........Well A daa like it, quine. An thi wis on thir best behaviour—like they wis at Jess's fur Sunda denner or somehin."

"But they're aa right?" Rae's voice was anxious.

Izzie laughed. "Thir aa recht aa recht. It's jist they ken somehin thir no lettin on an (she made her voice breathless and sexy) ye ken how A *hate* thon." She paused. "Oh aye, an A near forgot tae tell ye, yer front room windae wis blawed oot, but A reddit up the mess an A've phoned Maxwell's the glazers ti fix it. Thir comin this efterneen. A hink they shoulda gie'd us a bulk discoont fur the amount o gless they've sellt here the day. That okay?"

"Yes. Aye. Yer a hon, hon."

"A ken, A ken. See ya later."

Rae fidgeted and agitated all afternoon and slipped off at five on the dot—which was by no means her normal habit—and drove like the bars all the way along the winding country lanes back to Auchpinkie. The scene of devastation that greeted her when she drove along The Street horrified her and, once she'd drawn into Fountain Square and parked, she stood outside the car for a long time looking at the pile of rubble and allowing all sorts of dreadful might-have-beens to annoy her before she shook herself and went indoors. The window had been repaired, as Iz had said it would be, and there was no sign of damage within the house. And there was no sign of Willie either. Rae looked in his bedroom and then out the back; no sign. "Hell and Damnation!" she thought. A kind of panic that she knew was entirely unreasonable was mounting in her. It was unreasonable because she already knew that her son was all right, that he had not been injured, that he had gone to school in the afternoon. But she could not get rid of it. She shook her head and stamped her foot. "That laddie!"

Iz stuck her head out the door just as Rae's hand was descending to knock on it. She was wearing a shocking pink shell suit, had her hair up, and was, as usual, dripping with gold. Izzie, as Peem was wont to make somewhat wry mention of, had a fine collection of jewellery, and none of it costume. She liked to show it off, even if the only people who saw it were

her kids and the milkman. It's a bit of a habit in these parts that's probably considered gauche by refined city tastes. "A seen ye comin," she
said, and kissed Rae. Izzie kissed everyone. At least, everyone she was on
first name terms with it. She just liked it. Which was fine because she did
it very well and everyone liked being kissed by her. She had the knack of
kissing you just the way you'd want your best friend's favourite sister to.
Just dangerous enough to be thrilling. "C'way in, A'm jist gie'n the twins
thir tea."

"Thanks for the gless. Hiv ye seen Willie?" Izzie ushered Rae
into the kitchen, which looked out onto the square, and returned to the
task of coaxing macaroni cheese into the mouths of her matching six-
teen-month old twin daughters. Rae sat down at the table out of range.
She was quietly glad that this task, at least, was behind her; but then they
were so delicious with their golden curls. Without thinking, she leaned
forward and took one of the nearest twin's feet in her hand.

"Urna thir feet jist—*scrumptious* when they're at wee," Rae said,
more to herself than to her friend. The twin smiled at her and gurgled.

"A ken. A could jist eat thum. Oh, Willie's up the stair wi Ian.
An daa ask me fit thir up tae; A daa daur ging intil the Bear Pit these days.
No while thir in residence, onywey." Iz was so calm that Rae felt the fear
and worry that had been gagging her subside. Izzie looked at Rae sympathetically. "Niver ye mind, ye'll get yer chance. An he's fine, be the wey."
She stopped shovelling food into the twin for a moment and looked
thoughtfully at Rae, who was still fondling the little foot, much to its
owner's delight. "Sometimes A wish they'd jist bide at wey. It wid keep
wis fae hivin ti ging through yon purgatory thi cry bein pregnant," she
said, quietly.

Something in her tone made Rae look up in surprise. "Plannin
more are ye?"

"Fit dae youse hink?" Izzie grinned.

"A thought you said this pair wis an accident."

Iz gave her a look that expressed how painfully disappointed she
was by this staggering demonstration of ignorance and then shrugged.
"Weel," she said, "A accident's jist like a hole i the causie ye daa cover up.
Still a accident if a body faas intil it. Ye no hink?" Then she grew thoughtful and waved the baby spoon at her friend. "See if ye made *choclate* bairn's
feet, though, they'd sell a storm." She laughed. "Thir nae a mum on the
planet could resist thum. Honest. We cid fill the insides wi gooey stuff—
ken like Chocolate Eggs ony pink an e'en mair," she narrowed her eyes
and pouted, "*Irresistible.* Like me. We could ging intae business. Youse
cid dae aa the clever stuff an A cid dae the quality control an hink up new
idears. A can see it noo; 'Swankie and Teviotdale's Choclate Baby Feet'."
She drew the sign with the spoon in the air in front of her and frowned.
"Naa, at's ower lang; we'll hiv ti hink o a better name. But they'd sell
themsels; we'd be millionaires in nae time an we cid be ladies o leisure."
She winked lasciviously and dropped her voice. "Or mebbe ladies o *pleasure.*" She giggled. Then she sighed. "But what *would* we do with Dedday,

my deeyah?" she asked the foot's owner in a mock English accent. "Pair hing's jist utterly an completely fushionless wi'oot wis, izzint he no jist?"

Rae was laughing, and nodding. But she wasn't really listening; rather she was simply letting her friend's enveloping personality lift her and carry her like a broad flowing stream. It was always the same with Iz. Rae could never remember a time when she hadn't been able to bring her out of depression or anxiety, without even trying, or so it seemed. And without invading her space, either. Suddenly it occurred to Rae that she hoped there was someone who could do the same for Iz, when she had bad times. Because everyone has bad times. She let go the foot and reached across the table and placed her hand on Izzie's free hand. Izzie squeezed it and looked at her for a long time. She didn't speak. Neither of them spoke. But it seemed to Rae that she could not let go, and all the time there were those eyes that were sometimes grey as a November sky and sometimes blue as an April one seeming to look right through her into her soul. Sye had those eyes, Rae thought, and then shook herself. "It'll be okay, ye ken," said Izzie at last. "It will. Hings aye work oot okay. Jist daa fash yersel. Let it flow ower ye. Ken like the story o the aik an the sauch-willae." She gave Rae's hand a squeeze.

Rae drew away but it did not hurt. "Aye. A ken," she said, and was surprised at the huskiness in her voice. Izzie was tapping her pursed lips with the back of the spoon. "Listen," she said. "How no lave Willie here a wee whiley, so's A can work ma magic on him. A'll get the pair o thum thegither an see fit A kin wheedle oot. Youse ging an hae a hot bath or fittiver else ye fancy. Relax an pit yer feet up. Hae a wee dram. A'll gie him his tea."

"You're no plottin anythin are ye?"

"Fa me? Daa be daft. *Plot?* Me?" Iz made the very notion sound absurd.

But suddenly there was a thunder of footfalls on the stairs, the front door banged shut, and the feet retreated across the square. Both women stood up.

"By!" exclaimed Iz. "Fit the blazes—" she crossed to the window and banged on it, but the boys did not deviate from their path and disappeared from view round the corner. Rae made for the door to follow them, but Iz caught her by the arm. "Naa. Let thum sort it oot. Yer ower late onywey."

"Aye but did ye not see," Rae's eyes were wide with amusement and concern at the same time. "Did ye no see whit they were wearin?"

"Aye A did, an A'll get tae the bottom o it yet, daa fash yersel." Iz shook her head. "Fitt'n the hell dae thi hink thi look like? Leddies! Honest ti goodness!"

At the far end of the village from the Auchpinkie Hotel, and as far removed in moral outlook, stood the worthy Victorian pile that was the manse. Here resided the Reverend James Jameson, Doctor of Theology, thumper of Bibles, and officially appointed upholder of the faith in an increasingly Godless world. The fact that the particular corner of that world where he resided and ministered was one of the more *spectacularly* ungodly was the source of a constant regret, and a certain cynical humour in his outlook.

Reverend Jameson was as traditionalist in matters of the life temporal as he was in matters of the life spiritual; (though, as he was wont to moot, upon a particularly poorly-attended service, in Auchpinkie the matter spiritual was of a very fluid nature). This was why he never ate dinner, but always "High Tea" which he took, with his wife Joan and his children, in the parlour which gave onto the front lawn via what the English call 'French Windows.' This evening he had just finished saying grace and was in the act of passing his teacup to his wife Joan for her to fill with the oak-dark infusion from the enormous and hideous china teapot, when a movement attracted his attention and he glanced through the window. He started, and the cup rattled in the saucer.

"My word," he said aloud.

"Do keep still, James," said Joan, who was struggling under the weight of the teapot, in an exasperated voice. "High Tea" had not the appeal to the Reverend's wife as it did to the Reverend. Joan herself would have been quite happy to put her feet up with a nice glass of white wine and listen to *The Archers* but she knew from experience that her husband was immovable on such matters.

"Sorry, dear," boomed the Reverend, who never spoke in anything less than his best pulpit baritone. "It's just that it would appear that we are about to receive a visit from two Jehovah's Witnesses and something that might be a dog."

"Jehovah's Witnesses?" replied his good lady. "Don't be silly. What would they come to a manse for? That would be like you going along to the—what do they call it?—the Kingdom Hall."

"Well, if those," and here the Reverend Jameson put down his tea-cup and pointed out the window at two figures in ill fitting suits who had tied the 'something' to the gate with a length of binder twine and begun to shamble up the rose-bordered path to the manse, "Are not Jehovah's Witnesses, pray tell me what they are. Mormons? It's very much the same thing, except better dressed. They seem to have no samples, so they cannot be travelling salesmen. Unless they are *dog* salesmen. Ho, ho. If they are someone ought to tell them to try another model. Whatever they may be, since they are heading with purpose for our front door, I can only deduce, my dear Watson, that they are coming here."

Joan swivelled round to look. "That's funny. One of them looks familiar," she mused.

"What's on what, Daddy," put in the youngest Jameson, Robert, who was recently four.

"I'm sorry?"

"You said," explained Robert patiently, stirring the yoke of his poached egg with the corner of a triangle of buttered toast, and regarding his father with blue eyes as big as dinner-plates, "That Mummy was on something. Well, what?" He bit off a hunk and began to chew it.

"I did no such thing," laughed his father indulgently.

"Yes you did, you said 'my dear what's on'. Well, what's she on?"

"Joan, is that child speaking in English?" The Reverend Jameson smiled kindly at his son. "I would have said 'who is on', my boy. 'What's on' is not grammar."

"But you said it, Daddy. You did. You said 'my dear what's on'." Robert chomped more eggy toast and nodded in agreement with himself..

"Watson, not what's on," sniggered Judy, ten, who was sitting at Robert's side. "He's a detective, silly."

"What?" Robert was even more confused by this, and he already knew his sister was baiting him. A piece of eggy toast flew out of his mouth as he spoke and splatted onto the forehead of his elder brother James, sitting opposite.

"Say 'pardon', dear, not what. 'What' is rude." A certain edge of alarm was present under Joan's urgently soothing tones as she felt that veneer of civilised, Anglo-Saxon domestic politeness that was but the thinnest of prophylactics against the Celtic anarchy that she knew fine well lurked under the surface of her life begin to crack.

"What's this," asked James, fourteen, "What's on my face?" His measured disgust could not hide his delight at finding a joke he could annoy his little brother with. He picked off the lightly-masticated piece of eggy toast and held it up between thumb and forefinger, glaring at his sibling with an expression that he hoped conveyed loathing and contempt but in fact looked more like constipation.

"What's what?" demanded Robert, unaware of the bolus' trajectory. He was getting a little ratty now and he pointed his fork accusingly at James. "Mummy, *he* said it *too*."

"That's not quite correct, Judy. You see, Sherlock Holmes was the detective. Watson was his companion and chronicler." The Rev. J. Jameson was a stickler for accuracy.

"There! You said it *again*! But what *I* want to know, what I *want* to know," Robert gathered up all the dignity of a four-year-old who is convinced he is in the right. "What I want to *know*....."

"Oh for goodness sake, Daddy, I know who Watson was," cried Judy, who was going to be a detective herself one day. Or a brain surgeon. "I've read all the b..b..books."

"Here! Whatever it is, you can have it back." James Junior flicked the eggy toast back at Robert, using his dessert-spoon for a ballista.

"James! What was that?" Joan snapped. The ever-present undercurrent of chaos was too close to the surface for comfort now, threatening at any moment to burst out into her polite and civilised world.

"....Is *what* was on *what*" yelled Robert over the mounting cacophony. The eggy toast hit him in the eye and he howled in frustration,

"You never *ever* listen to me!" He thumped the table in imitation of the gesture his father used when expounding one of his theories, but his aim, in the heat of the moment, was erratic. His little fist caught the edge of the plate and flicked the rest of the poached egg and toast onto Judy's lap.

"Look what you've done *now*, you little b..b..beast!", screamed the furious recipient, stuttering in rage. She swung her arm back and aimed a good one at the back of her brother's head; but he had the keenly honed instinct for self-preservation of the youngest child and ducked. The whizzing haymaker overshot and connected with the water-pitcher instead. What a pity it was full; the contents described a shining arc and fetched up on the eldest Jameson, drenching him instantaneously. He leapt to his feet and lunged at his sister with nothing less than bloody murder in his heart.

Just then, and in the nick of time as far as the Reverend James Jameson was concerned, the door-bell rang, and the dispenser of domestic peace and justice was obliged to leave his wife to cope.

On the manse doorstep stood two boys, both wearing suits that were too big and training shoes that appeared to have been hastily polished black. Their hair had been plastered down with what the Reverend could have sworn was Brylcreem, and they were both wearing paisley ties of a style that had not been seen in public for many years. It was some moments before the Reverend Jameson realised that he recognised his visitors. They were, of course, Willie and Ian, and frankly, the minister could not have been more astonished had he opened his door to a whole chapter of Jaffas having a Hail Jesus party on his front lawn.

"Well, well," he began at last. "Well, well, well. Messrs (he pronounced it phonetically) Teviotdale and—Swankie, is it not? If my admittedly startled eyes do not deceive me. My, but this is an unexpected pleasure. What can I do for you? I must say that most of the flock come to the Church, rather than the manse." This was not strictly true, since most of the flock did neither, but it sounded good. "We *are* open every Sunday, you know."

"Please, yer Refference, sir. We couldnae wait that lang." It seemed that Ian's voice quaked and he glanced over his shoulder frequently.

"Couldn't wait? As far as I can recall, you've been at least five years waiting already. What difference would five days make, boy?" He thought for a moment and regarded the boys' attire. "You're not in a *pop* group are you? Looking for somewhere to practise? Hm? If you are I have to tell you that the Church Hall is strictly out of bounds for that sort of thing. Too much trouble the last time." The minister shuddered at the memory.

"Naw, it's no that ava. An he's recht, Mister Meenister. We hud ti see ye the necht." Wullie leaned forward and gazed upward at the towering figure of the Reverend Jameson, the motion giving him an oddly supplicant air.

"Y'see wir..........Wir very mortal sowels thumsels is in awfy awfy danger!"

The Reverend Jameson looked down upon the boys for a long time, as he mulled this one over. He had ministered to the village a long time and he thought he was probably familiar with all of the conventional opening lines in current use by now. He pursed his lips and raised first one eyebrow, and then the other, and then both together. This was a new development. And there was no doubting the lads' nervousness. What *could* they want?

In a guarded voice, and after careful consideration, he said "Mortal souls? I take it you mean 'immortal souls'? Hm? That's not a term to be used lightly, you know. I hope you two are not speaking in vain."

"Aw, mister yer refference, sir, please! We *hivty* talk ti ye. We jist hivty." Ian's voice was quite definitely shaking. The boy seemed on the verge of tears.

"Aye! An no *oot here!*" Willie pleaded.

"Why not? It's a pleasant evening. And I must say I was just about to take tea. Why don't you come back a little later—say eight o'clock?" Jameson began to swing the door to.

"No! Ye cannae! A mean ye cannae lave wis oot here! He mecht ging an dae hit again!" Ian's voice was now cracking in pure funk.

For all his bombast and theatrical style, the Reverend Jameson had seen real fear before, and he knew its face. Whatever this pair were up to they were not on the hustle. At least, not with pecuniary motive. And it might well be interesting; perhaps amusing.... he reflected on the civil war that even now was taking its nightly course in the parlour. "Might go and do it again?" he mused. Then he said, in a gentler voice, "Is somebody threatening you, my boy?"

"Aye, ye *cid* pit it at wey," nodded Willie enthusiastically. "But no *somebody*. A mean no *jist* somebody," Ian dug him sharply in the ribs and Willie jumped and glanced over his shoulder. "A mean *mair*'n jist *some*body. An youse ur—A mean you are wir *only* hope. We need ye tae inter....inter......We need ye ti talk tae *Him* fur wis!" Here the boy rolled his eyes heavenwards in a gesture so droll that Jameson could scarcely contain himself. He bent slowly downward until his own eyes were only a little above Willie's, pointed one finger up at the sky and raised his eyebrows in mute question.

"Aye! That's recht! Ye've goat it noo! Wullye help wis, please, mister meenister yer refference sir?"

"However could I resist?" replied the minister dryly. "You had better come in to my study." Whatever it was, this was going to be good, he thought as he stood aside to admit the two lads, the twenty-two inch flares of whose trousers flapped a broken-legged syncopation as they walked. It was certainly going to be good.

CHAPTER NINETEEN
Riparian Retribution

A gloom had settled over Balgownie Grange that had nothing to do with the lengthening evening shadows. Andrew Anshaw paced and fidgeted and his face was one thunderous mask of biliously evil humour. There had been too many guests for them all to have gone out on the water on this their first day, and so they had been divided into groups. One group had gone to the casting school, one had played golf, one had been driven up the moor to spend the afternoon catching glimpses of the disappearing behinds of the Estate's red deer, and the members of the last had all been allocated a gillie and sent out on the Pinkie to try their luck. Of these four groups the first three had returned smiling and full of cheer and were now gathering in the Conservatory Wine Bar to discuss the day and refresh themselves. The last group, however, had returned with long faces and glum airs; not a one of them had had so much as a tickle all afternoon, and this was the source of Andrew Anshaw's ire.

Anshaw called Geordie to the Estate Office at seven, by which time all the guests had returned and were being served drinks in the lounge. He was furious.

"What went wrong, George? Where are all the fish you promised me?"

"Well, boss, A keep tellin ye it's no really like at. Heh, heh.... Mebbe these guys arenae ony guid, ye ken..."

Anshaw cut him off. "Nonsense! What are the gillies there for? I thought the idea was that they would show the guests exactly what to do—even down to helping them cast. So," he shrugged his shoulders and held his hands out, palms up. "So what went wrong?"

"Weel," Geordie scratched the top of his head. "Thir no muckle fish in the watter, an........."

"George! There's what?"

"A mean no many fish in the river. Heh, heh."

"I don't see that it's a laughing matter. All week you've been telling me there would be more fish than we'd know what to do with."

"Aye, well, aiblins A wis wrang an the Run's a puckle late this year, heh."

"Pickle? What's pickles got........George, will you kindly speak in English?"

"Aye, sir—A mean yes, sir. I mean, maybe the Run's been delayed. Heh, heh. I don't know why," he added hastily, "There could be lots o reasons."

"You said there were plenty of fish last week."

"Aye, but like A keep tellin ye, sir, they dinnae hing aboot like, heh. See they bide—stay here jist long enough so they get used tae the fresh water. Then they go upstream, right up to the smaa wee burns in the glens an then they....."

"I know what they do, George. I know that." Anshaw ran a hand through his thinning hair. "A biology lesson I do not need." He drummed his fingers on the desk. "Right. What now?"

"Try again the morn's morn, boss, heh, heh. Nuthin else we kin div."

Anshaw got up from his chair and sat down on the edge of his desk in fronnt og Geordie. He glared at his head bailiff and folded his arms, a gesture which Geordie had already come to realise boded No Good at all. "Are you aware that the Chairman of Alba Life Assurance is coming on Friday?" he said.

"Aye, I'd an idear."

"And do you know that he is a very keen angler? And that he is coming back from New York to fish the river on Saturday morning before the farewell lunch?" Anshaw's voice was silky with veiled menace now.

"A heard that an aa, sir."

"Either he catches a salmon or you're on the dole. That'll be all, George."

Big Sye ate salmon for his supper. He hacked himself off a big tail and poached it and then ate it and it was just braw. Pluto didn't usually eat fish, but he thought the salmon was just fine and dandy too. Big Sye's Ma and Da, and Peem and his brood and all the relatives they were speaking to at the time ate salmon too, and they all thought it was a rare treat. The village cats gorged themselves on fish bones in an orgy of eating until they were so stuffed they didn't even bother running away from the dogs any more.

"No the necht, leds," they seemed to be saying. "We'll play wi yiz the morn, but gie's a bit peace an quiet the noo, eh?" And the dogs gave up and sulked.

Sye looked out the window of his front room. Eck, his Da, was making his way home after his medicinal six pints of export. For his digestion. It was heavy weather the night, thought Sye. Eck was not making his usual more-or-less-direct-but-with-a-wee-bit-weave-and-a-Woops-*steady* way from the bar to his cottage, a distance of no more than twenty yards as the drunk sways, but was instead traversing the front wall of the Hotel, feeling his way along unsteadily with both hands on the reassuring surface of the stone. He knew from experience that if he just went on long enough in the westward direction he would inevitably fall into his own front doorway, where with any luck Nan would rescue him. He always left the front door open for this express purpose. Once, in a careless moment, Nan shut it, and Eck, who was being particularly buffeted by the waves that night, traversed the length of numbers One, Two, Three, and Four before falling into the doorway at Number Five (In Auchpinkie the numbers went up one side of The Street and down the other) and had crawled into Jean Smith's bed. Jean was a widow and getting gey long in the tooth, so you'd have thought she might not be that fashed to find a man in her bed, but not a bit of it, she raised a stooshie that didn't settle for months. Maybe she had a thing against the Swankies. Anyway, Nan was careful never to let the door shut again—just in case.

That salmon was heavy eating. Sye shoved Pluto off the couch and settled himself down for a snooze. He was tired, and he slept longer than he had meant to; it was after half nine before he woke, and stretched himself into life. "C'mon Plute," he said to the dog, who had sneakily got back up on the sofa and was now using his jawbone to cut off the circulation to Sye's legs. "Less ging an get some air."

The pair stepped out into the cool darkness. Far below they could hear the rushing of the surf on the beach, and the wind had got up. Sye felt its breath refresh him, and his mood lifted. He turned up the collar of his pilot-coat, for there was already a smirr of rain in the air, and he set off towards Fountain Square with Pluto skipping at his side. It was amazing how that dog's bad hip would get better when there was a walk in it.

Peem yawned as he answered the door. Across on the other side of The Street, near the ruins of the cludge, they could see an open dustbin rocking from side to side. It was clattering on the paving and the nether quarters of a yellow dog protruded skywards from it, its hind legs wriggling and kicking in the air. Sye turned to Peem.

"Queer-like business thon, wi Boab," he mused. "A've been that busy the day A've niver hud a meenit tae find oot fit's the story."

Peem stretched, folded his arms, and leant on the doorpost. "Iz says it wis on the news it wis ges."

Sye chuckled. "Boab wis aye fu o ges. But A niver thocht he'd dee o hit."

Peem laughed and yawned again. "Naa, it wis somehin ti dae wi the drains. Typical bluidy Cooncil, eh? Build a cludge thir. Aabody kens the clift's rotten thir."

Sye started and looked across the road again. The dustbin had fallen over with a bang and scattered rubbish all over the pavement. The yellow dog reversed out, its prize, a salmon carcass, clamped firmly in its jaws, had a quick look around and took off along The Street. Sye furrowed his brow. "We'll need ti watch thon," he mused. "A daa hink we'll hae ony mair boather fae the polis, sae lang's we daa dae onyhin daft, like, but yon Gilchrist, he's anither can o worms athegither. A dinnae trust him no ti stert snoopin aboot, like, or worse, forbye."

Peem had not met Gilchrist, and he only nodded. "Fan d'ye want tae git the gear," he asked. "The noo?"

Sye shook his head. "Ach, A slept langer'n A meant, an thir nae pynte daein it noo. Are ye game for a wee bit necht work again?"

Peem shrugged. "How no? Wir no takin the boat oot the morn,

ur we? Thir thon weldin job tae feenish, but if it blaws up the wey it's threitnin, it'll be ower rauch."

Sye nodded. "Weel, let's hud on till the tide's recht in an we can git the pot-boat in aboot the cave. Save a lot o ersin aboot."

Peem nodded. "Means ye'll loss the Dory if wir nabbit, mind," he cautioned. "Mair loss'n thon auld Zodiac."

"Fit aboot yer motor, min?" replied Sye. "At's worth mair'n the twa thegither! Onywey we'll no get nabbit. A feel lucky."

"Fine. Fit time aboot? High tide's, lemme see, an hour later........ hauf-een-ish? Drap by at een?"

"Aye," agreed Sye.

"Fancy a pint the noo?" Peem didn't sound enthusiastic.

Sye smacked his lips. "Naa. A dinnae, ta. A hink A'll awa doon the port an hae a wee deek ower the Dory. Da's been yasin hit, an he's fell coorse, so he is." He turned, and began to walk along The Street towards the track that led down to the beach. He had a hankering to see the sea; the fresh westerly breeze with its scent of the tropics and its promise of rain had made him want that. He had often thought of how it was that the sea and the wind were such big things. Why that air that swept in across Scotland from the Atlantic had started off, days or weeks or maybe even months before as a great scoop of warm tropical air that had been cut off by the cooler air to the north. Then it had voyaged hither and thither in the form of a depression, an anticyclone, a huge spinning mass of air hundreds of miles across, but always making its way north-east-ward. And it was here, and it was true; you could smell the hot humid jungles and the spices of far away places upon its balmy breath. Sye loved this west wind, even though he knew that it meant bad weather.

Lost in thought, he soon found himself at the shore. The moon moved in and out behind ragged clouds and there was now a real smirr of rain and salt spray in the air. He breathed in deeply and strolled for a while towards the harbour, where a solitary light burned. The sucking and sighing of the sea was all about him and he felt his blood stir. The sea......Seamen are supposed to be unromantic, pragmatists to a man; but we know of none, and we have known many, who are not stirred by a night such as this. The elements dance and dwarf us, and the sea, play-ful as a mighty bear, rustles and tickles the shore, knowing with what shocking violence it can smite, should it be driven to.

Sye stood for a long time by the light on the pierhead, while Pluto investigated, his nose and one eye, as always, fixed intently on the ground in front of him like a myopic detective. The gusts whipped and tugged at Sye's hair, and out to sea he could see now how the distant light of the Easter Rock lighthouse disappeared and reappeared in an unfamil-iar rhythm, while the billows, like dancing elementals, rose in response to the cry of the wind.

"Gingin ti catch it the morn," mused Sye, and jumped down onto the deck of his Dory. He switched on the battery lights and opened the engine compartment. Diesel, oil, okay. He stepped under the shelter of the cuddy and thumbed the starter. Once, twice, the Lister three cylinder motor turned, before he dropped the decompressor and it burbled into life. Nothing wrong there. Sye let it turn a while to top up the battery and then pulled the strangler. He closed the engine hatch and moved around the boat, checking the docklines. It's such an instinctive thing for seamen to do that they don't even notice they're doing it. When he was satisfied he climbed up the rusty steel ladder to the harbour wall and whistled on Pluto as he walked back on to the beach. He whistled again, and swore. The wind was noisy now and the damned dog was likely digging in about something dead and smelly and either didn't hear him, or didn't want to. He shrugged. Pluto knew his own way back to the house, that was for sure.

The road up to the village is not well lit but Sye thought nothing of it, his footsteps guided by long familiarity. Near the top the track passes through a deep gully, whose sheer sides rise almost vertically twenty-five feet up. Sye was near the top of it when he heard the voice.

"Kent ye'd come this wey. No even youse ur gallus eneuch ti ging the ither wey at necht."

Sye froze and peered into the darkness ahead. Then a shadow detached itself from the inky blackness of the gully wall and approached. In the dim light Sye recognised Geordie Baird and his eyes narrowed. Something made him turn and look back down the path. There was another figure in silhouette, which could only be Alan Gilchrist. Alarm bells rang in Sye's skull but he didn't let on.

"Ye didnae even ken he wis there, didye," mocked the Head Bailiff of the Balgownie Estate. "Walked recht past him blythe as ye like." He stepped closer and Sye could smell the drink on him. "Christ, youse ur a canty bastart so ye ur! But ye're no hauf as smert as ye hink. We seen yiz gingin doon thir. So fit hiv ye done wi the fish?"

Sye shrugged non-committally. "Fish? Whit fish?"

Geordie shook his head. "Daa stert wi yer shite. A ken it wis youse poached the river lest necht, youse an thon cloon ye hing aboot wi. A ken it wis youse, even if A daa ken fit wey ye did hit. But A'll tell ye ae hing; ye poached the bastartin Run *oot*. An A *ken* it wis youse. It shair as hell wisnae yon fushionless loon fae Montrose wi nabbit. So daa stert. Fit wir ye daein doon thir at the herbour?" He paused. Sye thought quickly. Geordie was drunk—drunker than Sye had ever seen him—and that made him unpredictable. But bushwhacking was not his style. So maybe Gilchrist had been winding him up to it. And that meant that Gilchrist was the one to watch. Geordie started up again. "Ma joab's on the line cos o youse an yer bluidy cantrips! Aye, A seen yer boat this morn. A'd a hud tae be blin no ti see yis. An so did the skipper o yon boat even if he sez he's no shair noo. An if it wisnae fur the fect that youse hiv got the luck o Auld Nick hisself, ye'd be in the clink recht noo, an ye ken fine. Noo, fit izzit ye wis daein doon thir?"

Sye shrugged and looked up at the darkness overhead. "Weather brewin, Cousin Geordie," he said quietly. "A jist ginged doon tae check the lines on ma Dory."

"Mak it ready ti ging an fetch yer haul, mair like! A'm hinkin maybe A'll ging doon an luik yer boat ower masel. Mebbe fix it recht!"

"Ye ken the rules, Cousin Geordie. Youse lads are obliged ti keep tae the laa, or else risk yer conviction. An ye cannae convict a poacher but ye nab him in the act, or in possession o teckle or game ye can show ti be illegally teen. Ye've goat none o hit—nae fish, nae poachers, an nae proof. Noo if ye daa mind A'll awa hame till ma baid."

Geordie stepped closer, so close that Sye could feel his breath, and smell the drink on it forbye. And could see in the dim light how his cousin's face was twisted into a mask of rage.

"Aye," hissed Geordie between his teeth, "Thet's recht. Ye'd hiv made a bonny kind o a dockside lahyer, youse. A've no enough to get ye. No in a coort o laa, onywey. But A've plenty proof eneuch fur this, ya smartarsed bastart ye!"

Sye doubled as the blow from the lead knuckle he hadn't seen hit him hard under the ribs and he twisted, not a second too soon, and a booted foot that would otherwise have broken his nose glanced viciously against his cheek. He reacted quickly and swung his own boot and enjoyed the grim satisfaction as he felt the steel toecap crunch into Geordie's tibia. But then another blow jarred the breath out of his body as Gilchrist brought the butt of his staff thumping home again and again into his kidneys. He spun, but too late, and the staff clattered him again, in the temple this time, and his head rang and flashes of coloured light spangled the night. He brought his hands up to protect his face and Geordie's lead knuckles thumped again and again at his stomach. The staff jabbed him once more from behind, this time in the back of the knee, and Sye knew he was in real trouble as his left leg folded. But Gilchrist closed too soon with his cover dropped and just before he went down Sye got three rapid-fire, hard, punches in at his face and his heart was gladdened as he felt the skin split and the meat mash against the bone. Then the pair of them landed on Sye at once and he went down, knowing what was coming as they set to with their boots, and curling into a ball to protect himself.

Then, suddenly, as he neared unconsciousness under a hail of kicks and clouts, Sye heard Gilchrist yelp and his staff fall to the ground. "Jesus *Christ!* A've been bit!" he yelled out.

There was a snapping, snarling hell-beast, almost invisible in the inky dark, that had exploded into the fray. All you could see of it was the green flashing of its eyes and the white of its fangs. It left Gilchrist and went for Geordie, who did not see it coming and knew nothing until it sank its teeth into his backside.

"Ayah ma *arse!*" he howled. "Fur Chrissake whassat! G'aff!"

Geordie twisted and there was a loud tearing noise as the seat detached from his pants. But he was not free for long, because Pluto—well, who else—warming to the task, nipped him twice on the hand for good luck and then locked his jaws firmly onto the bailiff's forearm.

"Holy Jesus Christ widje get at hing *affofme*!" wailed the stricken bailiff, beginning to panic.

Sye heard a boot thump hollowly and a muffled snarl from Pluto. It brought him to life. He scrambled to his feet and as he did so his hand fell on Gilchrist's staff. It was his lucky break, and Sye was never a loon to let one of those past. He grabbed the staff and swung it from a low kneeling position and dirled its owner a dunt he would never in all his life forget, catching him right in the face as he prepared to land another rib-breaking boot in Pluto's side. He staggered, fell backwards and groaned. "Ma neb! Ya bastart ye ye've brak ma neb!" The front of his jacket was soaked—apparently instantaneously—with blood.

"A'll brak mair'n at in a meenit," muttered Sye grimly, and let Gilchrist have another wallop on the side of the head as the stricken bailiff tried to get up. The head made a sound like a coconut and Gilchrist stopped trying to get up and slumped forward, clutching his skull with his bloodied hands. Then Sye, who was now on his mettle again and feeling a long way less than charitable, blootered him a right toe-ender hard in the mouth for good measure, on the principle that if you kick a man when he's down, he's less likely to get up and annoy you again. It worked, too.

Geordie, meantime, had got his arm free, leaving the sleeve of his jacket behind. He swung his boot at Pluto, but his timing was all to hell in the drink, and Plute promptly bit him on the leg. Then the fearsome hound grabbed a trouser leg and began to tear it, tugging at it in that way that we find so amusing when we see puppies playing with towels, but is no joke when it's for real. It was all the terrified Bailiff could do to keep his balance, his hands grappling at the loose soil and turf of the bank of the cutty.

However, the noise of the stramash had not gone unnoticed. Nan had, some hours before, decided that she could take no more of Morag's ramblings, fascinating though they were. Bad for her nerves, she said, and she had enough bother getting to sleep nights already. So she had gone back to her cottage after wrapping Morag up in bed with a nice—and generously laced—cup of tea and another Valium. There was nothing more she could do, she reflected; the puir wumman had gone clean gyte and no mistake.

Now it happened that the same Morag's bedroom overlooked the cutty, and the noise had disturbed her. (Like Nan, most of her friends had lately decided that she *was* disturbed.) She threw back the covers on her bed and slipped her feet into her baffies, her jaw set in outrage. As if she hadn't tholed enough the day without this! Something had to be done. Morag, a pink whale in her quilted goonie, fished under the bed for her late father's hammerlock twelve-bore, pulled back the hammers, and threw up the sash of her bedroom window.

"Fazzat?" she shrilled, and waved the gun at the darkness below. "Fitz gaein on doon thir! Murther! Rape! A'll shoot, A tell ye! A wull! A'll shoot afore A submit ti yiz! Ye'll niver tak me alive! A'll defend ma honour ti the lest! Honest A wull!"

"Aw, Jesus Christ Al-bluidy-Mechty, no *hur*!" yelped Geordie, who had managed to grab a tree root that protruded from the steep bank with one hand and was desperately holding onto his trousers with the other, while Pluto—who was really enjoying himself now—tugged and tugged and snarled and snarled. This really was the final straw for the beleaguered Bailiff. "She's no recht!"

Morag, who was still, and to put it mildly, er, aviating as a result of the whisky and Valium cocktail, pondered this for a moment. This was not what she had expected the lustful hordes of leering satyrs that populated her dreams to say. For some reason she could not have explained, even had she wished to, they had always appeared to her with more genteel accents, maybe like yon actor boy Richard Burton she'd seen in films. Ach, fit a braw spikkin voice at loon had an nae mistake. Mind, he was Welsh, no like the coorse cheils fae roon here ava. Anyway, at the sound of the voices her face twisted into an expression of even greater outrage. "Here, fa d'ye hink yer cryin 'no recht'?" she squawked, like thoroughly ruffled broody hen. "A'll gie ye 'no recht', so A bluidy wull!" With that she keeked along the barrels of the shotgun and jerked the trigger.

A blinding flash of orange flame stabbed down into the darkness, accompanied by a deafening roar that gave poor Morag such a fleg she wet herself on the spot. The charge of No. 4 shot whistled through the air between Sye and Geordie, who had instinctively—all thought of their battle now forgotten—leapt sideways for cover when they saw Morag shouldering her ancient piece, and smacked into the wall of the cutty, a swarm of little ricochets buzzing like mosquitoes. Pluto, whose active life had left him with a thing about being shot at, instantly left go Geordie's breeks and bellowed viciously at this new assailant, letting her ken in no uncertain terms what he would do to her if she tried *that* again. At the same time there was a shriek and a muffled thump from inside the bedroom as Morag sat down heavily under the violent shove of the recoil, and another *flash-bang-shriek* as she shot her bedroom ceiling with the second barrel, coincidentally blowing the light-fitting into smithereens and plunging her into darkness. A cloud of white plaster dust puffed out into the night air, which was now filled with the furious barking of all the village dogs.

"*Jeesus!* Let's get the hell oot afore yon skelly bitch re-loads!" exclaimed Sye, he and Geordie looked aghast at each other in the almost dark, and the pair of them took flight, leaving Gilchrist to stagger up the path behind, nursing a sore face and spitting out bits of teeth.

CHAPTER TWENTY
Wounds of War

Rae did as Iz had told her. She went back to her cottage, and poured herself a hot bath with a large gin and tonic on the side. She put a Billie Holliday record on loud and left the bathroom door open. Rae liked hot baths, and she sank into this one up to her nose, letting her long hair hang over the end so it wouldn't get wet. She liked G&T's too, and the sound of the ice-cubes clinking and the heat of the water and the strains of *Nobody's Bizness* belting through the corridor made her feel pleasantly decadent. Whatever her rascal of a son was up to, it would come out in the wash; and she had not forgotten that Izzie's talents in the extraction of information department were formidable. She shaved her legs, and took her time so she only nicked herself the once and there wasn't too much bleeding. Then she got out of the bath and wrapped herself in a thick towel.

She dried, and tried on the yellow shantung dress and the shoes, and then looked at herself in the full-length mirror on her wardrobe. Needs a hat, she thought, pulling her hair back to show her shoulders. Or maybe just a hairband. But otherwise fine. But not for tonight. She hung it carefully in her wardrobe and then considered her naked self in the mirror. She leaned towards the mirror and squinted—Rae was slightly short-sighted but she hated wearing glasses—with distaste at the few grey hairs that had begun to appear in her thick raven-black hair. She always kept her hair long, partly because she thought her ears stuck out—they didn't—and now she piled it up on top of her head with her hands and smiled her smile of even white teeth.

She pondered her long nose, turning her head a few degrees from side to side, and her very dark eyes with their long lashes. She pouted and examined her full lips and high cheekbones, and stretched her slender neck. No wrinkles. She let her eyes take in her slim, fine-boned body. She had hardly any stretch-marks from her pregnancy, but she bore the scar of an appendectomy. Her skin was naturally dark, and when she sunbathed it turned to deep mahogany, but now she thought she looked a little pale. Then she turned sideways and pulled in her tummy and tucked in her bottom. She stretched up on her toes; it made her legs look better, longer, and she had good legs to start with. And though her feet were delicately formed, they were long-boned like the rest of her, and she had always thought they were too big; which was why she usually tholed heels in public, though she preferred to loaf around in bare feet. She examined herself again, and nodded. "Not bad," she allowed herself, "Not bad at all." She pushed out her chest and was pleased by the confirmation that her breasts were still firm and well-shaped, even if they were smaller than they once had been, a result of motherhood. She thought "Still a nice handful, though" and then stopped herself, firmly..... She shook herself and jerked open her knicker drawer. A feeling that made her tingle all over had intruded and she was very anxious to shut it out.

Rae dressed sensibly, in jeans and an old shirt. She made herself a tomato omelette and had a glass of wine with it. Then she got out the painting stuff and went on with repainting the gloss on the kitchen doors. She liked painting; she could lose herself in its slow rhythm, and the time passed quickly. She heard the door banging and glanced at the clock on the cooker. It was after eight. She waited for Willie to come rushing into the kitchen, but he didn't come. It worried her. She put down the paint pot and put the brush into a jar of thinners; then she peeled off the rubber gloves she'd been wearing and washed her hands to get rid of the bitter smell of the rubber.

She climbed the stairs as quietly as she could. There was no sound from Willie's bedroom, but the door was slightly ajar and she could see light flooding through. She moved closer, and pressed with her fingertips against the door so that it swung open a little more. She did not dare push it any further for fear of it squeaking. It suddenly occurred to her that Izzie would have oiled the hinge, and the thought almost made her laugh; but she stifled it just in time. She applied her eye to the crack and peered into the room. Willie was kneeling by the bed, dressed in his pyjamas. He was saying his prayers. Rae felt a sob grab at the back of her throat, and her eyes moistened. Then Willie got up and sat on the bed. Rae pulled back, wiped her eyes and counted to ten. Then she knocked on the door and entered. Willie looked up at her. He looked funny; lost, and a little scared. Rae sat down on the bed beside him and ran her fingers through his hair.

"Were ye goin tae go tae bed withoot seein me?" she asked.

"Well, A, aye.......no, A kent ye'd come up. Sorry."

"Didn't ye want me to come up?"

"Oh, aye. It's no that. A jist.........A wanted tae dae somehin."

"Whit?"

"Oh, nothin, Mum. Disnae matter."

"And did ye manage to dae this mysterious somethin that ye'll no let on about?"

Willie stuffed his hands between his knees and looked at the floor. After a while he sniffed and shook his head.

"Whit wis it then? Maybe A could help."

He looked round at her quickly. "Naa. Ye'd jist hink A wis daft."

"Promise A won't."

Willie looked at her searchingly and then shook his head. "It's aa recht. A'll be okay." He looked away, and then back. "Mum, is it true Izzie's ma auntie an Peem's ma uncle?"

Rae laughed. "Is that whit's been botherin you?" Her eyes

searched his and she saw that it wasn't. But at least this he would talk about. "Well, sometimes when people are right good friends they tell thir bairns they're their uncles and aunts. They're no really, but it's a wey o lettin a friend ken ye love them. That's aa."

"Oh. And are you a freen of Auntie Iz?"

"A've kent Iz syne we were lassies thegither. She's ma cousin, older than me, by two years. But we were aye best pals. Funny, she's older, but it wis aye me that got us in bother." She laughed. "Yer Auntie Iz has pulled me out o more scrapes than I'd like tae tell ye." For a moment her expression darkened.

"An whit aboot Uncle Peem? Are ye a freen o his tae?"

Rae smiled. "Peem grew next door to that house they live in noo; an A grew up in this one. I've kent Peem as long as I can mind tae. Why?"

"Oh, nae reason." Willie pondered and he frowned. "He's nice."

"Who?"

"Uncle Peem."

"I ken."

"He says he'll tak me sailin syne the boat he's daein up's feenished. A *can* go, can't A?"

Rae frowned, and then nodded. "We'll see. I must admit there's no many folk I'd let tak ye out on a boat, but he's one o them." She smoothed her son's hair. "Ye got hamework to do?"

"A done—A did it at Ian's."

"Really? This I must encourage."

"He helps me." Willie grinned. "He's better at Maths'n you."

"That's no surprise! Done yer teeth?"

"Uhuh."

"Bed, then." She stood up and turned down the covers for him to get in, and then sat down beside him again.

"Mum? A luve ye."

"A love ye tae. Go to sleep." Rae kissed him and left the room, turning out the overhead light so that the only light in the room was Willie's little night-light. She had to run down the stairs. She didn't want Willie to hear her crying.

When she recovered, she crept back to his room. The boy was fast asleep and didn't budge as she tucked him in. She went back downstairs and wrote a note and left it on the kitchen table where he would see it if he came looking for her, and then grabbed her coat from the hook and slipped out into the night. She was in desperate need of some fresh air. She walked up past the square and Mae's darkened shop, to where the tarmac ended, and then on up to the top of the Ness and stood at the wall, that place where long syne the women of the village would wait to see the bright-painted hulls of their men's boats plunging homewards with the white horses. The wind was freshening and it moistened her face with the spray it had already lifted. She looked for a long time out over the water, away across the Firth of Tay; there the lights of St. Andrews, and there, further, appearing and disappearing like a mirage, the lights of Dunbar. She looked long and hard into the night; but it contained no answers and she turned back to the village.

There was a light on behind the curtains at The Chateau. She did not know what impulse made her do it, but she tapped on the door. There was no reply, except a rumble that might have been a dog growling or a snore. She tapped again and there was no reply again. She turned round on the step. Across the square was the Hotel, all flooding warm and welcoming light into the night. She looked up at the illuminated clock on the steeple. Just one, she told herself, and crossed the square.

Rae had thought to have herself a quick livener to fight off the cold that had somehow entered her bones even though the night was mild; but she had not counted on John MacTaggart, the sewage engineer from the Cooncil. John had taken a latish supper in the lounge. He had meant to leave directly afterwards, but somehow or another he had just kept wandering up to the bar and getting himself another bottle of Pils. He was an unhappy man; his marriage was going through one of those rocky patches that everyone's does as the parties knock the corners off each other. John hadn't been through enough of these yet to realise that that was all it was, and the prospect of going home to a cold welcome made him glum. Besides, it was nice and cosy there in the bar and nobody knew him.

Rae came in and sat down on a stool at the end of the bar and ordered a brandy. John, who was feeling adequately gallus, being adequately lubricated, examined her out of the corner of his eye. Tallish, slim, lots of very black hair; bones fine as a bird's and beautifully, beautifully formed. Olive skin. Looked less than happy. He smiled at her and said "Good evening." And Rae, in an unguarded moment, made the mistake of smiling and saying "Hi" back.

To cut a long and tedious story short, when Rae tried to make her escape on the grounds that it was getting late and she had to work the next day, she found herself being escorted along the street, and short of kicking the sewage engineer in the shin and calling for help, she could think of no way to prevent this. It appeared that he took her insistent requests that he stay in the bar and finish his drink as some sort of coy politeness which he was honour bound to disregard. While they approached Rae's cottage, she rehearsed her lines for getting rid of this man, whom she thought was rather sweet but who was also quite drunk and whom she suspected of being very married. She hoped he would not be difficult, and she already had her keys in her hand, and she was fidgeting with them uncomfortably. Then, suddenly, she heard the sharp report of a shotgun being fired, close by, and then another, and then the sound of running feet. Running feet that seemed to be getting closer. From the far end of The Street she heard more ruckus with car doors slamming, and then a big vehicle started up and took off up the Arbeg road. For a moment Rae was almost thankful for the presence of the sewage engineer (who for his part felt his courage waning fast), but not quite enough to grab his arm or anything. And then, out of the darkness and into the pool of light under the street-lamp at the cistern, who should appear but Big Sye, his torn pilot coat all covered in mud, jeans and checked shirt bloodied from the cut that Gilchrist's staff—which he now carried as a trophy of battle—had made on his temple, and limping a little. At his side strutted Pluto, rumbling basso-profundo and baring his fangs at anything that dared move. They made as unlikely-looking a pair of saviours as you can imagine.

"Sye!" cried Rae, stepping forward, "Whit's happened tae ye?"

MacTaggart was drunk all right, but not so drunk he didn't know when he was beat. He gazed in sheer horror upon this denizen of nightmare that had materialised in the form of a lanky and lantrin-jawed gorilla daubed in gore, at whose side was some hellish black beast with slavering chops and gleaming green eyes and a fearsome growl. He saw at once that the target of his lust was acquainted, worse, familiar, with this apparition, and the guilt of his carnal desire put it in his head that it might be Rae's big brother, or worse. He almost keeched himself at the chilling thought. One thing he knew; any chance of him getting off with Rae had just gone out the window, with bells on. He sobered up right quick and backed off at speed, mumbling frantic goodnights that no-one heard.

He staggered back to his Ford Sierra, collapsed into the back seat, and spent a lonely and bitter night in freezing and fitful slumber. When he got back home at six the next morning—still over the limit by a long way but unable to stand the pain any longer—he got merry hell from Mrs. MacTaggart. She had had waited up all night, in increasing anxiety. By the time her errant husband got home she had forgotten that her original intent was to apologise, promise to make it up, and seduce him. Not any more. No way was she going to believe that he'd done nothing wrong. John found it hard to argue his corner. After all, he may not have done it, but he'd sure as hell thought it.

But we will leave the MacTaggarts to patch up or no, because it is none of our business, noting only the moral, and return to the scene outside Rae's house. Rae was so shocked by Sye's appearance that she ushered him inside at once, insisting on salving his hurts.

"Eh—Y'shair?" he asked, regarding the retreating figure of MacTaggart with some curiosity. "A hope A'm no interruppin somehin, like, A wis jist on ma wey hame."

"Yer no. Not at all. *Really,*" insisted Rae, who was in truth very glad her cousin had appeared, a sentiment that in a less pressed moment might have gart her stop and think a wee; but at the time she had no thought of it, and instead led the way to her front door and unlocked it.

Pluto looked up quizzically at his "master" and his ears asked, "Yer no........Ur ye?"

"Awa hame, Plute," said Sye, by way of a reply. "There's a good led. A'll no be lang."

"Ye shair? Eh mean Eh could come in an keep ye company, like." Pluto thrust his enormous head in the open doorway and sniffed hard. "Here, smells no bed in thir. Bit clean beh your standards though."

"Plute! Awa hame!"

"Eh, weel, if thet's the wey ye want hit like," grumbled Pluto and ambled off. He stopped and lifted his leg against the corner of the house. "Eh suppose even youse kin mak it hame wi'oot gettin in boather fae here." His amble changed into a trot as he thought of the leather settee. "Jist bawl a halloo if ye need me mind!" said his tail.

That dog was going to be insupportable for days.

"Okay," smiled Sye, stepping into Rae's house. "Ye've twistit ma airm. Fa wis at lad, like? No meanin tae pry."

"That," said Rae dryly, closing the door behind them. "Wis nobody. The product o a moment's weakness."

"Fit dae ye mean, Rae?"

"Just that whiles a man offers to buy ye a drink an he disna ken enough tae let it drop there. And dinnae act so innocent, A'll give ye a pound til a penny ye've done the exact same thing yersel mair than once."

Sye nodded. Rae led the way into her kitchen, and pulled out one of the chairs. "Sit down," she instructed. "A'll get the First Aid kit oot."

Rae turned and started digging in a cupboard and told Sye to take off his shirt. This he did with difficulty, wincing a little as the cuts and contusions nipped. He was developing a slight shake and his limbs were beginning to stiffen up, signs that the adrenaline was wearing off; he knew he was going to feel a lot worse in the morning. Rae turned round and suddenly another Very Naughty Thought struck her. But she shook herself and suppressed it at once.

She busied herself mixing up some antiseptic in a bowl with water as hot as she could stand it, and brought it to the table. She swabbed at Sye's cuts to clean them.

"Ye should mebbe have yon stitched," she observed, indicating the cut on the temple.

"Naa. Heid cuts aye look worse'n they are. Jist clean it but lave the clot an it'll be okay." Sye had other reasons for not wishing to attend the Casualty Department of Arbeg Hospital that night, as you may perhaps imagine, but he refrained from mentioning them.

"You seem tae ken more about this than me," said Rae. "I'm not sure that's a good thing. Ye've been in a fight, hivvint ye? Nae fibs now."

Sye smiled. "Ach, it wisna really a fecht, Rae. A wis jumped."

"It's different?"

"Aye. It means yer no asked first. An the reason A ken aboot these hings is cos A'm a Master Mariner. Ye hae ti ken First Aid. No cos A'm foriver gettin intae fechts, like. In case ye wis wonderin." This latter was a debatable point, but Rae let it lie.

"I'm glad tae hear it. You're too auld for this nonsense. Who did it?"

Sye paused. "Daa ken," he lied. "A didnae get a recht deek at thum."

"Them?"

"Thir wis twa. It's recht derk doon thir." He chuckled. "A thocht A wis in recht bother an then Plute sterts in at them and the neist hing auld Morag lets fly oot her wundae wi yon blunderbuss she keeps under the baid an hinks naebody kens aboot an aabody legged it tootsweet."

"A heard the shots."

"*Aabody* heard the shots. A widnae wonder if we hud a wee visit fae the boys in blue ower the heid o't. An a could fair dae wi'oot thon efter the necht A've hud. Christ A've no been in a stramash like at for donkey's years. A'd forgot fit wey it hurts an aa."

Rae perched on the table and continued swabbing. She frowned. "D'ye think maybe somebody should go over an see if she's all right? Morag I mean."

Sye shook his head firmly. "Nae wey, Rae. The skellie besom mecht jist no miss the next time, if ye get ma meanin."

"Surely no!"

"Ah weel, A wis jokin, like. But *A m* no gingin ower, at's for shair. Youse ging, if yer that gallus."

Rae rummaged in her box and found a self adhesive plaster large enough to cover the cut on Sye's head. The wounds on his torso would hurt, but they would be better left open to breathe; they were not serious, though he was going to have some cracking bruises. "There ye go," she said, when she had done. "Good as new."

"No A'm no, but ta onywey." There was a silence. Rae broke it. "D'ye fancy a dram? I think I've got a wee drop brandy somewhere."

"Naa. Hanks." Sye frowned. He knew well enough that the combination of alcohol and a declining level of adrenaline in his blood would be like knock-out drops, and he had not forgotten the salmon. But it seemed rude to refuse. "Tell ye fit, jist shove it in a cuppy tea; that'd be jist fine." He calculated that the stimulant and the depressant would just about cancel each other out. Rae laughed. As she put the kettle to boil, Willie staggered into the kitchen, dopey and full of sleep and rubbing his eyes. He did not seem to see Big Sye, who had put his bloodstained tee-shirt back on. The checked shirt was for the bin.

"Mum? A'm affa thirsty."

"Here I'll make ye some warm milk. That dae?"

"Uhuh." Willie realised that he was not alone with his mother and turned his wide eyes to Big Sye, who smiled. Rae crossed the kitchen and crouched down in front of the boy. "C'way. Back to bed. I'll bring yer milk up in five minutes."

When he had stumbled back out, Sye turned to Rae. "Yer loon? A didnae ken he wis big as at."

Rae was busy making the tea and did not look up. "They grow really quick, ye ken. It taks ye by surprise. They seem jist like tiny wee things, totally dependent, for ages, and then, bang— that's it, like— wee people. Here."

Sye took the laced tea and sipped it. It tasted good, strong and thick, and the hot brandy fumes were soothing and soporific. "How auld is he noo?" he asked.

"He's twelve. Why?" There was a cold sharpness under the surface of her voice. Rae always tried not to be defensive, but it was hard. She'd got used to people doing that little sum in their heads, estimating her age, subtracting Willie's age, and then raising their eyebrows when they got the result. She'd gotten used to it, but that didn't mean to say that she liked it any better.

"Nae reason," replied Sye quickly, noting the sudden chill, and made a mental note to steer clear of that subject, for the moment, at least. He was saved the bother of seeking a safer topic to break the silence that had settled by the swish of tyres on the road outside. He quickly moved to the window and parted the curtain just enough to see the police car draw up outside the Hotel. He nodded grimly as Rae joined him.

"Mind if A bide here till they buggers tak aff?" he asked, quietly. "Gin thi see me luikin like this thill be nae end ti thir speirin. No that *A've* done onyhin wrang, like; it's jist A've hud eneuch o they leds for the day."

He was aware of Rae's presence, though he had not turned to look. He knew that she was very close to him; there was that warmth, that aura, that tingling sensation of a body very close but not touching; as if his nerve-ends were reaching out, stretching as far as they could to bridge the gap. And he could smell her, too, and he liked that smell a lot.

He turned from the window. Her face was not six inches from his and to kiss her was a mere bending of the neck. They were very still for what seemed like an age and then Rae moved away. She stood by the cooker where the milk was warming and kept her back to Sye. "Sure ye can stay," she said, and her voice was thick. Sye did not move from the window but watched her carefully. He knew it was a time to be very delicate, and Sye could be surprisingly delicate. Rae turned to look at him and her eyes were flashing. "Can we not jist be friends? Is that possible? Can you dae that—with a woman?"

"Aye." There was no disappointment in his voice, but whether that was because he was really unconcerned or was just a very good actor, she could not tell. "Shair, Rae. Yer ma cousin." He grinned big and wide like a cousin should and she unwound with a bump. She realised that it was going to be very difficult to stay angry with this man; at least while he was standing right in front of her. And she had so many things to be angry about. Suddenly she caught herself asking 'What the hell's he doing on his lane with me in ma kitchen at this time of night onywey?' and then she remembered that she'd invited him in, and the thought sent a tingle through her.

"Ta," she said, quietly. Her mood had lightened, but she did not let her guard drop. That was a close one, she thought. Better not get that close again. She looked up. Sye was peering out of the window, and she moved forward to watch with him. The two bobbies had come out of the bar and crossed to The Chateau, tapped on the door, and then jumped back a full yard. Sye chuckled. That would be Pluto doing his famous Hungry Polar Bear impersonation. "Aw keech," he said.

"What?" Rae refrained from going to the window to look. Enough close shaves for one night, she thought. "What's the matter?"

"At buggers is comin this wey, that's fit. See if thi chap ye up— thir bound tae hae seen the lechts—see if they chap ye up, daa let on A'm here, eh? Please?"

"Course no. Should we pit out the lights?"

"Naa, that wid jist gar them mair interestit. Jist tell them ye daa ken onyhin an thill ging awa. Thiv nae reason ava ti chiz ye."

Sure enough, a few minutes later there was a knock on the front door. Rae left Sye and answered it. From his vantage point Sye could hear everything, and knew he could always slip out of the back door of the kitchen into the green if they came in. He chuckled when he heard the unmistakable sing-song West Highland lilt of the questioner. MacKimmie!

CHAPTER TWENTY-ONE
MacKimmie

Sergeant MacKimmie had been just about to finish his shift and was downing the last of a mug of tea when Duty Sergeant Mackay stuck his head round the door of the control room at Arbeg Police Station.

"Yer pals doon at Auchpinkie is at it again, Donald. Seems thir ructions doon thir. Ye'd better awa an hae a wee deek. Aye, A ken ye've near finished yer shift but that's kinda like your patch doon thir. A daa trust tae send onybody else efter derk. They mecht jist no come back, like. Think o the owertime an onywey, A dootna ye'll get a pint ootin hit."

"Aye, aye." MacKimmie sighed and pulled on his cap over his balding pate. "Right choo harr. And what haff my friendss been up to thiss time?"

"Ach, it's likely nuthin ava. Mrs Kennedy at Pitmeddoes says she heard shots. Likely it wis nae mair'n some motorbike back-firin. Ye ken fit she's like. Grand imagination an she gets lanesome nechts. Awa an drap in oan hurr jist so's she kens wir no sat on wur duffs here." The Duty Sergeant smiled grimly and lowered his voice a tad. "Tak oor Michael there, wullye?" he said, glancing at a much younger officer sitting at the end of the table. "Aboot time he got tae see some real polis work, an it'll keep him fae deevin me wi daft questions."

"Schots, iss hit?" said MacKimmie, standing up. He was a very big man, and moved with a certain ponderous grandeur that could be misleading. "Ochone, they're haffing a rare time to themselfs this week sso they harr, the good folks hoff Auchpinkie. You're likely right enough, though, Calum. It's likely nothing at all at all. Maybe somebody's heard a fox in aboot hiss chickens and had a pot schot at hit. Come along then Michael, ant you can trive."

MacKimmie and Cadet Michael Fernie stopped by the farmhouse at Pitmeddoes and took a statement from Mrs Kennedy; she was keen that they should come in and have a cup of tea and some shortie, but the sergeant politely declined, on the grounds that he was full of the brew already, and in reality because he knew fine well that if he accepted it would be an hour or more before he and Cadet Fernie got away again. He had known Mrs Kennedy many a long year, after all. Instead he ushered Cadet Fernie back into the car and they headed straight for the bar of the Auchpinkie Hotel.

Dave the barman was still polishing, and a puckle of imbibers had arrived, enough to make it worthwhile staying open; Uncle Gus and some Patersons and Teviotdales. They were playing a friendly game of darts. Davey stopped polishing when the two policemen walked in and instinctively cast a surreptitious eye at the clock. But he was licensed to one o'clock and it was just gone eleven fifteen.

"Cood efening, Tayfit. Chentlemen."

Dave regarded the new arrivals with patent suspicion and waited. MacKimmie pulled out his notebook, licked his thumb, flicked through the leaves and began. "Now where harr we? Hah yess. Habout ten-thirty this efening Mrs. Kennedy at Pitmeddoes heard schots, so she sayss. She thinkss they came from thiss tirection. Tid you hear anything, Tayfit?"

Dave the barman looked at him as if he were stark raving mad. "Hear onyhin? *Me?* Naa. Naehin ava."

"Titn't haff the folume on your hearing aid turned up, I suppose."

"Whit?"

"I set you titn't haff the folume on your........Oh neffer mind. I ton't suppose any hoff you latss," he said, turning to the darts players, "Heard any schots?"

"Whits?" asked Uncle Gus, perplexed.

"Schots. From a cun."

"Oh. Shots. Naa, no me." he turned to the other players. "You leds hear ony shots?"

There was a general accord of shaking heads. "Naa, sarge. Wiv been playin derts, like."

"Whith your earss?"

"Fit?"

"I sait, 'Whith your.........Oh neffer mind, itss too late at night forr all that nonsense." The big sergeant leaned forward onto the bar, removed his cap and rubbed the bridge of his nose between his thumb and forefinger. "It'ss peen farr too long a tay alltogether so it hass, what with you people plowing up pensioners ant I ton't know all what." He drummed his fingers on the bar and looked penetratingly at Dave, who was stock still as a rabbit that has just been confronted by a cat.

"Tchoo know, Tayfit, how pleasant it woult be to ask somepody a question in thiss fillage ant get a straight answerr?" he continued and drummed his fingers again. Dave did not move again. This was getting beyond a joke. MacKimmie caught sight of himself in a mirror and there at his side was a police cadet with his cap on. He groaned.

"Take your capp off, Michael, there'ss a coot latt. You're confusing the poor mann. Put hit on the parr peside mine. There you are tchoo see. Much more comfortaple."

"Yaseyell?" muttered Dave.

"Aye, that'ss most chenerouss off you. A pint off your most excellent eighty shilling. And Michael—I mean, Catet Fernie—here will haff a wee sota ant lime. He's triving."

As the two policemen left the bar after their drinks, Cadet Fernie, who had until then been silent, spoke. "You didnae pey fur at."

"Pay forr hit? Whyeffer would I haff tun that? He gave it to uss. Hit wass a cift."

"But is that no...... corruption?"

"Only in Etimpurgh. Here it'ss called courtesy. And pie the way, wheneffer I take off my cap, *you* take off *yourss*." He stuck his hands deep in his pockets and rocked on his heels, sucking a tooth thoughtfully. "Unter normal circumstancess I woult call hit a tay at that. Putt what with all the ruckus today and since I know that Inspector Ness hiss hinterestet, maybe we'll chust see if we can't chap a few boties up ant ask them if they heard anything. They won't haff, put it'ss cood practise for you. Hant an extra half-shift iff we keep hit coing till one."

MacKimmie crossed to The Chateau, and peered through the window into the darkness within. Then he banged on the door and at once there was a roaring and snap-snarling and a scratching of claws and the sounds of great draughts of breath being taken into some mighty lungs. Cadet Fernie jumped back from the door as if he expected the Hound of the Baskervilles to come crashing through the panels.

MacKimmie, who had moved back with a little more decorum but no less velocity, clapped him on the shoulder reassuringly. "Neffer mind. Hit's chust Pluto. Sso Alexanter iss nott at home."

"Could he no jist be sleepin?" Fernie suggested, helpfully, but MacKimmie wagged his finger.

"Nott at all. Alexanter woult not haff a tog in the house that made a row like that while he wass sleeping."

The boys in blue ambled down the street towards the space where the Convenience once had been. There were lights on in Rae's cottage, and the Sergeant rapped on the door. Rae answered, but apparently she had heard nothing. MacKimmie, who was of the old school of police work, nevertheless noted the following points: Rachel Swankie, who had left the village many years before in what could charitably be described as a hurry, was back. She was painting the house so she meant to stay. She was no longer a skittish but bonny teenager, but a woman of considerable poise whose girlish good looks had developed into something much more interesting. She was not wearing a wedding ring and there was no mark on her finger where one might have been. She had had a drink but was not drunk. And she was hiding something. But MacKimmie satisfied himself with a quick squint into the house. Whatever she was hiding she did not look the type to go running around discharging shotguns in the middle of the night. He welcomed her back diplomatically, tipped his hat and moved on to Number Three, Peem and Izzie's, where a light was showing in an upstairs window and there emanated the definite sounds of a woman shrieking, though not from pain; more like hysteria. The sergeant knocked firmly on the door; noted the abrupt cessation of hilarities; and heard Peem's feet thundering down the stairs.

Peem flung the door open wide, laughing. "Christ yer fell sherp, Sye, Izzie's......" His laughter ceased and his face fell as the light fell on the two policemen standing there. MacKimmie noted that Peem was perspiring, was struggling with the zip on his jeans, was bare of both chest and foot, and appeared to be wearing a bra on his head. And the reference to Big Sye did not escape him either.

"Coot efening, William. Were you expecting someone? Ant how iss Issabel?"

Peem looked for a long time at MacKimmie and then shrugged. After all they had known each other for twenty-odd years, and it had to count for something, even if they had been on opposite sides of the law for most of them. He grinned, leaned forward and whispered conspiratorially, "Weel, Sarge, Sye's meant ti come roon tae talk aboot the joab the morn's morn, an Izzie's, well, Izzie's kinda *tied up*, like." At this he winked most lasciviously. "An A'm, A'm....." Peem had to stop; or else he was going to choke from holding back the laughter. He wiped his eyes.

MacKimmie wagged a big finger jovially. "You ton't neet to tell me any more, William," he intoned. "What you ant the delightful Issabel get up to iss certainly none off our concern, ant in any case I'm *quite* sure thatt it'ss not suitable for the earss off young Michael here. I meant in a more cheneral way." Cadet Fernie flushed to his roots and MacKimmie, smiling inwardly, went on. "Far pe it from me to trag you away from whateffer it iss that you were toing, putt my colleague here ant I are investicating a report of schots peing fired in the area."

"Whits?

"Schots. From a cun. Ant for coodness sake stop........Neffer mind. Titchoo hear anything, yourself? Apout half past ten?"

Peem scratched his head and for the first time realised he was still wearing the bra. He snatched it off with a sheepish grin. "Hauf ten? Naa. A didnae hear onyhin, James. Mind, A wis fell busy, like." He winked again.

"Tear me tat's an awful tic you haff there," sighed MacKimmie, putting away his notebook. "I'm sorry to haff disturped choo, William. Especially at such a moment. Please pass on my recards to your lady wife."

Peem closed the door and the two policemen heard the hammering of his footsteps pounding up the stairs followed by the slam of a door and a shriek. Festivities had apparently re-commenced.

"I've known coats whith less hormoness than that mann," mused the Sergeant as they turned away.

"Ye've kent *whits?*"

MacKimmie turned on the hapless cadet. "Now look here. Tchoo see I'fe chust apout hat enough of you East Coasterss taking the mickey out off my accent. You shoult listen to yourselfs sometime. *I* ton't efen *haff* an accent. Why it'ss well known thatt the PPC think tat we West Highlanters make the pest newssreaters. Now maype there'ss nott much I can to to stop theess other clownss, putt you I'fe cot rank on. So watch it!"

"Sorry, Serge," stammered the hapless Cadet Fernie. "A didnae mean it personal, like."

"Yess, yess, your apology iss acceptet, Michael, putt............"

At that moment they were distracted by the sudden appearance of another person in the little square. He appeared to be male, with shoulder length black hair, wearing a duffel-coat and sneakers. His face was one great eruption of adolescent acne, and he was making his way along the street at some speed. He appeared unaware of the policemen. MacKimmie put out a hand and tapped him on the shoulder as he sloped past.

"Christ! Fazzat!" yelped the newcomer, jumping at the touch and spinning round to look at MacKimmie with sheer horror. "Fittirye efter?" he managed after a few moments. His right hand dived into his coat pocket and nervously fiddled with something.

"Ah! Young Martin Paterson! Hant how are we tonight, Martin?"

Martin's phizog revealed nothing but consternation and his jaw dropped open.

"Tear me, tear me, it's terrible tings these arr," said MacKimmie kindly, reaching out his hand and slipping the walkman earphones from Martin's ears. At once the square was filled with a relentless hissing, swishing rhythm. "Now why ton't choo switch it off until we haff a little chat, there's a coot latt. Tchoo know you'll make yourself teaf with tat."

"Och, aye," said Martin, his voice shaking. "By, at wis some fleg ye gied me." He opened his coat and fumbled at the switches until the racket stopped.

"There, now, that'ss petter. Now, Martin, I want to ask you some questions."

Martin swallowed. "Um, A'm, er, like, me Ma's....."

"Hoch, thiss won't take long at all at all. Where haff you peen this efening, Martin."

"Eh......Um, A've been wi ma freens."

"Och yess, putt where?" repeated the sergeant, leaning closer. The youth's eyes widened in confusion and terror. "Haff you peen up at the school pike shet? Mmm? With these freindss?"

Martin looked round and considered running, but MacKimmie, who had not been twenty-five years on the force without learning something, put his hand on his shoulder and rooted him to the spot with a shackle-like grip.

"Well?" he repeated.

"Aye," whispered Martin. "But we wisnae......We wisnae daein naehin'...."

"Oh, I'm sure, Martin. Now, tell me, titchoo hear anything while you wass all there tocether with your friendss toing nothing at all at all?"

"Fit....Fit kinny hing?"

"Schots, Martin. Schots from a cun," clarified the sergeant when he saw the youth's eyes cloud into even deeper confusion.

"Naa," replied the Martin emphatically. "Nae shots."

MacKimmie narrowed his eyes. "Putt you tit hear something, issint that right?"

"Eh, oh eh aye, noo ye come ti mention hit A mechtae heard somehin. But it wisnae us!" Martin stopped suddenly, seemingly surprised by the length of his speech.

"Off course it wass not choo at all at all. Now, tell me, where they came from?"

"Whit?"

"The schots."

"The whit? ....Oh aye!" Martin's brow unfurrowed. "The shots. Fae doon thirr." He pointed towards the track end. "Oh, eh, A mean......."

MacKimmie just waved his finger. "And then what?"

"Eh, some fowk cam runnin up the track. Twa o them got intil a motor an drove aff. Een o them wis hirplin."

"To you know who they were?"

Martin balanced the twin terrors of being rousted by the police and being sorted out by Big Sye and shook his head. "Nu'. It wis ower derk."

MacKimmie, who knew full well what was going on inside Martin's head, nodded. He reflected a moment and decided that, since they could always continue the interrogation later and there was no evidence of anything more than somebody discharging a gun at an unusually late hour, there was little point in applying the thumbscrews. Not just yet.

"And that iss all?"

"Aye."

"Hmmm. Well, thank you, Martin, for all your help. Coot night."

"Izzat—izzat it?"

"Wass there something else that choo wanted to tell uss?"

"Nu'."

"Well, coot night then, Martin. You run along to your mother like a coot latt."

"Aye, okay." Martin's mood suddenly became positively jovial. "Necht, then, sarjint." He moved away in the direction of his house, his footfalls increasing rapidly in tempo as they retreated.

"Serge.....Serge, did you no see his een?" hissed Cadet Fernie urgently.

"What apout hiss eyess?"

"Weel....they wis like denner plits an they wis aa bloodshotten. Yon fella wis oan somehin, A'm shair o hit. An he hud somehin in his pooch he wis tryin tae hide."

"Yes, well. Ant what to you think I should to apout it?"

"Weel, mebbe he's oan drugs or somehin.....?"

"On trucks?" MacKimmie laughed. "On trucks? You ton't say! Michael, that lattie wass so out of hiss prains it'ss a miracle he could speak at all. To you want to know something?" MacKimmie continued without awaiting a reply. "There used to pe a Pobby stationed perma-nently in this fillage. That wass the cottage pack there, see? I wass sta-tioned here for near on twelf yearss myself pefore they went onto panta patrols ant then onto no patrols at all. To you know what the young latss who were nott olt enough to trink in the Par used to to in the efenings in those tays? Hm?"

Cadet Fernie shook his head.

"I'll tell you, since you seem to pe such a nice latt. They used to trink three pottles of Carlsperg Special followed py a pottle of Collis Prowns cough mixture—with Coteine, mark you—ant then run up ant down the street hitting each other on the hetts with pits of two py four ant preaking wintows ant walking over cars ant all sortss off nonsense that choo would not efer imagine in all your tays at all. Oh it wass terriple emparrassing so it wass, I wass alwayss haffing the Plack Maria from Arbeg out here to pick them up."

He shook his head at the memory. "Now they hang apout in the school pike shet ant smoke their whacky paccy ant they ton't efen pother to make a nuisance out off themselfs. If it wass me making the lawss ant not these plasted politicians, I would not chust make the stuff legal, I'd make it compulsory. Now, let'ss co ant haff a look town on the track."

The policemen walked to the track and switched on their rubber torches. There was, at least, no sign of any bodies. After a few moments MacKimmie stooped and picked up a piece of cloth.

"Fit's at, serge?" asked Cadet Fernie.

"It'ss the sleef off a chacket that's somepoties torn off. Ant it iss all coveret in," he wiped his hand on the grass. "Slavers. Tog slavers, if you ask me, or else there iss a werewolf loose in the fillage."

Michael looked around quickly. "Ye daa really hink *that*, div ye?"

"Och Michael tchoo know you watch too many off these late night films. You should co to ped early with a nice Horlicks ant not give yourself theess ideas. I wass chust choking. I'll tell you something, though," he added, illuminating the dark patch on the path where Gilchrist's nose had spurted blood with his torch, "They'ff peen haffing a proper scrap to themselfs here tonight."

"Aye, but fit aboot the shots, Serge?"

MacKimmie waved his torch up at the darkened windows of Morag's house. "The schotts? I wonter. Let's co ant see if Morack can enlighten us, hmm? Maype she heard something."

Morag took a while to answer their knock, partly because she wasn't as quick on the move as she used to be, partly because she was *still* aviating as a result of the Valium, but mainly because of the ridiculous number of locks she had on the door. When at last the final tumbler clunked open she opened the door only as far as the two security chains would allow and peered out. She was covered from head to foot in white dust.

MacKimmie regarded her with an air of kind curiosity. "Cood

efening Miss Paterson. I wass chust talking to your nephew. My, haff you peen baking?"

"Fittin the hell ur ye oan aboot min? Are ye daft? Wakin a body at this time o necht. Bakin, sez he."

"It'ss chust that you seem to pe all covered in flour, that'ss all. Are you sure you're quite all right?"

Morag wiped a plump hand across her cheek and regarded the plaster dust that came off with some confusion. "Ach, jist a bit stoor, that's aa," she said quickly. "Fittdye want?"

"We've hat a report that somepody fired a cun, Miss Paterson. I ton't suppose you heard anything?"

Morag glowered at him sulkily. "Fit if A hiv?"

"Firing cuns in a built up area iss against the law, Miss Paterson. Are you sure you titn't hear anything at all?"

"Weel thir wis a row doon in the lane syne. Some buggers fechtin."

"Putt no schots."

Morag avoided his eye. "Nu'. Nae shots."

MacKimmie nodded thoughtfully, and then made as if to ask another question; but then he thought better of it, shrugged, touched his cap, and said, "Well, coot night, then, Miss Paterson. You chust away to your ped now ant ton't be catching the cold." With that he turned away.

MacKimmie and Fernie made their way back down The Street towards the Hotel and their car.

"She wis coverin somehin up, serge, A ken it," chirped Cadet Fernie enthusiastically.

MacKimmie stuck his hands in his pockets and rocked back and forward sagely. "Ochone, Michael," he said at last, "When you've peen on the force as long ass I haf you'll realise that in a wee little fillage like thiss *eferypoty* is covering something up. They can't liff any other way. They all know eferything apout eferyone else ant it cets tiresome. Eferypoty hass to haf *some* secrets, ant in a wee community that's not easy. Tchoo see, they all haf things to hide—not chust from uss, putt from each other. In fact, mainly from each other. That makes them fery careful apout what they say. Sso we haf to make allowances. Now I know, ant you know, that Morack Paterson iss acting in a suspicious manner, ant not letting on all she knows, putt that's not reason enough for me to scare the poor botie out off her wits at this time off night. Especially ass we ton't really know if there were schots or not. Nopoty—well nopoty closer to the planet than Martin Paterson—ant I't like to see you make him into a witness that woult stant up in court—iss coing to admit to hearing them, far less tell uss where they came from, that'ss for certain."

"How no?"

"Pecause they all haf secrets, Michael. Ton't you listen? Let uss suppose that Morack heart a fracass ant fired a schot or two to scare the puccers away. Nopoty's coing to tell uss cos they're that scared that Morack might let on something apout them that they might like to keep quiet.

They ton't like us ant they ton't like outsiters raking through their affairs. A fight, tat's nothing. Tat's not illegal, not really. Putt cuns is ant cuns means trouble ant polis all ofer the place ant cootness knows what might fall out of the press. They ton't want to know. I wouldn't mind betting that there is quite a few illecally helt shotcuns in the fillage, putt short off searching all off the houses we'll nefer know, ant even then we propaply wouldn't find them all. In any case, the whole thing might pe chust Mary Kennedy's imachination. There's nott a week coes pie putt we get a call from her. So, in the meantime, since we ton't have reason to do anything else," he glanced at his watch, "Another pint off peer and we can call it a night. Come along."

CHAPTER TWENTY-TWO
Sye and Peem again

Big Sye waited until he saw the police car glide out of the village. He had left Rae's and returned to *The Chateau* while the Sergeant and his colleague were making up their half-shift in the bar, and now he knew that if he and Peem were to get the Fish, they would have to do so quickly. Already the wind, which had so recently been playfully and agreeably tugging at hair and clothes, was becoming violent, and Sye knew that if they didn't go now they might have to wait a day or maybe two before the sea subsided enough to safely manoeuvre through the rocks to the cave. By which time the salmon would be ruined. When, from his darkened front room, he judged the coast was clear, he donned an olive green slicker jacket and trousers and went to get Peem.

Peem was waiting for him. They exchanged few words. Men who have been up all night, have had four hours sleep and who find themselves turning out again at one in the morning in a rising storm tend to the laconic. They jumped into Peem's Volvo and headed for the harbour. Without fuss and practically without saying a word, they started Sye's pot-boat, warmed the engine, slipped the lines and set off to sea. When they worked together the two men showed the evidence of all the years they had done so; each knowing the tasks to be done, neither getting in the other's way. The fresh breeze whipped at their cheeks and the spray it drove slapped the tiredness out of them and charged them with a kind of elation as Sye guided the boat expertly towards the cave. With the tide fully in they could make the boat fast right at the entrnce to the cave, but still the fish had to be brought out of the cave in boxes, gruelling and slow work, dangerous too, for the narrow ledge that they had to traverse was awash and slippery with the tide so high, and they dared not show a light outside the innermost part of the cave lest unwelcome eyes should observe it.

So it was near four in the morning by the time they got finished; the dory loaded, brought back to the port, the boxes unloaded up into Peem's Volvo, and all the fish brought up to the village to hide in safe places. The wind was really starting to howl by then; Sye judged a Force Six while they were moving the fish in the dory, a Force Eight when they got back to Peem's, and he felt it in his water that it would go well past Force Ten before it grew tired of being boisterous. The storm was taking its time to get going, like, and those ones are the ones that hang about. When they come on quick they can be fantastically violent and do just as much, if not more damage, but the slow ones are the ones the sailors dislike. Still it was exhilarating and took the dullness off the fatigue. Peem helped Sye stack the last of the salmon in the bath at The Chateau and joined him for a deoch an doris. Then they went to their beds, tired as they could remember ever having been.

CHAPTER TWENTY-THREE
Rae and The Minister's Wife

ae's part-time job at Swankies' occupied her two and a half
days a week, one whole day and three half; which was fine by
her. Tues-day was one of her half-days, and by the afternoon the
gale had mostly worn itself out, leaving in its wake a spring day of beauty
when the whole world smelled fresh and of the earth and the sea and the
coming of life to the world. And it was warm, warm with the breath of
tropical air. Rae put on her new yellow dress and shoes and went for a
stroll along the cliff-top path, out past the old Coastguard cottages. Everywhere the primroses littered the grass and the gorse popped and crackled and filled the air with its scent and shouted the yellow of its flowers.
Rae had her heart filled with joy by the shrilling of the laverocks in the
fields on one side of the path and the wailing of the maws and other sea-
birds as they wheeled around their nests in the cliff-face far below, by the
pleasant warmth of the sun, and the breeze, which though still strong,
was pleasant. She felt more alive than she had for years.

As she returned to the village, feeling the sun on her back and
idly enjoying the way that her dress brushed against her bare thighs, she
was stopped by two little Teviotdale girls sitting on the sandstone wall
opposite the school. Their satchels hung loosely from their skinny shoulders, and their white socks were about their ankles. They looked at Rae
with that mixture of shyness and curiosity, and one of them managed a
smile of perfectly even and perfectly white little teeth. The other kept her
mouth shut because she had lost the two front ones and the new ones
hadn't grown in yet and it made her embarrassed.

"By, at's an affy bonny dress ye've got oan," said the one with
teeth.

"Aye! Foo muckle did it cost ye?" put in the other.

Her sister elbowed her in the ribs and she yelped. "Daa be
coorse!"

"Never you mind," said Rae, laughing. "And it's all right, you
dinnae need to be so rauch." She smiled at the girls. "Well, are ye not
goin to introduce yersels? Here, I'll go first. I'm Rae, and I've moved into
the cottage in Fountain Square."

"Far auld Mrs. Swankie yased tae bide? The een that deed no
lang syne? A'm Jessica but aabody cries me Jess. She's Shona but she'll
no smile cos she's nae teeth. She's ma sister." Jessica beamed at Rae
again and Shona punched her in the ribs.

"Aye, that's me. Mrs. Swankie was ma mither. I'm Rae Swankie."

The girls drank this in. "Ur you the een that gingit awa?" lisped Shona in a voice filled with awe.

"Uhuh."

"But yer beck noo?"

"Uhuh."

"Good. Ma sez ye gingit awa til Embro. Is it no fell big there? By thon must be somehin. Fit wey did ye want tae come back here fur?"

Rae couldn't help laughing. "Aye, well, it's a wee bit bigger than Auchpinkie," she allowed. "But why good? No that I take it amiss."

"Ach jist cos yer that bonny. A want ti be bonny like youse fan A grow up," said Jess, her eyes wide.

"Kin ye tell wis shomehin, mishus?" chirped the toothless one, her breath whistling through the gap. "Shee, we're haein a row aboot fither ye can or ye cannae. A say ye can an she shez ye cannae."

"Cannae what?"

"It's a shecret."

"Well I cannae help ye if ye don't tell me whit it is ye want tae ken," protested Rae, wondering how much longer she could resist bursting out laughing.

"Promish tae no let on? See if A whisper it wull ye keep it a shecret?" Shona's dark eyes were pleading.

"She wants tae wad wur cousin Jeemy fan she grows up an A say she cannae," squeaked Jessica in a hysterical sing-song; she could stand the suspense no longer. At once Shona flung herself at her sister in blind rage and the pair of them fell off the wall into the weeds behind.

Rae thought about this as the children clambered back up, still glowering at each other. "I think so," she said when the girls were once again perched on the wall. "I think so—but I'm no just right sure, now ye ask. No sure enough tae settle an argument like that." She paused and a serious look crossed her face, and when she spoke it was to herself, in thoughtful tones. "D'ye ken, I dinnae think I iver asked onybody masel. Is that not queer now?"

The vagueness of her reply did not seem to be exactly what the girls wanted to hear. They shrugged their shoulders and kicked the leather off their heels on the wall and looked about glumly with an air of disappointment.

"We hivtae be shair, y'see, missus," said Jess at last, her tone matter-of-fact. "We jist *hivtae*,". She added in a voice that left no doubt that this was a matter of life and death. Rae thought for a moment and then nodded over to where the noise of hoeing was emanating from the manse vegetable-garden. Mrs. Jameson, the minister's wife, was a keen gardener, and she was busy setting out her lettuces. Rae remembered Mrs. Jameson from her mother's funeral. "But there's Mrs Jameson doin her gerden. How d'ye no ask her?"

The two girls huddled together. "We're ower blate," whispered Shona.

"Aye. We ur," agreed Jess mournfully. "Here, A've an idear!"

She brightened up. "Youse could ask hur fur wis! Widye missus, *please?*"

"Aye, goannie ashk her fur wis, pleashe, mishus, pleashe wullye?"

Rae laughed. "Ach well, okay. A wanted tae drop by jist to say hello anyway."

The Reverend James Jameson had spent a large part of his afternoon deep in reflection in the study of the manse. At last he went out to speak to his wife Joan, who was at the lettuce seedlings. At times when the complexity of a question of morals defeated him, he liked to run it past her. As he stepped outside the house a dark-haired woman came through the garden gate and stepped lightly up the path. The Reverend squinted at her curiously. She was wearing a yellow dress that shouted 'Spring!', and her hair was up in a pony-tail. The minister narrowed his eyes more and then smiled as he recognised the visitor as Rachel Swankie, a newly arrived parishioner.

"My word, Miss Swankie," he said in surprise. "How well you do look. Quite the picture of a spring day. A very good afternoon indeed."

"Guid afternoon, Mr Jameson," Rae replied, smiling her best killer smile hugely. Ministers, she reflected, were allowed to go on like that. Ministers and ancient lawyers. "I'm sorry to disturb ye........I just dropped by to say hello. I was on my way tae ask Mrs. Jameson something, but likely you could tell me and save me getting ma shoes all muddy."

"Oh good. I wanted to see you, too. Fine boy, you have, Miss Swankie. A credit to you. Quite devout, it seems." Another bum on a pew, with a bit of luck, thought the minister to himself.

Rae was pretty near dumfoonert by that last one, but she didn't let on; no, she took the compliment in her stride and made up her mind to have it out with her son later. "Really?" she laughed, and smiled again at the minister. She did hope this was not going to be an awkward interview; Rae had no objection to the Kirk, but she had no desire to get involved in it either. But she was good with people, was Rae, much, much, better than the Reverend Jameson was prepared for, and very quickly he found himself talking about his roses, the weather, how much more pleasant life was in the country and the two silly lassies at the gate who were just dying to know the answer to a certain question........

When the Reverend Jameson finally got to see Joan, and Rae was striding back down the path with the sun glowing a yellow halo all around her, he was positively exhausted with confusion.

"Joan, can I talk something over with you?"

"Yes," replied Joan, without pausing in her trowelling. "Who was that woman?"

"Rachel Swankie. You know, Etta Swankie's daughter. You met her at the funeral. Tell me, about those boys who came the other night........ I'm having difficulty with them. You see, they are under the impression that they are the subject of direct heavenly intervention of an intensely personal nature. Now there is no question that this has had some effect for the good upon...."

"*Who* did you say it was?" Joan had stopped trowelling and was sitting back on her haunches looking in the direction of the gate.

"Rachel Swankie......Some effect for the good upon their natures. In fact you might say that they are changed boys. Now the question is this. Do I tell them that.........."

Unnoticed by her husband, Joan had got to her feet and was intently watching the figure in yellow, who had stopped to talk to two little girls sitting on a low sandstone wall. "Well, what's she doing *here?*" demanded Joan. "I thought Etta swore blind she'd will the house to the Cat Refuge before she'd let her daughter at it."

"Well, for all that, the same girl's moved into the same mother's old house. Look, dear, I'm trying to explain. Do I allow them to continue to believe that God has directly intervened in their lives, in the hope that this belief will make them into better people, when according to *The Scotsman* the explosion to which they refer was caused by some freak build up of gases, or do I disabuse them, in which case they will certainly go back to their old....."

"James! A moment, please. Isn't her son one of the boys who came round last night?"

"Why yes. Yes."

"And what did she have to say about it?"

"Nothing. We didn't discuss it."

"What? Her son comes here and tells you he expects the wrath of God to descend upon him any minute and you didn't say anything? Don't you think that's a bit odd?"

"Well it's a very delicate situation. That's what I'm trying to talk to you about."

"Delicate my foot! Ian Teviotdale—for that matter the whole tribe of them—is about as delicate as a Sherman tank and it doesn't take much nouse to work out that this other one—what's his name?"

"William Swankie."

"That this *William Swankie* is of the same mould. Whatever they think now I promise you in a week's time they'll have forgotten about the whole thing. They're a pair of complete little....*whittericks*, and living in the fear of some awful heavenly vengeance for a few days is not going to do them any harm at all. You might even get them to come to the kirk before they rumble you. But really, James, I think you should have told her. After all, she came round to see you about it—"

"Ah but she didn't."

"She didn't? So what did she want? The Swankies, if I recall, have never been great ones for the kirk, except Etta of course. And if you ask me *she* had ulterior motives."

"She just dropped by to pay her regards, that's all. Very charming young woman. We chatted and she asked me if cousins could marry. My she has a way with her, you know. Now about these boys......"

Joan gave her husband a look that would have frozen water and thumped her forehead with the heel of her palm several times. "James, tell me; do you live in the same world as the rest of us? Never *mind* about the boys. Don't you think that *other* little item is so much more interesting?"

"What, the bit about the cousins? Oh but........."

"Of *course* the bit about the cousins. Oh my goodness! And what did you say?"

"I said yes it was. It's not very common, but there's nothing against it. I think maybe the other lot have some sort of dispensation you have to have, but marrying your cousin is quite in the tradition of the Presbyterian Kirk......... Where are you going, dear?"

"I'm going to find out what in the blazes is going on!" shouted Joan over her shoulder.

"I don't think you should concern yourself, dear; I don't think she was interested personally. I mean, she *said* she was asking for those two.........Oh, dear." He sighed. Joan had disappeared into the house and was clearly not listening.

CHAPTER TWENTY-FOUR
The Hag's Huddle Gets Its Act Together. Sort of.

Joan Jameson walked past The Chateau on her way to Mae's shop, and noted the odour. Now Mae, in addition to being shopowner, postmistress, and unofficial convenor of the Committee of Social Etiquette, was the village gazette. If ever you wanted to know anything that had to do with the life of Auchpinkie, you just went into Mae's, bought a box of firelighters or a packet of tea, and gently pumped her. Coincidentally (as attentive readers will have noted) she was Sye's auntie, and forbye that, retail outlet for the salmons.

"Peculiar smell in the square this afternoon," remarked Joan while she counted out the money from her purse. "I do hope we're not going to have another of these awful accidents. Mind you, that smells more like fish."

"Oh?" Mae sniffed. "A canna recht say A've taen tent o hit masel."

Since most people's olfactory glands were instantly stunned into insensibility by the overpowering odour of cats that caught you high in the chest soon as you opened the door of the little shop, this revelation, I think even Joan would have had to allow, was hardly surprising. But she held her tongue.

Mae clucked and leaned her plumpness across the counter, her considerable bosom bulging under her cardigan as she did so. "Wid it be a nice wee bit salmon yer efter, like, Mrs. Jameson?" she rasped conspiratorially.

"Salmon? Well, I....I don't know." Joan doubtfully eyeballed Mae's hands with their shining patina of grime and printer's ink. "I didn't know you sold fish, Mae."

"Och it's a braw bit fush so it is Mrs Jameson," said Mae, brushing aside the last query. "Ma nephew jist catched it this morn. Honest. That caller it's still kickin. Here, hae a deek at this." She squeezed out from behind the counter, shooing cats before her as she went. She swept a couple of them from the top of her ice chest and opened the lid. With some ceremony she lifted out a fish from where it lay with several others (which she made sure that her client did not see) on top of the raspberry ripples.

"Izzint that no braw? Shair an the Reverint widnae like a wee bit o't fur his suppir the necht?", she wheedled, holding the salmon up. The cats immediately formed a swarm about her feet and a few of the bolder ones made a start on the ascent of her pinnie.

Mrs Jameson was insufficiently slow of wit not to realise that something, er, fishy was going on, but the salmon looked good and it was cheap—suspiciously cheap; but she adored salmon and could not resist it. While Mae wrapped it up in a yesterday's *Press and Journal* that was still warm from the cat that had been sleeping on it, she angled.

"Have you seen Morag Paterson today, Mae?" she enquired innocently, while regarding with feigned interest a postcard showing two Scotty dogs with tartan scarves on from a rack labelled 'Souvenirs of Scotland'. "Only I really must drop by and see her. The Reverend went by this morning but I'm sure she'd appreciate a visit from a woman. It must have been awful, poor old Bob being blown up like that, right outside her window."

A vision of Morag wielding her yard-broom flashed before Mae's eyes before she could stop it. She tried to stifle the cackle, but too late and she choked. She doubled up over her counter with her eyes popping and her blubber wobbling as she coughed and spluttered explosively, her face purple and her fat cheeks streaming with tears. Joan became quite alarmed, and discreetly took a position in the lee of a rack where she was sheltered from the spittle. "Cat hair," croaked Mae at last, thumping her chest. "Happens aa the time. Far wizza? Oh aye. Aye weel, mebbe. Morag. Aye." She coughed and cleared her throat. "Pair sowl."

"You know, Mae, I was always sorry for Morag. The poor woman had such a time of it with her mother......Rest her soul. But it's been over two years since she died and Morag has been locked up in that house all along." Joan replaced the Scotty dogs and picked up a postcard showing a Highland bull standing on a mountain with a quizzical look on its face. "Yes, I really must drop in and see her." Joan moved onto the ground she really wanted to know about.

"You'll never guess who dropped in to see us today, Mae."

"Yer recht A'll no an aa."

"That nice girl who has moved into Etta Swankie's old house. Her daughter, I believe, though I can't say I'd seen her before. Except at the funeral, of course, but that's different."

"Rae Swankie?" Mae's eyes drilled into Joan's head. "Aye A suppose she's aa recht efter her gate."

"She looked just marvellous, Mae. I hadn't realised how attractive she was. Mind you, you don't, at a funeral, do you?"

"Weel she wis aye a bonnie-like quine fan she wis younger, like. Aye weel pitten-on. An she used ti be a recht cheery sowl tae. Kinda wild, though. A thocht Etta'd soored her fur guid." Etta had been married on Mae's brother-in-law, and there was no love lost. "Mind, *yon* limmer'd hiv soored a pint milk jist lookin at hit."

"Oh, Mae, you really mustn't speak ill of the dead, you know." Joan had picked up a postcard of a piper with a barrel chest and magnificent knees.

"A niver spak aboot her ony *ither* wey," muttered Mae, tying up the parcel with string. "An A'm no aboot ti stert noo. She was a thrawn auld besom if ye ask me, an the milk o human kindness wis positifely conjeellified in her sowl." She snipped off the string with a vicious motion that did not escape her interrogator. "An A wis under the impression that Rae wid likely turn oot a miserable greetin-fiss jist like her forbye, muckle though it grieves me."

Joan frowned. This was not the direction she wanted the conversation to take. But she knew you had to be careful with Mae, and let her do the talking.

"It's no at A blame the quine, noo." Mae was warming to the task. "She hud it recht teuch wi yon auld carlin. An then her faither—ma brither-in-laa Wullie—weel, Etta pit him in the grun fan he wis herdly forty year auld. Rae wis jist a bit lassie."

"But surely that wasn't Etta's fault....... I'd always heard he'd died of cirrho—of a liver complaint."

Mae cackled like an old hen and wiped her hands on her apron in a manner she had when she was Ginging Ti Say Somehin. It was clear from the marks thereon that this was something she did regularly, too. "Liver complaint? Heh, heh. Thir wis nuthin wrang wi Wullie's liver. Heh heh. It jist cam oot on strike in protest at aa the work it hud ti div. Heh heh. Fegs, A'll bet ye a pun til a penny it's like spleet new still, it had that muckle booze shoved intil't."

Joan laughed nervously, and picked up a postcard showing two girls in kilts doing the sword dance whilst grinning at each other. She had never worked out how they managed to do that.

"Naa, Mrs Jameson, A ken Etta niver *eckchully* killed him. If she hud of she'd a picked a cheaper wey. But jist ask yersel fit wey it wis he got a drouth on him like thon? Christ it wis leejundary. A'll tell ye fit wey; cos o hur an her constant nip-nip-nippin. She drave Wullie ti the drink."

"And Rachel?"

"Kennin Etta A thocht she musta been anither een o they immaculint conceptics—no meanin ti be coorse, like. An be the wey, aabody cries her Rae. She hinks Rachel's stuck up. At least she yased til, an A jalouse she's ower auld ti cheenge her gate noo. Ach, Rae wis a fine lass until Wull deed an then she sterted, weel, she got wild. She had a hale wheen divilment ti get ootin her system, an she an Etta yased ti fecht like cat an dug. An then ae fine day she jist ups an aff she gings an naebody, but *naebody* hears a cheep fae her till she turns up at Etta's plantin. An the next hing ye ken she's shiftit intil Etta's auld hoose sonsie as ye like, wi yon laddie o hurs. Thir a tale thir an aa if we could get ti the bottom o hit." She leaned over the counter again and her breasts stretched the fabric that contained them threateningly. She lowered her voice. "Ken Etta niver meant fur her ti get the hoose. That's Gospel—eh, beg pardon, A wisnae mindin. But efter aa the auld limmer ginged an deed intesticulate."

"Intest—oh. I see. I didn't know that."

"Aye. No mony fowk div. But thir wis nae ither affspring, see, so Rae got the lot. Quite recht tae, but it's no fit Etta said she wanted. Only she cowpit hur creel afore she'd gotten roon ti makin a will tae leave Rae ootin. Heh, heh. Served the auld besom recht. Me, A hink she wis at grippit it wis jist hinkin o fa the hell else she mecht a left her siller tae that done fur her."

"Oh, I see," said Joan Jameson. "Oh, well, I just thought that Rachel—Rae looked......I don't know, refreshed, today. Alive. It made me think something romantic might have happened to her. But maybe it was just the sea air," she added hurriedly.

"Romantic?" Mae wheezed deeply and leaned on the counter. She drummed her fingers thoughtfully. "Here noo ye come ti mind me A seen Agnes this mornin, an she sez that Rae wis in the Hotel bletherin tae some fellae fae the Cooncil." She leaned forward and once more Joan prayed under her breath that the fabric could stand the strain. Mae adopted her conspiratorial rasp. "Ken een o they cheils at cam doon ti hiv a shufty efter yon splosion. They left the place thegither, like. Him an Rae A mean."

"Really?"

"Oh, aye. An A daa like ti cast axpersions, like, seein fit wey she's ma niece an aa, but ye ken Wally Guthrie wis in syne threipin he'd seen the same fellae's motor tak aff up the road like a scaldit cat at some ungodly hour the next again morn. He's terrible trouble wi his kidneys ye ken, the pair sowl's up hauf the necht wi thum."

Joan was startled. "Who? The man from the council?"

"Naw, Wally Guthrie acoorse."

"I didn't know she had a cousin with the council," mused Joan, aloud, and could have kicked herself. But too late.

"Fit did ye say?" Mae's eyes gleamed like one of her cats as she pounced on this delectable wee snippet.

"Oh, nothing. I was thinking of somebody else." Joan hurriedly covered her tracks. It was time to end the interview before Mae started to pump her. "How much do I owe you for the fish?"

"Och, aye, a body siccan yersel must hae that mony hings tae hink aboot, bein the meenister's wife an aa. That'll be ten note—eh, pun—fur cash."

Joan Jameson pushed the ginger tom that had settled on the wrapped up fish onto the ground, ignoring the fearful yowl, took it under her arm and swept from the emporium full of smiles and polite fare-thee-wells.

Mae watched her back recede with her lip curled. She hated that. When folk came in and tried to milk her and as soon as they started to let on something juicy themselves they were off. It wasn't fair. Oh, aye, she kent fine what thon stuck up lang bag o banes o a meenustir's wife was intil. Cousin? Wi the Cooncil? Blethers! Mae's brain whirred into overdrive. Rae Swankie had only one male cousin who was not thoroughly attached. Mae would ken fine, since she was aunt to the both of them. Through the glazed shop door Mae had a perfect view of the front door of The Chateau across the square. She pondered while she slipped the two fivers into her purse. Maybe Wally was wrong; after all he was not the most reliable of informants, on account of his lifelong passion for alcohol.

"A'll hae ti keep an ee oan that een," she muttered to herself.

A little later, Sye came out of The Chateau and closed the door behind him. He was carrying a black bin-liner and even at that range Mae's practised eye could tell it contained several good sized fish. She watched impatiently as he sauntered along the street away from her, and clapped her hands in delight when he disappeared from view round the corner of Fountain Square. Mae clapped her hands in delight and waurstled her way through the shop to the phone This news had to be called in. "By the cringe!" she exclaimed gleefully as she picked up the handset, "Izzat no jist somehin!"

Rae had just washed her hair and was drying it when she heard the knock on the door. She swore and wrapped a towel round her head and went to answer it. In front of her stood Big Sye, looking sheepish and holding a black plastic bin liner with something in it in one hand.

"Hello, Sye," she said, and smiled. "I wis jist thinking about ye. Come away in."

Sye coughed and shuffled. "No the noo, ta. A cin see yer busy, an onywey A've ti see Peem aboot somehin. A jist brocht this ti ye ti say hanks, like. Fur patchin me up, like." He held out the bag and grinned. "An no lettin on ti the polis an aa." He placed the bag on the doorstep. "Weel, A'll see yiz later, eh? An hanks again."

"It's me should thank you for rescuin me fae that bloody man," laughed Rae and looked in the bag. "Salmon? Oh, here, that's ower much, Sye." Her eyes widened. "There's three—no, four o them here."

"A thocht ye cid shove a puckle in yer freezer. A hope ye like salmon?" he added anxiously.

"I love it. So does Willie. But really, Sye, A canna...."

"It's aa recht," Sye went on. "A've mair'nn A need."

"More salmon than ye need? You *are* a man worth knowing." She grinned at him. "Sure ye'll not c'way in for a wee dram?"

"Na, honest, A said A'd see Peem. A wis jist passin."

"Okay, well, if ye'll no come in, would ye let me buy ye a dram at the Hotel sometime?"

Sye's brow furrowed a little. "That's no how A gie'd ye the salmon," he said, quietly.

"I know. I wouldnae ask ye if I thought it wis. Tell ye what— Sunday? How wid that be?"

"A'd like that fine, Rae." He leaned forward and gave her a peck on the cheek, cousin-style.

Unremarked by the two participants in this innocent scene, Jess was peering through the curtain of Number Five Fountain Square, Nan was at the door of Number One The Street, and if Mae had craned her neck any further in her vain effort to see round the corner she'd have broken it. Shortly after Sye had set off for the beach and Rae had with-

138

drawn to blow-dry her hair, a meeting of the Committee took place in Mae's shop.

By six o'clock the same evening the news was out to an astonished village that Big Sye was courting Rae, official. Naturally nobody let on a word to the parties involved.

CHAPTER TWENTY-FIVE
The Fish Makes Its Presence Felt.

By Thursday morning the last of the storm had shuffled off, a poor and timid shadow of its lusty arrival, leaving the country refreshed and the sea calm. The weather was settling into one of those periods of high atmospheric pressure with long days of warm sun and skies of liquid blue and air so clear you'd think it was water that can make early summer such a delight in Scotland. There was no denying that the warm weather pleased the village. Old bodies discreetly began to leave off their woolly semits, and the men began to leave their jackets at home and go out in their sark sleeves. But not everyone was so gladdened by the promised fine spell. At The Chateau, Big Sye stood at his bathroom door and shook his head sorrowfully. The object of his dissatisfaction made its presence felt as soon as you opened the front door, and continued to assault your nostrils all the way up the stairs to the postage-stamp landing. Its pervasive presence was everywhere, and things could only get worse when the weather got better.

Sye had been into Arbeg to buy ice from the Fishie Soshie and now he hefted the bucket that he'd brought up the stairs and began to pour it into the bath. The sad fact was that despite his best efforts he could not get shot of all those bloody salmons that he and Peem had quite literally risked their lives, never mind the jail or an astronomical fine, to catch. Drew Gibson was doing his best, but it seemed that the market in hot salmon was a little weak; a puckle salmon here and a puckle salmon there was frankly not fast enough to shift this pile before they got themselves up and took off in the huff. Sye's freezer was full, Nan's freezer was full, you could hardly get the lid shut on Peem's and Mae was already feeding them to the cats. Dave the barman had been told in the strictest terms by Agnes that not one more fish was to cross their threshold on pain of legal separation. In any case the very word 'salmon' caused Dave to pale. He'd had salmon fried, poached, and baked, in pates and in omelettes and in sandwiches and the poor man had got to thinking that maybe he was in Purgatory and would have to eat salmon for all eternity as a punishment for short-changing the regulars.

As for Sye, his dreams were peopled by salmons, salmons of all imaginable trades and professions and shapes and sizes and all getting up to the most outlandish cantrips. Listlessly he spread the ice over the pile of gleaming fish. His bath was still a foot deep in the buggers and it pained him deeply. Even Pluto had had enough; he couldn't be bothered to steal the half-eaten tail that Sye had accidentally-on-purpose left on the kitchen table.

See, salmons are all very well when they've just been caught. Then they are nice and fresh and firm and their scales sparkle silver iridescence and they have the rich and heavy scent of the sea. But after a couple of days they start to get a bit restless, like. They start to think you've forgotten about them, and that makes them sad and a little indignant, and pretty soon they start reminding you that they're there. And pretty soon after that, if you still don't heed them, they get downright bumptious.

"Look here," they say. "This is just not good enough. You caught us. Now what are you going to do with us? We do hope you're not going to leave us here much longer, we really could not stand for that. We are, after all, the King of Fish, and we demand our due respect."

And then they begin to send their invisible odoriferous tendrils out into the world.

Earlier that morning the scale that the problem had already reached had been brought home to Sye with a bump, when he was accosted upon his own doorstep by Miss Doreen Farquharson, a venerable spinster of quaint hygiene and bottle-bottom glasses whose similarly unscoured yellow Vauxhall was the holy terror of the roads for miles around. She also happened to be Sye's next door neighbour but one.

"Fit's yon guff?" she had demanded. Miss Farquharson did not have a great deal of time for social niceties. "A cannae sleep nechts wi hit. Izzer somehin deid in thir? Y'got ocht stappit doon yer drains?" She screwed up her eyes and stretched her withered neck to get a look inside the door as she spoke. "A'll cry the Cooncil if ye daa dae somehin aboot it quick!"

Given Miss Farquharson's attitude towards washing, Sye was frankly astonished that she could smell anything but herself at all. But he'd dug her out a couple of good fish, and that had placated her for the time being. But that did not solve the problem.

Down by the shore there was a round pit about six feet across that had once been used daily for smoking haddock. In recent times, however, with the decline of the fishing from the harbour, it had fallen into disuse. It was a lot of work to start the fire and put on the damp oak chips, and you had to know what you were doing. Frankly Peem was having only limited success.

Mind, it had been his idea, so he had no one to blame but himself. After all, if you could smoke haddies like that, then why not salmons? And everyone knew how much smoked salmon went for. Why they could make a fortune with all they fish.

Peem had been at it since eight that morning and he was beginning to realise why smoked salmon was so expensive. It wasn't that he had failed; not at all. Well there *had* been a couple of disasters early in the day before he'd got the hang of the fire. No, he could smoke the fish all right, it was just that when they were done they bore no resemblance whatsoever to what Peem knew a side of smoked salmon *should* look like. They tasted okay, and the texture was fine— well maybe just a bit crunchy, but they were entirely the wrong colour and no matter what Peem did, insisted on curling themselves into spirals that just would not flatten out. It was frustrating to the point of distraction.

Late in the afternoon Sye arrived with a welcome fourpack of Tennent's lager. Peem was just finishing his last smoke.

"It taks furiver, this," he said, popping his ring-pull. "A daa ken how." He put the can to his mouth and swallowed half of it. "Fell drouthy work, an aa."

Sye nodded and threw back his. "A'm shair they dae them in ovens, like, the recht salmon smokers."

"Aye, A hink they maun dae, like, but we've no got a bluidy oven, hiv we. Here, mebbe A could knock somehin up ootin a forty gallon ile drum, though." He picked up a curled side and hacked off a large chunk with his gullie. "Hae bit gnaw at thon an tell us fit ye hink."

Sye cut off a slice with his own pocket-knife and popped it into his mouth. He chewed for a while and nodded. "No bed, Peem ma loon. No bed ava. Bit mair, weel, smokey'n yaseyell, but nutt at aa bed fur aa that. But is smoked salmon no yaseyelly a different colour'n this?"

"A hink it's somehin ti dae wi the temperature. It's ower het, A hink. A hink thi maun cool the reek some wey. Recht perjinckit fush, these salmons. No like haddies ava." Peem was reflective. "Y'ken A cid mebbe hae a shot at makin up a oven the morn. Fit d'ye hink?"

Sye pondered a long while and drained his can. "Suit yersel." He crumpled the can in his fist reflectively. "A cidnae be bothered masel. Thir's nae merkat fur salmon these days. It's the fermin that's killed it. Naebody'll pey a recht price. Drew sez it's aye the same story, his ti be fresh, no frozen, nae bruises, recht size—an efter he's tooken his cut—it's ower much trachle, min."

Peem nodded and sighed. "Weel, aiblins there is a bit mair til it'n smokin a puckle haddies on a stick efter aa." He sighed and looked out over the sea with narrowed eyes.

"It's takin up ower muckle o wir time, an aa," Sye went on. "We're gingin ti hiv tae look at yon weldin joab noo the weather's blawed itsel oot. We daa want ti loss the contrack, it's ower easy siller. An yon lootenant fae the Submarine base wis at me oan the ansaphone."

"Tint anither torpedae?" There was a torpedo testing range off the shore at Bervie Point, some miles to the south. The navy paid a generous reward for salvaged torpedoes that had strayed outside the test area; but you needed a pal on the inside to let you know where to look.

"Uhuh."

Peem laughed. "By thir some shower. It fair stounds me they iver hit onyhin ava wi the nummer o they hings thi loss. Still, it pays wir rent. Tell ye far he hinks thi tint it?"

"North o the boundary. Last reported heidin three three five degrees an no hingin back for nobody."

Peem nodded and sighed. Sye looked hard at him.

"Thir's somehin fashin ye. Fit is it? C'mon, spill the beans. Ye've no faan oot wi yer ma again, hae ye?" he demanded.

"Ach it's no that," Peem grinned.

"Weel, fit, then?"

"Ach, it's Ian, Sye. A daa ken fit the blazes has got intil thon laddie this week. Him an Wullie Swankie has been gingin aboot dressed up like a couple o Jaffas iver syne the village cludge blawed up. An noo he sez he's gingin till the kirk on Sundas. Weel, it's no that A've got onyhin agin the kirk, like, jist's lang as A daa hae ti ging masel, but......."

"But ye ken fine thir's somehin gingin on an it's annoyin ye cos ye daa ken fit," interrupted Sye. "I thocht thir was somehin up. A hivnae seen thum playin chickanelly or shooty-in agin the front waa of the Hotel aa week."

"Fegs, Sye, it's no jist that. There's a hale cetalogue o bedness that he's yaseyelly intil at the wee scamp has jist completely ignored. An it's no jist syne Monda. It's been gaein oan fur langer'n at. Sterted jist efter he took up wi Willie Swankie—ye ken, Rae's laddie." Peem looked quickly at Sye as if to make sure that he did, and then went on, "The pair o thum wis furiver skytin aff ti wir auld cave ower thir—they hink naebody kens, far they ging, like. Ian discovered it lest year, an he showed it tae Willie. I aye thocht if they wis doon thir they wis at least no causin bother some ither wey else."

"Hiv ye been up ti hae a deek?"

"Fit? Me? Sye, I hinna been in yon cave syne.......eh, weel, noo, lemme hink......." Peem scratched his beard. "It's gettin on twinty year, Sye. It cannae hae been lang efter the pair o wis wis up there wi the MacPherson twins, mind fan they let on ti thir faither they wis jist gingin til the fitba? An we took them up thir wi a puckle bottles o yer Da's hame brewed wine we'd sneckit fae his sheid?"

"Heh, heh. That wis some Setterda efterneen, recht eneuch." Sye smiled and then his brow furrowed. "Ye daa hink thir in trouble, dae ye? Ian A mean. An Willie tae. Pair Rae canna be very pleased, seein how she's jist lately flitted back."

"Yer recht thir. Her an Izzie's mountin a campaign. The hing's got the pair o wis bamfeezelt. Ian's aye been a recht normal laddie—aye in boather, but nae boather ava, if ye get ma meaning. It gies me the willies the wey he's cheenged, and that suddint, like. Somehin's gie'd the pair o thum a fleg, but naebody kens fit. Izzie pit the thumbscrews oan Ian lest necht, an ye ken fit? Monda necht the pair o thum wis awa up seein the meenistur. Ian an Willie tae."

"The meenistur? By it must be serious." He chuckled. "Fit's Rae sayin till't?"

Peem gave him a long look, and then shrugged. "A thocht ye

mecht tell me. Izzie an her's gingin oot fur a drink the necht ti talk aboot it. Weel, no jist that, ken. Hen necht. Us leds'll hivtae look oot fur wirsels."

"Jess lookin efter the tribe?"

"Naa, A'll bide in wi thum. A'm fair forfochent, this week, wi aa the capers wiv been intil. But cry roon, if ye like. Will hae a dram an a bit blaw efter the bastes is beddit fur the necht."

Sye nodded. "We'll see fit wey it gings." His gaze had turned to the northmost limit of the beach, and he seemed to be thinking about something. "Here, how no the pair o wis awa up thir recht noo an hae wursels a wee deek? Y'game?"

"Hae a deek? Fit at?"

"Wir auld cave. Youse *are* puggilt."

Peem laughed and drained his can. "D'ye hink we'll still be able ti get intil't?"

"Ach, yer no that stiff, ur ye? It's aa that guid grub Izzie gies ye." Sye poked Peem in the belly.

It did not take them long to clatter their way across the pebble beach to where Auchpinkie Ness pushed stubbornly out into the sea. At the top of the beach, just in the corner, if you like, was a deep cleft. A few well worn treads and handholds led vertically up this cleft for some little way, before the climber came out on a ledge about twelve feet above the beach. And here it became clear that there was more to the place than met the eye from below. For once on high you could see that the cliff was split; that is to say, there was a mighty leaf of rock, which had certainly been the wall of a tall and narrow cave whose roof had long since fallen in, to the right of the path, and to the left the cliff face itself. From the beach it was quite impossible to guess that there was a path at all, since the cliff appeared entirely homogeneous. A few paces along this narrow rocky passage and Sye and Peem arrived at the entrance to that little grotto known as Smuggler's Cave.

"Ye daa suppose thir in aboot thir, div ye?" hissed Sye as they approached. "A mind A'd a been recht fashed gin A'd thocht the grownups kent aboot this pliss."

"Naa. Ian's mowin his nan's green wi thon auld haund mower. He'll be at it for oors yet."

"Mowin the green? By A niver thocht hings wis that bad." Sye pushed past the gorse and then stopped. "See thon?" he said, indicating the scorched saucer shaped hole in the path.

"Uhuh. A see hit. A daa like it, but A see hit." Peem nodded his head slowly.

Sye led the way into the cave, backwards. It took him a while, for he had forgotten the nuances and twists of the passage, and also, to be fair, because he was too big. Peem followed him, scraping and puffing a little. If Sye was too long for the cave, Peem's trouble was girth, for though he was not exactly fat, he had the comfortable belly of the well fed married man. Once inside the inner chamber, Sye had to stoop sharply to avoid smashing his skull off the roof, though Peem could— only just— stand up.

It took a few moments for their eyes to adjust to the soft amber gloom of the cave and then they had a good look round.

"Hisnae cheenged ony ava!" Peem grinned in delight, his worries entirely swamped by the flood of memory. "By we hud some times here. Look," he added, picking up Hamish the spider in his jam-jar. "D'ye mind how I kept thum an aa? I'll gie ye a pund tae a penny it's Ian's"

"Wisna jist ettercaps wi youse," retorted Sye. "Ye had aa sorts up here."

"Aye, A aye liked ti hiv animals. Mind A hud a wee toddie?"

"Div A no jist! By, thon wis some guff. An ye had a futret but naebody tellt ye it wis a male. Thon near stank wis oot an aa." Sye looked around. "Here, they've got the pliss recht nice done oot, like. E'en got an ermchair." He was tired of banging his head and the constant stoop made his neck ache, so he sat down in it. The structure creaked ominously.

"Steady on, youse. A ken fit yer like wi furniture. The last thing we want ti dae is wreck the pliss." Peem continued prowling. "Ah-hah! Fit hiv we here?" he cried at last. He picked up a paper bag that had been hidden behind a pile of driftwood and let out a noise like a kettle coming to the boil, which was his version of a whistle. "Noo wid ye no jist ken it?"

"Fit is hit?" Sye held out his hand and Peem handed him the bag. "Sojum Klor-e-ate. By thir no intil at ur they?" Then he remembered the hole outside the entrance. "The wee buggers jist is, ye ken. That's jist fit thir intil. Pair o whittericks."

Peem put down the empty sugar bag he had discovered in the same place. "Ye ken fit? Mind fan you cam round fur a dram efter ye hud yon run-in wi Geordie Baird? The pair o wis got bleezin fou an we wis swappin the crack? D'ye no mind fit wey ye wis jaain oan aboot thon day fan we near got wirsels roasted alive ettlin ti burrin wir nims intil the gress at Arbeg links? Weel, A'll bet ye a pund tae a penny that thon wee rascal hud his lug at the keyhole aa the time. Wait till A catch him!"

Sye slapped his thigh and roared with mirth. "Fit ur ye gingin ti say, min? Daa dae as A dae, dae as A tell ye? Ye'll sound jist like yer Ma done an he'll heed ye jist as much."

"A maun be gettin auld." Peem could not help laughing, and rubbed his face wi his hands. "Yer recht eneuch." Suddenly a thought hit him. "Here ye daa suppose that it wis them that.......Ye ken.......The cludge..."

"Get real, min. Thon wisnae a wee hamemade squib. B'Christ there wis bits o cludgie landit up the Coastguard hooses. An besides it wis on the telly it wis a freak build up o ges done it. Ye tellt me yersel." He grinned. "An like A said, Boab wis aye fu' o ges."

Doubtfully, Peem shook his head. "Mebbe it wisnae them blawed the pliss up but A'm damned shair thir's somehin gingin on. Thir ower much o a coeencidunce, an A'm gingin ti hae it oot wi the wee tykes an find oot fit."

"Ach, tae hell, min, if it maks ye feel better, ging aheid. But yon cludge wis the biggest eyesore this side o the Owergate in Dundee, an it wis high time some bugger blawed it up. If it wis them done it they done us aa a favour. An as for Boab, it wisnae like he hudnae hud a fair kick o the baa, like."

"A jalouse yer recht," said Peem, and squatted down cross-legged on the palliasse. He put his hand into his inside pocket and drew out his leather tobacco-pouch.

"Hell, aye," grinned Sye after a few moments, leaning back in the chair despite its creaks of protest. He laughed. "Div A mind o that efterneen!"

"Fit efterneen?" Peem licked the paper of his roll-up.

"Yon efterneen! Wi the MacPherson twins."

"Oh, aye. Yon efterneen. Fit wey could ye disremember? Did ye ken Alexa wis in politics noo, be the wey?"

"G'aff."

"Aye. Izzie bumped intae the ither een—fit's she cried—Christine—Chris afore she got wad—no lang syne. She's married on a lawyer in Montrose, y'ken. Seems Alexa's a Cooncillor i the Labour Perty ower on the West Coast somewey." He lit up and inhaled deeply.

"Weel done her. She wis aye the gallus een, I'll gie her that."

"No half. D'ye mind how they missed the bus thon day an auld MacPherson—by, he wis a crabbit auld scunner, so he wis—hud ti come ower fae Carmyllie in his spleet-new motor ti pick the pair o thum up an hurl thum hame?"

"It's no the motor A mind, it's the wey Alexa got i the back o it. Mind o the mini-dresses the pair o them hud oan?"

"They drauchty eens that only jist cleared the fud? Aa the lassies hud them then."

"Ally's that lang, an aa. It wis a fell peety she'd niver figgered oot fit wey ti get intil a motor discreet, like. Specially fan she wis teeterin aboot on they fower-inch heels wi a guid skelp o Da's hame brew inside her."

"Aye, they great lang shanks o hers wis aa ower the pliss— jist like they hud been aa efterneen."

"An auld buggerlugs MacPherson wis birlit roon in his seat ti gie her a row, and crivvens did he no jist get an eyefu! D'ye mind on his puss?"

"Trust thon skellie bitch ti lave her scanties in her haunbeg!" Peem laughed and shook his head. "By, did A iver catch it thon day. A niver had a hammerin like at in aa ma days fae Ma."

Sye was laughing too. "Da hud me bleck an blue. Fegs A thocht he wid kill me. He wis that feared MacPherson wis gingin ti get wis the jile." He reflected fondly for a moment, and smiled. "Mind you, A'm no sayin it wisnae worth the hidin, like." He chuckled.

"Ah, come on, Sye, we wis jist siventeen." His eyes shone as the recall of distant pleasure warmed him. "Christ fan ye think on't tho' we didnae haulf tak some chances. We niver thocht twice. It wis aye a simple question o how in the hell wis ye gingin ti get eneuch time wi'oot yer folks or teachers or wee brithers an sisters tae eckchelly *manage* ti dae hit. An the lassies wis jist as gallus as we wis. Maist o thum. D'ye mind the boather ye hud ti git yer hauns on some Frenchies? Sneakin intae pub cludgies an half the time the bluidy machine wis brak an ye tint yer siller an it gied ye sweet Fanny Adams. Aye, aabody wis at it aa recht."

Sye nodded and cast his mind over twenty years of borderline living that intervened. "Aye, at's recht eneuch. It wis aye wis that got landed wi the blame, fittiver it wis fur. Mind, it's niver got bad eneuch yet at A've thocht o gie'n up an livin clean, like."

"That's jist cos youse daa hae bairns. Youse can div fit ye like cos the only bugger at'll iver miss ye is yon collection o spare perts ye cry a dug. High time you got yersel hitched an fund oot fit life's really like, boy." Peem was wagging his finger as he spoke. "Life's no aa jist ersin aboot, ye ken. It's *serious*." The thought was too much and he burst out laughing again. When he stopped he folded his arms and stretched out his legs. "Ach Sye, fan A hink o the cantrips we yased ti get intil, A daa hauf get fashed aboot Ian."

"Here, daa start gettin aa thon wey again!" exclaimed Sye. "We wis jist normal healthy laddies fu o bedness an foriver in the scrapes, an so's Ian. Soonds ti me like he's hud a wee bit fleg, but you look me in the ee an tell me youse niver got a fleg fan you wis thon age. Jings! D'ye no mind the day we sneckit thon new-fangled lawnmower ye could sit on fae the school jannie fan he wis awa haein his piece an ye wis cloonin aroon like yaseyell an sat on the haunlebars an fell aff afore hit? By Christ it's a wunner ye didnae shite yersel. The damned thing had yer spleet-new skale blazer minced inti shreds an wis jist gettin roon tae youse afore auld Smiler MacKechnie cid git in thir an turn it aff til ye. Hell's bells, an Smiler wis at couthie, ken—didna stop him gein wis a hammerin tho."

"A'd clean forgot thon een. A daa blame Smiler, like, we wis meant ti be daein sport but he'd let wis aff as yaseyell ti ging til the snooker jist sae lang's wi got him twenty Gold Leaf or fittiver it wis he reeked—"

"Players."

"Fittiver, the pair bugger kent fine he'd be for the high jump gin the Beak fund oot fit wis gingin oan. Christ he musta near shat himsel fan he come oot fur a quick reek an seen yon hing ettlin ti turn me intil respberry jeely." Peem laughed and shook his head. "An wis aa at boather no jist ower the heid o some quines wi wis efter a bit houghmagandie wi?" Peem stretched again and put his hands behind his head. He sighed. "Fit *wis* yon lassie's nim again? A cin see her noo. Ach, disnae metter— it wis a lang time syne." He lapsed into reverie and then returned to the subject at hand. "Yer recht, though," he said, his voice serious again. "Either A skelp Ian the wey Ma done me or Eck done you, or A figger oot somehin else. Heh, heh. An even supposin we wis wild— still are, mebbe— it didnae kill wis. No yet onywey."

Sye nodded and crossed his ankles. His hands were stuffed deep into his jeans pockets. "Peem," he said, after a pause. "Fittin the hell are we gingin ti dae wi aa they bluidy fush? A cannae herdly get in the front door o ma hoose fur the guff o thum. Wi canny jist gie thum ti the cats, an naebody's ony room left i thir freezer."

Peem stuck his chin forward and scratched it reflectively through his wispy beard. It was a poser and no mistake. He had to admit that all that his friend had said was true; the salmon wouldn't sell, and the smoking took too long. He thought for a while. This question of the salmon was indeed a tricky problem. A flash of genuine inspiration was required. They needed to get rid of the surplus fish, and neither of them could thole the thought of giving them to the cats or throwing them back into the sea. Not Salmons. Not after all that bother. But how? Suddenly he grinned. "Foo no let's hae a wake?" he said at last, with the air of a man inspired.

"A fit?"

"Fur Boab. A wake for Boab. A recht, auld farrant wake wi jiggin an aa that. Ken, a real blaa-oot."

"No mean *blaa-up*? Awa. Yer aff yer nutt." Sye's tone was mocking but Peem could tell he was interested.

"Aye A ken but at disnae mak it a bed idear."

"True. Be a kinda queer wake; he's nae faimly, has he? A mean, he's nae bairns, like. He niver wad. His old fowks deed lang afore Da wis born. A mean fa wid be the pallbearers?" Sye dug into his jacket pockets and pulled out two cans of Tennents. He opened one and passed the other to Peem, who nodded.

"Aye," he said, cracking it open. "A believe he did hiv brithers but they wis baith killed i the First War. An thir was aiblins a puckle o sisters but thir lang gone an aa. But the hing is, y'see, aabody kent him that bluidy weel. A mean he'd *aye* been thir. As a metter o fect a hink near aabody in the village is related ti the auld scunner some wey or anither. It wid be like fur aabody. We could draa straes fur the pallbearers, an y'see, the beauty o hit is, we can gie thum aa the salmon fur thir denner. See? Solves aa wir problems. Gets rid o aa they bluidy fish an we aa get a rare shindig ootin hit. Magic idear."

"Aye aye," mused Sye, who was warming to it. He liked a party, did Sye, and a wake is just a party where the guest of honour arrives already dead. Which is fine because at least you can be sure he'll not take the huff half way through. "Mebbe. But far'll we hae it? An fa the blazes is gingin till organise hit? "

"Likely we'll end up daein the organisin wirsels, jist like aahin else aboot here," grinned Peem. "But we cid get Ma an your Ma an thir pals tae muck in. An we'll hae it in the Hotel, acoorse."

"Agnes mecht hae somehin ti say aboot at."

"Daa youse worry aboot Aggie. See, A'll work on Ma, an youse work on Nan, an the pair o them'll get Morag an Mae on thir side, an the hale fower o them'll talk Agnes intil hit in nae time ava. She'll no hae ony chyce onywey, cos o the bar takins, which A jalouse'll be no an inconseederable sum, like. Even if Agnes is switherin, Divvy's ower grippit tae let thon pass."

"Aye, well A jalouse at mecht work, gin we can get the auld besoms ti lave aff yappin aboot aabody else lang eneuch."

"Aye, an Iz wid help," continued Peem, well into his stride. "She'll hink it's a grand idear. She'll get ti dazzle the hale village. A suppose A'll hae ti shell oot fur a new set o duds, mind— but fit the hell, it's in a guid cause, an A hiv til admit she kens fit wey tae pit on, does ma Iz. Here, A wunner if A cid talk her inti gie'in wis a bit sang? A niver heard onybody sing *The Skye Boat Song* like her. It'd be worth a new pair o they damned gowd earrings. We'll need ti get somebody tae play the piana tae. Fit aboot Uncle Gus?—he likes a good ceilidh. An we can get Tam Teviot ti dae the fiddlin an Chae Robb cin come ower fae Arbeg wi his squeezebox—he's still got the magic touch, ye ken, even if he is gettin a kinda fell lang in the tooth. The pair o them wis aye pals wi Boab. An Young Chae plays the drums, dis he no? By it'll be jist dandy! A can see hit noo. Here A wonder if Muckle Mel's got his pipes still? He yased ti be a rare piper, Mel. Yased ti win competitions at the skale. Mebbe we could get him ti dust them aff an gie wis a skirl. An you an R—" He stopped and looked at Sye. There was a long silence.

"Me an fa wid dae fit?"

"Ah, c'mon, Sye, am A no yer best mucker?" Peem's eyes were soft and appealing. "Hiv we no been intil mair scrapes than hauf a dozen ither fowk pit thegither? Hiv we no been roon the globe thegither an got drunk thegither in maist o the ports on the wey, no ti mention samplin the local talents thegither an gettin flung in the caboose thegither? Jeez, Sye, ye kin let on ti me. A'll no let on til a sowl."

"Fit's aa that ti dae wi the price o munce? Ye wis aboot ti say me an Rae wid dae somehin, wis ye no?" There was anger in Sye's eyes.

Peem looked hurt. "A wis jist gingin ti say youse an Rae could organise the jiggin. Ye yased ti be recht guid at hit the pair o yiz. A mind fan A wis courtin Izzie an we yased ti ging ti the ceilidhs in Forfar—the hale fower o wis in thon auld Jag ye hud then wi the exhaast that wis furiver drappin aff—youse twa wis aye the star couple at the jiggin. Ken me an Iz aye thocht—" Peem stopped, sensing that he'd gone too far. "Sye, A didnae mean ti fash ye, honest. Daa mind me; ye ken fit wey fan A git cerried awa like at ma mooth gings intil owerdrive wi the harns still i neutral."

Sye shook himself. Why was he being so touchy? "Sorry. A didnae mean ti bite yer heid aff. It's jist—look, Peem, thir naehin gingin on atween me an Rae. Wir jist freens. Thon's the wey she wants it, an at's fine be me." Only the swishing echo of the sea broke the silence that followed. Then Sye smiled. "But the idear o a wake, ma loon, is definitely a winner. C'way we'll awa up the village an see if we canna drum up a bit support."

CHAPTER TWENTY-SIX
Iz And Rae Hit The Town

There had always been a good measure of competition in Iz and Rae's friendship, which gave it a nice edge, so it will be no surprise that when Iz phoned Rae on the Wednesday to suggest a Hen Necht the following evening, the first time the pair of them had been out together for a very long time, Rae—who knew Iz well enough to know what she'd be planning—spent a lot of time thinking about what she'd wear. It gave her a tingly feeling that she hadn't had in years, and you'd have thought the plan was to hit the ritziest of Glasgow clubs rather than the lounge bars of Arbeg. A thorough overhaul of her wardrobe was soon effected. Rae knew that the order of battle would be risqué, with bells on, and she selected a navy blue woollen number that clung to her like glue and she hadn't dared to wear in years, with a roll neck and long sleeves. You got the impression that the designer had taken the cloth for the sleeves from the bit below the danger zone, because there was that little of it left. But then Rae was very proud of her legs. Add jacket, black shoes and some simple but strategically placed jewellery (Rae knew it was pointless competing with Iz there) and she was ready for anything.

Where Rae was tall and angular and dark, Iz was smaller and very fair of skin and built for comfort. She was curvy to say the least, with curves on her curves and dimples on top of those, and tight clothes were not for her. She went for the flowing look, and tonight she was in grey with cleavage and large quantities of gold. She looked Rae up and down appraisingly and nodded when they met outside in response to the taxi honking its horn. Arbeg had better watch out.

Some hours later the pair of them were perched on stools by the bar in the upstairs lounge of the Queen's; very sophisticated (for Arbeg) with quiet soul music and dim lights and a barman who knew how to make real cocktails—something of a rarity in this town—and the Gin Martinis were slipping down just a treat, so they were. On the way here they had passed through the town's only Italian restaurant—I mean sit down restaurant; there were plenty of fish and chip shops still run by the Latins— where they had bantered with the staff in fine style. A certain warm glow had settled over the pair, and the conversation was tending towards the confidential and sisterly. They had a lot of ground to cover, after all; twelve years is a long time out of anyone's life. And they had been busy years.

"You seem tae hiv got jist what ye wanted," mused Rae, in a quiet moment. "Peem's still daft about ye and the kids are great."

"Me? Och aye. A've still niver gotten ma villa i the sooth o France, but A suppose thir time yet. Need ti get at man o mine workin herder. But A ken fit ye mean. Bein married tae the Sex Fiend o the Western Hemisphere does hae its advantages. Sae lang's ye like at kinda hing." She pouted. "An A *love* it." She giggled. "Naa, the hing aboot Peem is A can read him like a buik. But A manage ti bamfeezle him still. Heh, heh. S'great." She swivelled round on her stool to look at Rae. "Can A let ye intil a secret, hon?"

"Whit?"

Iz smiled. She was definitely tipsy, but then so was Rae, and a lot more than she had been for a while. "A aye wanted ti look like ye. Wi yer hair. Y've got great hair, youse. An yer banes. An yer tan. Yon waiter wis recht teen wi ye."

"Ah, c'mon, Iz. Ye ken fine he jist noticed A dinnae hae a weddin ring. An you—yer the maist glamorous female A ken."

"Aye, but mines aa comes ootin a bottle. Expensive een, like, but still a bottle. Yours is natchral. Ye wis aye the guid-luikin een." This was not quite true; Iz was by any standard a good-looking woman, something she knew fine well, but it suited her mood to play it down.

"Bet ye daa git fehve-o-clock shadae fae yer cuits tae yer fud if ye daa shave yer shanks ivery ither day, though," giggled Rae, relaxing into the Scots she had grown up speaking, but had self-consciously begun to hide in order to please a succession of englified Edinburgh employers. The drink was certainly shaking out some dusty old memories tonight. Iz hooted with laughter, and waved her finger at the barman. "Ooh, he's affy bonny, him," she whispered. "See if A wis on the hunt, A'd......" She stopped. "Oh, eh, two more of your very fine Gin Martinis, barman." She stifled a giggle. "Ah hope ti hell he wisnae listenin."

"Whit wid ye dae onywey?"

"Daes a favour, Rae, an daa let on ye've lost mind o't." Iz narrowed her eyes. "Here, fan wis," she giggled and leaned forward and her grey blue eyes sparkled with mischief. "When *was* the lest tahme you got laid, dahling?"

Rae blushed. "Izzie! Hiv a hert! He's luikin ower here!"

"Daa mind him. He's jist servin drinks. He's a barman. He hears worse'n this ivery necht o the week. Naa, c'mon, tell us. Fan? Youse let on til yer big sister nou."

"No!" Rae giggled. "A mean, no lang syne."

"Fan wis at, like?" persisted her tormentor, her blue-grey eyes sparkling.

"Och, Iz, A daa ken—"

"*At lang?* Really? Jeez, hon, at's, at's jist *awfy!*"

"But A've no tellt ye yet!" protested Rae.

"Ye daa hae till. Onybody cannae mind the last time his been hingin aboot ower lang aaready."

Suddenly Rae looked very sad. Izzie stopped laughing and her hand reached out. "Daa mind me, lass. Ah didnae mean tae.........ye ken. Ye ken A widna hurt ye."

Rae touched the hand. "Whit is it wi youse? Fit wey is it ye can get at close at quick? Naebody else can dae it. Ma mither couldnae—no iver, no e'en when A wis a wee bit lassie. Ma Da, he cid dae it, but A daa mind much o him nou. He deed that lang syne. But you— A hivnae seen ye in ower ten—"

"Try twal."

"Okay, twal year...... An here twa weeks later ye ken hings aboot me A even hide fae masel! Fit wey kin ye dae that? Hiv ye got the segint secht or somethin?"

"Naa, A daa hae at, quine. Thank God, if thir is een. A daa need ti ken fit's stored up fur me. A daa want tae. Naa." She thought for a moment. "Ken somehin, Rae, the twa o wis is good an pished noo, so fittiver we say's no gingin ti coont fur naehin the morn's morn. But see when ye buggered aff like thon—Christ A thocht A'd niver forgie ye. Ye hurt me mair'n onybody has iver hurt me afore or syne. Ye wis sib til a wee sister ti me aa they years—an then *Paf!* Disappeared. Wi no even a notey for a cheerio."

"A'm affa sorry, Iz—"

"Daa interrup, hon. A ken fit wey ye done it, so it's aa recht. It took me lang eneuch, but A figgered it oot. See, Peem was i the Merch they days, an A *hated* hit. A could niver staun aa they months on ma lane. An A hud ti thole Jess bidin next door—tell ye, we hud some battles afore she got the message ti bide affa ma patch. An yer mither, she wis twa door doon the ither wey. A tell ye A hud a hale heap o lang nechts hinkin aboot fit wey the twa fowk A luved the best was at lang awa fae me. A widnae like ti ging through thon again, A tell ye. An niver e'en a wee notey. Fit did ye hink? A'd klipe on ye til yer Ma? Tell her far ye'd joukit awa til?"

"No. Niver." Rae's voice was breathless. Somehow she had known that this moment would come, sooner or later; but it didn't make it any easier. "A jist wanted ti forget everythin. A wis that happy here. An then, efter, everythin was that bad—A couldnae staun it, Izzie, A jist couldnae. Ivery time A thought of you, or Peem, or Auchpinkie, A jist wantit tae greet an greet. An A hud a bairn tae luik efter. A had tae be strang. An ivery time A thocht on ye, aa the wee bit strength A'd built up went awa fae me. A'm sorry."

"A ken. A ken ye are, or A'd no be here with ye the necht, tellin ye foo muckle A luve ye, ye ken. A daa dae this wi aabody."

"But ye dinnae ken *how* A left, Iz."

"Aye A div. Ye daa need tae tell me. A ken fine." Iz' voice was quiet, and there was a strange darkness in it that Rae didn't like.

"But no *really* ye dinna."

"Aye really A *dae.*" Izzie looked hard into Rae's eyes and Rae realised that the heart-to-heart was about to get a lot more intimate than she wanted, and that it was her fault for not backing off earlier. Izzie laughed, shortly. "God youse are some gallus, so ye are. Onybody'd hae ti gie ye that."

"Comin back, ye mean?" Rae sounded a bit hurt.

"Aye that. But no jist comin back. Thon ither hing tae. Tell me, dis it no occur ti ye that yer no bein jist entirely jonick?"

"Fit wey dae ye mean? Fa til?"

"A mean til aabody."

Rae's voice was suddenly quiet now. "Fit dae ye mean, Iz?"

"Ken, youse cin be recht like yer mither at joukin questions whiles. A'd watch at." Iz took a big swallow of the rocket fuel. "Listen, hon, daa you imagine for een meenit that A'm at much smerter'n the rest o the fowk at neen o them'll click. It'll tak them longer, cos they daa ken ye the wey A div. But thill get thir fur aa that. Thill figure oot this story aboot fit wey ye gaed awa til Embro on a whim—like ye iver did ocht on a whim—an got yersel bairned be the first boy at cockit his laig ower ye is nuthin but a pack o lees. Then fit ur ye gingin ti dae?"

"It's no lees ava. It's the truth!"

"It bluidy is *nutt*. Jeez, daa act like A'm gyte. Tell us, fan wis the lest time ye had a shag? Hm? A lassie wi yer looks, yer harns, aa that ye've got an thir no a man i secht. Nou, at could mean een o twa hings, an if it's the first een A'll awa an be a nun." Iz stopped herself and thought a moment. "Naa, scratch at last wee bit. Onywey, this is the lassie at's supposed ti hae drappit her draaers fur the first likely loon at glimmered at her? Dae me the courtesy, eh? A'm no that daft, an ye weel ken." Iz had been looking at her glass, and she flashed a glance up at her friend, and for the first tie Rae saw a flash of deep, dark anger. "You didnae lave Auchpinkie ti ging an drap yer draaers up some close an get yersel bairned. You left because ye wis *aaready* on yer road. Recht?" Iz stopped. Tears had started from her eyes.

"Aiblins A hinny got the segint secht, but A'm no blin, ye ken!" Suddenly Iz grabbed her coat and rushed out, leaving Rae speechless.

"Thir a problem?" asked the barman, solicitously

Izzie had not gone far. From the door of the bar Rae could see her. She was heading towards the taxi-rank with her arms crossed and her head down. Rae ran—well, after the fashion of a woman wearing four-inch heels with half a bottle of wine and several gin martinis in her—after her, her footfalls echoing along the street ahead. She ran in front of the other woman and stopped. "Iz! Hud up!"

Izzie stopped abruptly and glared at her. "Listen, A ken fit happened! A ken. A tellt ye, A had a wheen time on ma lane ti figure it oot. Fan wis it? Afore me and Peem wis wad? No that it metters, like. A'd jist like ti ken fan, so A'd ken whether it wis ma husband or jist ma fiancee at shagged ma best freen." She pushed past Rae, who was clean dumbfounert. No other word for it. "Daa fash yersel, hon, A'll be fine the morn," she hissed through her teeth. Rae had to stride quickly to keep up with her.

"That's how ye niver wrote!" Iz went on, between bleating little sobs. "Ye wis ower guilty. Weel, A tell ye, Rae, A forgied ma man. An a thocht A'd forgied youse, an aa, an it's jist the drink on me talkin. Aahin'll be fine the morn, daa fash yersel." She stopped and turned to Rae, her eyes flashing. "But ti tell ye the truth A would, really, really like ti ken *how* ye done a hing like at ti me."

"Izzie! That's *eneuch!*" exclaimed Rae, in total exasperation now. This farce had gone far enough. "Me and Peem! Peem an *me*? Jesus, Izzie, daa be bluidy *ridiculous!* In the name o the wee mannie it wisnae Peem *it wis Sye!*" Whereupon Rae howled and burst into hysterical sobbing herself and buried her face in her hands.

Izzie's mouth dropped open. She ettled to speak, but nothing came out, and her mouth just opened and shut like a goldfish. She swayed slightly, and then sat down quickly on a low wall at the edge of the pavement. "Fittdye say," she whispered at last. "A mean at last hing ye said. Say it again."

Rae looked up and gasped. Tears were streaming down her face and big, hard sobs were shaking her slender frame. "It wis *Sye*, Iz. It wis Sye. It wis yer big brither. A—Izzie A've kent Peem aa my life; A hink he's a fine lad an great company, but A niver, iver fancied him. It wis *Sye*. It wis aye Sye an naebody else."

Izzie swallowed hard. "Bastart! But A *tellt* him no tae lay a finger on ye! An onywey, how did ye—here, how did ye cry yer laddie Willie, then? Hm? Tell us? How did ye dae at?"

"For ma *faither*, Iz. No for Peem. A *promise* ye A wid niver hiv........." Rae struggled to get a grip on herself, teetered on her heels and sat down on the wall beside Iz. "It wis on yer waddin necht, gin ye must ken aahin." She sniffed and pulled a hanky out of her bag. "It wis real romantic, Iz. Really. Mind at Sye wis Peem's best man an A wis the Maid o Honour? Well, A gied masel tae him that necht. See, afore that we wis only thegither cos o youse twa. We really *wis* jist freens. Actually we wisnae even at." Rae shook her head miserably. "A wis aye jist the daft wee lassie dragged alang tae mak up the fowersome 'cos Peem wid niver ging onywhere wi'oot Sye an onywey Sye wis keepin an ee on fit youse twa wis up tae. But he acted—Christ he acted like he wis *ma* bluidy big brither." She sniffed hard. "A've had plenty time tae hink aboot it, an A hink it wis cos he wis that much older than me; A mean, it disnae seem much noo, but fan A wis saxteen an he was twinty-three—ye ken. He aye acted jist like he wis ma big brither. Kinda like he felt *responsible* fur me. Hud tae luik efter me so's A didnae get in boather. But at wisnae what A wanted." She grinned weakly at Iz. "An *nou* ye tell me ye'd tellt him tae lay aff? Thanks a bunch, like."

"By, mony's the necht A've greeted masel tae sleep for the want o somebody tae luik efter me syne—but onywey, that necht A gied him aa A had tae gie. A wisnae takin nae refusal fae him that necht! Ach, we'd baith had ower muckle drink, an youse an Peem wis jist wad an A wis rotten jealous o ye—Jeez ye were a bonny bride—an A jist decided A'd waited lang eneuch an A wis gingin tae have him an at wis at. An—an it wis jist lovely, Iz, so it wis. We did it up on the tap o the Ness an aa the starns wis oot– Oh, A mind o they stars shinin thon wey; A've niver seen....." Rae stopped and dabbed her eyes again. "Onywey A jist dragged him up there; A wis gingin ti hae him an nae nonsense—ma mind wis made up, an A gart him dae hit. He'd nae choice ava. Ach, Iz, ye see, there wis youse in yer bridal suite an A wanted Sye inside me *that necht*. Thir wis naebody else A kent wis hauf the man he wis. A they loons at the skale an i the village—jist daft wee laddies, aa o thum. But Sye wis— he wis a *man*, see. A real man, no a laddie playin at bein a man.

"A really really wanted him. A luved him. At least, A hink A did. Gin he'd asked, A'd hae wad him the next again day, but fit does he dae instead? The bastart pissed aff ti Rio-de-bluidy-Janeiro an niver a word. An twa weeks later A missed ma monthly. An nae use me talkin tae ma mither; she'd a jist showed me the door onywey an gied me dog's abuse forbye. She'd aye sayed at's fit she'd dae gin A got masel bairned afore A wis wad. It wis ony the eence, tae. Jeez, thir's weemin canny get awa for luve nor money, an A spread ma legs *eence* and whoops-a-daisy an at wis me. So A took masel so's she'd nae the satisfaction. Whit wid youse hae done?"

"Lemme get this strecht," said Izzie, speaking very slowly, and tapping the fingers of her left hand with the index of her right as she made her points. "A've been haein waukrife nechts fur twal year wunnerin fit him at A wad an youse got intil, an aa that while it wis thon great muckle lunk o a brither o mines that A'd tellt tae keep his paas aff ye? Hiv A got that recht noo?" She shook her head. "Jings, Isabel, for a smert cookie yiz can be some thick whiles." She looked round at Rae, who was greeting pedal to the metal again, and flung her arms round her. "Aw, hon A'm that sorry. Please forgive me. It's jist—me an Peem cam back fae wir honeymoon an Sye'd shipped an you'd lit oot—A didna ken fit tae hink."

"It's aa recht, it's aa recht. It's jist at bluidy *gin*. Fer Chissake it aye does this ti me an A shid ken better." Rae rallied herself. "Fit wid youse hiv done, Iz? Eh?"

"A daa ken. A'm some gled A wis niver at stuck. But it mecht hae been a better idear til ask me then an no wait till nou."

"A ken. But A wis that jeelous o ye bein married. No o Peem— A mean, like A sayed, A like Peem fine, but he wis niver fur me. It wis jist youse bein married. A niver thocht A'd be jeelous, but A wis. An then when Sye shipped like thon it wis worse. A felt like a skellie wee lassie that had gotten hersel in boather an you wis a wiselike married wumman. It wis like ye'd been cheenged, suddintly. A couldna e'en bring masel ti spik tae ye aboot it. An A've niver iver felt that stupit in a ma puff. We wisnae like we wis afore, twa lassies that tellt een anither aahin, ony mair."

"Yer no noo, A hope. Jeelous, A mean." Iz smiled cheerfully and smeared her eye-liner with the back of her hand. "And ye *can* tell me aahin. In fect, ye'd bluidy better."

"No, A'm no jeelous, an A kin see A wis skellie. But A wis aye skellie, ye ken," replied Rae with a crooked smile. They both laughed, and Izzie fell against Rae's shoulder. Then they looked at each other and grat again. A while later, Iz recovered herself. "Ah, see that *gin*—Jeez it's deadly so it is. A aye end up greetin ma heid aff wi it. Or hysteerical. Or the baith." She wiped her eyes, with her hanky this time.

"Tha's better," she went on. "Hings is aye better wi a bit greet. But Rae, Rae, *Rae*—fit'n the hell wis ye hinkin? Did ye no hink ti yase somehin? A mean, me an Peem didnae hing aboot till wi wis wad, like, but A aye made damned shair ti tak precautions. Did ye no think o yasin— ye ken—een o they hings?"

"A Frenchie? He got een fae the machine in the Hotel but it luiked at feechie A wouldna lave him yase it. A didnae want ma first time tae be wi a feechie horrible bit rubber hing like thon onywey. A wantit *him*. It wis *contact* A wis efter. A didnae want *onyhin* atween me an him. Nuthin. Jist him. An aahin he'd tae gie me an aa. A ken fine it wis a daft hing ti dae, so daa chiz me aboot it."

"Skelly besom. Ye wis aye ower romantic, and did A niver tell ye it'd land ye in boather? But yer recht aboot Etta showin ye the door. She aye hatit Sye like the pox. Mind, she didnae ken yer condeetion."

"Mebbe she had reason tae hate him. Mebbe she kent he'd ging an dae somehin like thon." Rae's bottom lip was trembling and no matter how hard she tried she couldn't stop it; the quiet of the evening was broken by her wails yet again.

Izzie petted her and soothed her. "Rae, Rae, daa be soor. D'ye no ken fit wey it wis e'en yet? Sye got his Mate's berth. The first time he'd shipped as a Mate. Christ ye ken foo muckle he'd ettled fur it. An they tellt him ti be at the airport at Dyce in twa oors cos the ship had ti sail fae Rio the next again day an the recht mate had brak his laig. Hell, Rae, ye wis at the skale daein yer bluidy Highers. Fit wis he meant ti dae, drap by ti see ye—'Scaise, me, Miss, A hud the leg ower een o yer lassies lest necht an noo A've ti catch a plane tae Rio, d'ye hink A could hae a word wi her?' Come *oan*. Eck an Nan wis awa ti Torremolinos an me an Peem was awa wir hinnymune. An he'd a kent fine he couldnae lave a message wi Etta."

Rae blew her nose and nodded.

"An neist hing is we heard aa they stories fae Etta about youse gettin knockit up by some flee-bi-necht. It wis aa ower the village. Ye'd hink Etta'd want ti keep thon tae hersel, but no a bit o't."

"Ach but Iz; how did he no lave me a notey? Or send me a letter? Christ jist a postcerd fae Rio wid hae done. A hud nae wish tae be some sea-widda, Iz. A didnae want fowk gowkin at me an sayin there gings the lassie at's man shipped tae get awa fae her. An A didnae want onybody merryin me oot o peety, or cos o fit ither fowk sayed. Ye ken fit thir like in Auchpinkie aboot hings like at."

"Sye niver gie'd ye ony reason ti hink thon wey, hon."

"Fit dae ye cry hit then? Een necht o passion an the next again day he fucks aff? Am A missin somehin here?" Rae let out another pathetic wail and it was some moments before the conversation could continue.

"There, there. A daa ken, hon. Thir a side o Sye even A canna get close til. An he can be een o the maist thochtless glumphs A've iver kent. An the next meenit cherm ye again so's ye'd hink butter widnae melt in his mooth. Ye'll hae til ask him yersel." She paused. "Hae ye tellt him?"

Rae shook her head. Her eyes were closed and she bit her lip.

"Rae, ye'll hae ti let him ken. It's no fair."

"A'm feared."

"Fit o?"

"Him. Fit he'll say. And o me, too. Fit wey could A tell him? A wish A'd niver come back. Fit a mess. Oh, God, Iz..........A've hud ither men. But A gie'd up wi hit. It wisnae ony guid. D'ye no see? A *hud* ti come back. A didna *want* ti come back. A couldna bide awa. A didna want ti come back—och A made up aa kinds o reasons, A ken, but A didna want ti come back. A wis ower feared. But A *hud* tae. A imagined hings bein jist like they wis, but thir no. Jist pals again? Hah! Jist pals. God A'm a bluidy mug. O, Izzie, fit if he disnae care? A ken it's selfish, but's lang's he disnae ken mebbe we *can* jist be freens an it'll niver come tae the bit. Ye ken. But soon as he kens he'll hae ti choose. An A'll hae ti choose. An ye've nae *idear* how much that scares me. Aw, Izzie whit hiv A done? Whit am A gingin ti dae?"

"Noo daa stert up yon again or ye'll get me gingin an aa, an ma mak-up's aaready a disaster area. But yer recht, fur eence. Ye *are* in a bluidy mess." Iz paused and thought a moment. "But ye ken somehin, Sye's niver been really serious aboot onybody else. Och A ken he's had his leg ower a wheen lassies, an a puckle o thum e'en hung aboot wee whilies, but he couldnae fool me. An recht eneuch, sooner or later thi wis on thir way, like. Niver een o them at cid really get him interestet. A cid tell. Thi'd nae chance. Suin as he kent thi wis ettlin ti get hitched, that wis it, like. Ta ta."

"D'ye hink he wis serious aboot me?"

"Och, aye. That's how this hing's sicca guddle. A think he really wis serious aboot ye. If he hudnae been, then hou come he's been the wey he his aa these years? A mean some o they lassies his been fine eneuch quines, belave me. Ma brither's got guid taste an he's niver hud ony boather pullin weemin, amazin tho' it seems. Peety the pair o ye are sic canty buggers, cos A tell ye, yiz ur gingin ti hae til eat some humble pie whitiver happens, or else......."

"Or else?"

"Or else yiz lave the morn, flog the hoose an niver iver come back again *iver*. No muckle chyce, A ken, but that's it. Ye bide, an sooner or later it'll aa come oot i the dobie. An the langer it festers the worst it'll be i the end. Rae, A luve ye like ma wee sister, but A wid tell him masel if a thocht ye wid tak advantage. Sye's done naehin wrang—"

Rae gripped her arm tightly. "Ye widnae let on til him. Ye wid *nutt!*" Her voice and regard were so supplicating that Iz, who thought she'd gotten a hold of herself, began to bawl again.

"Nim o Christ Rae, yer jist efter tellin me Wullie's his *son!* He's *bound* ti finnd oot some time or anither *onywey*. Ye jist *cannae* keep a secret like at. Honest, luve. No furiver. An ye ken A widnae klipe on ye. A wisnae hinkin."

Rae's grip relaxed. "The bit o it is yer bluidy recht. Yer recht through an through an A *hate* it. How dae ye hiv tae be recht aboot aahin?"

"A'm no. But A'm recht aboot this. An fit aboot Willie?"

"A'm mair feared for him'n A am for masel, A hink. Pair wee scrap! A'm feared he finds oot an then somehin bad happens—fit would A dae then? That's why A thocht, if we could jist be freens........."

"God yer *gyte* youse. Widje jist kindly forgit this freens hing? Sye's quite capable o bein a freen, an a good een. But no tae *youse*. Youse ur jist a scaur at's gingin till itch at him till he picks it aff. An A canna really believe at's fit ye want, onywey." She hugged Rae again. "An be the wey, did ye ken thir aare#ready fowk in the village threipin thir somehin gingin on atween youse an Sye?"

"Fit? There is nutt! Fa's sayin at, Iz?"

"Ach nae doot the hing'll hae come fae yon rumour fectory itherwise kent as Auntie Mae's shop far yon bunch o interferin tongue-waggin bachles—ma mither an ma mither-i-laa includit—ettle ti arrange wir lives fur wis. But fit did ye expeck, hon? Ye cannae jist vanish ae fine day wi aa the siller ye'd saved up i yer Post Office accoont fae yer Setterda job an then turn up twal year later an naebody bats an ee. Git real, eh?" She shivered. "Look, it's gettin fell cauld an yon bit cloot ye've got on maun be lettin the drauchts whistle in aboot somehin sair. An aa this greetin's begood ti mak me drouthy agin. We cannae ging back in thir luikin like this, sae c'way we'll get wirsels a taxi back oot tae the village an hunker doon i the Hotel lounge an gnaw at the bane till it's recht clean. Then it's no sicca far stagger at flingin-oot time." She got to her feet and held out a hand to Rae.

"Iz, A've ti work the morn," protested Rae. She blew her nose hard and then pulled herself to her feet. "God, Izzie, they gin martinis are *lethal*. Maybe A shouldnae hae ony mair drink." Izzie put her arm through hers and steered her towards the taxi rank at the steeple. "Daa gie me at guff. This here is a Hen Necht, A'll mind ye. We hiv ti figger wirsels a wey ootin yer wee bit bother ye've got yersel intil. Youse jist lippen on yer big sissie. An onywey, A need ti talk tae ye aboot the bairns. Efter we've figgered oot fit we're gingin ti dae wi youse twa."

"Aye, well mebbe jist een wee white wine an sodae. But nae mair o that *bluidy gin!*"

"Ach tae hell, quine, A hinny had a recht greet in yonks. Taxi!"

CHAPTER TWENTY-SEVEN
Back to Mae's

In the foetid warmth of her post office and grocer shop, Mae was locked deep in conversation with her cronies. This meeting, which took place on the Friday morning, had two items on the agenda. Item one was the funeral reception for Lanky Boab. Sye had spoken to Nan the evening before, and Peem had chizzed Jess; and, as they had foreseen, their respective mothers took up the cudgels. But there was much to be done; in the first place, Agnes had to be persuaded to let the thing happen in the Hotel at all, and secondly she had to be convinced that they would eat the salmon, which was after all, the whole point of the affair. Agnes would have liked to have avoided this, because she knew it meant that she could not charge for the meal; she had not lived in Auchpinkie all these years without realising that any attempt to charge for preparing it was doomed from the off. However, and as our heroes had guessed, the thought of letting the bar-takings go elsewhere was the deciding factor since she knew damned fine that if she refused they would just hold it in somebody's byre and get pie-eyed on moonshine and supermarket beer. So, after much huffing and puffing, Agnes bent to the will of the village, and it was decided that the reception would be held at the Hotel at 1pm the following day. Boab's remains were due to be interred at 11.30, so that would give everyone time to get a couple of refreshers in before getting down to the serious business.

The other item on the agenda was of a far less mundane nature. The committee had to consider the unexpected (and totally erroneous) news that Big Sye Swankie, well known poacher, freewheeler and general hell-raiser, was courting his cousin Rae. The committee was divided on this. Nan, being of the opinion that the sooner that her son got married the sooner she could call her house her own, was thoroughly in favour of a match. Any match. Any match *at all*, and to that end she was even prepared to countenance her son getting hitched to a certain wee limmer that had gone and gotten herself knocked up. You understand that except *in extremis*, Nan would have had something to say about that. But her cronies had tellt her to zip her lip and keep it that way. Agnes was deeply wary of Sye. From her brief meeting with Rae at the Hotel on the night of the MacTaggart incident, she had formed the opinion that Rae was, well, a cut above, shall we say (rather like the way Agnes viewed herself but not quite so much) and it seemed a bit of a waste to throw her at someone like *Sye,* even if she had made regrettable errors of judgement in the past. Jess Teviotdale, who had no time for Agnes' notions of social station, which she considered utter bull, thought it would tidy things up very neatly. Plus it wid snib Aggie's latch but *good,* and that was always a selling point with Jess.

Mae was in difficulty with the moral consequences of a liaison between such close relatives, but this difficulty, which might have been valid anywhere else, was laughed off by the others. This was Auchpinkie, after all. Any stranger arriving spent the first few days having the uncanny and unnerving impression that he kept meeting the same people over and over again, just with new names (well, not even that sometimes,) so closely did the population resemble each other as a result of *centuries* of close marriage. Anyway, as Jess averred in a low growl, while puffing a cloud of cheroot-reek in Mae's direction, "It wid tak a quine born an bred i these airts ti settle at laddie's hash," a statement that was undeniably true. Morag—who was feeling much better now, thank you, and had taken to light constitutional exercise—was, unsurprisingly, as suspicious as Nan of any unmarried person who had children; a suspicion that was entirely matched by her complete mistrust of Big Sye. But none of her friends were listening to her.

Nevertheless a decision would have to be made, and quickly; for everyone agreed that the ideal opportunity to make a match would be at Lanky Boab's 'reception'.

"Yiz daa hink at's ower suddint, like, dae ye," muttered Mae, who was a stickler for propriety. "Kinda fleet?"

"Y'ken aiblins it's no the recht time efter aa. A daa ken if it widnae be unchancy— it bein a plantin an aa." These things bothered Morag deeply.

"No a wake, a reception," put in Agnes. "Wakes is heathen."

"Weel, if A ken Sye, if he's interestit he'll no need ony hertenin," added Mae, who *did* know her nephew. "A daa ken fit wey ye're that bothered." She pondered. "Onywey, did thi no yased ti hing aboot thegither? Mind fan Peem wis courtin Izzie? Ach it'll be recht romantic, like."

"Aye, but that wis afore she gingit awa an got hersel bairned," observed Jess. "A aye thocht at wis a queer hing ti dae recht eneuch."

"Ochone, A ken, tsk tsk," nodded Morag. "A hink thir somehin fer wrang wi a lassie at wid dae a hing like at."

"Aye, weel we aa ken fit youse hiv been hinkin o daein, so keep a lid on it," retorted Jess. Morag looked hurt.

"A cannae help fit a dream aboot fan A ging ti sleep," she protested.

"Dae ye mind them through the day, but?" demanded Jess in response. Morag turned bright red. "Aye well, there ye ging then. Yer in nae poseetion ti spik aboot onybody else. Fittiver the lassie done it's no the hauf o whit ye've been hinkin o daein. Fegs, yer harns is triple-X-rated, wumman."

Nan was pleading. "Och, daa be sae hard on Morag, Jess; she canna help it. A aye thocht the hale hing aboot fit Rae done wis a bit peculier masel, but Sye niver spak aboot it, an Etta niver had a guid word ti say aboot her fae the day she upped an left. No that she hud onyhin guid ti say aboot mony fowk. A must say's far as A mind o Rae she wis a fine eneuch quine, even if she wis a bittie wild." The future mother-in-law was getting herself used to the idea.

"Bittie wild? Thir wis loons got inti less scrapes'n her," Mae broke in. "A mind she yased ti ging sea-maw's eggin oan the cliffs, an she wis aye the maist gallus. So the laddies said onywey. She aye got mair eggs'n ony o thum, A ken that. A yased ti sell thum afore they gart it illegal. As if we didnae hae eneuch maw-skite aaready."

"Och, you an yer sea-maws' eggs. A could never stand them," Agnes made a face at the thought. "How can ye eat an egg that tastes of fish?"

"She's recht aboot the skite, though," observed Jess. "Thir no a day gings by but A hing oot ma laundry an een o they blastit maws keechs on it. A hink we should shoot them like we yased till."

"Listen, dae youse lot mind keepin ti the point," demanded Nan. "A daa gie a fiddlers aboot the bluidy sea-maws. A'm jist petrifeed yon ditherin loon o mine's gingin tae miss the chance, like. A mean, if A canna get rid o him ti Rae, fa the hell am A gingin ti get rid o him tae? Jings did we no gie him thonder hoose an noo he's got it jammed that fu o his junk he's got nae chyce but clutter up mine? Christ thir's twa motor-bikes in bits in ma bunker yet—hiv A tellt ye afore?"

"Ye hiv at. Mair'n eence."

"Ach, youse dinnae ken fit it's like ava. Eck's bed eneuch, but the twa o thum—A tell ye, it's deeabolical. An syne he's gotten his bath fou o salmons he jist daunders ower an has his bath at me, an he disnae e'en fetch his ain fiss-cloot. Ye want tae see the wey he laves the bathroom an aa. Naa. High time some ither pair wumman had the tholin o him." Nan sniffed and pulled a hankie from the sleeve of her cardigan.

"Noo, noo, Nan, daa get yersel aa emotional, like," Mae smiled soothingly. "An ye ken he's a recht hertie loon."

"That's aa recht fur you ti spik! Aa yourn were married be the time they wis echteen, an if A recall, thir wis nae hingin back neither. An A ken there's naebody mair hertie'n Sye. But A jist wish tae hell he'd settle doon so's A cid lave aff deevin masel wi worry aboot fittin the hell he's gingin ti be intil next."

"A hope yer no insinyoueytin nuthin aboot ma dochters," rasped Mae. "Thir baith o thum had the full nine month afore thi drappet thir bairns."

"Achtaehell thir's aye been a wheen pre-mature bairns roon here," growled Jess. "An gin A mind recht yer Young Rab's betrothit drappit her first een guy quick. Daa ye bother gettin up on yer soapbox, Mae," she added, wagging her forefinger warningly. "We've aa got steens ti hurl if we hiv tae. The bit o't is, Sye's aye been a bed influence. Ony time ma Willie's been in boather, ye ken fine weel fa's been at the root o hit."

"Here, fit ur you sayin aboot ma laddie?"

"She's sayin he's trouble an he needs sortin oot by somebody." Mae was keen to get her own back.

"Ye'd better no neither o ye be castin nae axpersions here!

"B'Christ, Nan, A'm on your side. Git aff yer high horse willye?" snapped Jess. "An can we no mebbe keep aabody else's bairns ootin this fer fehve meenits?"

"Aye, well," said Nan, smoothing her rumpled feathers back into place. "A jist daa like ti hear onybody miscryin ma laddie, that's aa."

"And ye're sure that this lassie would be able tae.... Are ye *sure* she can cope?" asked Agnes, "With Sye, A mean. A mean, his habits are—well, so peculiar."

"Weel say fit ye like aboot her, she's raised yon laddie aa on her lane wi nae help fae Etta or his faither, fa iver at mecht be," mused Mae. "An shairly some o her mither's thrawn nature his rubbed aff. A ken she left hame fan she wis jist turned sivinteen, but tholin yon auld scunner e'en at lang maun hae teuchened her up a bit. Would've teuchened up an auld buit, if ye ask me."

"Mae! You can't speak like that of the dead!" Agnes was shocked. "Have a wee bit respect!"

"Blethers! Ye threip on like at ilka time A spik aboot thon hackit auld hooer, an it's jist cause yer ower taffee-nebbit. You couldnae suffer her ony mair'n the rest o wis, sae daa stert yer shite," retorted Mae.

"I don't think you should call me toffee-nebbit. And I suppose yer right enough......Mind, that pair lassie....." Agnes' final objections were being overrun and she knew it. "Well, then," she said. "I suppose that's it then."

And so unofficial committee on social etiquette not only gave its blessing to the match and decided that it might be a Very Good Thing After All, but went on to discuss the detail of how the thing would be done.

And meanwhile, the subjects of all this conniving were none the wiser.

Big Sye and Peem worked Friday, even though Peem was feeling a little delicate because of being wakened at one-thirty in the morning by his beloved, up to the ears in gin and white wine and in an even more frisky mood than usual. He then had to turn to at half four to catch the tide. Despite his feeling like a half-shut knife as a result, he and Sye had at last finished the welding job, and then returned to Auchpinkie; they had a lot of organising to do. Muckle Mel and Uncle Gus were in the bar when they got there. They had stayed on after lunch, just like they always did on a Friday, for a bit news and a game of darts. They both thought the idea of a wake was grand, and Mel agreed to play the piobreachd for Boab. But Dave the barman was puzzled, as usual.

"Wake? Fit wey can ye hae a wake?" he demanded.

"Weel, fur Boab, like. An it's high time we hud a guid ceilidh," replied Peem.

"Aye, A ken at," said Dave, who instantly thought of the bar takings. "But ye canna hae a wake. No a real een."

"How no?" asked Peem with a measure of impatience. This was his plan and he did not like to see it criticised.

"Cos yer gingin ti plant the auld bugger the morn's morn, at's how."

"So whit?"

"Weel fit wey can ye wak him if he's aaready i the grun, min?"

"Here, yon's recht eneuch," rumbled Muckle Mel, who had a voice that boomed like distant gunfire. "*A* mind noo. The hale idear is ye hiv the deider there, an ye send him aff, like. A kent thir wis somehin up wi't" He paused while he swallowed a third of his pint with one gulp. "At's recht. A mind playin the pipes at a puckle wakes lang syne. But the kirk didna like it so they stopped it. That's how thi daa really hiv them these days."

"Naa, that's no the reason," chipped in Uncle Gus. "No roon here onywey it's no. Div neeno yiz mind fan they plantit Mae's Da? Thon wis the last recht een here. D'ye no mind at, Mel?"

"Naa. At wis fan A wis awa in Aden wi the Bleck Watch gittin shot at bi the baith sides."

"Ah, weel, ye see, we aye had recht wakes here until that een. That een feenished it tho," chuckled Uncle Gus. (He was not, by the way, an uncle to anyone present; indeed he was that rarity, an only child. He got his name from his habit of sitting in and quietly commenting on other peoples conversations till somebody bought him a drink. As in, "Oh, aye, an een for the uncle an aa.")

"Fit wey?" Peem's curiosity was getting the better of his pique at his idea being found to be flawed.

"Heh, youse boys is ower youthie. Weel, we hud a recht wake, wi Mae's Da in his kist i the lobby so's aabody cid say ta-ta like, an then the paalbearers set aff fur the kirkyerd wi the kist, like. But the buggers wis that skeeched at hauf wey up the rack the seaward side gingit ae wey an the landward side poo'ed the tither, an the pair auld sod i the wuiden jeckit gaed fleein ower the wa an ower the clift intil the sey. The meenister— auld Ferguson, like, noo there *wis* a meenister, he hud ye shakin i yer buits ilka Sunda—far wizza—O aye, onywey, it wis Ferguson pit the kybosh on it efter at. Sayed it wis ower wild an disrespeckfu. At's fit wey we daa hae recht wakes like at noo. An A tell ye somehin, A daa see yon lang streak o misery alang by lettin wis awa wi hit either."

"A mind o thon," noted Dave the barman. "At wis no lang efter we bocht the hotel. Heh! A'll tell ye somehin else, thir nae wey Agnes'll hae a deider in aboot here noo. Hink o the Health an Safety, deiders in aboot far thir grub."

"Oh," said Peem, crestfallen. "So it'll no be a recht wake. At's a fell peety. But we kin still hae wirsels a braw ceilidh." He sighed and supped his pint. "Mind, naebody's gingin ti let on ti the Health and Safety, ur thi," he mused hopefully. "An we widna let Boab in aboot the grub ava, wid wi? He'll be oot i the lobby, like. Shairly Agnes widna mind at?"

"Aiblins," allowed Dave, polishing thoughtfully. "But e'en gin ye cid talk Agnes intil it, ye've still niver gotten by the meenister. An ye cin bet yer bottom dollar at een'll pit his fit doon like Gus says."

Peem nodded glumly. This bother of the minister was a poser and no mistake. It wasn't as if they could kidnap him or anything, after all; the rules said that Boab had to have a Christian burial, and that required the presence of a Minister o the Kirk.

Sye had been silent throughout the exchange, regarding himself intently in the mirror while he listened, as was his habit. At last he spoke. "Ach we'll jist hae ti fix hit, then," he said, quietly. "Ken fit A mean? Fix it so we *cin* hae a recht wake, like."

Peem grinned happily. He knew Sye well enough to know he had already thought up a ploy.

Not long later, Muckle Mel, Uncle Gus, Big Sye and Peem left the Hotel with purposeful gait and set expressions.

Now, it happened that the person charged with the responsibility of tending Auchpinkie's verges, sweeping The Street, clearing drains, removing cats from trees, mowing the kirkyard lawn and most importantly—as far as we are concerned—digging the graves, was one Joe Forbes, who, technically at least, was employed by the Cooncil Parks Department. But since, as far as anyone in authority in Arbeg was concerned, Auchpinkie was a blank space on the map with the legend 'Here be Devils'—no that far fae the truth, really—Joe had for many years enjoyed considerable latitude in how he organised his week's work. The one appointment that was entirely fixed in time and place was when the Parks Overseer came out on a Friday afternoon at two thirty to meet him at the little shed in the lane behind The Street where he kept his tools. For this reason Joe was always very careful not to have too much beer on a Friday lunchtime; not a difficult task, since he habitually spent all his money by Thursday night, and Dave knew better than to give him tick.

This appointment was in itself immutable because of the immutable routine of the Cooncil. Joe—who had never been the possessor of a bank account, and was never likely to be—was paid in cash. In this he was by no means unique as the council employed many parkies and gardeners whose liking for the feel of real money would not easily be replaced by the modern love of bits of plastic and monthly statements.

But it did rather inconvenience the Parks Overseer. The Cooncil Wages Office in Arbeg could under no circumstances be persuaded to start giving out the little brown wage packets before two o'clock on Friday afternoon, even though they were made up on the Thursday. Two o'clock had always been the time, and pleas of inconvenience fell on the ears of the wages clerkesses as they might have on the cold stone of the hideous Victorian building they inhabited. If two o'clock had been the time since before any of them could remember, what right had they to interfere with Cooncil tradition? The Cooncil was not just any employer: the Cooncil was the Local Authority, a very bastion of tradition. The ways of others in this modern and corrupt world were not to pass within the shining portals of The Cooncil. Oh no, indeed. And so the Parks Overseer, who had to deliver the wage-packets to the men, waited patiently (*he* was paid by electronic transfer once a month) in the queue of other functionaries with similar duties until, on the stroke of two by the steeple bell, the squeaky shutter flew up and the packets were passed across, signed for, and put into the little brown leather satchels designed for the purpose. And then the sundry and several Overseers would begin a hell-for-leather dash around the countryside, especially the Parks Overseer, for he had to deliver the packets to employees in several outlying villages, and he himself finished at four on a Friday.

Since the Parks Overseer, being in the employ of the Cooncil, was a Very Very Very Busy Man and the whole of his week was just brim full to bursting of Very Very *Very* Important Things, he had long since rationalised his weekly schedule. The men, he figured, who worked in the outlying villages had been doing the job so long that they did not need any telling what to do; and if they did, then it was probably too late to get the message through in any case. The Overseer knew his lads, after all. So he combined his supervisory meeting with the handing out of the pay-packets, listened to a brief resume of what they'd been up to that week, made certain suggestions for what they might like to do the next, if it didn't rain, cast a quick eye over the policies, and then pished off to the pub.

And you know what? It suited everybody fine. The men got on with the job and never ever had the annoyance of a supervisor near them, and the Overseer could congratulate himself on the efficiency of his management. Why he could write a book about it. That particular Friday he had a special bit of good news for Joe Forbes at Auchpinkie, though, for a funeral the Saturday meant a grave had to be dug; and a grave being dug on the Friday certainly meant overtime. Time-and-a-half the digging on Friday afternoon and Saturday morning and double time the backfilling on Saturday afternoon. A nice wee bonus.

Perhaps, had the overseer noticed the four men descending upon Joe's shed as he bumped and bounced his van along the rutted track that led back to the Arbeg road and his next meeting, he might have spared the time to be a little curious. And had he known what was their plan, even worried, perhaps. But there was no way that he could have known what skulduggery was afoot, so he can't be held to blame for what happened. But it just goes to show you, doesn't it?

CHAPTER TWENTY-EIGHT
Deek White Again

A t the Northern Scottish depot, Deek White got out of his battered Escort and wandered up to the office. The place seemed
deserted, which did not surprise him, for it was nearly eight
o'clock. He was to pick up his old bus; the panel shop had straightened it
out and the replacement vehicle he had been using had been recalled.
The bus keys were kept in the outer office in a locked cupboard, to which
all the drivers had keys. Deek let himself in, opened the cupboard and
picked up his keys. He sat down at the desk beside the parcel scales and
the racks of timetables and rubbed his forehead. Actually the run to the
fish-factory was not that bad after all. The first night had been pretty
rough, but things had settled down after that. Those women could give
some stick, all right, but they were really a pretty couthy bunch, when all
was said and done, and it has to be said that Deek really *was* a right hand-
some loon, and a charmer with it. They had quite taken to him. In fact
they seemed to think he was far too skinny by half, and had taken it upon
themselves to feed him up; the last two nights there had been little parcels
of sandwiches and flasks of tea discreetly left for him. And, being the
resourceful sort of a lad that he was, he had struck up something that was
more than friendship with one of them, a petite brunette in her mid-
twenties with startling green eyes and interesting curves. Her husband
was in the Merch and she did the fish because she was bored and her
auntie worked there. Asides of which it gave her pretty good spending
money, paid cash, which didn't have to go through her joint account.

And bored sea-widows with spare dosh were definitely up Deek's
alley.

Upon the desk in front of him was an *Evening Express*, and Deek
picked it up and began to turn the pages idly. As he read he became aware
of a curious smell. He swivelled the seat round, his nose twitching. Smelled
like burning—like smoke. But there was no sign of anything untoward in
the office. Becoming more convinced of his senses and alarmed in equal
measure, Deek searched for the sources of the worrisome odour. There
were two doors leading from the office, one out into the garage and the
other into the Depot Manager's inner sanctum. A quick look out into the
garage confirmed there was nothing awry so the smell must be coming
from Ramsay's office. But that was always locked at night, and only
Ramsay and Sheena had keys.

Deek was a curious lad and he was getting worried forbye, so he
tried the door anyway. It wasn't locked at all. He opened the door and a

blast of hot air and choking smoke hit him in the face. The lights were
still on and through the thick smoke he could see the cause of the fire.
Ramsay's wastepaper bin was ablaze, flames leaping six feet into the air.
The paint on the ceiling had already begun to crinkle and brown, and the
mountains of paper on the desk had caught light too. Deek grabbed the
fire-extinguisher from the wall and began to blast at the flames. Once the
fire on the desk had died down a bit he shoved the blazing bin with his
foot out into the garage where it could do its worst, and then returned
and thoroughly damped out the smouldering embers on the desk. He
heaved a sigh of relief—it had been an exciting few moments, and Deek
was impressed with his cool handling of the situation—and then chuckled. It was not the first time that Ramsay had set fire to his wastepaper
basket by his habit of tipping cigar ash into it, after all........But usually
Ramsay was around to sort it out himself. Now that was curious. It doesn't
take long for an overflowing wastepaper bin to burn; Deek had been sitting in the outer office for some time, and he knew Ramsay had not passed
him. And anyway Ramsay finished at half-five and he was not a man to
hang about after work, especially on Fridays.

It was only then that our Deek asked himself, "So how come the
lights were on and the door unlocked?"

He had a good look about as the smioke cleared. There was no-
one else in the office. But on Sheena's desk he found an empty bottle of
sherry and two plastic cups. One of them had lipstick on. Behind her
desk there was another door, to a boxroom where the files were kept. His
curiosity piqued, and a definite hunch forming in his mind, Deek went
behind the desk and put his ear to the door. Yup!

From within he could hear the unmistakable sounds of human
passion.

It was a question of timing, and Deek's was perfect. He waited
until the sounds were in crescendo and then threw open the door and
snapped on the light.

"Onybody there," he inquired, all innocence.

"Nooooooo!" wailed Sheena's voice.

"Jesus Christ fit the .....Uh!" replied Ramsay's.

They were, as they say, *in flagrante delicto*. The twin white hills of
Ramsay's arse, delicately spotted with plooks, mounded south of his shirt-
tail and north of his crumpled trousers, whilst Sheena's ample, shapely,
bestockinged thighs rose and encompassed them to east and west. Her
bare arms were wrapped round the slumped body on top of her, and
looking over Ramsay's shoulder, Deek could see her eyes gazing back at
him, crazy with horror, partly at being discovered, but mainly at the loss
of an orgasm that been stolen from her on the threshold of explosion.
Deek suddenly felt sorry for the poor quine. Maybe he would sort her out
himself sometime to make up; he'd always had a bit of a fancy for her. He
made a mental note of it.

Meantime, though, he just smiled cheerily, waved, and said "Fit
like, Sheena. Sorry ti boather ye. 'Scuse me, Ramsay, min, but d'ye hink

A could hae a wee word wi ye? Just finiver youse twa his feenished up, like. Nae rush ava." and shut the door. He was going to have some fun with this one, that was for sure.

Big Sye returned to The Chateau at about the same time as Deek made his discovery, feeling very satisfied with himself and his afternoon's work. He was surprised to find Tam Teviot in front of the little house. Tam, as far as he could recall, had left the bar at least an hour beforehand. His bike was propped up, as usual, against the front wall of The Chateau; but tonight, so was Tam. He had his hands on the bars and his right leg raised as if about to swing it over the bike. His right foot was resting on the saddle, and he seemed to be in a position of perfect, if precarious, balance. He was stock still, and stared with his watery eyes down The Street.

"Here, ye aa recht, Tam?" asked Sye, a little concerned. Tam was a very old man indeed, after all.

"Aye, m'fine, shon. Zhisht fine." Tam's intent gaze (he was trying to make two lamp-posts into one) did not waver.

"Can A gie ye a haun?"

"No, 'sh aa recht, shon. A'm zhisht recoverin ma he—ma heckway libryum."

"Yer whit? Oh, aye." Sye grinned.

"A wizh zhisht gittin on ma bike, shon, an it kinna gaed awa fae me like. Sho A'll hae ti bide here till hit comes back." He looked very sad, as he said this, as if regretting the fickleness of his senses. "She, if A try an get aff an lave go the bike A'm feared A'll losh it aathigither an A'll faa doon, an if A try an *go* the bike A *ken* A'll faa doon, sho A'll zhisht shtay here till hit comes back."

"Till fit comes back?"

"Ma heckway libryum, shon. Ma heckway libryum. A'll be fine. Shoon ash A've got it back A'll be on ma road." A thought seemed to strike him and he turned his head slowly to look at Sye. "Here, A hope ye daa mind if A lean ma bike againsht yer wa, shon."

Sye laughed. "Ye can carry oan, min. Ye've been daein it ivery necht syne A biggit the place. A reckon it'd be mean ti stop ye noo."

"Yer a fine laddie, sho ye are. A'd shack yer haun but A'm ower feared A'll cowp if A lave go the bike."

"Anither time. Ye shair yer okay?"

"Zhisht fine, shon."

"Here ye'll no forget an bring yer fiddle the morn eh?"

"Fiddle? The morn?"

"Fur Boab's wake, mind."

"Fit? Boab'sh deid. Pair Boab. He wizh a recht jhonick auld craitur sho he wizh."

Sye realised that further conversation was futile. "Aye, Tam. A'll send A laddie tae mind ye the morn's morn," he said, clapped the old man on the back—gently, so as not to knock him over, and went into the house.

Rae, at the same moment, was stretched out on her sofa in the lounge with the curtains drawn closed. There was a glass of Andrew's Salts by her side. With her right hand she gently swabbed her forehead with a damp cloth. Work, that day—Friday was her full day, being pay-day for the casual staff—had been hell. On wheels. She could think of no other apt description. The effort of maintaining a smiling and relaxed presence in the office had near as dammit killed her, and she made a mental note to send the biggest bunch of flowers she could find to Gayle, who had taken one look at her, remembered the phone call from Iz, and made four. She had put Rae in conference and fended off all calls, and supplied her with stiff and repeated doses of aspirin and coffee. She was a wonder, that girl.

The doorbell rang. Rae froze. It rang again, and a herd of elephants crashed out of Willie's room, thundered down the stairs, and flung open the door. Then it turned round and stampeded back up the stairs, and there was an explosion as the bedroom door slammed shut.

When the echoes had died down, Rae became aware of the presence of another in the room. She raised her dark glasses and lifted her head so she could see. There was Iz, and she was looking full of life as a week-old lamb. She had a litre bottle of *Blue Nun* in her hand.

"Ohh," said Rae, letting her head fall back onto the cushion. "Fit did ye dae ti me." It was not meant as a question. Rae knew.

Iz squeezed down on the edge of the settee. She was clearly delighted about something and she wiggled her copious bottom into Rae's side to make room for herself. Rae grumbled a protest. "Poor wee baby," crooned Iz, sweetly. "Are we feeling so tewwibleh bayed?"

"Ohh. *Ohh*. Ohh my God! How can ye be that bluidy *cheerfu?*"

"Ach, weel, A got ma medicine fan A got hame last necht." Iz winked meaningfully at Rae. "Nothin like a good dose o hormones ti gar ye feel yersel again. Pair Peem had ti get up at fower tae catch the tide, though, an he's the een that's feelin rauch noo. Heh, heh." She slapped Rae on the thigh.

"Dinnae!" moaned the recipient. "Please dinnae!"

"Guess fit, hon?" continued Iz, ignoring her victim's supplications. It was obvious to Rae that Iz had something to tell her, and that she was not going to go away until Rae listened, and showed appropriate enthusiasm forbye. Rae painfully dragged herself up, propped herself on one elbow and swigged the Andrew's Liver Salts. "Fit ur ye daein drinkin at muck?" demanded Izzie. "Best hing for a hangower's anither drink. Well, segint best hing." She giggled. "Far's the corkscrae? Ye *hiv* got een, hivvint ye? Else A'll hae ti ging back alang by ti get een an His Nibs's no in best humour, like." Rae's already ashen face seemed to pale even further at the thought. "Ach, weel. Jist youse lie thir an A'll sort ye oot. Youse jist lave the hale hing til yer big sister." Iz got up and went into the kitchen. Rae heard her singing to herself as she opened drawers and cupboards. Rae fell back on the sofa and pulled a cushion over her face. But it was no use, and Rae knew it. Iz was not to be thwarted that easily. The same girl returned with two glasses of wine and removed the cushion. Then she sat down again. "Drink up, noo, ma pretty baby, an nail back yer lugs, cos hiv A got some news for you."

CHAPTER TWENTY-NINE
Joe Forbes' Assumption

Joe Forbes awoke to a Saturday morning that fair dazzled with glorious sunshine. Above him the sky was blue and glistering in the shining light of a northern spring day. He looked up and wondered at the sparkling beauty of it and did not move. It was so beautiful that it made him want to cry (at least, *something* gart him want to greet.) He looked up at it and smiled. It was some time before the thought crept, kinda sidewise like, into the murk of his brain, that where he could see that sublime patch of heaven, there should have been the cracked plaster of his bedroom ceiling.

Now our Joe was not what you would call a man of imagination; he took a long, deep, scientific look at the patch of blue, concluded he was seeing things again, and turned onto his side.

But this time, that didn't help, for instead of the dust-covered bedside table with the alarm clock that had stopped at 3.36 more years ago than he could remember, and the bedroom wall with the fading rose-patterned wallpaper and the plastic crucifix with his long-disused rosary hanging from it, he saw a sheer, blank wall of deep brown earth. He waited till the jangling of bells that his movement had set off inside his cranium subsided, squeezed his eyes up tight shut, held them that way, and then opened them. First the left, and then the right.

But that didn't help either. The wall of earth was still a wall of earth, and the patch of blue, he quickly confirmed, was still a patch of blue and not a lath and plaster ceiling in need of refection.

It occurred to Joe that there was something not quite right here, and he sensed a thing that approximated fear. And then he heard voices, sweet, angel's voices, that descended to him from on high. The cold hand of dread gripped him tighter. So this was it, then. He raised his head. Someone—or something—banged on the top of his skull with the vigour of a Gordon Highlanders Drum Major and it was several minutes before the echoes died down and he could think again.

He understood now. He was in Purgatory (where else did they have pain like that?) and the powers of light and dark were fighting over his soul. Well, okay, so maybe Joe wasn't the brightest spark on the planet, but he sure knew that where he was it was cold and damp and smelled of farts, and up above it was clear and blue and shining and there were magical beings with sweet voices, and he had no trouble working out where *he* would rather be. With a superhuman effort he heaved himself to his elbows, fighting off the hammering in his head and the waves of nausea, and sat up.

When he opened his eyes, he found that his nose was just above the level of a grassy sward. There were, as he had feared there might be, gravestones all around him. Right in his line of vision and not ten feet away, were the angels. Well, so he presumed, though their attire was not quite what he'd expected. They were acting angelically enough, arranging some wild flowers in a jam-jar atop the neighbouring grave. The suits with bell-bottom trousers and the paisley ties were a surprise, but then Joe (who was rational to the point of the obtuse) figured that they must have some queer-like fashions in heaven, too.

The angels appeared to have no interest in him; they were probably too busy saving the soul of the occupant of the next lair. But pretty soon Joe began to be impatient, for he felt that he had suffered enough to pass through Purgatory onto the next stage of his journey. He decided to attempt communication. Remind the angels that he was there, like. In case they forgot. For a moment he thrashed around the rusty recesses of his aching harns in search of a phrase that might suit, and then he smiled and nodded.

What he tried to say was "Hail Mary, Mother of God." What actually came out is not easy to transcribe, but it married many of the qualities of the bark of a rutting stag with the hoot of the steam whistles of the ferries that had, in his childhood, plied to and fro across the Tay.

It did *not* have the desired result. The two angels spun round, looked at Joe, looked at each other, dropped the jar of flowers, looked at Joe again, opened their eyes wide and their mouths wider, screamed, and fled. Joe, in despair, raised his hands onto the ground, tried to pull himself up, slipped, and fell back. As he blacked out, two thoughts filtered through to him:

The first was "Ach yer jokin, daa tell me the bastart Proddies wis recht efter aa."

And the second was "Y'ken A could sweir A've seen they twa somewey afore."

Nan looked up at the sound of running feet and saw, through her kitchen window, Wullie and Ian belting past at full steam. She narrowed her eyes. She was not at all persuaded by the boys' recent conversion and remained convinced that they were Up Tae Somehing. She went back to her ironing. She was a troubled woman, Nan. Despite all their deliberations, she and the other members of the Hag's Huddle had yet to come up with a sure-fire scheme to get Sye and his cousin together. Worse, since Sye had presented a bin-liner full of salmon to Rae on the Thursday evening, there had been no report that they had even met each other. And had they done so, *everyone* would have known. Nan dearly hoped that this was not going to be another of her son's passing fancies, and you can rest assured that the network was working flat out on the problem.

Agnes was proud of her abilities as a cook. And she had good reason. She was a woman of talent and imagination; who knows to what heights she might have risen anywhere else in the world but Auchpinkie? But it was rare for her to have the opportunity to show off even before her fellow villagers, since their idea of refined cuisine ended at mince and tatties and deep-fried haddock and chips. So, despite the fact that the canny side of her told her that she was a mug and she should charge the buggers for the food, once she had accepted that, in the interests of economy and having a good party, they would eat of the salmon donated by Big Sye, she determined that she would prepare it herself. In any case, she had seen the inside of too many of her neighbours' kitchens to trust anyone else with the task.

She had perhaps not been quite prepared for the scale of the operation, which she had only fully realised when Big Sye had trundled three barrowloads of salmon across the square the evening before and decanted them into a huge mobile troch that was usually used for the dishes. But Agnes was a hardy soul who made a point of never showing the slightest surprise at what the villagers might do, and certainly not of being defeated by them.

She had pored for hours over her thick catering textbooks, noting and adapting recipes and techniques as she went along. One thing she was determined about—this repast was to be one that would be remembered. Smoked salmon paté, salmon mousse, salmon en croute, salmon baked, poached, in pies, in sauces, glazed, moulded, you name it. If salmons could be turned into it, it was there. The pride of place upon the board was to go to an enormous salmon paté, moulded into the shape of a four-foot long salmon, and covered with thinly sliced lemons and a glaze of reduced fish stock. It was so big it had had to be cooked in three parts and then married up later.

Copelands Funeral Directors and Morticians of Brechin had the task of arranging the technical side of the affair. They had picked up Lanky Boab from the mortuary at Arbeg Infirmary on Friday, and they had turned him out proper. One of his suits had been cleaned, and was almost unrecognisable. And Boab himself looked healthier than he had for twenty years, with his cheeks delicately rouged and his lips carefully lipsticked. He was to be delivered to the kirk at Auchpinkie at nine-forty-five so that the mourners could pass and pay their last respects before the service began at ten-thirty, with the burial an hour later. At nine o'clock the driver and his assistant creaked into life, brought the coffin out on its trolley and slid it into the back of the venerable Daimler hearse. The driver swept a speck of dust from the gleaming bonnet with his impeccably white-gloved hand, and they set off.

The Reverend James Jameson was adjusting his robes in his dressing room when he heard the frantic hammering on the front door. "Joan, dear, can you get that?" he called. But Joan was out in the garden and did not hear, so the Reverend sighed, finished dressing and made his way downstairs. The hammering on the door had reached a frantic tattoo, and he flung it open with some ire. There was no one there. "What the....?"

"Please sir, help," came a small voice from below. He looked down. Willie and Ian were kneeling on his doorstep. Their faces, pale with terror, stared up at him.

"What on earth are you doing now?" he demanded, his irritation patent. "I have a service to conduct this morning. Can't this wait?"

"Oh, no, no, yer refference, sirr, it'll no wait ava," squeaked Ian, nodding his head vigorously. "Somehin awfy's jist happened."

"Something—like what? What have you been up to? And please stand up. You're giving me a slipped disc."

"We done like you said yer refference sir, honest we did." said Ian, scrambling to his feet and looking around nervously. "We've been really *guid*. A even mowed ma gran's green like she's been askin me tae. An we've never the eence poked the skale an wiv *even* done wir hamework." This last was impressive.

"An A pentit the fence i the back green," added Willie. "An then this morn we went ti pit some flooers on his granda's grave an, an,..." He grew even paler and swallowed.

"And what," queried the minister with evident annoyance. "Get on with it, laddie."

"An the Deil hissel come ti git wis! Jings, A never thocht we wis that bad, yer refference."

"*WHO?* Who did you say came to get you?"

"The Deil! *Ye* ken, yer reference, Auld Nick."

"The Devil? On Monday it was God and now it's the Devil? My word you two are favoured. What on earth do you take me for?"

"Yer a meenister," observed Willie, without the slightest trace of irony. "An it wis Cloots aa recht. A'm shair o hit. In the kirkyerd. We seen him, he come risin up ooty the grun recht afore wis, so he did. He wis, he wis horrible so he wis. He wis aa bleck......"

"Aye, bleck wi soot fae the *Fire*, A dootna," interjected Ian in a voice that shook with portent. "An his hair wis aa staunin up on hits ends an his een...."

"Aye ye wanty see his een, yer reference sir. They wis, they wis hidjus, sae thi wis. They wis brecht reid an they wis stickin ootin his nut like bull's-een."

The Reverend James Jameson shook himself. He knew not whether to laugh or to be furious, and could only stand with his arms folded, his eyes moving from one urchin to the other while they spoke.

"Aye an his lips wis aa bleck an his teeth wis aa yellae an his voice...." Ian rattled on.

"Aw, dinnae, dinnae, it wis— it wis that *scary*. Ken like a, like a wild beast."

"Aye an some fowk dae cry him The Beast, daa they, yer refference, sirr? Auld Nick A mean. Izzat how?"

"Enough! That is quite enough!" The minister clapped his hands in exasperation at their relentless clamour. "Do you two really expect me to believe that the Devil himself has manifested *in person* in the Auchpinkie kirkyard at half past nine on a Saturday morning?"

The boys looked at each other, thought about it, and nodded. "Aye, yer refference, sirr. That's jist exactly hit. We seen him." Ian made it sound like an everyday occurrence. He nodded and waved his hand in the direction of the kirkyard just to make sure the minister had got the message.

Willie leaned forward and quavered. "Aiblins he's still there!"

"Well then," said the minister somewhat drily, looking at his watch. "We have just enough time to go and see if he is indeed still in residence in my kirkyard before the service begins. Shall we go?"

"Aw, naw," wailed the boys in unison. "Ye *cannae...!*"

"Oh yes but oh! We are going to sort this nonsense out right now. And what better way than to beard the Devil in his very lair." The Reverend Jameson chuckled at his own witticism. He was rather prone to doing so, although Joan thought it impolite. She herself came sauntering around the side of the house at that moment, and he called out, "I'm going to the church now dear. To attend to a little something. I'll see you along there a little later, shall I?"

Nan looked up from her ironing again. There was the minister, with a hand firmly grasping the respective collars of Willie and Ian, making full speed the other way with his black gown flowing resplendently from his shoulders. She clucked her tongue. Disapprovingly. All this cerry on afore a funeral.

The Reverend James Jameson approached the open grave, literally dragging the boys by their scruffs. His own heart, despite himself, knew a frisson of fear. His hapless captives both had their eyes screwed up tight and they were whimpering like kittens and their hands were so tightly clasped in supplication that the knuckles were white. The minister noted the broken glass jar and the strewn flowers and nodded grimly. That much, at least, was true. His pace slowed as he made the last few steps. He peered into the grave and let out a gasp of surprise, and at the same time let go of the collars. But the boys were by now far too terrified to run. They screwed their eyes tighter shut and prayed as many prayers as they could remember. Then they heard the minister laugh.

Willie cracked an eye just open and looked around through the filter of his eyelashes. He could not see into the grave, but he could see that the minister was apparently in paroxysms of mirth.

"He's gone sterk ravin gyte at the very secht," thought Willie in awe, shutting his eye hurriedly. "A kent he should niver hiv keekit doon thir." He squeezed up his eyes ferociously, lest Clootie should try to prise them open by main force.

And then the boys heard the minister say, when he had recovered himself, "Forbes? Is that you? Forbes? Are you all right? Forbes! *Forbes!* Wake up, man. I say, your resemblance to the Devil had never struck me before. But now it's been pointed out, well, heh, heh, you know, you make rather a fine devil. Forbes! Wake up! Forbes!"

"A didna ken the Deil wis cried *Forbes*," gasped Ian, too amazed to remain silent.

"Wheesht!" snarled Wullie out of the corner of his mouth. "D'ye want ti get us roastit an aa?"

Joe had had a large black void since his last conscious thought. And now he heard his summons and remembered where he was. A great smile spread across his face as he realised that his name was being called from above and he opened his eyes to take in the glory. The first thing he saw was the imposing figure of the Reverend James Jameson blotting out the sky above him, his black robes flapping gently in the breeze. The smile froze and he had another thought. From which he deduced, in passing, that he was no longer unconscious.

"Ach, bluidy hell," went this thought, "Is that no jist typical o the bastart Proddies? No eneuch ti ken they wis recht, like, luik fa they've pit on the welcomin comattee. Yon drivellin Embro git. At's really rubbin yer neb in it til ye."

And then another thought forced its way into his thumping head. It occurred to him that he had no recollection of the minister's death; so how was it that he had got to heaven in advance? As a matter of fact, he distinctly remembered speaking to the man only....... When he started digging....... Digging the grave for Lanky Boab..... Joe made his eyes scan his limited field of view, not without suffering. There was a shovel, just on the edge of vision, stuck in what appeared to be (from his perspective) an upside down heap of earth, with a jacket that bore a strong resemblance to his own hanging on it. There was something shiny sticking out of the pocket, something that seemed strangely familiar. He took a few moments to assimilate this, and then looked up again. The minister appeared to be reaching a hand down to him. Joe decided that Proddie or no, this was not the time to spurn a helping hand, and he reached up his own. There was a peal of thunder and a flash of lightning inside his aching head. But he did not let go his grip, and, with much suffering, dragged himself to the edge of the hole, which was only about three feet deep. Slowly, and with a good deal of help from the minister, he levered himself into a sitting position on the grass with his legs still hanging over the side.

There he remained, in silence, allowing the sun to penetrate the chill of the grave, until the pounding subsided. Then he turned and examined the shiny object in his jacket pocket.

It was an empty forty-ounce bottle of *Hundred Pipers*.

"Ah, Holy Mother, dis this mean A'm no deid efter aa?" Joe groaned and dropped the bottle. "Here'n wis A no jist gettin ti hink it mecht be a no bed idear?"

He squinted up through the sunshine that hurt his eyes. The angels were back, he noted, but they had been transmogrified into those little buggers Wullie Swankie and Ian Teviotdale, both standing stock-still with their eyes shut and their hands clasped in attitudes of prayer. Joe realised, dimly, that his saviour was trying to communicate with him. He turned his bloodshot gaze to the man, with an expression of piteous suffering upon his phizog. He could see the minister's lips moving and he could hear the voice, but the words could have been in Icelandic for all the sense Joe's thundering head could make of them. He lifted one cheek and farted noisily.

"Oooh, it's really too much!" exploded the minister, driven to excess by this latest assault upon his dignity. "Forbes, I have to bury a man in that hole in two hours, and it's not half dug yet!" He regarded Wullie and Ian venomously. "Will you two kindly open your eyes at *once,*" he snapped. "And for pity's sake *stop praying.*"

There was such a tone of adult authority in his voice that the boys, contrary to their habit, did exactly as they were told. Both dropped their jaws in amazement at the sight of Joe Forbes sitting at the edge of the grave, shaking his head slowly from side to side and wondering if he was really going to die, and if it would not be in any case a preferable alternative to his present condition. For once in their lives they were too confounded to think of anything to say.

"You two," said the minister in a weary voice, "Go down to the Hotel and ask Agnes for two pails of cold water. I think our man Joseph here needs to freshen up."

CHAPTER THIRTY
The Missing Corse

The Copeland's Daimler hearse swished to luxurious stop. They were in plenty of time, and Auchpinkie could be no more than a couple or three miles down the road. The driver got out. "Hing on, Meekil," he said, somewhat superfluously for Meekil showed not the slightest hint of any intention to move, "An A'll see whit the boather is." He put on his top hat and walked towards the cause of his concern. A tractor, still attached to its bogie, was blocking the road. As he got nearer, the man from Copeland's saw that one of the tractor's wheels had been removed, and there was what *might* have been an enlarged version of a human being footering with some part of the machine's innards. Some *very oily* part. The man from Copeland's stopped at a safe distance and waited to be noticed. When, after several minutes, it became clear to him that he would not be, he cleared his throat, and the giant turned to him. The man from Copeland's could not help noticing how small the head was on those gargantuan shoulders. (He was used to measuring people.) But then he realised that the head was of perfectly normal size, it was just dwarfed by the sheer scale of the torso and limbs it went about with. However, prudence suggested to the man from Copeland's that he had better not remark on this.

"Ye gingin ti be a affa lang whiley wi at?" he asked. "On'y we're gingin til a funeral ye ken."

"Yer no."

"Aye we are. Me an Meekil tae."

"Here an A thocht ye wis awa til a waddin. Silly me." Muckle Mel, for it was none other, straightened to his full height, and the man from Copelands began addressing his third shirt-button.

"Aye, at Auchpinkie, tae. We daa want ti be late."

Muckle Mel scratched his head thoughtfully. "Weel, ye see nou, the limited slip differential knuckle joint cotter pin's U.S. A'll need ti get a boy oot fae Geddes's wi a new een."

The man from Copeland's looked sad. "Dis aa that mean ye canna shift it?"

Mel nodded once.

"Weel izzer ony ither wey til Auchpinkie? See A dinna ken hereaboots masel, an Meekil's fae Fife."

Mel nodded sympathetically and pointed a nine-sixteenth ring-spanner back up the road. "Thir a cross hauf a mile back alang thir. Ye tak the recht." He waved his right hand to make sure the man had understood which one. "Ye cannae miss the kirk."

Meantime, Geordie Baird—you'll remember him—was walking the chairman of the Alba Life Assurance Society up the side of the river to a pool where he had seen, to his enormous relief, a good sized fish at half-past-six that morning. He only prayed that it would still be there.

The Chairman was a small and dapper man of monkeyish features and steely grey eyes enlarged like fish in bowls by his spectacles. He was also deeply sensitive to the people around him; he was one of those who know that a successful company has a motivated staff, and to motivate your people you have to understand them. And David MacGarvie was possessed of a sensitivity for the feelings of others that was uncanny, and would have made him an unbeatable poker player, had he been a gambling man. He had instantly understood that the Bailiff felt awkward being called 'George', and so, not knowing which familiar was used, called him 'Baird' quite naturally. And he was satisfied to see that the Bailiff relaxed perceptibly.

And when he saw that Baird knew his water as well as the back of his hand, he deferred to his advice without comment. MacGarvie was no novice angler and he knew the value of experience such as Geordie's. So while they quietly passed several delightful pools that tugged achingly at his heart for him to cast a fly over, he said not a word, and let not a cloud shadow his brow. At last they arrived at a pool where the river slewed round a sharp bend. MacGarvie clucked his tongue. He had rarely seen a more difficult pool.

On the far side was a sandy bank that was deeply undercut, and the trees on the near bank seemed to push at his back as he stood in the shallows. An overhead cast was out of the question, and a straight sidecast would foul the scrub downstream. The water under the bank was as dark and velvety a brown as the deepest of burnt umbers, and the water moved in a slow and mesmeric eddy. From the opposite bank it was quite impossible to guess how deep the pool might be.

"If ye'd like ti hae a wee shot ower there, sir," murmured Geordie, "There wis a bonnie fish there this morn—could hae been twenty pun, mebbe mair. Ye'll hae ti side-cast like, and get yer flee ti come doonstream at him. It'll no be an easy cast," he added, with an edge of concern.

Geordie moved back into the trees as MacGarvie moved a little way out into the stream. He nodded approvingly at the relaxed motion while the Chairman false casted, a barrel-roll cast, the rod-tip, the line, and the big Silver Butcher all describing an infinity sign in the air, until the length was right and the angler let the whole uncoil onto the water.

Time stood still. There was only the deep rustle of the water, the breathing of the air in the first greening of the trees and the hooting call of the woodpigeons. The angler gathered the line in big loops in his left hand. He was as taut as a bow string and yet in perfect balance, all of his nerves humming.

"No deep enough, sirr," offered Geordie as the cast swam down level with them and MacGarvie picked it up and began again to false-cast out the line. "A ken it's no easy but try and cast deeper in under the bank and gie it time ti sink in the slack water afore it comes intil the current."

He was right. It *was* no easy. The second cast was better, but not good enough.

"Deeper in, sirr. Ye need ti get recht doon. That pool's mebbe twal fut deep and you're herdly gingin doon sax."

The third cast was not enough, and Geordie bit his tongue; but the fourth was good, a bold cast that put the fly a foot short of the bank where it fell quickly before being drawn into the eddy by the weight of water pushing on the line.

"Spot on, sir! Wind in on the reel, noo, cos if he hits ye herd he'll hae the skin aff ye."

The fourth, the fifth, and the sixth were all good; but not a tickle was felt. MacGarvie began to be afraid that he'd put the fish down; Geordie that it had buggered off altogether. Then MacGarvie moved two paces downstream and slightly out into the river, so that the water was up to his waist. He could feel the weight of the water shoving him and he knew he dared go no deeper without risking a ducking or worse. But he had the measure of his tackle now, he had his rhythm, smooth and slow, and with a cast as sweet as you like he popped the fly in six inches from the bank right at the upstream extremity of the undercut. It was such a delightful cast that Geordie couldn't help breaking out a wide grin, the first, he thought, he'd grinned all week. The fly sank deep, deep, deep, and then began to move fast into the eddy, on a different line, the water this time dragging it further down and MacGarvie felt his pulse quicken and his mouth dry; this was it, the shoot, where the water moved fastest and plunged deepest—and this is where you'll be, my beauty! This is where you'll be!

MacGarvie had fished a lot of rivers, but this was the first time he'd fished somewhere so close to the sea, where the salmon were mad with the taste of the salt water still. And when the King hit him he couldn't believe the force of it. No mouthing, no tickling, no 'Count to five' and then tap the hook home, just Bang! and he was on. He struck with such violence that the hook set itself, and it was hard to know how it was he didn't break the line there and then. And then at once he was away, driving powerfully upstream, knowing he was tricked and ready to take the angler on.

Sometimes a big salmon will sit on the bottom with the hook well set and wait for you to go away, being canny enough to know that you'll never pull him out of there by force, and sometimes you have to throw stones at him or slide weighted rings down the line to annoy him into action. But not this one.

No, this one *wanted* a fight. MacGarvie heard his reel scream and his thumb burned on the flange while he braked all he dared, his rod arced into an inverted 'U'. Still the salmon took line and MacGarvie began to move upstream after him, braking hard on the reel and praying that the fish would not take all he had. His movement became faster and faster as he came out of the deep water and felt his limbs lighten, then splashing through the shallows, until he was almost running, his rod bent nearly double under the load of that mad upstream dash. It was dangerous; one slip and he could have smashed his brains out on a boulder. And behind him a corner of his mind heard Geordie, his voice tight, but steady.

"Brake, sir, brake! Keep him tight! Put yer rod over to the side! Try an turn him!"

MacGarvie did as he was told and swung the twelve foot rod over to the bank side in a desperate effort to put a sidestrain on the fish, but he just kept going, going, going, burrowing through the water like a torpedo. MacGarvie did not dare look down at his reel, for fear he would miss his footing, and no less for fear of seeing that he was out of line as well. He had no idea of how long that first violent, brutal run lasted, but suddenly, as abruptly as it had begun, it was over. MacGarvie swore instinctively as the rod whipped straight and the line slacked. There was a sudden and awful silence in his head. Broke me!

"Pull in! Pull in! Pull in!" Geordie's voice had mounted to an anguished yell and MacGarvie began to crank frantically at the reel.

"No! Ye'll niver get fast enough to get a hud o him! Ower-hand it!"

MacGarvie pulled at the line, great handfuls rippling through the water, letting the coils fall at his side and extend downstream. But he knew it was hopeless.

And then there he was! Suddenly he was in contact with the fish again. He had turned and was bucketing downstream towards him at an unbelievable speed. MacGarvie hauled line as fast as he could and still could only just keep up with the headlong rush. And then the line went slack again and the blood pounded in his ears. What now!

Suddenly the mighty, glorious King of Fish leapt in his shower of sparks, a curving silver knife that cut a rainbow through the air not twenty feet in front of the amazed angler.

"Drap yer rod! Let him tak aa he needs!"

The fish, shaking its head all the time, splashed down after an age in the air, and MacGarvie didn't need to be told. Rod up! Get in touch again! The fish sounded deep to the bottom and then skyrocketed up into the air and then back to the deeps. He used all his strength and his wiles. He hugged the bottom and sulked for ages and then exploded into a fury of twisting and turning. Once he stayed down for nearly ten minutes, with MacGarvie straining at him as hard as he dared in a relentless tug of war. And then he charged off upstream almost—but not quite—as violently as before. And the cycle was repeated, and repeated, and repeated, until MacGarvie was soaked in a muck sweat and the muscles in his arms and back cried out for relief. But he was gaining, and he knew it.

At last the salmon, beginning to tire, was dragged to the surface, every inch of the way a dour and sullen heave. He still had fight left in him, but after a few charges to the bottom, and then slowly being brought again to the surface, he showed the silver of his flank in defeat and Geordie snapped out his telescopic tailer. He slipped the noose around the great flukes, and heaved the salmon ashore. From his pocket he pulled a short metal priest and with a single blow to the back of the head, delivered the coup de grace.

MacGarvie slumped onto the bank, shattered. The fight had lasted for over an hour and every part of the man hurt. Geordie, exuding delight, pulled out his hip flask and passed it over.

"Yer health, sir. That was as weel done as A've seen." MacGarvie swigged and felt the heat go through him and revive him. He rose and passed back the flask, and Geordie toasted him. He had produced a pocket balance and was hefting the fish on it.

"Luik, sir," he said proudly. "thirty-five pun eleeven oonces."

"How much? Are you sure?"

"Tak a luik for yersel, sir. It's no a record for the water, but it's close. The auld Laird—the een afore Mister Thomas, like—hud een that wis the ither side o forty in 'sixty-three. A wis jist an apprentice, an ma faither wis the Bailiff then. But it's the best syne, A'm hinkin. Ye'll mebbe get the Weight o the Year wi that, ye ken."

"It's certainly a record for me, Baird. And thank you."

After some moments in which the two men reflected quietly, Geordie spoke. "What dae ye fancy noo, sir? Try again furrer up?"

"We won't see anything like that again today, will we, Baird."

"No, sir, A dinnae hink we likely will."

"Well, if it's all the same to you I'd leave the fish and the tackle and just walk up the bank. One mustn't be greedy and the pleasure of seeing the river will be enough for me." He chuckled while he unstrapped the waders. "In any case I doubt if I would win another battle like that."

The two men set off slowly, Geordie explaining in quiet tones the run of the stream and the tales of the river, and MacGarvie listening and asking the occasional question. As they returned, later, to collect the catch, he said, "Baird, did you know I had a stretch of water? I daresay not. It's on the South Esk. It's the next up from Lang Braes."

"Guid watter, sir. Ma faither kent it."

"Could be better. There's some woodland and a bit of rough shooting too. It really needs someone like you to put it in shape. It's been in my wife's family for generations but they've let it go a bit."

He stopped and faced the Bailiff. "Look, I'm not in the business of poaching staff; but if you were ever to fancy a change....." He pulled out his wallet. "Here's my card. Let me write my home number...There. I'll better anything you're offered here."

"Ach, A've been aa ma days here, sir. Thank ye kindly, but.......A daa hink A could shift noo."

"Well, if you ever change your mind........ Phone me at home. This number." He pressed the card into Geordie's palm. But not before he'd wrapped it in a fifty-pound note.

CHAPTER THIRTY-ONE
Planting Lanky Boab—Or Mebbe No

By quarter to eleven a large crowd of villagers had gathered in thekirkyard. Everyone was turned out in their best, and if it was the case that their best, being reserved for visits to kirk on occasions such as this, was reminiscent, collectively, of a sartorial history of the previous thirty years, this did not make the net effect any the less splendiferous. Fur coats and veils abounded amongst the distaff, and the men, universally, wore suits with black armbands and black ties. Agnes Paterson, in particular, caught the eye. She had met her culinary deadline by a hairsbreadth, and had retired to her chamber to apply her warpaint. She spared no effort in her preparations and was suitably rewarded, for all eyes turned as she sailed, majestic as a galleon, up the path to the kirk.

But if the tongues clucked when Agnes made her entrance, they positively quivered in hissed comment when Morag appeared. There had been some swithering about whether she would come at all (not least in her own mind), but the gallus side of her had the upper hand that morning, and she had turned out to see her late tormentor planted.

Rae arrived with Izzie, and splendid she was, too. She had spent all the previous evening altering and mending and rummaging through boxes and wardrobes under Izzie's supervision and had succeeded in creating an ensemble that was at once suitably sombre (being entirely black) and at the same time thoroughly *attirant*.

"A cannae wear at til a funeral, Iz," Rae had protested. "A'll luik like a tart."

"No ye'll no. Youse ur utterly incapable o luikin like a tart. *A* wid luik like a *tart*. Youse'll jist look pure deid gorjis. Trust me. An onywey it's no a funeral it's a wake."

"Thir a difference?"

"Och aye, a funeral ye hae ti pretend yer no gingin ti hiv ony fun intil aabody's done greetin an the body's plantit an the drink's flowin. But a wake, naa, a wake, aabody kens thir gingin til hae a ball. It's mair honest. So A've heard onywey. A've niver been til een masel."

"But ye said most folk daa ken."

"Neither they div." Izzie tapped the side of her nose. "Jist the important eens kens. But naebody gies tuppence fit the rest o thum hinks onywey."

Rae twisted in front of the mirror. Iz had been right; two glasses of wine and she no longer had a hangover. It was worrying. Iz, who was rooting through her wardrobe as if it were her own, gave a whoop of triumph and emerged with a black feather bonnet with a veil. "Perfect! Jist perfect. D'ye no hink veils," she popped it on her own head and struck a pose, "Mak a lassie look aa innocent an virginal?"

Rae grabbed the bonnet. "It'll tak mair'nn a wee bit nettin tae mak youse look like a virgin. An onywey ye've pit it on backside foremost."

"Ooh! Catty!" Izzie stuck her tongue out, and Rae stuck hers out back. Iz adopted a thoughtful pose. "Here, youse open anither bottle o wine—A hope ye've got anither bottle, be the wey, else we'll need ti ging ti the Hotel an they cherge an arm an a leg fur cerry-oots. A'll be beck in fehve, hon. That's if the Bears daa swallae me up."

When she came back she had a large brown paper parcel. She unwrapped it on the bed and Rae's eyes widened. It was a magnificent black mink stole with a white ermine border. Rae let out a low whistle.

"It wis ma great gran's," explained Iz, holding it up. "A niver wear it cos black's ower severe for me. Maks me luik auld. But you'll luik like serious class."

"Ye mean A'm no?"

Iz smiled. "Ye are that. Ye jist hiv bother seein it whiles."

Mae and Jess were talking when Rae arrived. They looked her up, and they looked her down, and Jess's eyes narrowed to slits.

"By Christ, the quicker we get her tied doon the better," she hissed. "Thill be some trouble gin we dinnae." She had noted the way that those menfolk who were not still in the bar downing their liveners followed the newcomer with their eyes as she glided up the gravel path. Rae was not particularly trying to glide; the studied poise of her movement was more to do with the unnerving sensation of walking on half-inch ballast in heels.

"Aye, yer recht," growled Mae. Rae may have been related, but...... "Thir's nae tellin fit a lassie that wid dress like at ti ging till a funeral mecht get intil."

"Ken her mither aye had a side til her at aye liked ti show aff," mused Jess. "Afore she got religion, like."

"Ach, yon wis a hooer till the day she deed, Jess. She wis jest ettlin ti mak hings easier for hersel on the ither side."

"Wheesht, Mae! Ye canny sae hings like at in a kirkyerd."

"Oh, can A no, but!"

Ma Henderson had lived in the same cottar-house in Auchengask since before anybody else could remember, and to tell you the truth, she couldn't have told you how long herself. Her daily routine was cast in stone and it was a rare day that anything at all happened to make it seem any different from all the rest. Auchengask was, if you'll believe it, even quieter than Auchpinkie. Auchpinkie at least had the attraction of being a road-end with a hotel to wet the thrapple; Auchengask you just drove through, and you had to be lost to do even that. Once there had been a little community of thirty-odd souls, but that had been before the Great War, and the population had been dwindling ever since, so that now there was only Ma, a certain Major Geddes who lived at the Mains and was as skellie as a maik watch, and two rather nice young men from Dundee who lived in three cottages they'd knocked into one.

Every morning Ma left her cottar-house with a bucket of mash for the pig she kept in the vestibule of the old Free Kirk. She always wore the same outfit, topped off with a greasy flowered pinnie, woolly hat and wellie boots. As she passed the kirk door she thought there was something awry; and while she poured the mash into the pig's troch, she made up her mind to satisfy her curiosity on the way back. She didn't have a lot of curiosity, did Ma, and what she had was not an urgent thing with her. But something was awry, and wanted to know the meaning of it.

So, when she hirselled her ancient frame through the gutters past the gleaming Daimler hearse parked outside the kirk for the second time, she steered her bent body towards the two gaunt figures in black who were leaning against the vehicle smoking reflectively.

"Aye, aye, leds," quo she, "Fit's daein the day, like?"

The taller and apparently elder of the two top-hatted figures measured her. It was a gesture the man couldn't help, and he meant no harm by it, but it was still a little off-putting. "Here, ye dinnae ken onyhin aboot a funeral, dae ye?" he said, at last. He had a voice like two dry stones being ground together.

"Well, no here, exactly," growled Ma, "An ye kin lave aff luikin at me aa yon wey. It'll be lang eneuch yet afore youse buggers gets yer hauns on me."

"Because," the other continued, without seeming to hear her, "Because we've been waitin here for near twa oors an naebody's showed up like." He had a slightly petulant air with him, so he did.

"Izzatso? Ye pair hings. Ken, A didnae hink thi still yased this kirk," mused Ma aloud, by way of a hint.

"And A'm gettin fell hungery," went on the skeletal figure, who, it became more and more clear, though he may have been pointing his head at Ma while he spoke, was not actually engaged in conversation in any real sense of the word. It came from spending too many years talking to dead folk. "Half-ten the memorial service and half-eleeven the plantin it says on the line, an here'n it's gone twal and nutt a sowl except youse. Did ye say ye were gingin til a funeral?"

"No A'm no, an no here neither."

For once the man appeared to catch what she said, for he looked puzzled. "Ochone, that's a fell peety. Sure ye'd no like ti jist bide here for this een? Seems kinda teuch ti plant the auld craiter wi oot a audience, like." He cocked his head to the side and took in Ma's attire. "Aiblins ye'd like ti pit on some ither shuin, tho, no meanin ti be farrit, like, missus."

"Awjince?" Ma cackled out loud. This was the best laugh she'd had in years. "Awjince? In Auchengask? Fegs min ye've niver a meenister nur a howff atween yiz. Fit'n the hell widje dae wi a *awjince* gin ye hud een? Furtae luikit youse twa staunin thir like tint sheeps? Heh heh heh."

"Because it's a cold an a lonely place, the sod," went on the man from Copeland's, "An it's nae kindly til an auld bodie ti let him ging til his eternal....Fit did ye say?"

"Fan?"

"Jist the noo. Efter yon bit aboot fit wey ye wisna gingin til a funeral no here neither."

"A sayed yer short a meenister *an* a howff, at's fit A sayed. Ur ye deef, laddie? An at's a lang road short a funeral be ma racknin."

The man looked hurt as he pondered this.

"Fit dae ye mean?"

"A mean thon's the auld Free kirk, ye daft gowk. Thon hisnae been yased fur years, min. A've bade here syne afore ye wis borne, ma bonnie loon, an A'll tell ye ma faither afore me couldnae mind o hit bein a kirk. It's been a mealstore an a ceenema an Jones the plumber fae Wales hud his gear in it till he deed, but it's no a kirk. A mean it *wis* a kirk but no ony mair if ye get ma meanin, like. It's been deconsacrecated or some ither sic guff."

The skeletal one thought about this with evident sadness, and then he looked at his colleague, whose silence was relentless. "Hiv ye got the line on ye, Meekil," he said, gently. "Wid ye mind jist terribly ti gie me a wee bit deek at hit a meenit, in a general kinda wey, heh? Thankin ye kindly like."

Meekil shrugged and drew a folded paper from his inside pocket, and passed it to his colleague, who looked at it for a long time and then at the fading sign behind him. "Parish o Auchpinkie an Auchengask," he said, at last, stabbing his finger accusingly at the line.

"Aye," snapped Ma, with mounting exasperation. "But this is Auchengask, ye numskulls. Auchpinkie's a mile an a hauf doon the rack. Gie's a look at yon bit line." She snatched it from a claw-like grip and read it. "Luik! A kent it! Robert Paterson Smith at Auchpinkie parish kirk! At's the funeral A'm no gingin til. Jings, an here's youse twa dunderheids hingin aroon wi auld Lanky Boab in the beck o yer motor ootside o the wrang kirk!"

The two gentlemen from Copelands looked at each other for a while. Then they looked at Ma, who was laughing so hard she risked becoming a customer herself. At last the skeletal one spoke. "Meekil, ye ken thir some fowk in this world no entirely honest, A'm hinkin." His voice betrayed a hint of weariness. "Dearie me an A jalouse aa the mourners'll hiv been waitin aa this time." His sadness deepened. "Aye, weel, it's done noo, an forbye, Mester Smith's no in a fell hurry." He returned to Ma. "Far did ye say the recht kirk wis, missus?"

The Reverend James Jameson was in a state of some agitation by twelve-fifteen. He had already phoned the Copeland's office in Brechin, to be told that yes, the hearse had left on time and would he kindly not mind hurrying things up because there was another stiff due to be planted at Arbeg the same day and they were needing their hearse back. So it was with great relief that he composed a quick prayer of thanksgiving and silently committed it to his maker when at last he saw the black Daimler hearse wheezing its way along the Street. The crowd outside the kirk had been getting increasingly restless, despite the fact that it was such a fine morning to be out (as they all had said several times) and if that was not bad enough, the minister had recently become more and more aware of the hovering presence of Agnes Paterson, whose liberality with the Eau de Givenchy made it impossible to ignore her. It seemed she had something on her mind, and the minister had the notion that when Agnes had something on her mind, it were better not to be her target.

Moments after the hearse passed the Auchpinkie Hotel, a stream of men who had reckoned it more pleasant to bide inside warming the bar than to hang about in the kirkyard getting thirsty, trooped out and made their way up the hill behind it. The last to leave was Dave the barman, who snibbed the door firmly shut behind him.

About the service of remembrance itself there is little to say; the crowd squeezed into the little church with its plain white walls and oaken pews, filing quietly in past the open coffin, and saying their few words of farewell. The place hadn't been as busy since the last time a villager died, and would not be again until the next. Rae and Big Sye, by some quirk of chance that neither of them could work out, found themselves sitting next to each other. Sye discovered, as the service progressed, that his reverentially downcast gaze was frequently drawn towards Rae's knees, or more particularly the several inches of bestockinged thigh that was visible above them, and that his consideration frequently wandered, despite his best efforts, to the further delights concealed under the mounding black fabric of her dress. He was fair chuffed when the service was over and he could get out in the coolth again.

The choice of pallbearers had caused plenty of argument. Tradition decreed that the pallbearers must all be men; and normally the closest relatives stood service. But since Boab had had no offspring and none of his nephews or nieces—whose very existence, indeed, was only presumed—could be tracked down, some detailed consideration of his family tree had been required. After long debate the list had been set at Big Sye, Muckle Mel Paterson, Peem, Dod Spink, and the Young and Auld Eck Smuths. It was not the most practical arrangement; Sye was big, by any measure, but Muckle Mel was a legend, a man-mountain, a great towering bulk of bone and meat. Peem was, well, as you know, Peem was kinda normal, and so was Dod Spink, but the two Eck Smuths—predictably father and son—were somewhat short in the arse, as it were.

It worked well enough, though, after a bit of rearranging of places, even if Boab's passage from the kirk to his final resting place was rather more on the incline than you might think usual. The coffin was carefully laid beside the grave and the three silken ropes passed through the handles. The minister took his place at the head of the grave with the Bible open in his hand. The congregated village crowded round, and the ladies dabbed their cheeks politely with their handkerchiefs. It was a bonny sight, under the blue sky and atop the red headland of the Ness. No one noticed the darkening frown on Joe Forbes' face.

At last came the moment to lower the body into the grave and the six pallbearers heaved up on the ropes and swung the coffin over the hole, and began to lower it in. The coffin, however, appeared to have other ideas, and remained hovering over the hole, even though all the ropes were quite slack. Morag began to feel herself faint; it was enough to have brazened the village tongue-wags (she ignored the fact that she was just as happy to wag her tongue about others herself) and to have looked her erstwhile tormentor in the face, without the thrawn old sod refusing to let himself be planted before her very eyes. Muckle Mel, who was not the most delicate of characters, gave the coffin a surreptitious tap with his toe that would have stove in a barn door. Still it did not budge. The Reverend James Jameson was frozen in consternation, one hand raised ready to give the benediction. The rest of the congregation squeezed closer to get a right look at this queer thing. Joe Forbes quietly began to reverse out of the tightening huddle until a hand fastened on his collar and he heard Jess's gravel-pit voice rasping in his ear, "And far dae ye hink *ye're* ginging, ma wee loon?"

Meanwhile, those closest to the grave were locating the source of the trouble.

"This hole's no near lang eneuch!" rumbled Muckle Mel.

"Aye, yer recht, at's fit the metter is, aa recht," chirped Young Eck Smuth. "A kent hit fan A seen hit, A sez ti masel, 'Thon hole's ower nippit,' so A did."

"Didye? How did ye no let the rest o wis ken then, ye daft bugger ye," observed Mel.

"Spickin o daft buggers, far's the een that caad this hole," demanded Peem, who was beginning to feel a drouth that made him impatient.

"A've got a hud o him here, daa ye fash yersel, Willie," rasped his mother from behind. "An A'll no loss him."

Muckle Mel scratched his chin. "Here, fit about we pit him in on the angle, like?" Mel was a practical sort of a man. "On a slope, ye ken. Diagonal, y'see?" He made a shape in the air with the shovels he had for hands to illustrate. "That wey he'd ging in, fur shair."

At this the minister mastered his horror. "We can't do that!" he exclaimed.

"How no?" demanded Nan Swankie. "He hud a worse list on him maist o his days."

"No, no, we can't. Such a thing would be unthinkable. Where is Forbes? Forbes! Come over here."

A very sheepish Joe Forbes found himself propelled through the crowd. He had his cap in his hands and he twisted it up as he presented himself before the minister. He was still giddy from his exertions in getting the hole dug, and if there was one thing Joe hated it was getting a public bollocking from a Proddie. Something told him that that was just exactly what he was about to get. And him with a nippy head too. "A'm recht sorry, Mr Jameson," he muttered. "A cannae figure fit's gaed wrang. Yon's a standard size Coonil graft. Aabody's meant ti fit intil hit. Naebody tellt me the auld ba—eh, the *deceased* wis at big."

"Daa gie me at!" snapped Peem, whose thirst was beginning to press. "Ye held up the bar alangside o him eneuch. Ye maun hae kent he wisnae wee, like."

"Aye, weel, fit dae ye purpose we div noo wi yer standart size graft," growled Muckle Mel. "Mebbe we could hink o pittin ye in hit yersel?"

"Naw hanks, A've been thir aaready the day." Joe shivered. "A'll caa it oot the extra fut'na hauf jist as quick's A can. Naehin else fur it. Daa suppose ony o youse leds wid gie's a haun? Nu'? Ah weel." With that he headed off to fetch his tools.

Not for the first time that day, the Reverend James Jameson found himself engulfed in an advancing cloud of Givenchy. Agnes spoke quietly. "And what are we all going to do in the meantime?" she inquired, levelly.

"Well, perhaps, Mrs. Paterson, we could all return to the kirk and spend the time in prayer......." suggested the minister.

"We will *nutt!* We will do no such thing, Mr Jameson. For your information A have been up half the night getting the lunch ready and if ye think I'm going to let it all be ruined and go to waste just because yon drunken Dundonesian sot cannae dig a right grave and they twa cadavers fae Copelands cannae find the right kirk, ye don't know Agnes Paterson. We shall all retire to the Hotel, and Boab can be planted—buried, *after* lunch."

Reverend Jameson saw in this proposal a possibility of catastrophe greater than his wildest imaginings and he shuddered. The dire warnings of the previous incumbent on the danger of the admixture of alcohol and funerals were loud in his ears. He was about to protest when he felt the light touch of his wife, Joan, on his sleeve. "James, dear, I do think you had better do as Agnes says," she said soothingly. And then in a quieter voice that was electric with urgency, "Because we're already so late that if you don't they'll all just disappear to the Hotel anyway and leave you and Forbes to sort things out on your own!"

Her husband sighed. "Very well. I suppose we could all do with some refreshments. It's been rather a fraught morning. But what are we going to do with the deceased? We can't leave him out here. It wouldn't be right."

"Ach, lug him doon the Hotel an aa, yer reverence," butted Jess, who had arrived beside Agnes. "Foo no let the auld scunner at least watch frae in at the warm?"

"Aye," wheezed Mae. "At wey it'll be a recht wake, wi the deider thir an aa. We hinny had een o they syne ma faither deed."

"Yer recht," put in Nan, "An ye ken how, divint ye? Cos the drunken sots at wis daein the paalbearin let yer faither slip ower the kirkyerd wa an cowpit him recht ower the clift an they hud ti get the Arbeg lifeboat oot ti fish him ootin the sey afore they could plant the pair auld craiter. Sailin aff oot ti sey in his kist, so he wis, like een o they Vikings. Mind like in thon picter wi Tony Curtis an Kirk Douglas in."

"Christ, A mind at. Bluidy guid joab the tide was in or they'd a hud ti scrape him affa the rocks." Jess paused. "Mind, ur ye shair it wisnae the *deid*boat, an no the lifeboat but?"

In the general roar of laughter that followed, nobody heard Agnes' protestations about dead bodies in her Hotel. And they would have ignored her anyway, so it was probably just as well.

As they shouldered the coffin down the track to the Hotel, a conversation that would have interested the minister took place amongst the pallbearers.

"Jings A thocht we'd blawed it thir," said Peem with evident relief that they had not.

"Aye an efter aa that boather wi the tractor A hud," added Muckle Mel. He chuckled. "A wonder fa it wis tellt they twa walkin corses far the recht kirk wis?"

"Aye an fa wid hae, A mean fa wid hae thocht Forbesy wid hae caad a graft near twa feet ower nippit? Eh? Fa?" squeaked Young Eck Smuth. "Some lucky, eh? Eh no?"

Sye was grinning despite himself. "Here, youse ken somehin, daa ye," rumbled Mel. "Tell us or A'll drap this kist on yer nut."

"Weel, ye ken Forbesy's no fit ye'd cry smert, exactly? Aye, weel, did ye ken fit wey he measures the grafts? No? He's a stick he keeps in his toolsheid. It's jist the recht width fur a graft an twa an a hauf o it mak the recht length." He laughed and pulled something out of his jacket pocket with his free hand. "Weel, that's ti say, it *yased* ti be the recht length." He passed the object to Mel. It was the first nine inches of a yardstick, very neatly sawn off.

"By yer a fly bastart so ye are, eh? Heh, heh."

"Ach weel, A didnae want ti tak ony chances, ken," replied Sye with a chuckle. "No wi somehin important like this." He reached up and tapped on the coffin affectionately. "See the lengths we've gone till ti gie ye a recht send-aff, Boab?"

CHAPTER THIRTY-TWO
Showdown At The Auchpinkie Hotel

eordie Baird was quite content when he got back to the office; after all, fifty bar tips have an effect like that on the best of us. There was no one else there, but he had not expected there to be. He had given Gilchrist the rest of the week off sick after the farce of their set-to with Big Sye Swankie, on the grounds that he looked too bad to be seen in public. In fact he had a broken nose and several stitches in a cut on the temple, not to mention being short two teeth. But these were nothing compared to his psychological hurts. Gilchrist was nursing a wrath that was splendiferous to behold.

Geordie, on the other hand, had been able to get away with it, saying that the bruise on his cheek and his bandaged hand were the results of an accident. To be quite honest, our Geordie was ashamed and embarrassed about the whole thing. Not that there was the slightest doubt in his mind that Big Sye and probably Peem had somehow or another managed a poach of historic proportions, but Geordie disliked tactics like that. Gilchrist had talked him into it, and Geordie, with his arse being regularly chewed by Anshaw, who appeared to think that all old ways were bad ones, had finally agreed, albeit only after a wheen of drink. It was not, mark you, that Geordie had the slightest qualm about giving a poacher a good hiding; but he had a quaint set of values. A poacher caught in possession of tackle, or of gun or snare or most importantly of game, upon Balgownie land, could take what he got and Geordie would say he'd asked for it. But to go and seek a man out, with no real proof, on his territory, was just not the name of the game. And especially when the man in question was family. That side of things was police work, and Geordie liked to keep it that way. He was beginning to find Gilchrist's ways far too heavy-handed to be getting on with.

It was unfortunate, he reflected, that Gilchrist seemed to have made such a good impression on the new owner of Balgownie. They were both of the same ruthless ilk, untramelled either of them by the complaint of mere conscience. Geordie hung up his coat and hat and stretched. Then he noticed the note on his desk. He picked it up. Apparently Mr. Anshaw wanted a meeting. Geordie sighed. That man would have had ten meetings a day. How could he not just let folk that had been doing their job twenty years and more just get on with it? Geordie had a dram from the bottle of the Fiddich that he kept in his bottom drawer and then put his jacket and hat on again. Pointless prolonging the agony and at least he had good news for the boss.

He walked the short distance to the Grange from the lodge where the Estate Office was, and indicated to the reception girl that he was going to see Anshaw. When he got to the office, he was rather unpleasantly surprised to see that Gilchrist was already there and that if he did not miss his guess, he and Anshaw had been deep in conversation. "Aye, Alan," he offered. "Feelin better A hope."

"Sit down, George." Anshaw regarded Geordie malevolently as he took a seat opposite him. "I thought you told me that Alan here was ill."

"A did."

"But he was not ill. He was injured."

"Ach weel, it comes tae the same hing, tae ma wey o hinkin. Couldna really hiv him walkin aroond frichtin the guests lookin like that, noo, could we, sirr?"

Anshaw glared at him, but then continued. "That's for me to decide. The interesting thing is how Alan came to be inj...."

"It's no, sir. No ava. Wi aa due respect, it's fur *me* tae decide. The management o the Estate staff is *ma* preserve. Sez so in the contrack ye gie'd me. A wis readin it lest necht, sir, sae A ken."

Anshaw scowled at Geordie again. "Well, well, never mind that now. The point is how he got hurt. Now Alan says that he got hurt by a poacher."

"Suspected poacher."

"By a poacher, and that you were there. Now why didn't you tell me this?"

"Cause we couldna prove nuthin. So it wisna worth the bother."

"How can you say that? This man is responsible for the fact that during the opening week of the Country Club there have been no salmon for our guests to catch, and you say that that's not important?"

Geordie turned to Gilchrist. He expected support, but his blood ran cold when he saw the look on the other man's face. "Ach, so it's that wey, Alan," he said quietly. "Ach weel, taks een tae ken een, as they say."

"What did you say, George," demanded Anshaw.

"A said 'It taks een tae ken een,' sir." Geordie did not feel like speaking "English" today.

"It what—oh, never mind. That's not important now. What is important is that we go and find this man and finish off the job that you two seem to have so comprehensively bungled. And then we can deliver him to the police. Now you, George, get together the three gillies, and take them in the Landrover. I'll take Alan in my car."

"No, sir."

"I beg your pardon?"

"A said 'No, sir'. Gin ye ging and dae that ye'll be committin a criminal offence. Fit we done the ither necht *wis* a criminal offence. We hae nae proof that this fellae done it. We hivnae ony proof that onybody done onyhin."

"Ach come *on,* Geordie," burst out Gilchrist, his voice mocking.

"The pair o us seen yon Zodiac takin aff like aa the deils o hell wis efter hit. The skipper o yon Protection boat saw it tae, even if he did chynge his tune later. An iver syne A come here A've heard tales aboot how this Big Sye character is sicca braw poacher there's no a trickle watter nur a skelp grun in the hale coonty he cannae set his hand ower if he taks the whim. It's high time he wis sorted oot fer yince an fer aa." Gilchrist shook his head and sneered. "By youse hiv cheenged yer tune. Ur ye feared? Izzat it? A'm no feared an A got waur as ye. This time A'll tak ma gun an shoot the bastart's dug afore we stert."

"Naa, Alan, A'm no feared. All A'm sayin is we hiv *nae proof.* We hivnae eneuch proof tae tak the man tae court. You wis thir. Ye heard whit thon polis said fan we hud a deek i Sye's hoose. The fect o the metter is at ye've made this intil a personal affair an at's preventin ye fae usin yer professional judgement." Geordie was getting roused, and a couthy man roused is always dangerous. "Ye've pestered an niggelt at Sye Swankie fae the first meenit ye met him, A daa ken how, aiblins jist ti prove somehin. Yer wey ooty line, Alan. It's the same story wi thon poacher we did nab reid-haundit. Ye gied him sicca hammerin the polis his advised me tae drap the cherges cos gin we divint, he'll press cherges o assault. If ye'd a laved him alane like A tellt ye til it woulda been cut an dried."

"George!" Anshaw's patience snapped. "That will do. You go and get the men."

Geordie smiled. "Did ye ken the Chairman o yon Insurance company caught a salmon, sir? He's recht chuffed, so he is."

"Oh. Very good, George. Now, we don't have time to rest on our laurels, do we. You go and get the men and we'll see you in—shall we say—ten minutes on the drive?"

"Look, sir, gin ye want ti dae somehin, wid it no be better ti ring the Polis an get them ti meet us?"

"Yes. Very well." Anshaw's eyes were narrow. "I'll phone the Arbeg Police while you organise the men. That will be all."

"Very well, sir."

It was after he had left the office that Geordie realised that he had lost his deferential attitude and nervous squeak when addressing Anshaw. He nodded. He went to the reception desk and asked the girl to page the gillies for him. Then he went back to the Estate Office to get the Landrover.

Now, a wake is like no other kind of a party. The point with most parties is that everybody arrives intending to have fun, and maybe they'll end up greeting. But at a wake, everybody comes along for a greet, and then, with that out of the way, proceeds to have a ball. It's as if having done the greeting first it clears the air, like. Lets you concentrate.

Agnes had done her guests proud; her board groaned with the product of her labours, and pride of place was given to the four-foot long salmon paté that lay, glistening and pinkly resplendent, every one of its scales sculpted by hand, on a marble slab in the middle of the great table. The whole of the restaurant and the Lounge Bar had been commandeered to make enough space for what amounted to the entire village, or at least, all of the villagers. Bob was given pride of place by the juke box and a young member of the Paterson family was stationed close by with instructions to prevent anyone from sitting on the coffin, resting their drinks on it (with or without coasters) or tipping their ash inside it. At both bars, business was brisk, with the villagers taking on board liquid fuel as fast as they could. It was a drouthy business all that hymn-singing.

It was a curious fact that when Rae and Sye sat down, why did they not just find themselves sitting next to each other again? Sye was not so daft as to put this down to coincidence, and he made a mental note to have himsel a wee word with his mother when circumstances would permit.

In the square outside the Hotel, Willie and Ian were discussing their future. Ian was leaning against the whitewashed wall and Willie was shying stones at a cat sitting on a wall on the other side of the square. The cat must have known him very well, for it regarded the whole undertaking with utter contempt.

"Christ A've niver felt sae daft in aa ma puff fan A seen yon auld goat Joe Forbes gettin ootil at graft," bemoaned Ian.

"Ach it wisnae that, it wis the wey the meenister wis laughin at wis. Ken somehin? A bet he's been stringin us alang iver syne Monda."

"Yer no serious!" Ian glanced around instinctively.

"Helpmaboab, widje kindly no start aa yon again, neither, eh?"

"Ayebut..."

"Nawbutnaw. Ken fa A wis speakin ti yesterda? Naw? Weel A had me a wee crack wi Mr Robinson, the chemistry teacher. Ken fit he says? A'll bet ye dinna."

"Nu'. A dinna. An A hink ye should......."

"He sez it wis in the pippers that it wis a build up o ges that caused yon splosion. Stick that in yer pipe an smoke it."

"A fit?"

"A build up o ges min. Goad niver hud a lookie-in. It wisnae nuthin ti dae wi him ava. It wis jist a simple exydunt."

"Aye but Goad's omnipi...omnipitocious. He couldae done hit an gart it *luik* like a exydunt."

"Ach daes a favour. Yer on the raips an ye ken it."

Ian's eyes flashed. "An fit wid youse ken, smart-alec?"

"Aye an see how ye went oan aboot Auld Cloots this mornin— loadae guff min. Ye almost hud me believin ye."

"A fit? Ye wis aheid o me! Fit wey could A hae hudye believin onyhin ava fan ye wis that far awa? Fegs min ye were near the ither end o the street afore A goat ootin the kirkyerd." Ian chuckled. "A niver seen ye run at fast afore. By, even Badger couldna keep up wi ye."

It was Wullie's turn to rankle. "You're no cryin me a cooerd ur ye?" he demanded. "Jist as lang's we ken, like?"

"Och, no, no, nutt at aa, nutt at aa," replied Ian, all innocence. "But ye ken fit they say aboot ceps fittin."

Wullie's knuckles were already white. "A'll show ye fit kind o a cooerd A am!" He moved to the centre of the square and held his hands up to heaven. "Here! Oy! Goad! Y'upthir?" he bawled at the top of his lungs. "Kin ye hear me? Hallooo! Ahoy thir! A daa hink yer ony mair'n a fragment o the imagination. Fittdye hink? Fittir ye gaein ti dae aboot it? A daa hink yer thir ava. Goannie prove hit, gin ye ur? *Goannie?* A'm a recht easy terget, eh? C'mon an zap me, then, Goad!"

"HERE! YOU!" thundered a voice from behind and Willie flung himself to the ground.

"Sorrysorrysorry! A didnae mean it honest A didnae!" he cried into the gravel.

"Awtihell, Wullie, luik!" exclaimed Ian.

"Whit?" moaned Willie, still supine.

"Get up an luik ahent ye, ye galoot." Willie turned slowly and looked. Not God, but another figure, not much less terrifying, stood not ten feet from him, and he was not laughing.

"Jings it's the new Baillie fae Balgoonie. Whit'r we gonnae dae?"

"Youse distract him while A tell ma Da!"

The rising tide of chatter was stilled in an instant and all eyes turned to the door. There stood Ian Teviotdale, still dressed in the ridiculous 1970's suit he'd been wearing all week, with a look of panic printed on his face, yelling, "Da! Yon new Bailey fae Balgoonie's here!"

"Fit!" cried Peem, skelling a good quarter of his pint in shock. "Fit, here?"

"Aye. He sez he wants ti spik til Uncle Sye!"

Sye, who was sitting at the table, fixed his eyes upon the pink mound of salmon flesh that rose in front of him; Agnes, who was busy directing latecomers to their seats, saw his glance and clapped her hands to her cheeks. "Oh, my God! We cannae let him see that!"

"Ach, it'll be okay," Sye reassured her. "I'll awa oot an see fit he's efter."

"He's maybe efter settlin the business he sterted the ither necht, Sye," came a basso-profundo rumble. "D'ye want me ti tak a daunder alang tae?"

"S'arecht, Mel. A'll bawl oot if A need ye," Sye grinned at Muckle Mel and made his way through the crowd to the Hotel door. He felt calm. If Gilchrist was here for a square-off, man to man, then fair enough. He could have one. It surprised him a little that Geordie had not come too, but he put it from his mind, knowing that he had the comforting presence of the three times Grand Champion of the Braemar Highland games at his back, along with a few other handy lads.

"Fit like, Gilchrist," he said, stepping into the hallway, closing the door behind him. He could hear the rush of frantic activity commence as he did so. "A believe yer needin a bit crack wi me?"

Inside, Agnes, who, until the moment the lounge bar door swung shut, had been rooted to the spot in consternation, snapped into action. "We'll have ti dae something with that, to start with," she said firmly, pointing at the salmon paté. "There'll be all hell ti pey if he sees it."

Out in the square, Gilchrist spoke. "Mr. Swankie the poacher. Better if we talk *ootside*, A think."

"No fancy a dram, then?"

"No fae you."

The two men moved slowly out into the square in front of the Hotel. Sye felt his big knuckles tighten and his frame slacken into a loose prowl and he bit back the surge of adrenaline. Gilchrist was in front; for him to make the first move. He walked slowly, his hands plunged deep into the pockets of his breeches, out of the blue shadow cast by the hotel into the sunny half of the square. They were moving towards the corner of The Street, where they would be out of sight of the Hotel. Instead of following Gilchrist as he rounded the corner, Sye walked straight ahead, so that he could see along the Street and still be in full view of the eyes which he knew were observing everything from inside the Hotel. His mouth was dry.

Gilchrist turned. "A've a bone ti pick wi youse. A've a score ti settle. Mebbe yer ower feared o me wi'oot yer dug, though. Mebbe ye dinna want ti get yer fancy duds aa clarty. See scum like you? Thir nothin bad eneuch fur ye." He stopped, noticing that Sye was veering off so he could get a look down the street. But there was nothing to see, just the Estate Landrover parked a little further along. "Whaur ye gaen?" Gilchrist demanded angrily.

"Ah, weel it's fair dumfoonerin the hings that cin lowp oot at ye these days. Naa, naa, Gilchrist, A'll tak ye oan man ti man, but recht here, i the Square."

"So aa yer buddies kin come oot an kick ma heid in? A've come across yer wey o daein things afore, ye ken."

"Thill be nae interference fae them, A assure ye," said Sye through gritted teeth. He shook himself. Gilchrist was able to needle him better than anybody he'd ever known. But why? Why now?

"Ach yer jist yella. A gutless, cooerdly poacher is aa ye are."

The blood was beginning to pound at Sye's temples. Gilchrist goaded and goaded, at the same time moving into the blind space in The Street. Sye moved towards him. He could see no-one else. He gathered himself and paused. "Here, tell us far ye've left Cousin Geordie the day? No be hingin back ahent the ingle, eh?" There was a chuckle and the same fellow appeared, shaking his head.

"Here A am, Cousin Sye. A wid jist cry canny wi the bearin yer heidit oan if A wis you."

"Ye mean thir mair?"

Gilchrist spun towards Geordie. "Whit are ye tryin tae dae?" he snarled. "Ruin it aa?"

Geordie turned to him. "A tellt ye i the office this wisna the wey, Alan. A'm yer boss, mind."

"Yer no ma boss ony mair."

"Oh aye?"

"Aye, Mr. Anshaw's made me Estate Supervisor. Ower yer heid. Ye tak yer line fae me noo."

"The hell A div."

Sye flung back his head and laughed. "Wid youse twa cloons tell me fit the blazes is gingin on?"

"I'll tell you," came another voice, and Anshaw walked into view. His face was black with fury and he stared at Geordie as if he was vermin. He made a gesture with his hands and the other three men appeared. "It appears that you have taken something of mine."

"A canna *imagine* fit ye mean. A daa even ken fa ye ur."

"I think you do. And we are talking about salmon, my friend. Salmon that you poached. My salmon."

"*Your* salmon? Am A no recht in hinkin a salmon is a wild fush? Ken A've niver been able ti see fit wey it comes aboot that somehin wild belangs ti somebody jist cos it happens ti be on his land. Fa's salmon wis it afore it wis i the Pinkie? Eh?" Sye grinned. "An as fur the poachin bit, ye should speir at Cousin Geordie. He'll tell ye ye've nae proof an no a hope i hell o a conviction." Sye avoided consideration of the vast quantities of salmon in the Hotel, not to mention several freezers full to bursting. "An gin yer hinkin o mair o the same nonsense as the ither necht, A tell ye, ye'll be a sorry man."

"Cousin Geordie? George—is that true?" Anshaw was knocked a little off balance by this revelation.

"Aye weel he is, kinda, weel, it's a puckle times removed, but, aye....."

"So that's what your hesitation is all about. My what a nice set up. The Head Bailiff of the Estate and the most famous poacher in the county are cousins. How very convenient. What does he do, George? Phone you up and tell you when he's coming so you'll know to stay out of the way?"

Geordie was so stunned he couldn't think of anything to say. It was Sye who replied. "Ma cousin has never spared ony effort tae catch...." He laughed quietly. "Yer a dangerous man an a canny een, A'll gie ye that. Fit're ye hopin? A'll gie somehin awa?"

Geordie looked at his hands. He suddenly felt very tired and he knew the time had come to lance the boil. "Naa, Sye. His wee scheme wis ti get Alan here ti provoke ye intil a fecht, an then he could hiv ye. An A dootna thir somehin i the boot o his motor that wid dae as incriminatin evidence. An then they couldae turned the hale place tapsalteerie. But A queered his pitch by showin ma fiss ower early. He didna let me in oan his scheme, see. He disna lippen on me ony mair. Is that no the wey o't, Mr. Anshaw? And then ye'd hae cried the Polis an let on fit wey ye'd caught this poacher in possession o whitiver an meantime he'd a go at yer Bailiff. That maks it aggravated an the jile. No?"

"You're dismissed, George"

"No A'm no. No wi'oot twa letters o warnin or fit's cried gross misconduct; an A hinna strayed ootside the laa, cept fur eence, an A'm sorry fur at noo. But it disnae metter cos ye kin stick yer joab up yer erse." Geordie nodded down the street and grinned. "An A've queered yer pitch mair'n ye ken forbye, A'm hinkin." Anshaw turned. There was a police car approaching. "See A didnae ken fit youse twa wis intil, but A kent it wis nae guid. So A jist made shair ye hud cried the polis like ye said. On the mobile phone ye sae kindly gied me. An ye hudna. Funny, that, eh no?"

"Ya bastart ye!" roared Gilchrist and leapt towards Geordie. But Sye put his foot out and the Borderer measured his length. He pushed up quickly and spun, but all he got was a kick in the face and that made him think about it. Sye noted how quickly, at the first sign of violence, the Hotel door swung open and a line of men came out, Peem first, then Muckle Mel, followed by six or seven others. Sye made a palm-down gesture, meaning that things were still okay.

Sergeant MacKimmie heaved himself out of the car and pulled on his cheesecutter with a gesture that said 'Official Business' very firmly. He was accompanied by another policeman, whom Sye recognised as the one who had visited him on the Monday morning. MacKimmie strode—with that manner of a policeman that looks unhurried and yet covers the ground with awesome speed—toward the centre of the scene. He addressed himself to Geordie.

"Now what on earth iss coing on here, Cheorge? No trouple I hope."

Anshaw stepped forward. "Sergeant, I'd like a word with you."

"Och, ant I'd like a word with you too. Putt it'ss customary for uss to talk to the fellow who called uss first, tchoo know."

"A hink hings is fine, Jim. Ye mecht like tae hae a wee deek i the boot o yon Jag at's parkit roon by. Itherwise hings is fine."

MacKimmie surveyed the line of men who were standing outside the Hotel. "It'ss all right, tchoo can co ant finish your trinks," he called. And then to Geordie. "What wass it that choo were planning for coodness sake? World War Three?" He looked at Gilchrist, who had picked himself up and was holding his mouth. Blood dripped steadily from between his fingers. "Och, you've not been falling over haff you?" the policeman inquired kindly. Then he turned to Anshaw. "I take it it'ss your Chaguar. Perhaps you'd like to open the boot for me."

"How dare you! I'll have your stripes for this. You need a search warrant."

"No I ton't. Not for a vehicle regarding which I haff information to the effect that it may contain articles pertaining to the solving off a crime. Ant since Mister Paird iss a Bailiff........" He smiled at Gilchrist. "Ant ton't you move a muscle while I'm gone. You other three," he added, raising his voice, "Can get back in the Lantrover now. The fun'ss ofer for today. Come along now Mr. Anshaw. Let's not make this tifficult."

Geordie's guess had been right. In the boot of Anshaw's Jaguar were a number of highly suspect items. Can openers with huge treble hooks tied on. A gaff with a barb in the hook. A length of monofilament net. And two salmon.

"Ochone, Mr Anshaw, tear me, tear me. Now where titchoo get this stuff?" He picked up the gaff and pressed his finger to the point. He whistled. It was sharp as a needle.

"It belongs to that man there!"

"Oh does it? Cheorge?" Geordie shook his head, and MacKimmie looked very hard at Anshaw. "Mr. Anshaw, now you'll haff to excuse me, I'm getting a wee bit deaf I'm thinking. What wass it tchoo were saying chust now?"

"One of the gillies found it this morning, sergeant. I was on my way to turn it in." Anshaw's voice was quiet, and this time it happened to be the truth.

"Aye. That'ss what I thought you said. Putt you thought you'd stop by here first." He put down the gaff and turned to face the owner of the Balgownie Estate. "First, all of this stuff is confiscated. I could haff the car too, you know. Gaffs with parps— tearie me, Mr Anshaw, tearie me. Who put it into your head to try this? Not Cheorge. He's too canny. He knows fery well that planting evidence on a poacher will not wash in the courts round here. Sso it must haff been our little wee friend from the south." He swaggered back towards Gilchrist with his hands in his pockets. Gilchrist pointed at Sye. "He's a poacher! Aabody kens that. Monday through the necht he cleaned oot the river. Dae yer duty!"

"Stevenson," called MacKimmie. "I wass lucky that Constable Stevenson wass on tuty today. I belief he can help. Titchoo haff a look round Mr. Swankie's house on Montay morning?"

"Aye A did that, Serge."

"Ant?"

"An nothin. Clean as a whistle."

"A'll bet it's no noo," shouted Gilchrist. "Search the bloody place, will ye, in the name o Christ?"

"No. Iff you chentlemen had come to me in the normal course of thingss ass I'm sure Cheorge advised you to, then I would. Pelieve me," he looked penetratingly at Sye as he spoke, "I ham quite happy to put poachers behind barss. They cause far too much trouble ant stir up all sorts of bad things that I haff no time for. Like all of this. Putt," he turned back to Anshaw, "I have already seen enough to convince me that a certain—*manipulation* of the law wass planned by you. Ant I have not peen on the force aal these years to put up with *that*. So I ton't think I'll pe looking arount Mr. Swankie's house today."

"That's bloody ridiculous! He's a fuckin poacher, man!" Gilchrist grabbed MacKimmie's lapel.

"You're unter arrest now. Assaulting a police officer in the course off his tuty. Take him to the car, Constaple." He stared hard into Gilchrist's eyes. "I atvise you not to make things worse than they are." He turned back to Anshaw as Stevenson bustled Gilchrist off to the car. "May I suggest you co home, sirr? Then I won't feel I need to make a report about the contents off your vehicle. I'll chust find them as a result off information received. As for your employee, he can spent the weekend in the cells until the Sherriff Court on Montay. Likely the Sherriff will admonish him on account of time served ant he'll be home after. I ton't think a bit off cooling off will hurt him. Off you co now, sir. Please."

Anshaw got back into the Jaguar with a look of thunder on his face, and then drove off.

MacKimmie watched him go and then pushed his hat back on his head with his thumb and turned to Geordie and Sye. "Ant you two? There'll pe no trouble?" The two men shook their heads. "Coot. So shake on it." His voice was warning. Geordie held out his hand and Sye shook it. MacKimmie nodded, and then took off his cap and tucked it under his arm. He fished a packet of cigarettes from his pocket and offered them round. Sye took one and the two men lit up from the same match.

"Ochone, Alexanter, I've heard some trettful things apout choo thiss week. Och, tearie me, tearie me. I can unterstant Mr. Anshaw peing annoyed, sso I can. Things woult not haff gone well for you if he hatn't irritated me like that."

Sye grumbled under his breath but MacKimmie ignored him. "Now, I'm coing to tell you something. I like to see peace. It'ss what I to. I protect the peace. That's my chob. Ant I have alwayss pelieved that in the pursuit off that end a policeman hass to use his wits ant his discretion. Which iss why I am *not* coing to look in your freezer, Alexanter. Putt now *you* owe *me*. Ant what you owe me iss no more ploddy nonsense or I will throw the pook at you. To you unterstand? See there's all sorts off little things that I can do to make your life very tifficult. Now I ton't want to do that, Alexanter." Sye nodded, and sighed. "Aye, Jim." He put out his hand.

MacKimmie shook it and then leaned forward and tapped him on the shoulder. "You know what choo want, don't choo," he asked in a conspiratorial hush. "You want kids. That would use up all that extra enerchy you use for getting into mischeif. That's what choo need. A nice wife ant plenty of little Alexanters. You're far too ploddy old to pe carrying on like a silly teenacher. Cood grief man you've cot your own pusiness and I ton't know all what, poats, cars.........Stop thiss nonsense pefore something really bad happens." Sye shuffled and looked at the ground.

When MacKimmie had finished his smoke and gone, Big Sye and Geordie Baird were left alone in the square.

"A kinda hink A'm due ye an apology," said Geordie, levelly. "Ye fit?"

"A'm due ye an apology. A shid niver hae jumped ye the ither necht."

"Aye yer damned recht thir; gin ye hudnae, Pluto widnae bit ye."

Geordie looked around quickly. "It's no that. An far is thon baste onywey?"

"I the hoose, A jalouse. Ye want me ti fustle on him, like?" Sye was laughing, but it was a bit too close to the bone for Geordie.

"Look, gie's a break, here. A ken fine ye netted the estuary Monday syne. Hauf the bluidy coonty kens. A canna fur the life o me figure oot fit wey ye done it, but A *ken* ye done it. We wis aa set for een o the best Runs A cin mind an then—" he snapped his fingers—"Nuthin."

"A suppose A'm due ye a apology masel. Specially seein as fit wey ye've been that jonick an aa. A shidna hae netted the river like thon. Aiblins it wis ower the tap an aa. We done it wi drysuits, be the wey— under watter, like, if ye want ti ken. Every ither year A've jist labbit a wee bit foulhooker in an teen ma twa-three fish like. Aye, well mebbe fehve- sax fish. But thon wis different. It wis ower much. But it wis yer ain blame."

"Ma blame?" Geordie was amazed. "Ma blame? Fit wey i the name o the wee man dae ye figure that?"

"Ye daured me ti dae hit, Geordie."

"Me? Fan?"

"Fan you wis here yon efterneen wi yon bastart Gilchrist. Ye stood in thonder bar an tellt me A durstna try it on this year, whit wi aa the extra bailiffs an aa that ye'd pit oan. Fit did ye expect me ti div? Especially wi yon dickheid gie'n it laldy."

"Ye near dredged the estuary, damned near got me fired an yersel the jile—aye, mebbe even killt—because.... Ye caused aa this bother jist cos A sayed ye durstna? Jim's recht, it *is* aboot time ye growed up."

Sye bridled. "Fit dae ye mean be at?"

"Ach, dinnae stert. Jist dinnae stert. It's jist....Well, jist let's say ye ging a lang wey tae git back at a man at's let oot a chance remark wi the drink on him."

Sye looked hard at Geordie. For the first time he could see the fatigue grained deep into his face.

"See, it's aa recht fur youse," Geordie was saying. "Yer a canny laddie, an ye've got yer ain boat an yer ain hoose an aa that an ye kin dae fit'n the bluidy hell ye like; but the rest o wis hivty work fur a livin. An fan ye get a new boss an he gits ye aa fired up an tells ye tae pit an end to the poachin or else, it gets ye a bit jumpy, like........An, A ken A fashed ye, an A'm sorry fur that too. A wis jist daein ma joab. As A seen it. But youse, ye wis jist daein hit fur a lark an tae rub ma neb in't."

"Aye, weel, ye mecht hae somehin thir an aa," began Sye, feeling uncomfortable.

"Ach A daa ken fit wey A waste ma breath; ye'd niver unnerstaun in a thoosan year. Onywey, it's neen o ma ingans noo."

Sye nodded. "Ye shair ye done the recht hing? Mind, A could

yase a bit help on the boat gin yer stuck......"

"That's recht jonick o ye, Sye," laughed Geordie, genuinely surprised. "Specially as A ken fine ye dinnae really need onybody. But it's aa
recht; A've somehin up ma sleeve. Naw, A couldna thole it ony mair
alang by. A've worked on yon estate syne a wis a loon an been recht
content wi ma lot. But noo it's cheenged an A'm no likin it ava. It's aa
cheenged an A'm ower auld a dug tae cheenge wi hit. Naw, yon fella fae
the Insurance company tellt me he'd a bit land ower by Brechin, wi a bit
watter needin sortit oot, so A'll gie him a try. An if no, A ken thir lookin
for good men on the Spey, an A'm weel kent."

Sye was dumbfounded.

"A still hink it wis a daft hing ye done, jist tae spite me. But at the
end o the day if ye hudna done it A'd a likely bit ma tongue an stuck it oot
wi him up thir, an A widna hae been content ava. But youse gettin ma
erse roasted—fur the first time in near thirty year, be the wey—Ach it's a
kinda complicatit, Sye. Ken you an me's been on the opposite sides fur
years an it wis aye a braw joke till it wis aa spiled. It'll niver be like at
again."

Sye nodded. "Ye'll no hiv tellt Mairi? Ye'd better come in an hae
a dram afore ye ging hame then."

"Aye, A'll tak a dram wi ye noo, noo that it's aa aff ma kist. Heh,
A daa ken fa ye'll hae tae dae battle wi next year. Mebbe Alan, but A doot
ye'll hae as much fun."

"A hink yer recht. Here, far did ye say ye wis ettlin ti get a joab?"

"A didnae. An gin A dae get it an A see youse wi'in five mile o
hit A'll shoot ye on the spot fur the poachin rascal ye ur!"

Inside the Hotel, every available space at every window that looked out
onto the square was occupied by a peering face, and Willie and Ian were
keeping up a running commentary for those who were not lucky enough
to have got a ringside seat.

"Jings! Thir shakin haunds again."

"Here, noo Sye's goat his haund on Geordie's shudder!"

"Helpmaboab, thir comin back in! Quick, aabody act normal!"

Geordie came into the lounge bar first and gazed upon the sea
of silent faces. "Afternoon," he said.

Agnes collected herself. "Would ye care for a wee dram, Mr.
Baird," she asked, quickly. "On the house, of course."

"Thank ye kindly, Mrs Paterson, I'll hae a wee low-flyer," he
said, and politely didn't notice that Agnes' hands had suddenly developed a tremor to rival her husband's. "But A canna bide lang." He also
ignored the audible sigh of relief from the company.

"A see ye hinna planted Boab yet," he said, indicating the coffin,
which was beside him by the door. "Aye, it's jist like the old times afore
they let thon auld bugger fa i the sea on his wey up ti the howff."

"Fa's he cryin a auld bugger?" whispered Mae indignantly. "At wis ma faither he's spikin aboot."

"Hudjer wheesht you!" hissed Jess, and simpered at Geordie across the table.

Geordie drained his glass. "Aye weel, be seein yiz." He replaced his deerstalker and squeezed it down on his skull. He turned, and as he did so he tapped the coffin. Everyone in the room held their breath. "Better plant him quick," he observed, "He's beginnin ti hae a bit guff aboot him," and breezed out. "Mind," he added, pausing at the door, "Hit's the first time A kent a deider stink o fish."

Agnes slumped against the bar. "By, aye, dae A need a drink!"

CHAPTER THIRTY-THREE
The Wake

Morag Paterson had been to powder her nose and as she left the Ladies on her return she passed George Baird in the corridor on his way out. When she got to her seat she realised, to her annoyance, that some old duffer was sitting in it. "Excuse me," she squeaked, shaking his shoulder, "A'm hinkin yer in ma sea....." The sentence never finished. Despite the lightness of her touch, the old body sagged under it, and his head swivelled round to look at her. Or so she thought. But the eyes were shut and she realised that she was gazing into the face of one very well made up and very well dead Robert Paterson Smith.

"Oh," she said, and fainted.

It was fortunate that Sye, whose seat was close by, had been following her, otherwise she might have been hurt; as it was he was perfectly placed to catch her under the armpits as she slumped towards him. He stopped there, for a moment, pondering what to do next. His experience with women in faints was, well, non-existent. Unconscious stupors yes, dead faints no. Especially women of Morag's bulk. He thought for a moment that he was going to slip a disc. But with a rapidity that in a less stressed moment would have astounded Sye, Izzie materialised at his side.

"Rae, Rae," she crooned. "Gie Sye a haun. A'll clear a way."

"Oh the pair hing," said Rae soothingly, and laid her hand on Morag's brow. Sye could not help thinking, as the blood began to thump in his temples, that maybe somebody in the line of Muckle Mel's size would be more useful. "We'd better get her somewey she kin lay doon fur hauf an hour. Kinye manage her, Sye?" Iz crooned, as sweetly as she could, and in the meantime silenced all offers of help with a glare that would have turned milk.

"A jalouse," Sye muttered, and heaved Morag's bulk up bodily. He was surprised at how heavy she was, and he hadn't expected her to be *light*. He caught Peem's eye, and it was sparkling with amusement. "Didye really *hivty* pit the auld bugger thir?" he grunted, turning so that he could go in reverse, with Morag's heels trailing on the ground.

Peem just shrugged. "It wis Ma's idear."

"This wey," said Iz, and Sye and his burden followed meekly, with Rae assisting the best she could.

By half-past one the wake was under full sail. Everybody had

had enough to drink to get their appetites going, and set about the salmon with relish. Course after course they ate, each succeeding culinary triumph sallying forth from the kitchen to a murmur of appreciation. Belts began to get tight and stays began to chafe under the weight of an orgy of consumption. After the salmon paté was a smoked salmon and orange sorbet; and the main course, the delight of it all, a salmon and laverbread *en croute* that was entirely as wonderful as it looked and smelled, but left everyone reeling. There was a short respite with the cheese, and then Agnes delivered the coup de grace—her mother's recipe sherry trifle, a glorious confection with the efficacy of a gastronomic atom bomb that left everywhere it passed quietude and glassy eyes.

A kind of beatific hush settled over the company after that; or perhaps you might say a shell-shocked silence. Men who had not spoken to each other for thirty years all of a sudden found that they were smiling across the battlefield of the table at each other and thinking that they might not be such dreadfully bad fellows after all, and women who on any other occasion would have slashed each other to ribbons with the scalpels of their tongues were chatting quietly like long-lost sisters. Even the Reverend James Jameson, who wholeheartedly disapproved of the affair, had to grant that it was having a miraculous effect upon the barbarous politics of the village, even if he did have a nagging hunch that this spirit of warmth and forgiveness would disappear in a haze of sorry heads the morning after.

We shall allow ourselves the indulgence of imagining that Lanky Boab—now safely returned to his coffin—would not have disapproved.

Sye and Rae dragged the comatose Morag, like a sack of coal, into the lift, along the corridor, and then into the first bedroom Iz could find. With a last great heave they threw the limp mass onto one of the single beds and sat down heavily on the other, panting. Somehow, Iz just disappeared, and Sye never even noticed. It was remarkable how she did that. Sye loosened his tie. He hated the bloody things and he was overheating. Today, he thought, was turning out to be quite a day. He became aware, as his heart rate returned to normal, that Rae was sitting on the bed beside him, saying nothing. He got to his feet. But then he stopped, arrested by the cool touch of her hand on his.

"Dinna gae yet," she said, and there was a tension in her voice that made him not. "Ye've been that......distant, since A came back—syne A came *hame*," she said, as if to herself. "Even when ye came round that necht after the fight......As if we were strangers meetin for the first time."

Sye sat down again, very slowly. Whatever hand had to be played, had to be played. There was no jouking the issue now. "And ye ken," Rae said, in the same quiet, gentle voice, "Och, it's jist—it's jist—Hell, I'm sorry, Sye. This is a daft idear." She stopped and breathed deeply for a little while. Sye felt an overpowering urge to put his arm around her and an absolutely irresistible force which prevented him. Rae still had a hold of his left hand anyway, but she seemed to have forgotten what it was, for she was twisting it up like a handkerchief. "A wis just going to say that aa this minds me so much o—ye ken—Peem and Iz's weddin—when we—" She stood up quickly, and made to leave, but this time it was Sye who stopped her.

"Yer no lavin noo," he husked. "No noo ye've opened at can o worms. A wis quite content tae be pals. How did ye hiv tae cheenge hings?"

"Were ye? Quite happy A mean."

Sye shook his head and loosened his collar for something to do. "Naa. *Course* no. But A'm good at games an A could hiv played thon een an naebody wid hae kent ony better, no e'en you. Content? Fittdye hink, Rae? Eh?"

"A dinna ken, Sye."

"How did ye ging? Niver a word, niver a note—"

"Why did *you* go? Oh, A ken, Izzie said—ye got a joab. Sye d'ye no think ye were due me the courtesy o lettin me ken? Whaur ye were goin—whit ye were plannin." She stopped and drew breath and when she looked at him her black eyes were irresistible. "Whither ye wantit me or no?"

Sye was nonplussed. "Fit the—A tellt Etta. A said til her A had ti ging."

"Can A believe ye?"

"Hell A sent ye a cable fae Heathrow an anither een fae Rio an then A wrote that many letters ti ye the skipper thocht A wiz skellie an A near tint the berth. Fittdye mean, let ye ken? Youse niver let *me* ken. A cam back here efter ma trip lookin fur ye an expeckin ye'd be here efter aa A'd wrote an b'Christ hud ye no skedaddled fur the big city. Thrown me ower fur some ither fellae that left ye up the road. An noo ye come back here an.......Ah stuff it." He got up, but Rae grabbed his arm..

"Oh, *Sye*! *Please*. Hing on a meenit. Whit cables? Whit letters?"

"The eens A sent ye." Sye sat down again.

Rae left go of his hand and covered her face, shaking her head. Sye could feel the sobs that wracked her shaking the bed they were sitting on. He didn't know what to do. He was angry but he didn't want to hurt her and yet it seemed he was doing just that. "Daa greet," he said, weakly, at last. "A'm recht sorry. A didna mean ti gar ye greet. Please daa greet."

"No, it's no you. Sye, A *niver* got ony cables or ony letters. Where did ye send them tae?"

"Yer hoose. Far else wid A hae sent them?"

"Jesus *Christ!* Weel, if they iver cam, ma mither must hiv hid them, for A niver saw a single een. Niver a one, A sweir."

"Yer jokin!"

"Well you explain it. Ye say ye sent letters, an A've little enough reason tae doot ye. God, fit wey could she *dae* that?" Rae bit her knuckle. Her black hair was falling down untidily and Sye was reminded—for the umpteenth time that day—of how much he was attracted to her. There was a bell ringing at the back of his head but he was too upset by the immediate revelations to figure out what it meant.

"So—so how *did* ye ging awa," he asked, at last. "How did ye gie up the skale—yer Highers—ye'd only a puckle months left; ye were aa set ti ging til the varsity.....Fit gart ye blaw it aa?"

Rae turned to face him. "Christ, can ye.no *guess?*" Her voice was harsh with anger, anger at herself, and anger at this man. "Can't you guess, Sye Swankie, *can't* you........." The sobs were coming quickly now and Sye could hardly make out her words. "D'ye no *realise* the mess A wis in *yet?*" And suddenly Sye did, and the bell made sense.

"Willie—he's—he's no—He's no *ma son*, is he?" Rae nodded. "Oh fer cryin oot bluidy loud," said Sye, staggered. He slapped his knee. "Dear *God* wumman, how did ye no get a ship tae shore call pit through if that wis the wey hings wis? Jesus *Christ* fit wis ye playin at?"

"A wis ower—Christ A wis seventeen, Sye; ye daa expect seventeen-year-olds ti be wiselike. D'ye no realise A didna want onybody merryin me cos thi hud tae? A rather'd dae it on ma lane nor live wi at. A ken fit happens; A've seen it, A ken the sea-widows at niver see thir man but twa-three month a year....Naa. An A figured at fan ye took aff wi niver a word like at, at wis whit wey it wis. Whit wey it wid be. A didnae want ony o't."

Sye was shaking his head slowly. This was all a little too much for him to take in, and his flash of anger subsided as he reflected on the hard years that Rae must have passed. "How, Rae? How did ye no let me ken?" he said, his voice quiet, and gentle.

"Izzie's recht. A'm ower canty." Rae threw back her head and swept the hair from her eyes. "Thir no muckle about me your sister disnae ken, A sweir. Funny, so it is. A wanted tae *hurt* ye, Sye. Ye'd hurt me. A wanted ye tae realise whit ye'd lost. A wanted tae gar ye greet ower me the wey A grat ower you."

"By Christ ye fair did that aa recht. Ye hurt me good, Rae. A grat aa recht."

"Are ye fashed.......Dinnae be; dinnae say onyhin. A wisnae gingin tae tell ye, Sye, A jist wanted......A daa ken whit A wanted. Noo it seems the stupitest thing—well no the stupitest, no really. But there wis A, in Embro, guid job, steady money, career aheid o me..........An A gied it aa up. An A tellt masel A wanted Willie tae be near his faither— A didnae mean tae put pressure on ye, honest—A wanted him tae grow up in the open...........A wantit hings tae be like they wis afore.......No, no that. A wantit hings tae be like they should hae been for me......But for him. D'ye unnerstaun, Sye?" She squeezed his hand and then let it go. "Look, A didna come here tae trap ye. A niver wanted ye unless.......See, wi me, A man wid aye hiv tae want me mair nor onythin else on the fiss o this earth. At's the way it's aye been wi me. A'll niver tak segint best, nor even less peety. So A'm sorry aboot this......this wee scene. A guess it's jist the funeral an aa. It's been a hell o a week. Maybe we better—Look, A really didna dae this tae trap ye. It wis aa Izzie's idear. A tellt her it wis da—Mmmf!" Further speech became impossible as Sye's mouth pressed against hers. With an alacrity that surprised both of them, she opened her mouth and let his tongue in, and then they were grappling with each other's clothes in a frenzy.

Morag came to, slowly. She looked around. She was in a strange room. From her left came rhythmic sounds of a nature she knew only from her dreams. She looked and saw; thon quine that moved in across the road was sitting astride Big Sye Swankie, moving slowly up and down with an expression of pure joy on her face, and very little on the rest of her. Morag did not at first associate this with the sexual act, partly because she had not realised that it would appear to be so pleasant, and then she realised, and froze. She squeezed her eyes up tight shut and wished she could faint again. But it did give her a certain thrill, and so she cracked one eye open just a peep.

Izzie, meantime, had taken up sentry duty at the entrance to the lift. A little time later, Jess and Nan came out of the party and spoke to her. They chatted in hushed tones, and then Iz nodded. Jess was delegated to go and have a deek, under the pretext of taking a cup of tea up to Morag. As Izzie observed, if Rae hudnae managed something by now the game was up anyway. When Jess got to the first-floor landing with the cup of tea and the Digestive biscuit, the first thing she saw was the ubiquitous Willie and Ian, who, having jouked Izzie by climbing up the fire escape, were now taking turns to keek through the bedroom keyhole. It was clear from their stifled hysteria that there was something worth seeing going on inside. Jess approached in silence and then applied her foot firmly to the nearest backside.

"Jings!" yelped Ian, and sprawled on the carpet under the blow.

"Awa ootae thir ye wee buggers afore A fung yer erses again!" rasped Jess, and swung her foot at Willie. But he was too quick and the lads took off down the corridor, giggling. Jess waited till they were safely out of sight, and then set down the cup of tea, hitched up her skirt, and, bending slowly so as not to set off her bad back, applied her own peeper to the keyhole.

She clapped her hands in delight, had another good look to be sure, and then waurstled off back along the corridor. This news *had* to be communicated.

"Staun doon noo, Iz," she growled as she passed, waving one finger in the air. "It's a goer."

"Fit aboot Morag?"

Jess laughed shortly. "A jalouse at's the nearest she'll iver git til haein a man atween *her* hochs, dear. A widnae like ti spyle her fun, seein how she spends at muckle time hinkin aboot it." This last one puzzled Iz—the secret of Morag's dreams being guarded carefully by the cabal of Mae's shop—but she shrugged and smiled in satisfaction. Time for a wee dram then.

Mae was awaiting the arrival of her second helping of trifle. She gazed listlessly at the empty space on the other side of the table where her niece and Big Sye should have been sitting. She was just wondering whether to go and recce the situation when Jess flung open the door and marched up to her.

"Hee, hee," she rasped into Mae's lug, her voice triumphant, "Ye'll niver guess fit A've jist seen."

Mae could, very easily, but she was too stuffed to mount her usual sarcastic reply, and let a condescending lift of her left eyebrow speak for her. Jess was far too pleased with herself to notice, and taking her seat again, she elbowed Mae with a vigour that would have winded a Scotland prop-forward.

"See gin at niece o yourn canna get her hooks recht set in him noo, A'd disown her," she cackled. "Och, A wunner fan we'll hae the waddin? A aye like a guid waddin ye ken."

Meanwhile, Agnes was following up the devastating Sherry Trifle, after a decent pause, with the First Aid; Gaelic Coffee, good and strong. That perked things up a bit, and even the Reverend James Jameson—who somewhat underestimated the alcoholic content of the brew—began to be good-humoured about the day. All around the table glazed eyes brightened, sagging jaws quickened, and fire and life began to flow once more to limbs that had become leaden under the onslaught. The babble of conversation began to mount again, and then—and no one was ever sure who it was—someone shouted:

"Fittaboot a wee bit music, like, an we'll hae a jig!"

Suddenly, the room came alive. Dave switched on the lights in the bar and braced himself as the crowd rose from their seats and closed in on him. Eck, Sye's Da, with practised fingers fiddled the counter on the ancient juke-box when he was sure that Agnes was too busy overseeing the clearing away to notice. He dialled in half-a-dozen Andy Stewart songs and half-a-dozen Lindsay Ross jigs and reels, and then put his hand over the bar and turned the master volume up full.

The crackling strains of *Nicky Tams* erupted from the machine with an ear-shattering bellow, and the wake awoke. Big hands, ready hands, came from nowhere, and tables and chairs were pushed aside in a tide of activity that swept past Agnes, though she tried, Canute-like, to stem it; but no real damage was done, only a wee bit paint scraped and a few tardy plates broke. Full glasses were passed over the bar into the crowd as quickly as empty ones could be picked up. After *Nicky Tams* Andy Stewart upped the tempo with *The Muckin o Geordie's Byre* and the party really began to rev its motors. The great space of the lounge bar was clear now, and the crowd was champing and tugging. And then came a long, drawn out chord of G on the accordion and Lindsay Ross's Scottish Country

Dance Band thundered out into the fray like a mighty ocean billow that carried all before it. The couples chose themselves and the room was filled with whirling bodies and the air was full of the sound of clapping hands and cries of "Heeeeeeyoouch!"

And if the dancing was not quite as Miss Middleton's dance class would have liked, she wasn't there and nobody was giving a damn what she would think anyway. What, after all, are a few toes trodden in the name of a good time?

After The Gay Gordons came The Dashing White Sergeant, and then, now that the blood was up, the company was formed into eights for a Strip-the-Willow.

Just at this moment Big Sye and Rae returned. They had indeed been having fun, but had begun to think that they might be missed and that they should perhaps adjourn till later. Take a breather like. And there was Morag to think of. In any case they were both feeling a bit drouthy after their exertions. There was a great whoop and a caterwauling of whistles and cries and remarks of a kind which, in deference to Rae's feelings, I will not here repeat, and they found themselves pushed to the head of the lead eight.

It was seven o'clock before the pace slacked enough for Agnes to persuade the pallbearers that they really ought to do something about Lanky Boab other than use his coffin as a shelf for their glasses. Morag, who had recovered sufficiently to come downstairs and take a little weak tea, though she kept looking about as if she expected to see something nobody else could, said she would feel more relaxed once her erstwhile tormentor was planted. Mind, as Jess remarked to Nan, nobody had noticed it getting in her way before, like. So the coffin was shouldered and weaved an unsteady path up the causie to the kirkyard, where the Reverend James Jameson was at last able to perform his duties. The rest of the crowd decamped to the kirkyard to see Old Rob (funny how death changes people) off; and a bonny like show it was. Tam Teviot played a slow tune on his fiddle at the graveside, a sweet and magical thing it was that he'd made special for his old friend, and it so plucked the heart strings that there was not a dry eye to be seen. And then Muckle Mel, who was standing atop the Ness, where the last rays of sunshine still played on him, struck up a lament that washed over all of them with the terrible sadness of its melody. It was a very moving moment, thought Joan, the minister's wife, and shut the door on the uncharitable reflection that after the amount they'd all had to drink, the whole *world* was probably moving.

But in the evening light it *was* bonny; even the minister thought so, and his proprieties had been more shocked than ever he could remember. At the end of the day, he thought, Robert Paterson Smith had been sent on to the next world from the midst of his friends, and the fact that the thing had not been done as the book prescribed it did not diminish one jot the dignity with which it was done, nor the sincerity, nor the love. Joan took his arm as they followed the crowd back down the hill, and even let her head lean on his shoulder, and the Reverend Jameson felt, for the first time it seemed, at home.

There was a sort of a quietness settled upon the crowd when they re-entered the Hotel, and Agnes thought, with a certain heaviness of heart in view of the bar takings, that the party might peter out.

But not a bit of it; for while she was thinking this the bar doors flew open and admitted an overpowering cloud of cheap perfume. In the midst of it stood Deek White and the merchant skipper's wife. Deek and she had spent most of the day helping each other have showers and other activities of a more or less fleshly nature, and now they were looking for a bit of light entertainment. But it wasn't Deek and the petite brunette that was the sauce the party was needing, it was the brunette's auntie and the rest of the nightshift from Cargill's that she'd insisted on bringing along for a night out. Deek—who, due to the hold he now had over the depot manager, felt that he could do as he pleased with impunity—had obligingly bussed them all to the Hotel, and now here they were, full of hell and not at all fussy how they got there.

"Sorry we're late, like," said Deek to no-one in particular, indicating the bustle of women all kitted out in their party frocks and heavily larded with make up. "Taks a fell lang while ti get this lot organised." He looked round at the faces staring at him in amazement. "This *is* the perty, eh, no?" he asked, a little uncertainly. *"Aye,"* roared Mel, whose blood was up after a good blow on the pipes. "It's ower early ti be hinkin aboot wir baids."

The still-bright embers burst into flame. Chae Strachan shouldered his squeeze box and with that and Tam Teviot on fiddle and young Chae on the drums they were all set; but the lounge bar seemed stuffy after the sweet cool sea breeze upon the Ness, so the three of them set themselves up outside in the square and gave it laldy. For hour after hour into the deepening night the company whirled and reeled and two stepped and foxtrotted and waltzed. Ten o'clock came and Mrs. Kennedy of Pitmeddoes complained about the noise. Sergeant MacKimmie was once again despatched, found his cap firmly removed and locked in a cupboard along with his car keys, and was at last posted missing by an increasingly impatient Duty Sergeant at two in the morning.

Around about midnight Iz was finally persuaded to take the stage, and her rendition of *My Love is Like a Red Red Rose* transported the rowdy crowd into reflective silence. Rae was so overcome that she dragged Sye off to The Chateau. She reckoned she had a lot of ground to make up and she wasn't for wasting any more time. Some three quarters of an hour later Peem noticed their absence, and upon investigation discovered that the light in Sye's bedroom was on. Peem had a wee word with Chae and Tam Teviot, and soon after Sye heard the strains of a version of *Moon River* being sung by male voice choir accompanied by fiddle and accordion with spoons courtesy of Peem, immediately under his window. Rae smiled at him and ran her fingers through his hair.

"We'll hae tae ging, ye ken," she whispered. "They expect it."

So they pulled on their clothes and made their way down; the villagers formed two lines and clapped and stamped a tattoo as they walked between them to the middle of the square. At the end of the two lines were Peem and Izzie, grinning like cats and each holding one end of a broom low down near the ground. Rae stopped when she saw them and grabbed Sye's arm.

"Ye ken whit it means if we step ower those, divvin't ye?" she hissed urgently.

"Aye," said Sye. "A div." He looked deep into her brown eyes, so dark they were almost black with pupils that merged into the irises; and then he laughed. "An A'm game if you are."

Rae just kissed him long and hard and they skipped over the brooms. There was a great cheer and Chae and Tam struck up a waltz and the couple led off. Nan cried harder than she'd ever cried before, Mae smiled beatifically, and even Jess got emotional. Only Morag was muttering something about they beck yerd waddins, but nobody was paying her any attention at all.

CHAPTER THIRTY-FOUR
And So To Bed

At last silence came to the little village; gone five in the morning and a metally blue-grey in the lift to the east. In the square before the Hotel the village dogs squabbled and snarled over the leftover scraps, the half-eaten sandwiches and the packets of crisps, and occasionally made sallies at the cats who, whenever they could, rushed in and snatched some tasty morsel.

In the bedroom at Number One Auchpinkie, Nan lay awake and thought soft thoughts that she would never allow herself to be seen thinking in daytime, and nestled against the mounding bulk of Eck, who slumbered oblivious. In the little cottage in the square, Jess contentedly sawed up her nightly logs, while in the neighbouring cottage Ian sprawled across his bed like a happy starfish and dreamed of mischeif.

Willie did something the same; he had not yet fully understood what had happened, but somehow knew that it must be good.

The Reverend James Jameson lay comfortably awake and pondered the indigo light of his bedroom window and listened to the rustle of Joan's breathing and wondered how to weave all that had come to pass into a sermon, struggling to wrest a moral from the jaws of chance.

Joe Forbes was awake, too, not pondering morals, but the voluptuous contours of the unclothed body of one of the Cargill's nightshift girls squeezed up tight beside him in his single bed. Over the undulating hillock of her breast, slowly rising and falling under the billow of the sheet, he could see his plastic crucifix glowing in the soft light of the bedside lamp, and he tipped a nod of thanks and farted his happiness.

Agnes dreamt dreams of salmon, and Dave dreamt legions of beer glasses and nips of whisky, and we shall leave them to it; outside the Hotel, Deek White and his petite, Sandra, lay piled together in a makeshift bed of coats on the back seat of his bus.

Down on the beach sat Peem and Izzie, nuzzling their familiar plumpnesses together in squashy content. They had been drunk, bleezing fou in fact, but that was hours before. The dancing and the time and the mood had taken them on somewhere past that. They were leaning against Peem's upturned dinghy, sharing a can of Tennent's lager from the stash under the boat. The clinker planking made awkward ridges in their backs and the pebbles of the beach uncomfortable dents in their doups, but they were much too happy to care. But then Iz sighed and looked at Peem, who raised an eyebrow.

"Here, A've somehin ti show ye," she said in reply to the mute question. She rummaged in the pocket of the jacket she'd fetched from the house and pulled out a bulging brown envelope. "Hae a deek in at," she said, and passed it over. Peem looked inside. The envelope was full of unopened letters, very old, with foreign stamps. He took one out and both his eyebrows shot up. "These ur—ur these fae Sye ti Rae?" Iz nodded and sucked in a cheek. "Fit wey did *ye* come tae hiv them?" asked Peem. Iz gazed studiously out to sea and avoided his eye. He couldn't remember her ever doing that before, and he was troubled. "Mind fan Etta deed thir wis naebody ti redd up the hoose? Aa her freens—those she'd left—wis ower auld, an thir wis nae faimly? An A said A'd dae it, jist fur auld lang syne? Weel, at's fan A fund they letters. An the cables. Thir in there an aa. The auld bitch had kept them aa. Ivery last een. So it made me feel better aboot this." She pulled out another envelope, much thinner, and passed it over. Peem made his kettle noise as he read the enclosed sheet with furrowed brow.

"Etta's Will! By the cringe she left aa her— she left aahin ti the Arbeg Cat Refuge! Jist like she aye said she wid. Ah jings, at's awfy.... Pair Rae..... The hoose..... Here A dinnae.....By A niver thocht she'd really—Far i the hell did ye get *this*, onywey?"

"Same place. It wis aa pitten far it wid be easy fund, Peem. Aa thegither. Like she meant it that way. Jist her ill-gittidness, A hink." Iz sighed and shook her head. "As if she wanted somebody ti find it that wid gie the letters ti Rae an then tak aahin awa fae her. Like she really wanted ti rub Rae's nose in hit. Ken fur runnin awa an gettin bairned like she done. Really hurt Rae cos Etta thocht she'd let her doon. A find it herd ti believe that onyone could be as spitefu an mean ti thir ain, but Etta wis a evil auld carlin at the best o times. Rae's bluidy lucky ti hae sae muckle o ma Uncle Willie's couthiness aboot her. Real saft centre, so she is. Ach she's got Etta's determination," Iz paused and nodded. "She's got that an no mistake. Eence she's made up her mind aboot somehin, she'll no gie up easy, oor Rae. But she's no nasty. She's niver been. Rae'll ging a lang wey ti no hurt a bodie—aiblins wind up hurtin hersel first. Be the wey, d'ye see how thon's een o they dae-it-yersel Wills thi sell i Menzies's? A've a feelin it's the on'y een thir is." Peem nodded in agreement without saying anything. He was too amazed. "A mean it's gone six month syne she deed, an A'd a thocht if thir wis a copy it'd hiv turned up be noo. A reckon Etta wis jist ower grippit ti pey a lahyer an so she done the hale hing hersel. See fa the Witnesses are?"

" Mary Smuth's mither an—an Lanky Boab!"

"Aye. So the ony three fowk at kent this Will o Etta's iver really wis—the rotten, nasty hing at it is—cept you an me—is deid. A widnae like ti miscry the deid, but thir nae a day passed lately A hinny been feared thon auld bugger'd mind o thon Will and then we'd aa hae been done fer," said Iz.

"Nae fear, hon," grinned Peem. "Boab wis that dottled he cidnae mind nothin that happened syne nineteen-fifty. An forbye, he'd likely a figgered it wis neen o his ingans. It wisna like Boab wis a pal o Etta's—

she likely slipped him twinty Capstan fur signin the hing, that's aa."

Iz nodded. "So fit dae ye hink we should div wi hit? The Will A mean. If onybody finds oot aboot it thill be hell tae pey."

Peem looked at Sye and Rae, who were perched on a rock near the water's edge with their backs turned toward him, and nodded slowly. "Yer recht. Canna hae at," he said at last, and pulled his Zippo out of his pocket. As the paper burned, he mused, "Christ A really, really *hate* cats. So A jalouse it wis yersel pit the ad in *The Scotser* that tellt Rae her mither wis deid, then?"

"On'y wey a could hink o gettin a hud o her wi'oot raisin a stooshie an the hale hing comin oot i the wash. Here, ur we criminals noo?" Iz indicated the crumpling flutter of ash with her eye.

"Ach, weel, A daa hink it. No as lang as the Cat Refuge daa find oot. An thir nae evidence noo. An forbye, even if we ur, it disnae mak wis bed people, noo dis it?"

Iz cuddled in close to Peem and took his hand and kissed it. "Thir a bonny pair, eh no," she mused, and took a sip of lager.

"Aye," agreed Peem, taking the can in turn. "A jist hope they niver find oot the connivin his gone intil aa this—or fa wis ahent it, like."

"Ach, Peem, wi fowk at's done's weel as they twa hud at ruinin thir ain lives, ye've ti gie them a bit leg up fae time ti time; it's only neebourly." She chuckled and then her voice grew harder. "An onywey A wis seek fed up deevin masel wi worry aboot the hings you an at brither o mine mecht get intil thegither jist ti keep him fae gettin bored. A've a fancy that Rae's complicatit enough ti keep at bugger busy fur a guid lang whiley. An A daa hink she'll be staunin for any nonsense. So yer on notice, the pair o yiz—nae mair o't. Rae'll back me ti the hilt, daa you fret." She looked into Peem's eyes and her gaze was troubled. "Hud tae dae somehin, hon. Aa they capers wis gettin oot o line. Yer ower auld ti be cerryin on like twa laddies. Jist daa say A'm as bad as Auntie Mae." She laughed, but there was something there that was not mirth that jarred. "A hud tae dae it—Especially fan A fund the letters an aa. Even though A— A.....". She stopped and looked away.

"Ye whit?" Peem's voice was gentle. He knew his wife well enough to know that he would have to coax her.

"Oh, hon, A had it in ma mind that you and—that you and Rae hud—ye ken."

Peem shook his head in amazement. "Fit? Me an *Rae?* Aw, c'mon, Izzie. Fit'n the hell gart ye hink at?"

"Ach, the wey it happened—her takin aff like at—niver a note— aa that. It wis ony fan A fund aa they letters A began tae figger it oot, an A niver really understood till Rae set me recht." Iz looked back at Peem and her eyes demanded the truth. "Ye niver fancied her? Honest A'll no be fashed."

"Rae? Naa. A sweir A've niver laid a finger on her, an niver wanted til. She wis aye the skinny wee hing fae alang by......A mean, she's a grand lass, is Rae, but she's mair corners on her nor a hex-head bolt, if ye get ma meanin. You're ma type, hon. Aye hiv been."

"Oh, good," said Iz, with a big grin. "That wey A'll no hae till divorce ye. On'y kiddin! Ken A could kick masel fur bein at daft aa they years. A'm sorry, hon. A'm sorry A misdootit ye. Jist—ye ken, whiles ye get an idear in yer heid an it'll no ging awa, disnae matter fit ye div."

Peem shook his head. "Furgit it. A'm jist dumfoonert ye niver speired at me aboot it afore nou. Daa ye iver keep a secret like at again, ye skelly besom."

"Shair ye're no fashed?" Peem grunted no and Iz sighed in relief. "Ach, A'm gey happy ti hear it, hon, cos gin it'd been the ither wey roon, A'm no shair A'd be that unnerstaunin. But then, that's fit wey A married ye. Weel, partly." She squeezed his thigh and whispered. "Mainly A jist wantit yer *body*." She gurgled merrily and looked down at Sye and Rae and nodded. Then she put her arms round Peem and hugged him.

In the salmony dawning light Rae gazed lazily into the rockpool. The creatures that hid so cannily during the day were still about their nightly dash of eating and hunting and fighting and procreating. Hermit crabs scuttled to and fro busily and the almost invisible shrimps jerked crazily through the water. The strawberry beadlet anemones waved their deadly tendrils and fished the water for their microscopic food, and several gobies rooted through the silt. Rae considered all this, and the brown skin of her slender foot, where her toes dipped motionless into the water, and then regarded the smoothness of her leg. She realised that she had not let her toes trail in such a rockpool where the chill water bit so thrillingly since she was a girl, and that she was a girl no longer, nor would she be again. She leaned closer in to Sye, upon whose knee she was sitting, and let her cheek rest against his head and her hair brush against his face.

Sye was thinking about this, in a warm sort of a way, and looking out, with his grey eyes, over the grey North Sea, to where the Easter Rock lighthouse stood darkly silhouetted, a last sentinel of the night, when the sun's disc breasted the horizon and the timeless red cliffs caught afire and illumined the scene with a suffused glow of reflected light, painting everything in burnished copper.

THE END

Glossary of Scots Words

Author's note: I swithered a long time before deciding to include a short glossary but on balance felt that it would benefit readers. Scots is a living language that is constantly re-inventing itself and I have tried to be true to this. I have not included words like *ma (my)* and *ain (own)* as I believe that if readers try to "hear" the voices as they read, then the meanings will be quite clear.

Readers who wish to extend their vocabulary of Scots should consider purchasing a copy of the excellent *Concise Scots Dictionary,* The Scottish National Dictionary Association, Polygon, 1985.

A

abune	above
ahent	behind
aiblins	perhaps
airts	parts, area
ashet	dish
ava	at all
aye	1) yes; 2) always

B

bairn	child
bairned	made pregnant
baudrons, pussy-baudrons	a cat
birl	spin
big, biggit	build, built
bike	wasp's nest
billie	young man
ben	through, into
besom	1) brush; 2) a woman
bleezin	blazing
blether, a	idle chatter
blethers	nonsense
bocht, bochten	bought
bogey; the game's a	it's all up, it won't work
bothy	cottage shared communally on a farm
braw	excellent
breeks	trousers

C

caa, caad	knock, dig
caller	fresh
canny	careful; *cry canny* go carefully
cantrips	tricks, capers
carlin	old woman

causey	path, road
chap	to knock; in dominoes, when a player cannot take a turn, he *chaps;* hence *at the chap,* sitting in the pub
chiel	person
chiz	pester, annoy
clarty	dirty
cleik	a metal bar shaped into a hook at one end
clift	cliff
cludge, cludgie	toilet
coorse	coarse, rude, uncouth
cowp	overturn
cowpit her creel	died
couthy	kind, gentle (of a person)
crabbit	short-tempered, irritable
craitur	person
creel	basket, lobster-pot
crivvins	mild exclamation of astonishment
cuits	ankles

D

daunder	wander
deek	look, squint
deeve	deafen, annoy
deider	dead person
deoch an doris	parting drink (Gael. door drink)
dirl	vibrate
doo	dove, pigeon
dootna	don't doubt
dram	drink (Gael.)
drookit	soaked
drouth, drouthy	thirst, thirsty
dunt	knock, blow
doolally	weird, crazy
dozent	dimwitted, slow
dunderheid	idiot

E

ettercap	spider
ettle, ettlin	try, trying

F

fankle	tangle
fash	annoy
feckle	confuse
feechie	disgusting

fegs	exclamation suitable for use in polite company, similar to *faith*
fell	great
fleet	quick
fleg	fright
forbye	besides, as well as
forgie	forgive
fou	1) full; 2) drunk
Frenchie, Frenchies	condom (French Letter)
fud	vagina
fung	kick, wallop
fushionless	useless
futret	ferret

G

gallus	cocky and self-confident
galluses	braces, suspenders
galoot	oaf, clumsy idiot
gar, gart	make, made
gaed	went
gey	very
gillie	one who assists an angler (Gael. *gille*, a boy)
gin	if
ging	to go
ginging	going
girn	cry
glaikit	stupid, distracted
glimmer	look
glisk	glance
gowk	idiot
graft	grave
grippit	mean
guff	1) smell; 2) nonsense
gullie	sailor's pocket-knife
gutters	mud and dirt
gushet	corner
gyte	crazy

H

hackit	ugly
haddie	haddock
harns	brains
haunle	handle
hertie	hearty, decent
hirsel	1) herself; 2) to move in a determined manner; 3)

	a herd (of cattle)
hoch, hochs	thigh, thighs
hooer	whore
houghmagandie	the act of sex
hurl (of transport)	to drive, give or take a lift (as in *A'll gie ye*
a hurl)	

I
ill-gitted	of an evil disposition
ingan	onion
ingle	angle

J
jaffa	Jehovah's Witness
jalopy	old car
jalouse	suppose, guess
jannie	janitor
jeely	jam (Eng.) jelly (Am.)
jig, jiggin	dance, dancing
jile	jail
jonick	nice, pleasant (of a person)
jotter	notebook; *gie ye yer jotters*, you're fired
jouk	duck, avoid

K
keech	shit (Gael. *cac*, ordure.)
ken	know
kip	sleep
kirk	church
kist	chest, coffin
klipe	tell tales
kybosh	refusal (from *knock back*, often shortened
to *KB*.)	

L
lift	sky
limmer	woman of dubious virtue
loon	boy
low-flyer	The Famous Grouse, a whisky
lug	ear
lum	chimney

M
maun	must
maw	seagull
meelie	melee
merkat	market

grandminnie	grandmother
muckle	big

N

nab, nabbit	catch, caught
nip, nippy	a half measure of alcohol
nippit	short, small
neb	nose

O

ocht	something, anything
ower	over, excessively

P

partan	crab
perjinckit	particular, fussy
pitten-on	dressed up
plant, plantin	to bury, burial
puckle	few, small number
puggilt	tired out
puss	face
pynte	point

Q

quine	girl

R

rauch	rough
redd, to	to tidy, to clean
reek	smoke

S

sair fecht	a real struggle
scunner	sicken, enervate
sea-maw	seagull
shoogled	shake violently
shufti	look
sic	such
siccan	such a
siller	silver, money
skeeched	to be addled with age or alcohol
skelly	daft
skids	underpants
sonsie	fair, cheerful
speir	ask
speirins	questions
spleet-new	brand new

stramash	rough-house, fight
smeddum	gumption, determination and ability
stappit	jammed, stuck
starns	stars
strand	beach
sup	eat, drink
swither, to	to be unable to decide
syne	since

T

tapsalteerie	upside-down
tattie-dreel	drill in potato field
teuch	tough
teuchter	ill-educated country-dweller
thole	suffer, bear
thon, thonder	that (over there.) Scots uses more degrees of separation than English; so *this, that, thon and thonder*
thrapple	throat
thrawn	ill-natured
threip	nag
tint	lost
tither, the	the other
tod, toddie	fox, fox-cub
trachle	trouble, bother, burden

U

unchancy	unlucky

W

wad	married
wake	a party held before, during or after a funeral
wheen	large number, amount
wheesht (hud yer)	be quiet
whiles	sometimes
whitterick	weasel; an incorrigibly wayward child
wifey	woman
willies, the	creeps
wirsels	ourselves
wye's	gentleman's undergarment.

Ordering

Poaching the River is available in either paperback form or as an e-book.

Copies may be ordered directly from:

Orders
PlashMill Press
The Plash Mill
Friockheim
Angus DD11 4SH
Scotland.

Please state clearly how many copies you require and remember to enclose your payment, full address including postal/zip code and a contact telephone number or email address.

Cheques, Money Orders, Postal Orders etc should be made payable to PlashMill Press. Prices stated are in UK Pounds.

For online orders and further details please visit the PlashMill Press website at **www.plashmillpress.com**

News of forthcoming publications, booksignings, offers and events are also available there.

You may also email **orders@plashmillpress.com** for more information.

Prices: Paperback   £11.99 (plus £1 carriage worldwide)
         E-book   £6.99

Payment from customers in the UK may be by cheque, postal or money order or in cash We also accept payment by credit or debit card or by bank transfer. Please see our website for further details or email **orders@plashmillpress.com**.

Trade inquiries are welcomed. Trade and bulk terms negotiated. Please see our website for further details.